# PHOENIX ON THE RUN

*The Shapeshifter Saga*
Book One

S. P. FOSTER

ISBN: 978-1-4669-5294-2 (sc)
ISBN: 978-1-4669-5293-5 (e)

Trafford rev. 08/17/2012

www.trafford.com

North America & international
toll-free: 1 888 232 4444 (USA & Canada)
phone: 250 383 6864 ♦ fax: 812 355 4082

# DEDICATION

This book is dedicated to my family for the support they have given during the writing. My wife Mary and my children Ariel and Nicholas.

# Acknowledgements

I would like to thank the following people for their assistance in preparing this book: My son, Nicholas, for helping with character and story development. My sister-in-law, Michaelyn Mann, for editing.

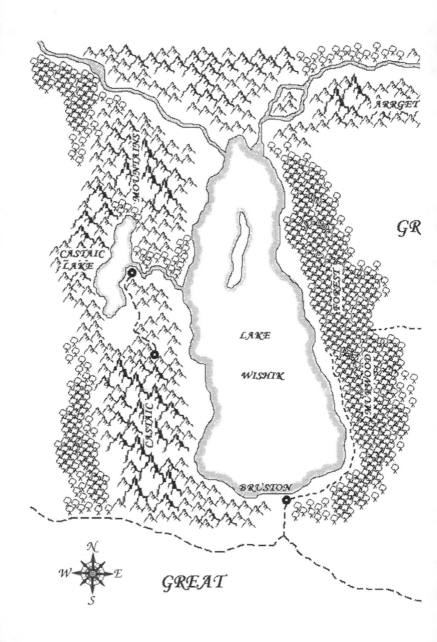

ÀRRGET NA

GR

CASTAIC LAKE

MOUNTAINS

LAKE WISHIK

FOREST

GOOMARTIK

CASTAIC

BRUSTON

N
W E
S

GREAT

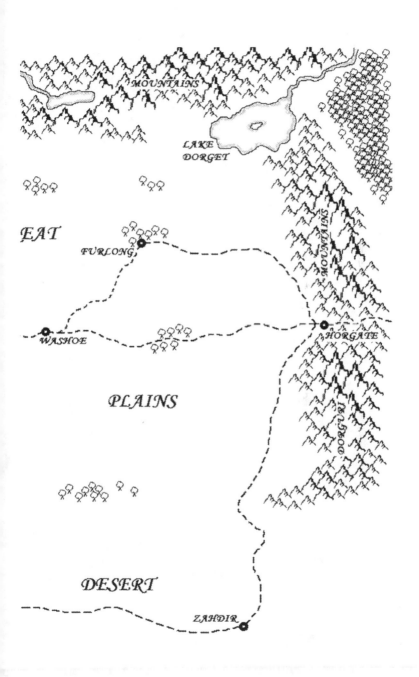

# CHAPTER 1

J'ORIK HAD BEEN running for his life for what seemed all night when exhaustion finally overcame him. He found a dense thicket of brush, laid down, and fell asleep. The next morning he awoke in a cold sweat. He'd been dreaming about the attack on the village. The memory was so vivid that he couldn't get it out of his mind. He sat there playing it over and over in his head wondering why it had happened.

The attack came at dusk. A horde of creatures, unlike anything he'd ever seen, simply overran the village. They were everywhere. Dark, hairy things dressed in black, heavy leather armor that matched the color of their skin. Their faces looked like someone had cut off the head of a boar and set it atop their huge shoulders. They only stood about five feet tall but with the steel helmets they wore and their massive size they appeared much larger. They came in from the beach like a swarm of bees and began destroying the village. People were screaming and running for their lives. Homes were being set afire. And these creatures seemed to be killing everything that got in their way, without any apparent reason. He fought back as best as he could, killing a few of the attacking creatures and being wounded several times in the process. He took an arrow in the arm and was cut several times. The pain was excruciating but he continued fighting. He pulled the arrow out and ignored the pain as he fought. He remembered thinking about the people that had raised him, the people he had come to call his mother and father. He wanted to go to their aid so he fought his way in that direction. The home was already on fire as he burst through the door. His father was gone and his mother lay on the floor dead. She'd been sliced open at the waist and her blood was pooled around her. Tears came to his eyes. He knew there was no time now to mourn He needed to get out of there and try to save himself. He grabbed the pack next to his bed that he kept ready for when he went hunting and strapped it on his back. He took one last look at his mother, tears still in his eyes, and headed for the door. There were heavy footsteps outside so he peeked out to make sure it was clear before exiting. The house was beginning to cave in and he knew he didn't have much more time before it completely collapsed so he rushed out with his sword ready. The house was near the edge of the forest, furthest from where the attack came from. Realizing there was nothing more he could do, he took one final look back at the village and the destruction that was being wrought. Then he turned and ran into the forest.

He had no idea who or what had caused the attack or even why his village had been the one attacked. All he knew was that he had barely gotten away with his life.

He was sore, not only from fighting in the village but from running through the night. He began checking his wounds and found that most of them were beginning to heal. The one wound he knew would take a little longer was the arrow he had taken in the arm but the scratches, cuts and abrasions had already begun to close and heal and the pain from the arrow wound was beginning to subside.

The forest around him was filled with the sounds of the forest beginning another day. He wasn't sure what time of day it was but it seemed like it was late in the morning. He was familiar with this forest—Murwood Forest. He hunted in it on a regular basis. He had traveled from one end to the other learning of its plant and animal life. Murwood Forest was long in a north-to-south direction stretching the full length of Lake Wishik along its eastern shore. It had an east-to-west spread of about a full day's walk along the road that cut through the middle of the forest. The trees were tall and had large, dense canopies of branches and leaves this time of year. There were some spots where the trees were so dense that very little light even reached the forest floor. The forest floor itself was just as densely populated with brush, fallen trees, and broken branches, so there was always enough wood just lying around to build a campfire when needed. He had never come across an open area big enough to be considered a meadow. The forest provided enough food for the animal life so there was always good hunting. There were deer, rabbit, turkey and quail. There were other, larger animals he could hunt but those were further north and less common or if he just happened upon them wandering too far south. There were only three well-marked trails running east-to-west through the forest, one each near the north and south ends and one running generally through the middle. The middle trail had been cut wide enough to accept wagon travel and was more like a road. The other two were more suited for foot travel. There was also a multitude of creeks that meandered through the forest from the Great Plains towards Lake Wishik with pools appearing periodically along their path. Lake Wishik bordered the western edge of the forest with the Arrget Mountains ranging across the northern end. Beyond the eastern edge of the forest the Great Plains spanned for almost a seven-day walk before rising up into the Dorguri Mountains. And at the south edge of the plains the Great Desert began, stretching south as far as the eye could see.

Since running from the attack on the village he hadn't been able to feel at ease, in fear that he'd been pursued by those ugly disfigured creatures that had attacked the village. He still took some time out to snack on a couple of biscuits that he kept in his ready pack. He always had a pack filled and ready to go with things that he needed when he left the village and went hunting. When he was hunting he never knew how long he would be gone so he always kept his pack stocked with enough food to last at least four days. The pack was also filled with an extra over-shirt, some first aid supplies, some dry biscuits wrapped in a cloth, a flask filled with water and a flint for starting a fire. On the outside of the pack he kept a bedroll and a length of rope attached, along with a knife and a small hand axe. He also carried a short sword, which was always at his side; a crossbow, which was his weapon of choice; and two knives, which he always wore attached to his boots.

After eating and calming down some he decided, that since the attack and the distance he had run, it was unlikely he had anyone, or anything, following him any longer. Gathering his things together he began another day traveling through the forest, thinking about the attack on the village and what might have brought it on.

The village was situated on the western edge of Murwood Forest a short distance from Lake Wishik. But now, because he had been running for his life and not thinking about where he was running, he was unsure exactly where he was. So, as he walked, he also took some time to look around and attempt to determine where he might be. He was familiar with the forest simply because he hunted in it on a regular basis. Not only was he a hunter, he was also one of the best trackers around, so it didn't take him long to figure out where he was. He was east and a little north of the village. Given the time that had passed and the fact that he had been running almost non-stop since the attack, he figured it was still a little more than a day's walk before he would reach the eastern edge of the forest and the beginning of the Great Plains.

He could see that the sun was beginning to near midday and decided he could take some time to hunt for food. He knocked an arrow in his crossbow and began looking and listening for prey. It wasn't long before he came upon a rabbit. He shot and killed it with ease. By the time he'd cleaned it and prepared it for cooking he could see that the sun had started to pass midday. From the hard running he'd done the night before, hunger was beginning to take hold so he stopped long enough to start a small fire, cook and eat his meal. Then he started off once again through the forest, away from the village. He had no desire to take the chance of encountering any of those creatures that had attacked the village.

After walking all day and encountering no one with evil, or otherwise, intent, he decided it was time to find a good place to set up camp for the night. He knew it wasn't much further to the eastern edge of the forest and he wanted to get there while there was still plenty of daylight left. He tracked, shot and cleaned another rabbit for his evening meal. While hunting he'd come across a small creek running through the forest. After stopping and refilling his flask, he decided to set up camp just out of earshot from the creek. He wanted to be sure that he could hear anything that might be out during the night sneaking up on him and knew that even the little noise coming from that small creek would be a distraction.

He started a small fire and cooked the rabbit he'd killed. The sun had nearly set, even though he couldn't see it directly he knew, and night came on. As he sat back to enjoy the rabbit, and the relative peace and quiet, he heard some branches snap off to the south. He knew it was more than just one of the indigenous forest creatures. After all, he hunted this forest on a regular basis and had for most of his life. He knew the difference.

As quickly and quietly as possible he extinguished the fire and knocked an arrow in his crossbow. He moved as silently as possible about ten paces away from where his campfire was in the opposite direction from where he'd heard the branches snap and lay down in the forest overgrowth to wait. He lay so that he was able to see back towards his camp—more snapping of branches.

He also had good night vision and as he lay there on the forest floor watching, listening to the snap, snap, snap of branches, a woman appeared out of the trees and brush near where his campfire was. She looked confused and scared and concerned that there was no one at the campfire. There was still a column of smoke rising up out of the ashes and anyone would know that the fire had just been recently put out. She squatted down low, her head jerking side to side quickly. He could tell she was searching for whoever had built the campfire.

The woman's hair was long and nearly ebony black. It was disheveled as if she hadn't cared for it in days. Her clothes were a mess as though she'd been wearing them for as many days. They were torn and had blackened areas as if they'd been burned. There was a strip of cloth wrapped around one of her legs. He thought she looked familiar but couldn't be sure, so he lay there without moving or making a sound and waited to see what would happen next.

Her eyes were still scanning the forest when she started, in a very low tone, to call out.

"Hello—hello, is anyone there?" She spoke with a very frightened look in her eyes.

He knew she had to know someone was nearby because the smoke was still curling up from the campfire he'd just extinguished. He saw her reach out towards the campfire with her hand and she quickly drew it back. She was checking how much heat was coming from the campfire. He could see she knew the fire had been very recently put out.

Again she called out. "Hello. I know someone's there." Her voice seemed to be getting braver. "Please show yourself. I won't hurt you." She spoke as if she was talking to a child.

He stood slowly, making as little noise as possible, and brought his crossbow up aiming it at the woman. She immediately turned in his direction and stood herself. She didn't seem to be as frightened as she looked, or as frightened as he thought she looked.

"Who's there?" she snapped. "I can't see you. Please come forward." There was fright in her voice.

He didn't move. He maintained his stance with the crossbow still aimed at her.

"Who are you?" he asked with as calm a voice as he could. He was standing behind a tree so she wouldn't be able to see him. "Where do you come from and what are you doing in the middle of the forest alone at this time of night?" He waited for her response without moving.

"My name is Lianna and I ran into the forest to escape the monsters that attacked my village." He could hear the fear in her voice when she mentioned monsters, and she continued, "My village was attacked yesterday and I was able to escape. I haven't stopped running since. I'm alone, lost, hungry, and I haven't seen or met another since running from the village. Please come closer." She sounded desperate.

He slowly came out to where she could see him but he kept his crossbow aimed at her. Before approaching too close he asked, "Please put your hands out where I can see them with your fingers spread and palms facing me."

She complied and he moved closer, still keeping his crossbow at the ready.

"I know you," she said when he got close enough. "You're one of the hunters from my village. Your name is J'orik isn't it?"

"Yes," he replied, surprised, "and it seems as if we're both in the same situation."

Feeling confident that she didn't present any danger now, he removed the arrow and lowered the crossbow.

"It would seem so," she began, "but I believe you have an advantage over me. You're a hunter and are familiar with the forest. You also have weapons and food, which I don't."

"I'm sorry," he apologized, "if you look closer the rest of the rabbit meat I didn't finish is laying near the campfire. Just brush it off some and it should be enough to take away the hunger."

She squatted near the campfire and found the remaining rabbit meat. She ate all that was left. After running in the forest for over a day without eating, the meat disappeared almost as quickly as she had picked it up. When she was finished eating the rabbit she looked up at him and said, "Thank you. I was very hungry, as you could probably tell."

He took out his water flask and handed it to her. "Would you like some water to wash it down?"

"Yes, thank you," she responded with a smile.

He sat down across the campfire pit from her, took out his flint, and restarted the fire. Once the fire got going and created enough light, he took a closer look at her. She seemed familiar to him but he just couldn't place her. She also seemed to be relaxing a little. She sat back against a tree and looked back at him.

"You seem to know who I am and what I do but I know nothing about you. You look familiar but I just can't figure out who you are."

"As I said, my name is Lianna," she repeated. "You may know my husband better. He was the village blacksmith. His name was Falder."

"You speak as if he's no longer alive," he said with some concern. "Did he not survive the attack?"

"No," she responded with tears welling up in her eyes. "He was killed. I saw it happen and there was nothing I could do." The tears started flowing freely then as she began relaying her experience. "I was visiting with some friends when the attack happened. It was so sudden and they just seemed to swarm into the village. We all ran screaming. I ran for home as fast as I could. On the way I passed by Falder's shop and saw two of those things coming up behind him. I screamed at him to watch out but it was too late. They clubbed him over the head and I saw him fall to the ground. After that all I had on my mind was getting to my children. I started running towards home again. Other people were running and screaming too. All of us were trying to get away from those monsters attacking us. They were lighting our homes on fire and killing anything that moved. I got close enough to my home to watch as Delia, the young girl I'd left to watch my children, get dragged outside, run through with a sword, and thrown to the ground. She was so young." She paused for a moment and cried, then continued, "I started to scream my son's name and then I felt a thick, sharp stinging in the side of my leg. I looked down and there was an arrow sticking out of my leg. I went to my knees because of the pain as I reached for the arrow. I turned and looked back at the house and saw my children being dragged out the door. I was afraid those things were going to do the same thing to them that they'd done to poor Delia, but they didn't. They just dragged them away. I started to scream again and then I felt something hard hit me in the back of my head. I fell, face first into the ground and everything went black."

"So your children were dragged away? They weren't killed?"

"Not that I saw," she replied.

"Go on. Obviously you weren't killed, so what happened next?"

"I don't know how long I was out, but when I came to it was still dark out. My head was pounding and my leg was throbbing. I just laid there for a few moments before trying to get up. When I finally stood up my eyes blurred and I felt dizzy. I fell back down to my hands and knees, feeling very weak. I was able to crawl over next to a woman lying on the ground near me. I sat up and tore a strip of cloth from her skirt. I didn't think she would mind since she was dead. I gritted my teeth and pulled the arrow out of my leg. The pain was excruciating and I wanted to scream but was afraid to, fearing that those things might still be somewhere nearby and come running to finish me off. I quickly wrapped the strip of cloth tight around my leg to stop the bleeding. While I sat there waiting for the pain to subside I looked around me. All the homes were either still burning or had burned to the ground and I didn't see anyone else moving. I was alone, scared, and my head was pounding. I reached behind my head and felt some moisture. When I brought my hand back around and looked at it there was blood on it. I realized then that I couldn't have been out too long or the blood wouldn't still be wet. All I could think about then was running as far from the village as possible. I didn't want to be there if those monsters decided to come back. So I got up slowly and stood on my one good leg and started limping through the village towards the forest. I figured that would be the best place to go since the attack had come from the beach. My head was still pounding but it was bearable now. I made it to the edge of the forest and turned to take one last look at the village.

Smoke was still billowing up from all the homes that had been burned. I turned back to the forest and started limping as fast as I could away from the village. I lost all sense of time. The pain in my leg eventually began to subside and I actually started walking. My head finally stopped throbbing and when I checked again the blood had dried. Eventually I got tired and sat down to rest. I must have fallen asleep at that point because the next thing I remembered was waking up to the sounds of birds and daylight streaming through the trees.

"When I stood up there was no pain in my leg anymore. There was no more throbbing in my head either and it felt almost normal. I heard running water nearby and found a creek. I washed the blood off my hands and out of my hair. I removed the strip of cloth from my leg to wash the wound and found that it had stopped bleeding and was almost closed, but I washed it anyway. I washed the strip of cloth I had used, wrung it out, and rewrapped my leg. I started walking again, away from the village, deeper into the forest. After a while I started running. It felt good to have some wind in my face. I kept thinking about my children, how they'd been taken, and Falder, how I'd watched him killed, and all the other unfortunate people in the village that had been killed. I ran and walked all day thinking about those things. Night finally set in and I hadn't eaten since leaving the village. I was getting hungry. That's when I spotted a light in the forest. It was your campfire, but I didn't know that at the time. I stopped and listened for a while, watching the fire light. I thought maybe I could sneak close enough to see who had a campfire out here in the middle of the forest. As I got closer it suddenly went out. I continued to move towards where the light had been and stumbled into your camp. From there you know what happened next."

"I'm sorry for your loss," he said with sincerity. "I did know Falder. He was a good man and a good blacksmith. I do remember he had a wife and children. He spoke of you and his children often. But now it's getting late and I can see that you could use a good night's rest." He undid his bedroll and handed it to her. "Here, tonight you can sleep on something other than the forest floor. I don't think we have to be concerned about any monsters getting us here in the forest tonight, so you can lie down and rest. I'll keep watch for a while longer before sleeping myself."

"Are you sure about the monsters?" she asked, still worried.

"Well, not absolutely sure," he answered, "but since I left the village I haven't seen or heard any. It's been a full day since the attack and I don't remember seeing any of them following me into the forest. So you get some rest tonight and tomorrow we'll awake refreshed and decide what to do next."

"Thank you, J'orik, you're so kind." Then she laid down and fell fast asleep.

J'orik sat there for a while longer watching her sleep before he himself fell fast asleep.

The next morning he awoke to find that Lianna was not there. He listened carefully and could hear some rustling in the overgrowth and snapping of branches in the forest. He turned towards the sounds and saw that she was nearby. It appeared as if she had gone out to collect wood for a campfire. She would bend over and when she stood again he could see that she was placing small twigs and branches in her other arm. He called to her to let her know that he was awake and she made her way back.

"Good morning J'orik." She greeted him with a smile. "I just thought I'd collect some firewood for breakfast. When I woke, you were still sleeping and I didn't want to bother you. I was being as quiet as I could. Did I wake you?"

"No," he replied. "I must have been really tired."

"I thought we could have a bite to eat before we started out. I also thought that since you're the hunter that you might be able to round up something for us to eat."

"I can do that," he said as he took out his flint from his pack and handed it to her. "Here's my flint to start a fire. While you're doing that I'll find us something to eat."

"Fantastic," she said with a sparkle in her eyes. "I'll have the fire ready when you get back."

He took up his crossbow and headed into the forest as she began putting the fire together.

He wasn't gone long before he spotted a large quail. He shot it down with ease and quickly cleaned it. Returning to the camp he noticed that she had not only got the campfire started, she'd also strapped the bedroll back on his pack and somehow cleaned herself up a little more. He figured she must have visited the nearby creek to wash herself. He came into the camp with a big smile on his face, holding up the quail he had shot and cleaned.

"I think this'll do for the both of us," he spoke with some pride in his voice. "Do you want me to cook it or will you?"

"You sit while I cook. It's only fair since you provided a cooked meal for me last night."

As she cooked the bird, he found himself watching her and wondering a little about this woman. Upon their first meeting last night she seemed so frightened and horribly upset about what had happened to her family. She had even cried while recounting what she'd seen. And yet, today, she seemed like a different person. She was smiling, had rummaged in the forest for firewood, cleaned herself, and now she was cooking for the two of them. He wasn't quite sure how to take all of this. Somehow, through the night, she seemed to have resigned herself to what had happened, accepted it, and was now ready to move on. He would have to question her about this but he knew now was not the right time. He would have to be gentle. The last thing he wanted to do was upset her.

She finished cooking the bird and they both ate quietly without saying a word. When they were done he extinguished the fire, put his pack on, and cleaned up the area so that no one could tell a camp had been made there. The last thing he did was to replenish the water in his flask from the nearby creek. He could tell she was watching him intently, watching every move he made, almost as if she was trying to learn.

After completing his tasks he turned to her and said, "Okay, ready to go?"

"Yes," she replied. "You lead, I'll follow."

He headed east again, aiming for the eastern edge of the forest. It was still early in the morning and he wanted to reach the edge of the forest by midday. He figured it would be less than half a day's walk, even if they were to take it slowly. He didn't want her to feel like she had to run to keep up with him. After all, he wasn't sure how much sleep, if any, she'd gotten through the night. They didn't talk much as they walked. Once in a while she would ask him about a particular plant and he would respond with an explanation of whether the plant was poisonous or not and if it had any fruit whether the fruit was poisonous or not.

About midday she asked him, "How much further before we're out of the forest?"

He turned and told her, "Soon." He also explained, "We're not just walking out the forest without first making sure it's safe."

It was soon after that that the forest began to thin and he knew it wouldn't be much longer before they reached the edge of the forest and the beginning of the plains. He started looking for a good spot for her to wait while he went to see if it would be safe for them to exit the forest. When he found it he stopped and turned around.

"I want you to wait right here while I go see whether or not it's safe to move on."

She looked at him with fright in her eyes and asked, "Why can't I go with you?"

"You will go with me," he explained, "but only after I've checked to see that it's safe. You'll be able to see me the whole time and if anything bad happens, at least by staying here, you'll have a head start if you need to run."

"But if something bad does happen, and I do need to run, I have no way of protecting myself."

He took the knife he kept attached to his pack and handed it to her. "Here, take this for protection. It's better than nothing and hopefully you won't need to use it. I don't think you will."

"Thank you." She took the knife and seemed to calm down some.

He turned and went the remaining distance to the edge of the forest. As he neared where the forest met the Great Plains, he was scanning the openness for anything that moved. He didn't spot anything within sight so he figured it would probably be safe for them to continue their travel across the plains. He turned and went back to get her. She hadn't moved and was still waiting in the same spot. She had a smile on her face when he came back and knew that he'd determined it was safe to keep going.

"So is it safe?" she asked curiously.

"Yes," he replied. "And I want you to keep the knife for your own protection in case the need ever arises. I have weapons enough for myself and one less knife shouldn't make a difference."

"Thank you again, J'orik, you're a very kind man. I don't know what I'd do if I was still alone," sounding somewhat sarcastic. "What lies beyond the forest? I've never been this far."

"There's a town that lies to the southeast called Washoe that I've been to. My mother used to take me there. Actually, both my mothers used to take me there, my real mother before she died and then the woman who took care of me after she died. My aunt and uncle run an inn there called the Dragons' Lair. The town lies on the road that goes back through the forest. It's the only town I've been to east of the forest. It's also where we'll be heading."

"What will we do once we get there?"

"We'll stop in at the inn run by my aunt and uncle. After we tell them what happened they'll be more than willing to help you. I'll be . . ."

"What do mean 'help me'?" She cut him short. "What will you do? Am I not staying with you?" she asked with a stern voice.

He thought for a moment before telling her. "I'll be returning to the village. I think it would be best if you didn't return with me. You'll be much . . ."

Again she cut him short. "I refuse to be left there all alone. I don't know them or anyone else there. And besides, I want to stay with you and go back to the village. It was my home too and where my family was." She began to cry.

He looked at her with sadness in his eyes. She was right. It was her home too and where her family had been but, it wouldn't be a safe place anymore, he thought. So he told her, "Yes, you're right, but you do realize that it probably won't be a safe place and we probably won't be able to stay there any longer."

"Yes, I understand," she came back at him. Her crying subsided with that and she told him, "Let's get on with it."

Before he turned to move on he told her, "We won't be getting to the town before dark and I'll be looking for food for the night so keep quiet, at least until I've killed our dinner. We'll be in the open most of the way so I want you to keep your eyes open for anyone, or anything, that might be out there. We should have plenty of time to prepare for any kind of meeting, you can see for quite a distance. Remember, though, we can also be seen from that same distance."

"I understand," she told him, and said nothing more.

# CHAPTER 2

THE CLOUDS OUTSIDE were roiling, thunder could be heard all around, and lightning would flash every so often. Rain was coming down hard and the wind would blow so strong sometimes that the rain seemed to be coming down sideways. The guards on the castle walls were getting drenched and were using their shields to protect themselves from the rain. They knew that if they tried to come in out of the rain that it meant certain imprisonment. Unless they were relieved they were to stand their post. Other than the guards there was not another soul to be seen outside in the weather.

Inside his room, K'orik was deep in thought. He had sent a small force over the mountains and across Lake Wishik to a small village at the edge of Murwood Forest. He'd been told that what he was looking for could be found in one of the villages around the lake. For nearly three decades now he'd been looking for his son. The woman who had birthed the boy had run away only five months after she gave birth. Every day since then he'd searched for him. Until now all the searches had failed and he was beginning to think that maybe the boy had died or been killed. But this time, he felt sure that this small village was where he would find him. He could not stand to fail again.

He knew that it would take about five to six days for the force he sent to travel to the village and back. They shouldn't spend much time attempting to locate the boy, or the man that he would have become now. He had given very specific details on how to identify the man, one detail in particular that would preclude any question that they had the right man. This man would be nearing thirty years in age, be very strong and fast, and he would bear a birthmark on the back of his skull. The birthmark would be unmistakable, a dark spot in the shape of a phoenix. K'orik himself had the same birthmark on the back of his skull, as did his father and his father before him and so on down through history. Because of the birthmark the phoenix had become the family symbol.

It was the morning of the sixth day now, even though it seemed like night because of the weather. K'orik was becoming more and more agitated. He was tired of waiting and wanted an answer. He paced back and forth in his room high up in the tallest tower. Periodically he would peer out towards the east looking for the return of the force he had sent, but today the weather made even that difficult. He decided he should take some breakfast thinking it would help to calm him down. He called for one of his servants and told them to bring him some quiche, biscuits and gravy, and a pot of coffee.

K'orik's room was plush, nothing but the best for him. Rugs from distant places covered the floor and were even hung on the walls alongside tapestries he had collected over the years. They helped to make it easier under foot while he paced. The bed was huge. The frame was constructed of solid ash. It was made up with silk sheets and down blankets and had several feather pillows tossed about. It was a four-poster with a canopy and set up against the wall equidistant from the adjacent walls. The canopy was a tapestry that he had made special. It bore the same image of the phoenix as was on the back of his skull. A large desk made of teak and mahogany set on one side of the bed turned so that he would be able to look out into the room with the wall behind him. Two unpadded wooden chairs and a table set in front of it. The chairs were comfortable enough for any guests he might have, but behind the desk was 'his' chair. It was actually more like a throne. The seat and back were padded and covered in red velvet. When he sat in 'his' chair he set slightly higher than the other furniture so he would be able to look down on anyone sitting in the chairs in front of the desk. On the other side of the room was a couch set against the wall with a large oak table placed in front of it. A chair set at either end of the table. The table was four legged and the top set about knee high from the floor. The couch and chairs were padded and covered in red velvet. All the furniture was ornately carved with images of phoenixes. Stained glass windows filled the openings in the walls; two on either side of the bed, one above the desk, and one above the couch. The door into the room was made of ash and set in the middle of the wall directly across from the bed. There was no opening, other than the door, in that wall. The door had the largest carving of a phoenix taking up the whole door and was on both sides.

K'orik was reclined on the couch in a red velvet robe. It was embossed with images of phoenixes and trimmed in white fox fur. He wore a solid gold medallion, embossed with the image of a phoenix, on a silver chain around his neck, which was the only piece of jewelry he wore. His eyes were a deep red rimmed with yellow and shadowed with thick, snow-white brows. His nose was of moderate size and rounded. It was flanked by high cheek bones. He had a small mouth with thin lips the color of flesh and no facial hair. The hair on his head was thick, white as snow, and shoulder length. He wore soft leather slippers. He was trying to relax as best as possible when there was a knock at the door. He hoped it might be Ogiloth returning.

"Enter," he spoke loudly.

The door opened and the servant he had sent for his morning meal entered the room. K'orik was disappointed it wasn't Ogiloth but he was glad his meal had arrived.

"Put it there," K'orik said gruffly, pointing towards the table. "Has there been any word of Ogiloth's return?" He demanded of the servant.

The servant spoke meekly, keeping his head bowed. "No sir."

K'orik huffed with even more disappointment and told the servant. "Leave me," waving his hand in dismissal.

The servant did as told and quickly left the room. Everyone that lived in the castle knew that it was best to do as told when K'orik spoke. He was not a nice person to those that disobeyed him.

The meal had come on a silver tray adorned, of course, with phoenixes. K'orik removed the domed lid from atop the tray, set it aside, and underneath, on a plate, was the meal he'd requested. He poured himself some coffee and sipped it, set the cup down and took a couple bites of the quiche and biscuits and gravy. He set the fork down, picked up the cup of coffee, and sat back in the couch to leisurely enjoy his drink.

He hadn't been relaxing too long when there came another knock at the door. This time the knocking was heavier and sounded more urgent. He felt sure that this time it would be Ogiloth.

"Enter," he said loud and quick as he stood.

The door swung open and Ogiloth entered his room. The doorway was just large enough for him to walk through. Ogiloth was a large, unpleasant looking creature. He was a true warrior. He always dressed in full battle attire which consisted of black, heavy leather armor matching the color of his skin and a steel head cap. Strapped to his right side was a two-handed sword which he was able to wield with one hand. On his left side was strapped a four foot long branch made from blackened ash wood. His armor was sleeveless, exposing his large muscular arms. He felt this intimidated his opponents. He could easily hold a human head in his hands and crush it. The soles of his feet were so thick and calloused from growing up in the mines that he no longer wore shoes. His mother had been a dwarf and his father an ogre. He appeared more ogre than dwarf. His body was hairless and his head set on a neck so thick it appeared as if he had no neck. His facial features were more like his father; large eyes black as coal, wide flattened nose, and a mouth as wide as his face filled with large brown teeth. He had no chin to speak of. It simply blended in with his large neck. The combination of the two races, though, gave him some very desirable characteristics. Not only was he large, he was strong, sturdy, and had a high resistance to magic. He was also intelligent, which is why

K'orik had chosen him to lead his forces. Next to K'orik, Ogiloth was the most feared by those living in and around the castle. He was still wearing the battle gear he'd arrived in and was drenched, which made his appearance even more unpleasant. Upon his return to the castle he hadn't waited, even a moment, to make contact with K'orik. He'd rushed as quickly as possible to K'orik's room because he knew he would be waiting anxiously for his report. He was, however, a little concerned about the reaction K'orik would have since he hadn't returned with what he'd been sent after.

"Did you find him?" K'orik questioned with urgency in his voice.

"No," Ogiloth responded. Before he could get another word in K'orik had flung his cup full of coffee at him. Ogiloth put his huge hand up just in time and the cup shattered into pieces. The coffee splashed him but it didn't make much difference since he was already soaked from the rain.

K'orik sat back down and glared up at Ogiloth. "What happened?" he asked disappointedly.

Ogiloth then proceeded to explain what had happened at the village. His force had landed on the east bank of Lake Wishik late in the afternoon of the third day after leaving K'orik's castle. They beached the boats about a mile south of the village, far enough that they wouldn't be seen from the village. He wanted to have the element of surprise on his side. He hoped there wouldn't be any villagers this far south doing whatever villagers might be doing. None were spotted, which made him feel more at ease. None had been out fishing, along the shore or in boats, so he felt he would have the upper hand. The sun was also beginning to fall behind the mountaintops. His force was a hundred strong and he felt it would be enough to completely overwhelm the village without trouble. Once the boats were secured and the forces were gathered he made it quite clear that there was to be no sound made. He reinforced that order by threatening to take the tongue of any who disobeyed. Everyone knew that Ogiloth did not make idle threats.

He had five lieutenants, each responsible for a group of twenty. He'd made it very clear to them that this was no different than the other villages they'd attacked over the last several years. It was not a pillaging excursion and they were told to convey this to their respective groups. He would not accept any mistakes. The women were to be slaughtered and the men and children were to be brought to him. The village was to be burned to the ground. If it was necessary to bludgeon the men that was fine, but they were not to be killed.

He and his lieutenants led them to the village. They didn't completely surprise the villagers simply because of the size of the force, but it was enough of a surprise that they were able to maintain the upper hand. They did overwhelm them, however, just as planned. Some of the villagers attempted to fight back and were able to kill a few of his warriors but, in the end, they overwhelmed the village.

Homes were set afire. The women were slaughtered. The men and children were captured and gathered just outside the village. The men were separated from the children and bound to prevent escape. His second lieutenant, Draiger, and his group took the children back to the boats while he and his first lieutenant, Olog, began dealing with the men. The other three groups had been directed to go back to the village and finish burning it to the ground. If they came across any that survived the first attack they were to abide by the same orders that had been given previously. Again, he made it clear that he would not accept any mistakes.

As the forces dispersed he returned to deal with the men that had been captured. One by one he scalped the hair off the back of their heads, being careful not to kill them. If they did not bear the birthmark as described, he had them taken, killed, and piled. One by one he did this and not a single one bore the mark. As he was finishing with the last man, the force that had gone back to the village returned. They reported no survivors and that they had made sure the rest of the village was left to burn. Having completed the task they all then returned to the boats.

Once back at the boats he questioned all five of his lieutenants, asking if they had seen a man that seemed to stand out above the others. Was he strong? Fast? Did he wield a weapon like it was an extension of his arm? The responses were all the same . . . Yes. He himself saw a man that seemed to stand out over the others. But, like his lieutenants had said, this man was lost in the mayhem. All the bodies had been accounted for and he was not among them. He thought that maybe this man had escaped into the forest, so he sent one of his groups into the forest to search. He told them that whether they found anyone or not they were to be back to the boats before sunrise.

Then he ordered the children to be bound in groups of four and loaded on the boats. While waiting for the search party to return they were to make ready for their journey back.

The search party returned just as sunlight was beginning to appear over the tops of the tress. They reported that they had found no one. Everyone boarded the boats and they made their way back across the lake.

Coming across the mountains took longer than expected because of the storm and the children.

Once they returned to the castle, he had the children taken to the nursery and then immediately came to make his report.

K'orik had sat quietly, listening to the report. He didn't say a word until Ogiloth was done and then he spoke.

"I'm pleased that you followed my instructions exactly," he said, standing up, "but I am very disappointed that you did not return with what I asked for." And then, in a more stern voice, "It seems as if what I sent you looking for was there, you just didn't capture him. Now I want you to assemble a small group of your best and go back and find him. You will find him and bring him back to me or not return at all. Is that clear?" He ended on a very harsh tone.

"Yes sir," Ogiloth replied.

"Now leave me!" With a look of disgust and a wave of his hand he plopped back down onto the couch.

Ogiloth turned and walked out of K'orik's room, making sure not to close the door too harshly. He was angry with himself but he knew K'orik was even angrier. The last thing he wanted was for K'orik to take his anger out on him.

# CHAPTER 3

J'ORIK AND LIANNA had been walking across the Great Plains for some time now enjoying the late afternoon sun. There was a slight breeze to keep them cool. He would look back to the west periodically to see if they were being followed, he saw nothing. He did notice, however, that the clouds were becoming very dark beyond the forest and thought they might just possibly get some rain later in the night. The Great Plains was a vast expanse of low, rolling hills with clumps of a reed-like grass growing everywhere they could see. These clumps of grass made for good hiding places for the small wildlife that roamed the plains. Every so often a herd of deer could be seen off in the distance, too far away for J'orik to shoot for dinner. Since it was just the two of them it didn't make much sense to even attempt going after the deer. Not once did they come across any water. Small, sparse groves of trees could be seen far off and he explained that water could be found near the trees. They passed a few rock outcroppings as well and he told her that when they stopped to make camp it would be in a rock outcropping, for safety if for anything. She made comments about the beautiful flowers that they passed on their way; blues, purples, yellows, and reds. The flowers provided a very pleasant aroma in the air and she would take in the smell with a deep breath and a sigh. He pointed north, towards the mountain range that could barely be seen from where they were at, and told her they were called the Arrget Mountains. They ran from the north end of Murwood Forest, east, to the north end of the Dorguri Mountains. At the intersection of the two mountain ranges was another large, roundish lake. It was nothing close to the size of Lake Wishik. In the middle of that lake was an island that rose as high as the mountains around. Looking east, they could only make out the tops of the tallest peaks in that range. And to the south lay the Great Desert which, he was told, seemed to go on forever. He'd learned about these places and their names from his uncle in Washoe. All in all, their trek across the plains so far was pleasant and uneventful.

The sun was beginning to near the horizon and another day was nearly done. They hadn't seen anyone, or anything, the whole afternoon. Other than pointing out a few things that were new or unusual to Lianna and telling her about what bordered the plains, they hadn't talked much. After all, he'd asked her to be quiet so as not to frighten any possible food away. She was beginning to feel as if he'd made that request because he just didn't want to talk with her.

Finally, shortly before sunset, he spotted a couple of rabbits and stopped in his tracks. she nearly ran into him. He quietly and quickly brought his crossbow up, knocked an arrow, took aim at one of the rabbits, and shot. The shot was true. The other rabbit was startled by the shot and dashed off. He went to retrieve the rabbit he'd shot and she followed right behind him. Even though things had been going well and she wouldn't be able to lose sight of him, she didn't want to be too far from his side. After retrieving the rabbit he started looking for a spot for them to rest for the night. He wanted to find a spot before the sun went completely down and there was no more light. It wasn't long before he found what he was looking for.

The outcropping of rocks was shaped almost like a horse shoe and rose about chest high from the floor of the plains. The rocks provided the protection they would need if anything were to happen. The open end pointed generally northeast. Since most of the wind came from the southwest, the rocks would provide protection against any heavier wind that might arise. At one time there must have been a tree or two that grew there because there were dry, brittle branches lying around and some gnarled roots still sticking out of the rocks. It couldn't have been any more perfect; protection from the elements and wood for a campfire.

"This is perfect," he said, satisfied. "I couldn't have asked for anything better."

"Yes," she agreed.

"How about you collect some wood for a fire," he suggested, "while I clean and prepare the rabbit."

"Okay."

He'd just about finished with the rabbit when she returned with more than enough wood. She gathered some grass, broke up some of the smaller branches, and composed the fire pit as she had seen him do. She took the flint out of his pack and lit the fire. He was impressed at how proficient she was becoming and how quickly she learned. Soon after, they were both sitting against the rocks, relaxing and enjoying their rabbit meal. By this time the sun had set fully and darkness had set in.

"We need to put the fire out," he told her. "We don't want to provide any way for anyone to see us out here in the open and the fire would be a dead giveaway in the dark."

It seemed like she was going to disagree with him, but then she agreed. "You're probably right."

After extinguishing the fire and letting their eyes adjust to the dimness, he untied his bedroll from his pack and unrolled it for her.

"Here, you take the bedroll," he told her, "I'll be fine just like this. It isn't that cold. In fact, it's not cold at all."

"Thank you," was about all she could say. But then she added, "You *are* a very kind man." And with that, she curled up on the bedroll and fell fast asleep.

He sat there for a short while just watching her. He did find her to be pretty and they did seem to get along well. But, for right now, he needed to concentrate on getting to Washoe and making sure she was safe. Protecting her was the most important thing to him right now. The other could wait until another time. He sat back and peered into the night sky, feeling the breeze blow across his face. It was quite peaceful. And then he was asleep.

J'orik woke the next morning with a start. A branch had snapped loudly nearby. He quickly looked around to see where the sound had come from. He noticed that Lianna was not laying on the bedroll and he became a little frantic. *Where had she gone?* he wondered. He stood slowly while scanning the plains around him and saw her wandering a short distance from their camp. She had a bundle of flowers in her arm and when he spotted her she was squatting down to pick up some more. He called to her and she looked up at him with a smile. He noticed she had made a ringlet out of some of the flowers and had placed them in her hair. *She looks even prettier with those flowers in her hair*, he thought.

She walked back to the camp and handed him a small bouquet of flowers. "Here, these are for you." She smiled again.

"What am I supposed to do with them?" he asked.

"Why, smell them of course," she replied. "They'll help you feel better."

He took them from her saying, "Thank you." Hesitantly he put them up to his face and smelled. They smelled wonderful and he did seem to feel a little better.

"Where have you been?" he asked her. "You look like you've bathed."

"I did," she answered, "sort of. Even though you said there probably wouldn't be any water around, I found a small pool of it over there." She pointed. "Enough so that I could at least wash the dirt off my skin and wet my hair. I was also able to get most of the grime out of my clothes too."

"You look very pretty this morning," he tried to be nice. "And you smell just like the flowers."

"Thank you. You should try it yourself. It feels wonderful not to be filthy."

"You're right," he agreed.

So he headed off in the direction she had pointed and soon enough found the small pool of water. He bent down and proceeded to rinse the dirt and grime from himself. Once done, he found that he did feel much better. He stood, turned, and walked back towards the camp. By the time he returned she had rolled up the bedroll and attached it to his pack. She had also removed any sign that there had been a campfire there. He was impressed. She was definitely a quick learner or she knew more about being in the wilderness than she let on. He preferred to believe she was a quick learner. The other option opened up some negative possibilities which he didn't even want to consider.

"Ah, you look much better," she complimented him. "Even handsome. If we put a few of these flowers in your pocket you'll smell as clean as you look." She walked over and tried to stuff some of the flowers in his pocket.

"I don't know about wearing any flowers," he told her, trying to gently stop her.

"I didn't say to wear them silly," she laughed. "I meant to put them in your pocket. They don't even need to show."

"Oh, right," he said with some embarrassment and stuffed a handful in his breast pocket. "There, how's that?"

"Perfect," she replied. She stepped closer to him, closed her eyes, and took a big sniff. "Perfect."

He smiled back at her and asked, "Are you ready to head out?"

"Whenever you are, kind sir," she responded with a smile.

He put his pack on and they continued their trek southeast across the plains towards the only town he'd been to east of the forest.

The morning was pleasant. A slight breeze coming from the southwest, a few clouds in the sky, over all what seemed like a very nice morning. Looking back to the west he noticed that the dark clouds he'd seen yesterday seemed to have dissipated. It didn't appear that there would be any bad weather coming their way today. He also hoped there wouldn't be anything else bad coming their way either.

They had only been walking half the morning when he spotted the town ahead.

"There's the town," he told her, pointing, "right over there."

"Where?" she asked, "I don't see anything except more plains."

He didn't realize that she might not be able to see as well as him. He forgot that his vision was better than most. He pointed in the direction of the town and told her, "There, right at the edge of the horizon. We should be there by midafternoon."

"Okay," she acknowledged, accepting what he said, "If you say so."

They continued walking. The rest of their journey was uneventful and they arrived in the town about when he'd said they would. The sun was about halfway between midday and the horizon.

They arrived on the outskirts of town where the road heads west, back towards the forest. Washoe was bustling this time of day. Looking into town they could see people walking about doing their business. Lianna had never been to a place like this, she'd never been outside the village. She was a little intimidated by it and immediately moved closer to him and grabbed hold of his hand. He didn't seem to mind or think much about her action, almost expecting it, so he just squeezed back.

"It's okay," he reassured her, smiling, "you'll be fine. Just stick close to me."

"I've never been to a place like this," she stuttered. "It's so much bigger and busier than our village ever was." Her head was moving side to side as she clung to him.

"Well, there are a lot more people," he explained, "and the town gets a lot more business and traffic then our village would ever get. People come here from all over so you might see some things that'll startle you. Just stay calm and close to me and everything will be fine."

"All right," she said, and squeezed his hand tight.

"I'm going to take us to the Dragons' Lair now," he began telling her. "You know, the place I told you my aunt and uncle have. They'll be able to set us up in a room for the night. Tomorrow I'll head back to the village while you wait for me there."

"What do you mean 'wait for you'?" she asked him with concern. "I thought we already talked about this. You don't think I'm going to stay here in a strange place, with strange people, while you go back to the village alone. I'm going back with you."

"I just thought it would be safer if I went back alone," he tried telling her again. "You don't want to run into any of those 'monsters' again, do you?" he asked, looking down at her with a smirk.

"Not really," she replied. "But it can't be too much different than being left alone in a strange place like this."

"I guess this is something we'll need to discuss some more a little later," he conceded. "Let's just concentrate on making our way to the inn." Then he turned and headed off down the road with Lianna in tow.

The town hadn't changed much from the last visit he'd made but he could tell it was making quite an impression on

Lianna. It was definitely different than the village; the sights and sounds, the number of people, and especially the clothes that the people wore. Every so often she would squeeze his hand tighter and look up at him with wonder in her eyes. She seemed almost like a child in this environment. They passed by a variety of shops and she would look inside each one to see what they contained. A few times she stopped him so she could take a closer look at something unusual she saw. It wasn't long before they came to the inn run by his aunt and uncle.

He stopped and turned to her. "This is the place I told you about."

He reached down and opened the door and, being the 'kind man' she said he was, he let her enter first. She still did not let go of his hand. Once they were both inside he shut the door and the noise level immediately dropped. The noise inside was different, more subdued. The interior wasn't what you would call plush, but it felt and looked very comfortable. The walls were painted a deep forest green and decorated with a variety of flowers. There was a short, purple, laced material that ran around the top of the wall where it met the ceiling. Hanging from the ceiling was a large, round, gold and silver chandelier with multifaceted crystals and candle holders hanging all over it. Two paintings hung on the wall to the right as you enter the room, both of a nondescript landscape. The front counter was straight ahead, no more than a few paces from the entry, and stretched from a stairway on the left to an arched opening on the right that led into another room. What noise they did hear emanated from that room. The front counter wasn't anything spectacular either but had a design that matched well with the interior. It was made of oak with a walnut stain and had a relief of two dragons in aerial combat, one red and one blue. The counter top had a glassy appearance and, upon closer examination, Lianna noticed that it looked like stone. There was a book in the middle of the counter with an ink well and writing quill. A large oval mirror hung on the wall behind the counter with a frame plated in gold and silver. She noticed that the frame also had a dragon pattern on it similar to the relief on the front of the counter. Above the mirror in large gold and silver lettering was the name of the inn—The Dragons' Lair. She also couldn't help but notice her reflection in the mirror. She just stood there in wonderment. It had been the first time she had ever seen such a clear reflection of herself. The mirror she used back at the village was nothing close to the clarity of the one she was currently looking into. She closed her mouth suddenly because she noticed, from the reflection, that it was hanging wide open.

A heavy-set man was behind the counter. He wore a plain white, long-sleeved shirt with a black leather vest over the top. His hair was well manicured into swirling ringlets and shined from all the gel in it. His spectacles were round with thin silver wire framing and his eyes seemed to sparkle for no apparent reason. He looked up from what he was doing and spotted J'orik. A smile immediately crossed his face and his eyes seemed to light up even more.

"J'orik," he spoke excitedly, "we haven't seen you here for quite some time. What brings you?"

"First, let me introduce you to my traveling companion," J'orik started. "This is Lianna, from my village," he said as he motioned in her direction, and then to Lianna, "this is Casper," as he turned back towards Casper, "my uncle Casper."

"It's nice to meet you, Lianna." Casper spoke with seeming sincerity.

"It's nice to meet you, Casper," she responded.

Casper then turned back to J'orik and asked again, "So, what brings you, and Lianna, here to our most humble establishment?"

J'orik did not have a happy look on his face. "The village was attacked a few days ago and, besides myself and Lianna here, I believe everyone was killed."

"Oh my." Casper now had a frown on his face and a look of concern. "What happened?" And before J'orik could respond, Casper waved his hands and told him, "Wait. Before you start, let's go into my office so there aren't any interruptions and I can hear it all without the background noise." Then he hollered into the other room, "Jarrel, come in here and take over at the counter for a while." There was no immediate response, so he hollered even louder, "Jarrel, did you hear me? Get in here!"

A young man dressed very similar to Casper entered from the other room and said, "Yes, Father. What is it you need me for now?"

"I need you to take over here at the counter," he commanded, "while I take these two people into my office for a talk. Make sure you stay at the counter this time. I don't know how long we'll be but I want you to stay here 'til we're done. Okay?"

"Yes, Father." The boy sighed as he moved behind the counter to take over.

Casper then motioned for J'orik and Lianna to follow him into his office. "Right this way." He lifted a portion of the counter top where it met the wall allowing them to come behind the counter. Dropping the counter back down, he opened the door to his office.

All three entered the office. Casper entered last and shut the door behind him. "Have a seat." He motioned towards a couple chairs set in front of his desk. Casper then walked around the desk and plopped himself down in a large, overstuffed chair behind the desk. Once he made himself comfortable he leaned back and turned to J'orik. "Now tell me what happened."

J'orik proceeded to tell him that a large force of ugly, disgusting creatures had overrun the village. How they had killed indiscriminately and set all the homes on fire. He explained that he had fought with all his strength until he saw that there was no way he would be able to survive if he stayed any longer. How he had found his mother killed in their home and he was unable to find his father. How he had escaped into the forest and run until he fell down exhausted and fell slept. How, the next night, Lianna had wandered into his camp and told him her story. Finally, how the two of them had made their way across the plains to Washoe and The Dragons' Lair.

Casper listened intently to every word without interrupting. He then turned to Lianna and asked, "How's the back of your head? Do you need to have it looked at?"

"There's still a slight bump but it's not sore anymore," she answered, "I think I'll be all right."

"I'm sorry to hear that this happened," Casper said, "but it doesn't surprise me. I've heard of similar cases throughout the realm. Villages being burned to the ground and the villagers killed. All of it being done by creatures as you have described. But there are a few details in those stories that I don't hear in yours. All the women are found slaughtered and lying about inside the village. All the men have been scalped and piled outside the village. But the most disturbing part is that there was no sign of the children, almost as if they just disappeared or, worse yet, were taken. Now, I know it's hard for you to imagine, but do you remember seeing anything like that?"

J'orik and Lianna both looked at each other in puzzlement then turned back to Casper and said in unison, "No."

"I left while the attack was still occurring," added J'orik.

"And it was still dark when I left. I was more concerned with getting away," Lianna told him. "But I do remember seeing my children dragged away, not killed."

"I plan on returning to the village," J'orik told him. "I'll be leaving tomorrow and I was hoping that you could put Lianna up here in a room until I return."

Before Casper could even respond, Lianna spoke up and snapped, "No. You're not leaving me here when I can travel back with you and see for myself what's left of the village. I could also help you if something were to happen."

"I don' know, Lianna," J'orik started. "We've talked about . . ."

"I'll not hear another word about it, J'orik," she demanded. "It was my village too. My friends and family lived there and I need to see for myself."

Casper had a wry look on his face as a smiled crossed it. "Sounds like your travel companion will be travelling back with you," he said to J'orik. "And believe me, once a woman makes up her mind to do something there's no stopping her." He ended with a chuckle.

Lianna gave J'orik a look of contempt and superiority, crossing her arms.

Casper saw her look and told J'orik, "And by the look on her face I'd say you have no choice in the matter."

J'orik just sighed and looked back at both of them. He could see that Casper was probably right. He didn't seem to have much of a choice. With that, he told Lianna, "All right then, we'll both go back—together." Then he turned to Casper. "Right now, though, I think we both need to get cleaned up, have a bite to eat, and then prepare for our journey. Do you have a room available for the night, uncle? I have no money."

"Bah," responded Casper. "After what you just went through, and the fact that you're my nephew, I'll set you up in a room at no charge. The question now, however," he asked, "is—do you want a room together?" A grin appeared on his face again.

J'orik said, "I don't see a problem. We've slept close together the last two nights and I don't see that one more night will make any difference."

Lianna just nodded in agreement. With that, Casper led them both back out to the front and signed them into a room.

He told them, "After you get situated and cleaned up come back down to the dining room and I'll have a meal prepared for you." Then he turned to J'orik with a smile. "You know your aunt Karin will be very happy to see you again. She'll probably fix you one of her best meals."

"I'm looking forward to it," he responded appreciatively. "Again, I want to thank you for all you've done for me—for us." He motioned towards Lianna.

"No problem," Casper said. "Family needs to stick together."

J'orik and Lianna then made their way up the stairs to their room. After settling in, which didn't take long, they took turns visiting the community bathroom to clean up. J'orik let Lianna go first so she could wash the dirt out of her clothes and have enough time for them to dry while he was bathing. He washed his over-shirt while bathing and hung it up in the room when he returned. He took out the extra one he had in his pack and put it on. After they were done they headed back down to the dining room to eat.

Casper was right. Karin was elated to have J'orik visiting. She served the meal herself. After the meal was laid out for them she turned to J'orik with a huge smile on her face. "I'm so glad to see you again J'orik. It's been too long since the last time you were here. Your uncle filled me in on what has happened and I just want you to know how sorry I am." Then she turned to Lianna with a look of sorrow. "I'm especially sad to hear about what happened to your family. It must have been difficult. If you ever need someone to talk with about it I'm here." She put a smile back on her face then and looked at both of them. "Enjoy your meal. I would love to stay and chat longer but I need to get back in the kitchen." She turned and walked away. On her way she looked back at them with a smile, winked, and then continued on her way.

They ate their meal with very little conversation. It was the first good, full meal they'd eaten since escaping from their village and Casper was right, the meal was fantastic. After they finished eating they returned to their room and fell into the bed completely exhausted. They both fell asleep immediately.

# CHAPTER 4

A FTER LEAVING K'ORIK, Ogiloth went to do as told. He gathered ten of his best warriors and ordered them to prepare to leave the next day. He wasn't sure how long they would be gone so they needed to organize for at least a ten-day journey. Their mission would be a search and recover and he would fill them in on more details the following morning before they started out. He reinforced what K'orik had commanded. They were not to return empty handed. He excused them to carry out his orders and then went to his quarters to prepare himself for the journey.

He went over and over all the details of what had happened when they had attacked the village. Everything seemed to point to one thing; who he had been sent for was there, he had just escaped. When he went back this time, though, he would not fail.

He ate his meal and lay down to sleep with all these thoughts ripping through his mind.

The next morning Ogiloth gathered his team of warriors together in a briefing room to go over the details they would need to know. He explained briefly what had happened at the village his previous force had attacked a few days earlier and that they would be travelling to the same village again to start their search. He told them who they were looking for and briefly how to identify him. He reminded them again that failure was not an option. Once the briefing was over he and his team left the castle and began their journey.

They made good time across the mountains. The rain had stopped the day before and by that morning the clouds had already begun to dissipate. The road, however, was still wet and slippery in places. They had to clear a couple of rock and mud slides, but these were nothing that impeded their journey. The warriors he had chosen were strong and ornery and the obstacles they came across were nothing for them to clear.

They arrived on the western bank of Lake Wishik late that night. He ordered his team to load the boat with all their supplies before retiring for the night. He told them they would be leaving at first light the next morning. They should get as good a rest as possible because they would need to make the eastern shore of the lake by the next night. He told them that if they pushed hard they should make it there by dark. He knew he'd assembled the best when none of them balked at the challenge. They all knew they were at the widest point of the lake and it normally took more than a day to cross, but they also knew they were on an important mission. None of them wanted to disappoint their leader. Ogiloth could be generous to those that followed his orders and did well. They all knew this and were anxious to please him.

The following morning they left at daybreak and began the push across the lake. The weather was in their favor, as well as the conditions on the lake. They made the eastern shore just as the sun was setting. Ogiloth was pleased that things were going well and he conveyed this emotion to his team.

Ogiloth was a born leader. He could be cruel at times, but only when warranted. He could also be generous. The forces he led for K'orik knew how he could be. K'orik knew how he could be also, which is why K'orik had chosen him to lead. Even though Ogiloth appeared to have a softness about him, the forces he led knew he was strong and led with a strong hand.

The boat was beached, secured, and unloaded. Camp was made before it was completely dark. Ogiloth wasn't concerned that anyone would see them because the nearest village was the village his previous force had destroyed. No one should be anywhere nearby. There were other settlements along the banks of Lake Wishik but they were either further to the south or north and he knew those people generally kept to themselves.

After settling into camp he gathered his team around the campfire to cover what they would be doing the next day.

"The first thing I want to say," as he looked around at each warrior, "is that I am well pleased with all of you. We have covered a long distance in a short time and all of you should be pleased with yourselves."

A shout went up around the campfire. "Huh! Huh! Huh!"

Ogiloth was good at lifting morale. He knew that a positive start was the best way to begin.

"But the real mission," he continued, "begins tomorrow. I know I've told you that failure is not an option and I still hold to that, but keep in mind that I am not the one you need to fear if you do not succeed. We all know who I speak of and he has told me that death would be a preference over returning empty handed."

There was a chatter of agreement and nodding of heads when he said that. They all knew who he was referring to.

After they all quieted down, he continued. "The first task will be to revisit the village and confirm that there are no survivors. If you find anyone alive they are to be killed. The only ones you are not to kill are the men. If you find any men alive they are to be brought to me—alive."

There was a low groan that went around the campfire. He knew that the group he'd put together much preferred the killing rather than capturing.

"Once the first task is complete," he carried on, "if there are any homes or other structures still standing, even partially, you are to finish destroying them. I don't want anything left to return to."

The team let out a shout again. "Huh! Huh! Huh!"

"Once these tasks have been completed," he continued, "we'll regroup back at the camp here. If we haven't found who we came for I'll inform you what we'll do next. Tomorrow will be a busy day so I suggest that you get a good night's rest. You've all worked hard getting here. I don't foresee any opposition," he added, "but if there is you will need to be at your best. Also, just as a precaution, I want a guard posted through the night. You'll take two-hour shifts until morning, beginning with you," he clapped the warrior to his immediate left, "and going in order from here." He pointed in a clockwise direction from the one that would begin the watch. "Whoever is on guard at daybreak will wake everyone else, beginning with me. And what I mean be daybreak is when first light appears over the tops of the trees."

After the briefing he excused them for the night. They all dispersed and went to their individual tents. Then he retired to his own tent. He spent a short time considering what their next move would be if they came up empty handed after surveying the village and then fell asleep.

# CHAPTER 5

THE NEXT MORNING J'orik and Lianna awoke feeling refreshed. They hadn't slept this well since their escape. The morning light was beginning to brighten the room. Both of them rolled off the bed, stood, and stretched. The bed was most comfortable and had offered them both a restful sleep.

"That was wonderful." Lianna yawned as she stretched. "I can't remember ever sleeping in such a comfortable bed. I don't remember waking one time during the night. How did you sleep, J'orik?"

"I feel the same way," he answered, yawning and stretching also. "But I've slept in these beds before and they are very comfortable. How about we head down to the dining room and see what Aunt Karin can whip up for breakfast. I'm starving."

"If it's anything compared to what she made for dinner last night, I'm looking forward to it."

They made their way down the stairs and into the dining room. As they passed by the front counter Jarrel greeted them with a smile. "Good morning. I hope you had a restful night."

"Yes," they both responded at the same time.

Before they could ask, Jarrel told them, "Father is in his office working on some business and mother is busy in the kitchen getting started for the day. Go on into the dining room and have a seat. I'll tell mother you're up and ready for some breakfast." He then headed into the kitchen to let his mother know.

There were only a few people in the dining room this early in the morning. It was quiet and they took a table near a window. The interior of the dining room was similar to the inn's entry. It was apparent to Lianna that it had been decorated with a woman's touch. Not so much, though, that a man would feel uncomfortable. The tables were of simple construction covered with a white cloth and decorated with a vase of fresh picked flowers set in the middle. A couple chandeliers similar to the one in the entry hung from the ceiling. The floor was hardwood and the windows had curtains embroidered with flowers that had already been drawn open for the day. Several paintings hung on the walls, again of nondescript landscapes. The bar counter was just like the one in the entry area. There were a dozen, three-legged stools setting in front of it and a metal foot rail ran the whole length. Behind the bar was another counter with cupboards. Shelves lined the wall on either side of another mirror similar to the one in the entry. A walk space was provided between the end of the bar and the wall common to the entry area and the dining room leading to the doorway into the kitchen. And, like the entry, there were images of dragons everywhere. This made her feel very comfortable, almost like she was home.

Karin came walking across the room with a smile stretching across her face. She was wiping her hands on her apron and, as she stopped at the table, she brought her hands together and asked, "What can I get for you two this bright and sunshiny morning?"

Before J'orik could get a word out Lianna returned Karin's smile and responded, "What do you suggest? I'm sure anything you offer will be wonderful."

"Well, first I need to know how hungry you are," looking at Lianna.

J'orik quickly interjected, "I'm starving."

Both women turned to him with stern looks on their faces. He recognized that look and quickly put his lips together and sat back in his chair. He knew he'd spoken too soon and decided it would be best if he just sat quietly and waited until his aunt asked him directly.

Karin and Lianna looked back at each other and Lianna said, "I don't think I'm as 'starving' as J'orik," glancing at him, "but I'm very hungry and like I said, I'm sure that whatever you bring me will be delightful."

"I think I know just the thing," Karin offered. Then she turned to J'orik. "And I think I know just the thing for you too young man." She giggled. "Would you like some coffee while you wait?"

They both nodded yes and she went and returned with two mugs and a pot of coffee. She set the mugs down and filled them. Leaving the pot on the table she smiled wide again and headed back to the kitchen.

J'orik and Lianna made small talk while sipping their coffee and waiting for their morning meal. Lianna would glance out the window periodically to watch the activity that went on outside on the road and on the adjacent sidewalk. For the most part, she noticed, the people went about their business without a care in the world. It seemed to her that, for them, this was the only place in the universe and that nothing evil could happen. She was thinking back to her village and the life she led there. She thought the same way she supposed these people did until the day the village was attacked. Then her whole world turned upside down and was changed forever. Her life would never be the same, and she knew it. She was gazing out the window lost in her thoughts when she was suddenly brought back to reality by J'orik saying her name.

"Lianna, Lianna," J'orik called to her. Then he spoke louder. "Lianna! Are you there?" And when she turned to him he said in a softer tone, "Breakfast is here."

Lianna brought her attention back into the dining room and their table. Karin was standing there with two platters in her hands, preparing to set them down.

"This," Karin told Lianna, "I thought you might enjoy." As she set the platter down she described what was on it. "It's one of my favorites for breakfast. It sounds simple, and it is, but it's perfect for starting the day. Scrambled chicken eggs with a medley of fresh garden vegetables mixed in, seasoned with ground pepper and basil; diced red potatoes covered with a white gravy sauce and whole basil leaves, the gravy is my own personal recipe; a couple of wheat biscuits fresh from the oven; and some apricot jam to spread on the biscuits. I hope you enjoy it as much as I do."

"It looks and smells wonderful." Lianna closed her eyes and took a deep smell. "I'm sure I will."

Karin then turned and set J'orik's platter down in front of him. "I know how much you like rabbit so I've prepared you an oven-roasted, butter-basted one stuffed with seasoned breading; a medley of fresh garden vegetables sautéed in butter with ground pepper and rosemary; a couple of wheat biscuits fresh from the oven; and strawberry jam spread for the biscuits."

J'orik looked up at his aunt with a big smile on his face. "You sure know how to win a man's heart." And then he began eating without another word.

Karin just smiled back at him and giggled. "I'll have Jarrel bring you some fresh squeezed orange juice to help wash it all down." Then she left and disappeared into the kitchen.

A moment later, Jarrel appeared with two cups of the orange juice and set them on the table. He just smiled without saying anything and left them to their breakfast.

They both ate their meals without speaking. Lianna could see that J'orik wasn't much interested in talking. He just kept shoveling his meal in his mouth like he hadn't eaten in days. But then, she thought, he really hadn't eaten a good home-cooked meal in days. She also enjoyed her meal. Karin was right. It was the perfect meal to start the day. She ate nearly everything realizing she hadn't had a home-cooked meal in days either. When she looked over at J'orik, his rabbit was nothing but a skeleton; the vegetables were non-existent; the strawberry jam had disappeared; and he was mopping up the remnants with the last bite of one of the biscuits. She just smiled as she watched him swallow the last bite. He picked up the cup of orange juice, which he hadn't touched yet, and washed it all down.

He sighed with contentment as he sat back in his chair. "That was fabulous," he said, looking at her. "Aunt Karin outdid herself this time."

She still had a little bit of everything left on her platter. She smiled and giggled and asked him, "Did you even taste it?"

"Of course I tasted it," he replied with a snort. "I just said it was fabulous. How would I know that if I didn't taste it?" Then he glanced down at her platter. "Are you going to finish yours?"

"I think I've had enough. Why, do you want the rest?"

"Yes," he replied quickly. "Can't let good food go to waste. And besides, Aunt Karin went to all this trouble. It would be an insult not to finish it." He pushed his platter to the side, reached across the table, grabbed her platter, and set it down in front of himself. Within seconds what was remaining on her platter disappeared as well.

About that time Karin came out from the kitchen and walked over to their table. She looked down at Lianna with a wry grin on her face and asked, "Did he let you have any of it?"

"Yes. But I ate enough to satisfy my hunger. It was delicious."

"Yes, Aunt Karin. I waited until she was done," he spoke up. "I must say, though, you've outdone yourself. It was most delicious." Then he belched.

Both women just looked at him with disgust.

"Excuse me," he offered apologetically.

Karin reached down and took the two platters. "Did you want more orange juice?" she asked them both.

They both nodded that they didn't and Lianna told her, "No, thank you."

Karin picked up the empty cups and went back into the kitchen.

They just sat quietly for a while letting their food digest. Lianna let her eyes wander back out through the window to watch the activity outside again. J'orik belched again, quietly this time but still loud enough to disturb her respite. He apologized again. She just smiled back at him.

"I think it's about time we start getting ready for our walk back to the village," he told her. "It's still early and if we leave soon we should be able to reach the forest before nightfall. We'll be travelling on the road so the walk will be shorter than the one we took coming from the forest."

She nodded in agreement. They both took one last sip of their coffee, rose from the table, and headed back to their room.

As they were passing through the inn's entry area Casper stopped them. "Well, good morning to the two of you," he said with a smile. "I hope you had a good rest last night. Did you find the bed to your liking?"

They both responded, "Yes," smiling back at him.

It seemed the man always had a smile on his face and it was difficult not to smile back.

"Will you be staying another night?" he asked.

"No," J'orik responded quickly before Lianna could speak. "We're heading out this morning after we get our things."

"Where will you be going from here?" he asked curiously. "I hope you're not planning to go back to the village."

"That's exactly where we plan to go," J'orik informed him.

"But I thought you said it was destroyed, burned to the ground," he said with some concern. "I don't see the sense in returning, plus it may not be safe."

"Safe or not," J'orik began, "we're going back. I need to make sure whether or not there were any survivors. If there are, then I want to help them." Then he noticed the glaring look he was getting from Lianna and added, "*We* want to help them."

"It sounds like you have your minds made up," he conceded. "Before you leave, though, I want you to see your aunt so she can put together a food package for you to take along. I'm sure she'll have a few words for both of you about going back to that place. And, she'll definitely want to say farewell."

"All right uncle, but it won't matter what she says, we are going back."

They made their way back up the stairs and to their room. They gathered their things together, headed back down the stairs, and made their way into the dining room. Karin was already there waiting for them with some food for their journey. She did not have a very happy look on her face. Both of them knew that Casper had been right about her having a few words for them about returning back to the village. They walked over to the counter and stood there looking at her, waiting for her to say something.

"Casper told me what you two are planning to do," she began. "I'm sure you know that it doesn't make me very happy.

I completely disagree with you returning," she continued. "I say 'what's done is done'. You need to look to the future and move on with your lives. You could stay here for a while and visit," she said hopefully, "See what happens. Maybe you might even decide to stay here in Washoe for a long while. Maybe even make it your home." Then she turned to J'orik. "You, I know, have many talents that would be very useful in a town like this. I know of several businesses that could use a man with your talents." Then she turned to Lianna. "And you, child, I'm sure you have just as many talents. You should consider staying. I know you lost your family and probably everything you possessed, but we're more than happy to take you into our family." Then she looked at both of them with a big smile. "Besides, I think you two make a lovely couple."

Both of them blushed with embarrassment at her last remark.

"Aunt Karin, I know you and Uncle Casper are concerned, but we both feel compelled to go back. There was something wrong about what happened and we both want to find out why it happened."

"I know, child." she sighed. "And that's why I won't try any harder to stop you. Like your uncle said I would, I've put together a food package for your journey back. It should last at least until you get back to the village. I'm assuming you're taking the road, which means it shouldn't take more than a couple days to get there. I wish you both the best and a safe journey." She kissed them both on the cheek. "Stop on your way out and say farewell to your uncle. Take care now." She turned around without anything further and disappeared into the kitchen.

J'orik placed the food package in his pack. He and Lianna walked out of the dining room. As they were passing through the entry area they waved to Casper and said farewell.

"I wish there was something I could say or do to get you to stay." Casper made one last attempt. "But it seems you have your minds made up. Farewell and safe journey. I hope to see you both soon."

He waved to them as they left the inn and stepped out onto the sidewalk.

It was midmorning and the town of Washoe was alive with activity.

"Is it always this busy here?" Lianna asked as they made their way down the sidewalk.

"Every time I've been here it's been like this," he responded.

"It seems so big. So many people," she said distantly. "I think I prefer the peacefulness of a small village. The people here seem so distant. At least in a village everyone knows everyone."

"I agree," he replied with a sigh.

They had reached the outskirts of town and the end of the sidewalk. As they were leaving town they both glanced back for one final look at the busyness they were leaving behind. A wagon came rolling by heading towards the forest and they turned their heads to protect their eyes from the dust that it kicked up.

"Have you ever ridden in one of those?" she asked him curiously.

"What, a wagon?" he questioned back. She nodded and he said, "No. But I've ridden a horse."

"A horse?" she probed. "Is that one of the animals that pulls the wagon?"

"Yes," he responded.

"What was it like?"

"Bumpy," he told her and they both laughed.

Looking down the road and watching the wagon disappear in the distance they could just make out the tops of the tallest trees in the forest. The day was getting warm already. There wasn't a cloud in the sky and just the slightest hint of a breeze.

"If we continue at this pace," he told her, "we should get to the edge of the forest by early evening. Once we get there we need to move into the trees, away from the road, and find a good place to camp. We don't want to camp along the road."

She just nodded her assent. "One thing we won't have to do today," she went on, "is look for our evening meal."

He laughed at that. "You're right about that. I'm sure Aunt Karin packed us some of her best trail foods. My pack feels twice as heavy as it should be," as he shrugged the pack higher on his shoulders.

They didn't see any more wagons as they walked. They began seeing more of the forest as they neared it.

J'orik had been right, she thought, as she looked up and saw the sun starting to drop down below the tops of the trees. She could now see the base of the forest and it wasn't much longer before they reached the shadows cast by the tallest trees. It was at this point that J'orik began to veer to the north away from the road. She figured he'd decided it was time to move away from the road as they entered the forest. She just kept walking alongside him, not questioning his actions.

As they entered the forest he turned to her and said, "We need to find a secluded spot to make camp. A place far enough away from the road, that a small campfire won't be easily seen."

She just nodded in agreement and they both began looking. It wasn't long before they spotted what they were looking for.

While she set up camp he went looking for firewood. When he got back she had camp set up and a fire pit ready to go. She had already taken the food package out and rummaged through it for their evening meal. He built a small fire and she cooked the meal. As expected, there was rabbit. There was also some diced potatoes and raw vegetables as well as some of Karin's wheat biscuits. Lianna stuffed the diced potatoes in the rabbit. She put the rabbit on a spit she'd crafted, and began cooking it. They sat and ate some of the raw vegetables while the rabbit cooked. After the rabbit was done cooking, they devoured it and a couple biscuits. Karin had already pre-seasoned the rabbit and J'orik thought it tasted almost as good as the one he'd eaten that morning.

As he sat back after finishing his meal he moaned with satisfaction. "I'm stuffed." Then he turned to look at Lianna and told her, "Thank you for the meal. It was wonderful. You did a great job." Then he let out with a belch. He smiled and excused himself.

"You're welcome," she replied with a smile. "And thank you for the compliments."

The two of them just sat there for a while and let their meals digest as the fire slowly burned down. Darkness began to take the forest and neither one of them put any more wood on the fire. They had agreed to let it go out so that it wouldn't attract any attention. It wasn't long after the fire went out that they both fell fast asleep.

The night passed without event. The next morning seemed to come too early. They were awakened when a gang of turkeys ran by close to camp gobbling loudly. J'orik's eyes snapped open and he brought his knife to the ready. Lianna saw what he had done and brought her knife to the ready also.

"Shh," he hissed at her.

They both began scanning the forest and listening for anyone, or anything, that might be chasing the turkeys that had just run by. They didn't see or hear anything out of the ordinary so they both visibly calmed down.

"That was startling," she said.

"Yes, it was," he agreed. "I thought for sure those turkeys were running from something, but it seems they were just running."

"Good morning." She smiled at him. "Did you sleep well?"

"I slept very well, maybe too well."

"We've been going pretty much nonstop since we left the village," she reminded him.

"You're right. And we still have a little over a day's walk before reaching the other side of the forest."

"And the road comes out south of the village," she reminded him. "So we have that much further to get to the village."

"You're right again," he agreed. "We'll go back out and walk along the road today but we should do the same as we did yesterday and move into the forest before nightfall. If we see anyone coming while we're out we need to duck into the forest too."

She nodded her agreement and they broke camp. As they left their campsite he glanced back and thought to himself how competent she was becoming in the woods. Only someone expert in tracking would be able to tell anyone had made a camp there. Then he looked at her and smiled to himself. He was really beginning to like this woman that stumbled into his camp not more than a few days ago.

Before stepping out onto the road he looked in both directions to assure that it would be safe. Once he confirmed it was all right they both stepped out onto the road and began walking towards the western side of the forest. The only thing that happened during their walk that day was they saw a wagon coming east on the road heading towards Washoe. They had enough time before it passed by them to take cover in the forest. They both agreed that they didn't want to be seen, by anyone.

The rest of the day was uneventful. As the sun began to set and darkness started taking the forest again J'orik left the road and started heading into the trees. Lianna had mentioned to him during the day that the rabbit was the only meat Karin had packed for them and she thought quail sounded good to eat tonight. Shortly after leaving the road he shot down two quail for their evening meal, one for each of them to eat. Again she set up camp and he gathered firewood. He returned and started a fire and she cooked their meal. This time, however, rather than potato stuffed rabbit, she prepared potato stuffed quail. She also crumbled a couple of the biscuits in with the potatoes. The quail wasn't seasoned like the rabbit had been, but it turned out very good anyway. Along with the quail, they finished off the remainder of the vegetables.

Just like the night before, they let the fire burn down to nothing as darkness fell on the forest. With their stomachs full and the peaceful sounds in the forest, they both fell fast asleep again.

# CHAPTER 6

A T FIRST SIGN of light, the guard on duty went to Ogiloth's tent and woke him as ordered. Then he went around to all the others and woke them.

Ogiloth stepped out from his tent and saw that the others had been awakened and were doing the same. Not a single member of the team that he'd organized grumbled or moaned about being awakened. This was another good sign to him that he'd picked the best. If any one of them had been hard to get started, he thought to himself, he would have made an example of him. But he saw that that wouldn't be necessary.

"All right," he shouted. "Everyone have a quick bite to eat and let's get started. You all know what needs to be done, so let's move."

Without any prompting they all gave a quick, loud, "Huh! Huh! Huh!"

One of the warriors, Gorog by name, asked, "Will we be breaking camp before starting, sir?"

Ogiloth glanced at Gorog with a wry smile on his face. "You know, Gorog," he began his response, "normally I don't expect any questions from those under my command but in this case I'll make an exception. I'm feeling generous this morning and you should feel fortunate." Then he looked at all the other warriors as one and continued answering Gorog's question in a very sarcastic tone. "Gorog, here, wants to know if we'll be breaking camp before we get started." He looked around and laughed. "How many of you know the answer to that question?" The smile disappeared from his face as he waited for a response.

Every single one of them shot their hand in the air.

He pointed to one of them randomly, "You. What's the answer?"

"No, sir," he responded with a snap in his voice.

"And why is that?" he asked the warrior, still with sarcasm in his voice.

"Because it was not one of the orders you gave last night, sir," he snapped his answer again.

"That's exactly right," he said looking around at them all. Then his gaze stopped on Gorog and a sneer crossed his face. "Does that answer your question?" he asked gruffly.

"Yes, sir," Gorog replied. "It won't happen again, sir," he added with a snap in his voice too.

"Good," he said, "Because next time you won't be so fortunate." He looked around at the rest and added, "All right, enough delaying. Let's move out." He turned and headed towards the village.

All the warriors on the team just glared at Gorog in disbelief. They couldn't understand why Ogiloth had been so easy on him. But then none of them knew that Gorog was Ogiloth's cousin.

The village was about five hundred yards north of camp and about one hundred yards from the shoreline up against the western edge of the forest. It only took Ogiloth and his team a few minutes to get to the village. There was a stench as they neared the village. A pile of bodies lay just outside the village to the south. He informed his team that these were the men from the previous visit. Flying insects were swarming about the bodies and all the warriors just curled their noses and continued on into the village. There were more bodies spread all about the ground inside the village and he explained that these were the women that had been slaughtered previously. Once inside the village they fanned out and began their search. It didn't take long because most of the homes had burned to the ground. After completing their search they reported back to Ogiloth informing him that they hadn't found any more survivors. Then he ordered them to demolish any remaining structures and meet him back down at the shoreline. They all dispersed back into the village and did as ordered while Ogiloth walked back down to the lake to wait, and to get away from the stench. After his team finished their task and met him back at the lake they all marched back to camp. All of this took less than an hour. His team of warriors was quick and efficient, which pleased him.

After returning to camp all the warriors gathered around Ogiloth to hear what they would be doing next. Some of them suspected what would happen next, but not a single one spoke or made a move. After what they had experienced this morning with Gorog, no one wanted to anger Ogiloth. They all knew that whoever tried to do what Gorog had done would most likely not survive the day. So they all stood quietly awaiting their next set of orders.

Ogiloth stood before them scanning the whole group before he began. This was easy for him to do because he stood about a foot and a half taller than the tallest of them. This made it necessary for all of them to look up at him.

"I want you all to know," he began, "that I am pleased with what we have accomplished so far. However, I am disappointed that we were unable to find what we came looking for. Even though I didn't expect to find him, I was hoping that we might have a stroke of luck and he would be there. This just means" he continued, "that it'll be necessary for us to look further, beyond the village. It's likely that he ran off into the forest to escape our previous attack. It's also likely that he would try to make his way to the nearest town once he reached the other side of the forest. So these are your orders." He began with the two trackers that he'd brought along. "Herg, Lorith, I want you two," directing his orders at them, "to return to the village and begin a search into the forest. I brought you two along because I was told you were the best trackers we had. Is that true?" he asked glaring at them.

They both responded with a snap, "Yes, sir."

"Good." Ogiloth smirked at them. "I don't want to see you again until we meet on the other side of the forest. When you get there I want you to make your way to where the road comes out of the forest. It will most likely be south of where you exit the forest. Now quickly gather what you need to take with you and go," he snapped.

Herg and Lorith left the meeting and headed off to follow his orders.

Then he turned to Gorog with a sinister smile. "And you, Gorog, since you showed so much interest in breaking camp. That'll be your task."

The others began to chuckle.

"QUIET!" he roared, looking out at them.

They all quieted immediately.

He looked back at Gorog and continued. "While the rest of us are gone you'll break camp and pack everything back onto the boat. You'll stay and stand guard over the boat and all of our gear until we return. Don't think that I'm doing this to punish you for what happened this morning," he assured him. "Someone needs to do this and since this is your first 'real' campaign you're the most likely choice for the task." He looked Gorog straight in the eyes with a big grin on his face and asked, "Do you have any questions?"

"No, sir," Gorog snapped his response, standing erect.

"Good. Now once the rest of us have left, you'll begin."

Then, turning his attention to the other seven warriors, he began explaining what they would be doing. "There's a road, a short distance south of here that runs through the forest, connecting the lake to the Great Plains. The rest of us will walk that road looking for any evidence of the man we came looking for. A town lies about a days' walk east of the forest on that road. I believe the man we're looking for probably went to that town. It'll take us about three days to reach this town simply because we'll be searching the forest along the road on our way. I want you all to pack enough to last that long. We can replenish our supplies if we end up going all the way to the town without finding what we're looking for. The people in the town will not be accepting of our kind but I don't see that we'll be going that far. I believe we'll find him, or evidence of him, before we get there. However, if we do end up going all the way to this town, I'll be the only one to enter it. The rest of you will stay outside the town, out of sight, until I return. I know this may be a lot of information for you to comprehend but I believe in all of you, otherwise I wouldn't have chosen you to come with me." He looked around at each one of them to see how they were taking all of this. None of them seemed to have a puzzled look on their face so he continued. "You all know what K'orik can be like. Well, this man we're looking for is just like K'orik. I want you all to stay alert and ready for anything. If at any time I give you an order to do something, I want you to respond immediately, without question and without thought. Just respond and do as ordered." He took one more look around and asked, "Do you understand?"

They all shook their heads affirmatively and in unison they responded, "Huh! Huh! Huh!"

"All right," he finished in a commanding tone, "let's pack up and move out!"

They all turned and went to pack their gear and supplies. Ogiloth did the same. Within a short time they were all heading south down the shoreline.

The next morning J'orik and Lianna woke as the sunlight was just starting to filter through the trees. They gathered their things together and packed to leave camp. Again they left the campsite as if there had not been one. They each ate a biscuit and started back towards the road. After assuring that it was safe they stepped out onto the roadway and started walking. It took less than an hour for them to come to the western edge of the forest. Once there, J'orik suggested they stop and rest and discuss what they would do next. As they sat there talking they both looked out over the lake and up and down the beach. The sunlight hadn't reached the beach yet so it was still a little dim. The trees were casting long shadows out across the beach like huge hands reaching for the water. As they continued to gaze out over the lake, the water started to brighten as more sunlight hit it. It was a beautiful morning and looked like it would be a beautiful day.

"I think we should stay away from the open and walk along the edge of the forest," he told her.

"I agree," she replied. "It's probably the safest. After all, we have no idea what's up ahead. Whether those monsters are still there or if they've left and even though I said I wanted to come back I'm not in a real hurry to see what's left of the village."

"Then why did you want to come back?"

"Because I do want to see what's left," she replied somewhat apprehensive. "I'm just anxious. And because I didn't want to be left behind to wait and worry."

"What is there to worry about?"

"You," She responded with a smile.

He just smiled back at that. He wondered again if maybe she hadn't somehow grown attached to him as much as he'd grown attached to her. The thought made him warm inside but he didn't say anything about it. He remembered what she'd told him about her family and what she'd witnessed. He wondered if maybe she was just reaching out for something, or someone, to hold onto. He'd be fine with that too and decided that if that was all she was looking for he'd be there for her.

"I think we should be on our way," he said as he stood up. He reached down with his hand to help her up. She grabbed hold of it and he pulled her up as she brushed the sand off her dress with her free hand.

"Thank you." She smiled at him again.

They started off towards the village, walking along the tree line. The village was about a mile and a half north of the road. A little over halfway there they both stopped suddenly and looked at each other.

"Did you hear that?" she whispered.

"Yes," he whispered back. "Let's move into the trees"

They both did as he suggested as quickly and quietly as possible. Once they were in the trees and hidden from view they both peered up the beach towards the sound they heard.

"What do you think it was?" she asked, still whispering.

"I'm not sure," he answered, still whispering himself. "But I'm going to find out. You stay here."

Lianna squatted down behind some bushes and J'orik began slowly making his way through the trees being careful not to make any noise. The sound seemed to come from out near the shoreline, he thought, so he kept his eyes scanning in that direction. It wasn't long before he saw what had made the noise. He stopped and hid behind a tree. There was a group of about a dozen of those ugly creatures that had attacked the village earlier. They had a camp set up at the shoreline. He noticed a boat tied off at the waters' edge. They were all gathered together. There was one larger and taller than the others doing all the talking. He guessed that he was probably the leader. He listened closely trying to hear what was being said. It sounded like he was giving them orders. The tall one stopped talking for a moment and pointed towards the village. He watched as two of them went to their tents, came out with packs on, and then headed back up the beach towards the village. As those two were leaving the tall one started talking to those that remained. From what he could make out it sounded like he was telling them they would be traveling the forest road towards Washoe looking for a man they thought had escaped from the village the last time they were there. He wondered if maybe someone else, other than himself, had escaped. Suddenly the whole group raised their hands in the air and made loud 'huh' sound three times, then dispersed into their tents and returned with packs on their backs. All accept one. He had a suspicion that that one was being left behind to guard their things while the rest went off in search for this man the tall one had been talking about. He saw that they were starting their way down the shore towards the forest road. He quickly made his way back to where he'd left Lianna. He found her still squatting behind a bush and squatted down next to her. Quietly, he conveyed to her what he'd seen and heard.

"There's about a dozen of those monsters up the beach," he started explaining in a whisper. "Two of them went back to the village, one was left behind to guard their things, and the rest are heading down the beach towards the forest road. I think we should stay right here," he continued, "hidden in the brush. You'll see the larger group pass by here soon. Once they've gone by and are out of earshot we can figure out what we're going to do next."

She just nodded her head acknowledging she'd heard what he said and agreed.

They both watched as the group of monsters walked by heading towards the forest road. She saw one huge monster out in front of the rest leading them down the shore. She glanced at J'orik with a frightened look on her face. He just put a finger to his lips indicating that she should be quiet. She peered back out and watched them pass by. After they were far enough down the shore that she could just make them out she looked up at J'orik.

"What do we do now?" she whispered.

"I'm not sure," he replied apprehensively. "I heard the big one say they were looking for a man that had escaped from the earlier attack. If that man isn't me then that means someone else may be out there and either wandering in the forest or somewhere along the lake."

"What do you think they'll do if they find him?" she probed.

"I'm not sure about that either. But if there's someone else out there we need to try and find him. There's a town further south along the lake that he might have headed for. It's about a two and a half day walk. If he made it there then that's where we'll find him. Before we go there, though, I want to go back to the village and see what's left of it. I might be able to pick up his trail there."

"What about the monster that stayed behind to guard the others' things? And the two that went back to the village?"

"I don't think we have to worry about the two that went back to the village," he told her. "The big one told them to start there and begin a search into the forest. The one at their camp, however, will be the only one we need to be concerned about right now. If I can get close enough I should be able to shoot him with my crossbow and eliminate that concern. It won't be easy though, there's a lot of open ground between the forest and the shoreline."

"What if we were to use me as bait to lure him closer to the forest?" she offered. "You could stay hidden in the trees and when he got close enough you could shoot him then."

He just looked at her with surprise. He couldn't believe she would be offering such a plan after all she'd been through.

"And what exactly do you have in mind?"

"Well, I was thinking that I could walk out of the forest straight up the beach from their camp. Walk towards the camp, disoriented, like I was glad to find someone still alive. Once he saw me, and saw that I saw what he was, I could turn in fear and start running back towards the forest. I wouldn't scream because I wouldn't want the others to hear me but I could certainly act frightened enough. I would think he'd chase after me then."

"What if he just takes up a weapon to shoot you down?" he asked concerned.

"I'll be looking back to see if he's chasing me, and if he does that then I'll fall down and he won't have a shot. Otherwise I'll just continue running back into the forest. Either way he'll have to chase me which will bring him closer to you hiding in the trees."

"If you're willing to take the risk then it sounds like a good plan to me."

With Lianna's plan in mind they both made their way quietly through the trees until they were straight up the beach from the camp. J'orik found himself a good tree to hide behind and knocked an arrow in his crossbow. They saw that the lone monster was packing things and loading the boat. J'orik indicated to Lianna that he was ready. She wandered out of the forest acting like she had said and started down the beach towards the camp. When she saw that the monster noticed her she put on a frightened look, which wasn't difficult, turned, and started running back towards the forest. The monster dropped what he was doing and reached for his sword. She kept glancing back with a look of fear on her face, a real look of fear. She noticed that he'd drawn his sword and was starting towards her. She didn't think he would try to throw the sword at her because of the distance but when he raised his arm and cocked it back like he was going to she immediately fell to the sand. When he saw her fall he started running up the beach towards her. She acted like she was trying to get up and when she glanced back she could see he was getting closer. She hoped that J'orik's shot would be true and find its mark before he reached her. Suddenly there was a whizzing sound and then a thud. J'orik had shot his arrow and she knew it had hit its mark. She glanced back and saw that the monster was still coming at her, even with an arrow stuck in his chest. There was another whizzing sound and another thud. She saw the arrow go straight into his mouth. He tried to scream but no sound came out and she watched as he fell to the sand. She quickly stood up and ran towards the forest where she knew J'orik had hidden. He was running out of the forest towards her while drawing his sword. He ran past her and continued towards the monster. She turned to watch just as J'orik plunged his sword into the monsters back. She came back down the beach and stood over the monster. J'orik had already extracted his sword and was cleaning it off. He slid it back into its sheath and turned to her.

"That went well," he said, pleased. "Your plan went off without a hitch. Almost exactly as you laid it out."

She looked down at the creature. "It's an ugly thing," she said, wrinkling her nose. "I wonder what it is."

"I don't know, but it smells awful."

Both of his arrows had hit the creature. One was sticking out the middle of its back. The other one had gone through its mouth and was sticking out the back of its head. J'orik removed the one that had gone through its mouth, cleaned it, and placed it back in his quiver. The one that went through its back had broken when the creature fell to the sand. J'orik always retrieved his arrows unless, of course, they were broken.

"I was worried there for a moment while I was lying in the sand," she said with concern. "He was getting closer and closer to me and I didn't know when you were going to take a shot."

"Well, like I said, it went well and we accomplished the task without either one of us being harmed. That's all that matters."

"What now?"

"We need to get rid of the body," he told her, "so when the others come back they won't know what happened. Let's drag him into the forest and cover him up. Then we'll come back and remove any evidence of what just happened."

They reached down, each taking a hand, and dragged the body into the forest. After covering the body with brush they came back and proceeded to eliminate any evidence of what had happened. Beginning at the camp where the creature had started after Lianna and working their way back up the beach towards the forest, they brushed away footprints and any sign of blood. J'orik noticed again that Lianna was becoming quite adept at removing evidence of any presence. Once they were done with that they tossed their brush brooms into the forest and continued making their way back to the village along the tree line.

It wasn't until they neared the village that they noticed a stench about it. They curled their noses at the odor and looked at each other disgustedly.

"What's that smell?" she asked. "It's disgusting."

"It's probably that," he said, pointing towards the pile of dead bodies at the southwest corner of the village. "That and the smoldering remnants of homes in the village," he added.

Smoke was still curling into the sky from the fires that had burned out. They walked a little closer to the pile of bodies that he'd pointed out and noticed they were all men, men from the village. Lianna had an urge to see if her husband was in the pile but couldn't bring herself to get any closer.

"J'orik," she looked at him mournfully, "I need to know if my husband is in that pile."

"Don't worry yourself," he told her. "I'll take a look."

It was difficult but he picked through the bodies and discovered Falder. He also noticed, with some disgust, that all of them had been scalped and run through with a sword. The meaning of it he could not understand. He returned to Lianna and told her he'd found Falder's body. Tears welled up in her eyes and she began to weep. She ran to him and wrapped her arms around him and wept. He stood there with her in his arms until her weeping subsided.

"Again, I'm sorry for your loss," he told her, with sadness in his voice. He didn't know what else to say.

She stepped back from him and looked up into his eyes. "I need to find my children."

As they entered the village they saw women's bodies lying strewn throughout the village. It looked like the village had been completely destroyed. They investigated further and discovered that there were no bodies of children. Lianna became frantic.

"I can't find my children." She began to weep again. "I don't see any children. Where did all the children go?"

"I have a feeling those monsters may have taken them. Remember, you said you saw them dragging your children away."

"Why would they take them? What would they need them for?" She shot back at him in frustration.

"I don't know," he tried to respond as calmly as possible. "And I don't even want to guess."

She ran to him and wrapped her arms around him like she had before and began to sob uncontrollably. He just stood there and held her in his arms until she stopped sobbing.

"It doesn't appear as if there's anything left worth salvaging," he said, looking around. "We need to leave this place. You stay here and I'll do a quick search to see if I can determine if anyone else might have escaped."

He searched for any signs that someone might have gotten away and didn't find any. He came back to where he'd left her standing.

"I couldn't find anything indicating someone might have slipped away during the attack on the village," he informed her. "But that doesn't mean no one didn't. There are a lot of footprints, making it hard to tell. I think now that we need to make our way to Bruston, the town at the south end of the lake, and find out if anyone did make it there."

She just nodded her assent. Her weeping had stopped and her eyes were beginning to dry.

"You're right, J'orik," she said, sounding more in control. "We just need to leave this place. There's nothing left for me here and I never want to come back."

"If your children are still alive," he tried to sound positive, "we'll find them."

She reached out with her hand and he took it in his. They walked out of the village down to the shoreline and didn't look back. They began their journey for Bruston.

# CHAPTER 7

OGILOTH AND HIS team walked the forest road for nearly two days searching for any sign of the man they were looking for. He had them spread out to about two hundred yards on either side of the road while he walked the road. At the end of each day he would listen to their reports. Nothing definite was reported by any of them. The most likely reason for not finding any sign was that the road did get traffic; wagons, animals, and foot traffic. The only thing that was remotely positive was that signs of two different sets of prints had been found each day. One set leaving the road and going into the forest for about twenty yards, and the same set returning. Unless he was now travelling with a companion, then it wasn't who they were looking for. Ogiloth could not be sure.

It was late afternoon of the second day that they reached the eastern edge of the forest. They set up camp just inside the trees, out of view from any traffic that might come by. They waited for Herg and Lorith, the trackers that had been sent searching through the forest east of the village. They didn't have to wait long. A guard had been posted to watch at the edge of the forest and within a couple hours after Ogiloth's group had stopped, the trackers were spotted. The guard on watch brought them to Ogiloth.

He listened carefully as they explained what they'd found. They found two sets of prints leading out of the village into the forest. The prints weren't together, at first, so they each followed a set. The prints were never more than about twenty yards apart, so they were able to maintain contact with each other the whole time. A little over half way through the forest the prints finally came together. They discovered a camp had been made where the prints merged. It wasn't easy to find evidence of the camp because whoever had camped there was very good had eliminating the evidence, but they found it. They also found signs that a rabbit had been killed nearby. There were also signs of prints leading to and from a nearby creek. They followed them until they reached the eastern edge of the forest, which was about a half-day walk from the campsite they found. From there they went in a southeasterly direction across the plains. At this point, they headed south along the edge of the forest towards the road, as they had been ordered. Throughout their report they constantly made comments about how someone not well trained would not have been able to find the evidence they had found. After they were done, Ogiloth just smiled at them.

"You've both done well," he complimented them. "I see that I chose well by bringing the two of you along."

"Thank you, sir," they responded in unison.

"Now get yourselves something to eat," he told them. Turning to the rest of the group, "It'll be dark soon. We'll make camp here tonight. Like we did back at the lake, I want a guard posted through the night. Take two-hour shifts again beginning with you," he pointed at the warrior to his immediate left. "And then in this order." He pointed to five more of the warriors.

As camp was being set up and the evening meal prepared, Ogiloth found a place to sit and think about all that had happened along the road and the report he had just listened to. After his tent was set up he disappeared inside to think some more. He took his meal inside with him.

*With the amount of time that's passed since our initial attack on the village*, he thought, *maybe the prints we discovered along the road might be the same as those Herg and Lorith found. They said the prints went southeast across the plains. There's a town along the road east of the forest that they probably headed for. If the prints we found along the road were the same as those Herg and Lorith found in the forest, that would indicate they were returning to the village, or at least heading back in that direction. I'll have to send Herg and Lorith out first thing in the morning to make that determination. Why would they return to the village?* he wondered. *Maybe they wanted to see if there were any other survivors. Maybe they just wanted to retrieve some of their belongings that may have survived. Maybe, just maybe . . .* There were too many possibilities. Now, though, he found he wasn't searching for just one person. Now he was searching for two people. Soon, he fell fast asleep thinking of all the possibilities.

The night passed without event. Ogiloth was awakened at first light by the guard on duty. The others had already started breaking camp, preparing for the day. He came out of his tent and stretched with a growl. He ate his morning meal while he thought about his next move.

It wasn't long before everything was packed and the team was ready to move out. They were standing around waiting for him to give the order. He stood up and called Herg and Lorith.

"I want the two of you to go out along the road and see if the prints we found are the same as those you found." He looked out on the other warriors and spotted the one that had found the prints along the road and called him forward. "What's your name warrior?"

"Traig, sir."

"Take Traig with you and have him show you where the prints were found along the road. Once you've made a determination, return here and make your report. Don't take too long. Go"

"Yes, sir." All three turned and left camp to do as ordered.

As they were leaving camp, Ogiloth looked around at the others. "The rest of you will remain here with me until those three come back. Keep the noise level down. I don't want anyone wandering in on us unexpectedly so you," he pointed to two of the warriors, "stand guard and watch towards the plains and the road."

The two he pointed at immediately did as ordered. The rest just sat around the camp and talked quietly amongst themselves.

It was less than an hour before Herg and Lorith returned. The last set of prints weren't that far down the road. They immediately went to Ogiloth to make their report.

"What did you find?" Ogiloth asked.

"Traig pointed out the prints you mentioned finding along the road," Herg told him. "We followed them and discovered a campsite left in the same condition as the one we found on our search. There are enough similarities that we're confident they're the same." He glanced at Lorith for confirmation and he nodded in agreement. He turned back to Ogiloth. "They're heading back towards the lake."

"Are you sure?" Ogiloth questioned, with a sneer on his face.

"Positive," he said without any sign of doubt on his face.

Ogiloth turned to Lorith with a questioning look and he nodded his head confirming, again, what Herg had said.

"Fine job," Ogiloth complimented them again. Then he turned to the others and shouted, "Prepare to move out. We are returning to the lake."

They all moved as one and headed towards the forest road.

Once they were all on the road Ogiloth shouted at them with another order. "Double-time today. I want to get back to the lake as quickly as possible."

As they all began jogging, one of them yelled, "Wagon!"

A wagon was coming towards them from the east.

Ogiloth immediately shouted, "In the forest! Hide!"

They all did as ordered.

The wagon rolled by leaving a cloud of dust in its wake. After it had passed and was out of sight they all came back out onto the road again and began jogging west, towards the lake.

Ogiloth pushed them hard all day. Not a single one of them grumbled or moaned about it. They knew that if they did he would have probably taken their head. They made good time and reached the western edge of the forest just as the sun was beginning to set over the Castaic Mountains. They didn't stop there.

"We're almost there!" Ogiloth shouted. "There's still enough light, we should be able to make it to the boat before it gets dark!"

They pushed on and made it to the boat just as the sun disappeared below the mountain tops.

When they got to the boat they were surprised at what they found. The camp they'd left was still partially set up. Gorog was nowhere in sight. He was supposed to have taken everything and loaded it on the boat. Ogiloth was furious. He couldn't believe that Gorog would have shirked his duty, let alone run off. He knew he'd embarrassed him in front of the others, but he didn't think it was enough to cause this. There had to be an explanation.

"You two go to the village!" Ogiloth growled, pointing to two of the warriors. "See if he's gone there!"

The two he'd pointed at immediately ran towards the village.

"It's too dark to do anything else now," he grumbled. "At least we don't have to set up camp again, but this isn't what I was expecting." He was angry and everyone knew it.

Within half an hour, the two that had gone to the village returned.

"Did you find him?" Ogiloth practically screamed at them.

"No, sir," they responded in unison.

He was going over in his mind what might have happened. *Maybe the two people we're looking for did come back to the village. They found Gorog alone and killed him. But, where was his body?* It was too dark now to make a search for him, so he decided to just rest for the night and make a search in the morning. Besides, he'd been pushing the team all day to get back and they could probably use a rest.

"We'll rest for the night," he told them. "In the morning I want a search done for Gorog. Get a good night's rest because tomorrow will be another long, hard day. Don't bother me until then. And I want a guard posted through the night with two-hour shifts, the same ones that did it when we first landed here and in the same order. Get a fire going and make me something to eat." His tent was still standing so he marched off in a huff and disappeared inside.

A campfire was made and meals prepared. One was taken to Ogiloth and the guard on duty. After eating they all went to their tents for the night.

As usual, Ogiloth was awakened at first light by the guard on duty. He came out of his tent in a cantankerous mood. The guard could see that today was going to be a rough day, even worse if they didn't find Gorog. He went around and woke the others letting them know that Ogiloth was not going to be pleasant to be around. They all had a bite to eat and anxiously awaited orders.

Ogiloth rose to his full height and looked around at them all. "I'm not pleased today. We've spent the last few days searching and have come up empty-handed. We've lost a member of our team. I don't want to spend any more time than is necessary to complete this mission. I'm sure you all feel the same way. You should feel proud for the work you have accomplished so far, though. You've worked hard. But we have little to show for that hard work except maybe sore muscles and my wrath. This is what we'll do today. I know the two of you went to the village last night." He looked at the two he'd sent. "But it was dark and I doubt you were able to do a thorough search. I want you to go back this morning and search again now that there's light. The two of you," he looked at Herg and Lorith, "will look up and down the beach for any evidence there. As for the rest of you, you'll spread out along the edge of the forest and search no more than fifty yards in. The search will not be any further up and down the beach than the distance from this camp to the forest road. If anyone finds Gorog, alive or dead, I want you to call out so the others will know they can stop looking. Regardless, I expect all of this to be completed before midday. Report back to me when you are done. Does everyone understand what they are to do?"

They all responded with a loud, "Huh! Huh! Huh!"

"All right," he shouted back. "Let's move!"

There were two reasons he was taking time to search for Gorog. One, he was his cousin and he wanted to be able to tell his uncle what had happened to Gorog and two, he didn't want anyone on his team to think they could just walk away without being chased down and punished for it.

It wasn't long after they'd spread out that a call was made that Gorog's body had been found. The warrior that had walked straight up the beach from their camp found the body only a few paces inside the forest. Ogiloth ran up the beach to see for himself. Gorog's body was found under some brush. The others gathered around to watch as his body was drug out onto the beach. They saw that he'd been shot through the chest and the mouth. The arrow in his chest was still there. He still had his sword clenched in his hand. Whoever had done this was a very good shot. It was obvious from the penetration of the arrow through his chest that a crossbow had been used. It was also apparent that he'd been facing his attacker. Ogiloth wasn't happy that he was dead but he was glad that he hadn't deserted. It showed that he had faced the danger and had not run from it.

Having found Gorog so quickly, Ogiloth decided that he could give him a proper burial. While this was being done he took Herg and Lorith aside to talk with them.

"I need one of you to go north, no more than two miles, looking for any sign of the two we've been looking for. The other will go south doing the same. Chances are they went south because there's a town at the southern end of the lake. Whichever one of you goes south should take a little more time tracking. I want both of you to be back here before midday. Now go and be quick about it."

They took off to do as ordered. Ogiloth went back to oversee Gorog's burial. After the burial he gathered everyone back at the camp and explained that he'd sent the trackers out. They were to wait until they got back before their next move was decided.

Both trackers got back about the same time. They were only gone about an hour after Ogiloth had sent them out. Just like Ogiloth had suspected, the one that went north didn't find anything much past the village. The one that had gone south, however, came back with a more positive report. He'd found evidence of two sets of prints going down the shoreline for a distance and then heading up the beach about where the forest road came out and turned south. The prints continued south along the road.

Ogiloth believed his thinking was correct. For whatever reason, the two people they were searching for had decided to return to the village. Most likely, they didn't find anything worth retrieving. They probably just confirmed that the devastation that Ogiloth and his forces had wreaked on the village was total. The village and all of its inhabitants were lost. They probably decided to move on.

Somehow they had slipped by him and his team. Most likely they knew they were being hunted. He would have to be more careful now. He would have to be more clever. It was a pretty good chance they were heading south. He decided that it was best not to leave anything behind again. Besides, it would be quicker to travel by boat. Maybe they could get to Bruston before their prey arrived.

"Break camp and pack up the boat as quick as you can," he bellowed. "We'll be travelling by boat now. The people we're looking for have a good lead on us but they're travelling on foot. If we move quickly, we should be able to beat them to Bruston. We'll be travelling non-stop until we get there. Let's move!"

# CHAPTER 8

J'ORIK AND LIANNA had been walking the road all afternoon. It was another beautiful day. Blue skies with a few clouds stretched out like sheets blowing in the wind. There was a slight breeze coming from the southwest that helped to make the heat of the day more bearable. The sun was getting low, heading towards the mountaintops. They hadn't talked much about the events of the past few days, they just kept walking.

"Aren't you getting hungry?" Lianna finally spoke out.

"I am," he responded. "How's rabbit sound?"

"I think I would rather have some quail again."

"Sounds fine to me." He came to a halt. "I thought I heard some in the trees. If you give me a few minutes I can go get one for dinner. You stay here and wait, I'll be right back." He headed off into the trees.

Lianna knew it wouldn't take him long. He was always pretty quick about hunting down food for them. She was right. It wasn't more than a few minutes and he stepped out of the trees with a large quail in his hand and a big grin on his face. Just as he was beginning to cross the road they both heard the loud whinny of a horse and turned to see a wagon coming south along the road towards them. J'orik quickly came across the road and stood next to Lianna.

"You know," he said, "we could get to Bruston quicker if we caught a ride on that wagon."

She looked up at him with a smile. "You know, I think you're right. Besides, I could use a break from walking. I've never ridden on a wagon before and I think it might be fun."

He just smiled back at her and they waited for the wagon. It didn't look like it was going to stop so Lianna began waving her arms.

When the wagon was almost on top of them, the driver pulled up on the reins and brought it to a stop. Most of the dust cloud that trailed the wagon blew off into the trees and as it cleared they noticed the driver reach under his seat and pull out a small hand crossbow. He aimed it at them and gave them a questioning look.

"Is there somethin' I can do for ya?" he asked in a gruff tone.

"We were wondering if we might catch a ride with you." J'orik replied.

"Is that a quail ya got in yer hand there boy?"

"Yes it is, sir." J'orik held it up for him to see it better.

"Normally I don't stop and give rides, but if yer willin' to give up that quail there I might consider it."

"That's not a problem, sir," J'orik told him. "We were going to have it for our meal but I can easily go get another one. Unless you would prefer rabbit?" he asked, with a questioning smile on his face.

"Akshilly I could go fer both. It's been a long day an' I'm perdy hungered. Besides, I usually stop before the sun goes down so's the fellas here can get a good night's rest fer the rest o' the haul tamarra." He pointed to the two horses and they just stamped their hooves and whinnied like they knew what he was saying.

"Well, then, I'll go get a couple rabbits and another quail."

"That sounds fine, son. But 'fore ya head off into the woods there, what're yer names?"

He put his hand crossbow back under the seat, set the wagon brake, and climbed down off the wagon. They introduced themselves as he was doing this.

"Nice ta meetcha, J'orik and Lianna. The name's Sammy, Sammy Drover, and this here's Buck and Handsome." He pointed to the two horses. "Best dang haulin' horses around."

The horses stamped their hooves again and blew out their mouths. Lianna thought for sure they understood what Sammy was saying.

He was dressed in heavy cotton pants, a blue long-sleeved shirt with a leather vest over it, leather gloves, and a wide-brimmed leather hat. The boots he had on were scuffed and looked well-worn. He dusted himself off, removed his gloves, and stepped forward reaching out with his hand in a welcoming gesture.

J'orik and Lianna both shook his hand and in turn said, "Nice to meet you Sammy."

"Ya better say yer hello to the boys here or they'll feel left out." He just smiled and looked at the horses.

They said hello to the horses and they just snorted back.

"Okay, 'nuf fer the intros. If yer gonna get them rabbit and quail ya better get started. I'll take care o' the little lady here. 'Sides, I gotta unhitch the boys here so's they kin rest."

"I'll be right back." J'orik handed the quail to Lianna and headed off back into the trees.

As Sammy started to unhitch the horses he told her, "Now, ya need ta git next ta the wagon behine me in case the boys here decide ta git a little frisky. Y'ever been round horses?" he asked her.

"No." she answered.

"Well then, I guess this is gonna be a treat fer ya."

He unhitched the horses and let them free. They immediately took off for the lake.

Sammy turned to Lianna. "Them boys love the water. They're perdy thirsty too."

She watched as they played in the water.

By the time Sammy had finished with the wagon J'orik came strutting out of the trees with a quail in one hand and two rabbits in the other, already cleaned.

Sammy looked at J'orik, impressed, "You a hunter boy? That was perdy quick."

"Yes, I am. It's all I've ever done. I've hunted this forest all my life."

"I see yuv already takin' care o' the nasty part. Let's git a fire goin' and git'm cooked. Like I said, I'm hungered."

Lianna dashed around the wagon and started collecting wood for the fire. Before long the fire was going and Lianna had both rabbits and quails spitted and roasting. She used some of the herbs Karin had given her.

Sammy took a long sniff and smiled, "Dang. That smells good."

"It's ready to eat whenever you are," she announced.

Sammy glanced down towards the lake to make sure the horses were all right and then reached over and took one of the spits with a rabbit on it. He tore a chunk of meat off and took a big bite, "Dang. Tastes good too."

Lianna just smiled at him as she and J'orik shared a quail.

Sammy watched them sharing the quail and asked, "So, you two a couple?" He continued devouring the rabbit.

They just looked at each other with a smile and a look of embarrassment.

"Uh-oh, looks like I might'a ast the wrong question. I jes thought since you was travlin' tagether you was a couple. Sorry if I embarrassed ya." He finished the rabbit and tossed the spit stick into the fire. He grabbed the spit with the other quail on it and sat back looking at them.

"No, we're not a couple. We've just been travelling together ever since our village was destroyed," J'orik told him.

"Ya know what? I think I might'a seen ya on the road comin' outta Washoe a few days back. Ya prob'ly dint think I seen ya dash inta the trees ta hide, but I did. Ya need good eyes when yer travlin' through the forest an' I got'm," he smiled. "Was that you?"

"Probably," Lianna responded.

"Ya know, I even seen a group of I don't know what yud call'm, but they was ugly as sin an' headin' this way. They tried hidin' in the trees too, but I seen'm anyway. Thought maybe they was robbers but they never came out after me.

The boys got kinda skiddish when we went by'm so I knowd they was there."

J'orik and Lianna looked at each other confused.

The sun had dropped below the mountaintops and it was getting dark now. Sammy had just finished the quail. "That was deee-lishus young lady. I haven't had a meal like this on the road since ferever" He got to his feet and told them, "Wait just a minute now, I need ta bring the boys in an' tie'm up for the night. You kin tell me yer story when I git back."

J'orik and Lianna started in on the rabbit while Sammy took care of the horses. He walked out onto the beach and whistled loudly.

"You don't suppose he's talking about that same group we saw the other day before we got back to the village, do you?" she asked him.

"I think that's exactly who he's talking about and, for whatever reason, they've decided to head back this way."

"I wonder why."

"I wonder why too."

As J'orik and Lianna watched, both horses came running to Sammy. He brought them up from the shore and tied them to the wagon on the forest side, talking to them the whole time. There was a trough hanging off the side of the wagon and he filled it with some hay. The horses began chomping away as he came back to the campfire and sat down.

"Okay, the boys're good fer the night. Now tell me yer story."

They looked at each other and then J'orik began. He explained how their village had been attacked by these ugly looking monsters. Their homes had been burned to the ground. Their family and friends had been killed. How they had escaped into the forest and met. They made their way to Washoe where his aunt and uncle own an inn, the Dragons' Lair. How they had made their way back to the village and found that the children were missing. The monster had taken them. They saw a small group of the same monsters when they returned but were able to escape being seen. The same ones Sammy saw along the road. They were able to kill one of them though. They decided they would make their way to Bruston because the monsters had headed towards Washoe on the forest road. Finally, how they had met him. Lianna would interject once in a while to tell her point of view. Sammy listened intently to it all. When they were finished he just looked at them in astonishment.

"That's one heck of a story. Sounds like you two've been through hell."

They both nodded in agreement.

"Ya know. I've heard stories 'bout somethin' just like what ya've told me. Villages bein' burned down an' all the people bein' killed. It's kinda why I keep that little crossbow on board, jest in case. Ya have any idea why this is happenin'?"

Both of them said, "No," nodding their heads.

"Well, it sounds like ya might have the right idea by headin' in the opposite direction of them monsters. But if'n it was the same group I seen on the road they musta picked up somethin' an' decided to head back this way. Maybe they found yer trail or somethin'. Bruston's a good place to go, lotsa people. I don't think them monsters would dare try anythin' there. Ride with me an' the boys and we'll gitcha there by tamarra late. Got plenty o' room on the buckboard fer the both o' ya," Sammy yawned big.

"We appreciate your kindness and the ride," J'orik told him. Lianna nodded her agreement. "But it looks like you're tired. We could all use a good night's rest."

"Yer right there, son."

Sammy stretched out right where he was and closed his eyes. Within moments they could tell he was fast asleep. They put the campfire out and laid down themselves. They gazed up at the stars as a subtle breeze swept across them. Soon enough they, too, fell fast asleep.

J'orik and Lianna woke up with a jolt. Sammy was hitching the horses to the wagon and was making quite a racket. The horses were stamping their hooves and snorting, making quite a racket also.

"Hey, you two!" Sammy shouted. "Ya need ta git movin' if we're ta make Bruston by late day. Wagon's leavin' as soon as I git the boys hitched. They're hankerin' ta git a move on and I'm not too keen on hangin' around here after the story ya gave me last night. I'll hafta make sure tha other driver knows what's happened so's he kin be aware."

They both stood and stretched with a big yawn and made sure they had all their things. They watched as Sammy finished hitching the horses to the wagon.

As soon as he finished he told them, "Walk 'round in front of tha boys and git up on the buckboard from tha other side. I'll be git'n up from this side."

They walked around the horses like he'd directed them. J'orik helped Lianna onto the wagon and she sat down on the bench. Then he climbed up and sat down next to her. Sammy had already gotten up and had the reins in his hands. He was ready to go.

"Ya ever been on one o' these contraptions?"

They both nodded no.

"Well, ya better hang tight cause when these boys take off yull be in fer the ride of a lifetime." He just smiled.

He let the brake loose, lifted the reins, and slapped the horses on their backs. They started out with a jolt and J'orik and Lianna jerked back in their seat almost going over backwards. They both quickly grabbed the front of the bench seat to bring themselves back to a normal sitting position.

Sammy looked over at them with a big grin on his face and started laughing. "I toldja ta hang tight didn't I?"

They both just looked over at him with a resigned smile.

The ride was bumpy but not near as bad as they thought it would be. The bench seat had springs holding it up which helped. The dust that was kicked up by the horses wasn't too bad either. They figured that the dustiest ride would be the one crossing the plains. For the first couple of hours they just rode and enjoyed the scenery. Sammy just sat there with the reins in his hands and his elbows on his knees. When they did talk they found they had to speak louder because of the extra noise from the wagon and the horses.

Sammy finally looked over at them and asked, "How ya like the ride so far?"

"It's a little bumpy but it's better than walking," Lianna answered. J'orik just nodded in agreement.

"What are you carrying?" J'orik queried. He looked back but couldn't see the cargo because there was a large tarp covering it all.

"Nothin' much. Most the time I don' even know what I got."

"Are you the only one that does this?"

"Nah. Me and my buddy Tommy work tagether. We haul stuff back an' forth between Bruston and Washoe. People always got stuff they need hauled. In fact, we jes might be passin' Tommy taday. Usually that's the only time we see each other is when we pass on tha road. Sometimes we happen ta pass when we got ta stop fer the night and we git a chance ta talk. I'll be stoppin' here in 'bout an hour or so ta let the boys take a rest. Gives me a chance ta git down, walk around and shake the ride off."

All three went back to watching the scenery pass by. Sammy only stopped twice before they arrived in Bruston. The second stop happened to be where a small creek flowed out of the forest down into the lake. It gave the horses a chance to get a drink. They never did see Tommy.

As they were coming into town, Sammy turned and asked, "Is there someplace in paticular ya want me ta drop ya?"

"Lianna hasn't ever been here before and I've only been here a few times," J'orik answered. "I guess anywhere will be fine."

"How 'bout ya jes git off at my first stop then. It's right close by tha sheriff's office. Ya might wanna stop in an' tell 'im what's happened to ya. I'm sure he'd be int'rested in that story ya told me."

Right about then they saw another wagon coming their way heading out of town. Sammy pulled up on the reins and stopped his wagon. He smiled as he waved down the other driver. The other driver smiled back and pulled up alongside Sammy's wagon.

"How ya doin' Sammy?" the driver yelled.

"Doin' jes fine Tommy. Gettin' a late start arncha?"

"Yeah. Took'm a little longer than they thought ta git tha last load on. See ya got some live cargo this time."

"Picked'm up on the road jes this side o' tha forest. Told me a story 'bout their village bein' torched and everbody bein' killed, 'cept them acourse. Was hopin' I'd see ya so's I cud letcha know ta be careful goin' back."

"Really, why's that?"

"The way they tells it it was some kinda monsters that attacked'm. I seen a group of'm on the road as I was goin' through the forest. Looks like they jes might still be 'round. Anyways, you be careful on tha drive back, keep yer eyes peeled. I'm gonna take these two an' drop'm by tha sheriff's place."

"Okay, will do Sammy. See ya on the return."

Tommy lifted the reins and slapped his horses on their backs and went on his way, heading back to Washoe. Sammy did the same with his horses and headed into town for his first stop.

Bruston was much larger than Washoe. Its main industry was fishing, but it also prospered on mining from the nearby Castaic Mountains. It was a bustling community with people, wagons, and a multitude of four-legged creatures. J'orik and Lianna's eyes were wide with amazement at all the activity and noise. Sammy wound his way around it all and it wasn't long before he rolled up in front of a large building and stopped.

"Well folks, this is my first stop," he informed them. "Tha sheriff's office is right over there." He pointed. "If I was you, I'd go tell'm everthin' ya told me. I'm sure he'd be interested. It's been nice meetin' ya and maybe we'll see each other agin' sometime. I got ta git ta work now." He climbed down off the wagon and headed into the building he'd stopped in front of.

"Thanks for the ride Sammy!" they both yelled at him.

"Yer welcome folks!" he hollered back as he disappeared through the door.

J'orik and Lianna just looked at each other and then climbed down themselves. They stood there next to the wagon for a moment taking in all the activity before making their way over to the sheriff's office. They had to dodge wagons and animals along their way but they were able to make it safely and in one piece. The sheriff's office was pretty easy to locate because there was a sign above the door that had 'SHERIFF' printed on it in big bold letters. J'orik opened the door letting Lianna in first. He followed her in and closed the door behind him. The noise level immediately dropped.

The entry had a waist-high fence directly across from the door with decorative rails extending up to the ceiling. There was a small table decorated with a vase of flowers in the corner where the fence met the interior wall on the left with a bench next to it against the fence. On the right there was a desk extending from the end of the fence to a gate that was attached to the same wall the door was. A clerk was seated behind the desk. They both glanced around the room beyond and saw three unoccupied desks. The walls were decorated with a variety of paintings, plaques, and shelves. The shelves were stocked with books and a variety of knick-knacks. The interior was painted a plain light-brown color. In the far corner of the room stood an empty coat rack.

The clerk looked up as they entered and asked, "Can I help you?"

She was plain looking and appeared to be an older woman. Her hair was a light-brown color but greying and hung below her shoulders. She was wearing a pale green, floor-length dress decorated with red and yellow flowers. She had a writing quill in her hand and appeared to be filling out some sort of form.

"We're looking for the sheriff," J'orik responded.

"Well, you came to the right place but he's not in right now, as you can probably see, but he should be back any moment. He stepped out to get a bite to eat. If you want, you can have a seat and wait." She pointed to the bench.

"Thank you." He smiled at her as he and Lianna took a seat.

She went back to doing whatever it was she was doing.

The clerk was right. They didn't have to wait long. The door opened and in walked the sheriff. His cotton pants and button up long sleeved shirt were a khaki color. His brown vest was made of leather and had a round silver badge pinned to the left breast embossed with the word sheriff. He wore a black, wide-brimmed, hardened leather hat. The black leather belt he wore had a three foot long wooden stick attached to one side and a short sword attached to the other side. His boots were also black leather with hard soles that came to a rounded tip.

He glanced at J'orik and Lianna then looked at the clerk.

"How long have they been waiting Clare?" His voice was a deep bass tone.

"Not long. They've only been sitting here for a couple of minutes."

He turned to J'orik and Lianna and asked, "What can I do for the two of you?"

"We'd like to talk with you about what happened in our village," J'orik replied.

"Okay. If you'll follow me," he motioned for them to follow him through the gate.

He swung it open and stepped through. He held it for them as they stepped through and stopped on the other side. He walked past them and they followed. He led them to the desk in the opposite corner of the office. There were two chairs in front of it and he motioned for them to take a seat. He walked around the desk, removed his belt and hung it on the coat rack, and sat in the more comfortable looking chair behind it.

"So what is it that happened in your village that brought you all the way to Bruston to talk with me?" But before either one of them could reply he added, "First, where is your village?"

"Our village is just north of where the road comes out of the forest at the lake," J'orik told him.

The sheriff just nodded. "Go on."

"Our village was attacked about a week ago by some sort of monster-like creatures. They burned our homes to the ground and killed everyone except us. We were able to escape into the forest and make our way to Washoe. My aunt and uncle run an inn there, the Dragons' Lair, and they put us up for the night. We decided to return to the village to see if maybe there were others that survived, but when we got there we found that none had." J'orik took a short pause.

The sheriff leaned back in his chair with his elbows on the chair arms and put his hands together forming a steeple. "And there's more?"

"Yes. The men had all been taken outside the village, scalped, killed, and piled up. The women we found strewn about inside the village. But the oddest thing was that we couldn't find any trace of the children."

"The men were scalped, you say? And you didn't find any of the children?"

They both nodded their heads affirmatively.

"You know, I've heard of incidents just like this in other places. The folks that I've talked with don't seem to have any idea why these things are happening. I don't have any idea myself. Do you have any thoughts why this happened?"

They both nodded negatively.

"There is one other thing I haven't mentioned," J'orik stated.

"And what's that?"

"When we did return to our village a smaller group of the same monster-like creatures were there. I was able to get close enough to overhear them talking. It seems they knew that I had escaped and they had come back to find me. Or, at least I assumed it was me. They mentioned they were looking for a man and I was the only man that had gotten away."

"Is there something special about you that would cause them to come back?"

"I don't know," he shrugged his shoulders. "Maybe they just wanted to make sure there were no survivors."

"Did they indicate they knew she had escaped?" he pointed to Lianna.

"No," he replied, shrugging his shoulders again.

"Well, I'm not sure that there's anything I can do for you except take a report of the incident. I'm sorry for what happened and I wish there was something I could do but, this is beyond my jurisdiction and I can't spare either one of my deputies to go that far to make an inspection. I need them here."

"But the children," Lianna cried out. "What about the children?"

The sheriff leaned forward in his chair and looked at Lianna with concern. "I understand ma'am and I do sympathize with you but unless you're positive the children were taken, and especially where they were taken, there's nothing more I can do."

She began to weep and looked up at J'orik. He just looked back at her with sorrow in his eyes.

"The children, my children," she said in between sobs.

J'orik reached over and took her hand in his, "I know Lianna. I said we would find your children and I won't give up until we do."

Right about then the office door swung open and a man dressed similar to the sheriff walked in. It was one of the deputies. "Sheriff," he said in a hurried tone, "I need your assistance down at the Lion's Pub, things are getting out of hand."

"Okay, give me a second and I'll be right there." He turned to J'orik and Lianna. "I'm sorry but I have to go now." He stood up, grabbed his belt off the coat rack, and started for the door. "Clare here can take your statement." And then he was gone with the deputy.

Clare stood up with her notepad and writing quill. She came around and sat down in the chair the sheriff had just vacated. They both looked over at her and they could see that her eyes were moist with tears.

"I can only imagine what you must be going through. I have three children of my own. If anything like what you described were to happen to them I would go to the ends of the world to find them." She placed her notepad on the desk and began writing. "Now there's no reason for you to have to repeat what you told the sheriff, I can see that it upsets you. I overheard everything you said. If you'll give me a couple minutes here I'll finish writing it down."

J'orik and Lianna sat there quietly while she finished making the report.

When she was done she looked up at them. "The last thing I need to complete this is your names."

They each said their names and she wrote them down.

"Now, do you folks have someplace to stay?"

They both nodded no.

"I know of a nice quiet inn at the south end of town you can stay. The owners are close friends of mine."

"But we have no money to pay for the room," J'orik told her.

"That's okay. I'm sure there's something that can be arranged. Actually, it's just about time to close the office anyway. If you'll give me a few minutes I'll walk you down there myself."

They nodded their agreement and Clare went about closing the office.

# CHAPTER 9

O GILOTH PUSHED HIS team hard all day. He was
pleased with their progress. At the rate they were
going he figured they would be to Bruston by the end of
the day. The weather had been good. It was blue skies with
wispy clouds. There was a slight breeze that helped to keep
it cool and the water calm, which made it less miserable
for each warrior working the oars. He thought about what
would happen once they reached Bruston. He knew that
in a community that size he would have difficulty locating
the man he was after especially since the majority of the
population consisted of humans, after all it was predominately
a fishing community. However, there was a small section of
Bruston populated by dwarves and he had some ties there.
His uncle Durog lived there.

The dwarves mined the southern part of the Castaic
Mountains which provided the second largest industry in
Bruston. His mother was a dwarf and some of his dwarf
cousins lived there. Even though he didn't visit much, they
accepted him, or rather, they tolerated him. Ogiloth was only
half dwarf. His father was an ogre and was chief over the

group of ogres that helped the dwarves mine the mountains. In his younger days, before he started working for K'orik, he worked in the mines with his father. The ogres lived in the mountains and rarely came into Bruston. The townspeople did not accept their presence. They frightened the women and children and were generally an unruly lot. Mining was also done in parts of the mountains further north along the lake, so there was a separate marina for the boats that made deliveries from those mines. This was where Ogiloth would be docking his boat. It would be less conspicuous and appear more like it was just another shipment of ore coming in.

He would need to be careful how he handled the situation because his warriors were not true ogres. They were a hideous mix of ogre, goblin, troll, and some other creature that Sarguroth had found deep in the earth. Sarguroth was a sorcerer friend of K'orik's that played with mixing different races and breeds and had developed the creatures he now had on his team. They were strong, obedient, and would work until you told them to stop or they dropped dead. They weren't overly intelligent but they weren't stupid either. They could be trained in a particular task and would excel at it. This is why he chose the two he had for tracking. The others were simply for brute force. Even Gorog had been nothing more than a grunt to him. He was his cousin, in a roundabout way, but Ogiloth never really did like him. When he was found lying dead in the forest it didn't sadden him.

Ogiloth was brought out of his reverie by a call from Olog, one of his lieutenants he'd brought along. "Sir, there's a wagon travelling along the road." He pointed like Ogiloth wouldn't know which direction to look.

He peered towards the western bank of the lake and could just make out a wagon heading north on the road. Even though they were too far away he was confident that there was probably only the driver and no passengers. He didn't think it was likely that the people they were searching for would leave town so quickly. After all, they had nothing to go back to. They would take time to at least make contact with the local authority and tell them what had happened, another reason why he would have to be careful.

He turned his attention back to the boat and told each warrior to just keep rowing. Looking ahead he could make out the tops of some of the taller buildings and knew it was only a couple hours before they arrived at Bruston.

Again, he felt they had made good time and he let his team know it. He wanted to keep up their morale because they worked harder when they weren't in a nasty mood.

They docked the boat as the sun was nearing the mountaintops. He stepped off onto the landing and turned to his warriors to let them know what would be happening next.

"You boys won't be getting off here. The people here don't accept our kind too well." A groan went around the group. "I need you to take the boat down the shore a couple of miles and make camp there." He pointed in the direction he wanted them to go. "I've been here before and the people recognize me. They tolerate me because I have family in town, family which I will be visiting. So my presence here won't seem unusual." He was careful not to make it sound like the people would perceive them as the monsters they were. With the stories that were being told he was sure that if his team was spotted the townspeople would make a connection and would expect the sheriff to do something. "I want you to make camp and stay there until I come and get you. For now I'll be the only one to continue the search. While you're waiting for me Olog will be in charge. Once I've determined whether the man we've been looking for is here or not that's when I'll be able to decide what we do next. There's enough light left you should be able to get down shore and make camp before dark. When I say a couple of miles down shore I mean a couple of miles down shore," he stressed, looking straight at Olog. "So shove off now while the light remains and I'll make contact with you when the time is right."

Another groan of dissatisfaction went around the boat but they obeyed and shoved off. He watched as they moved away and headed down the shoreline. He knew they would do as told but he watched for his own ease of mind. After they were far enough away he turned and walked the landing into town.

The sun had already dropped below the mountaintops when he walked into town. Lights were beginning to come on in the homes and buildings. The section of town he had entered was where the dwarves lived. They had their own section of town because the larger population of humans did not interact well with them. They just accepted their presence because of the commerce they brought.

He walked directly to his uncle's home. His uncle was his mother's brother. His uncle's wife, Ogiloth's aunt, had died years ago and his uncle hadn't taken another mate. He was an ornery old dwarf and most of the females couldn't stand to be around him anyway, so he lived alone. When he reached his uncle's home he walked up and knocked on the door.

"Who be there?" he heard his uncle grumble.

He didn't answer and just knocked again.

"Who be there I say?" His uncle's tone was a little more gruff and had some anger in it.

He ignored him and knocked again, only louder. He heard his uncle come stomping to the door. A small opening in the door appeared about eye height to a dwarf.

"This better be important," he grumbled loudly, peering through the opening. "It be you Ogiloth," he sounded a little less grumpy. "Why did ye not answer?" The door swung open.

"I wanted to see if I could make my favorite uncle even angrier than he sounded." He smiled big at his uncle.

"Well, ye was doin' a fine job at it. But I can't be angry at me favorite nephew."

They clasped in a strong handshake. His uncle Durog was still strong for being so old and he pulled him down into a huge bear hug. "How ye been boy?"

"I've been well uncle. And yourself?"

"I been doin' all right. Come on in boy."

He entered the home bending to walk through the doorway and the door was shut behind him. The door opened into a hallway with an arched opening on the left leading into a kitchen and one on the right leading into a study. There were a few paintings hanging on the walls. Walking further down the hallway it opened into the living area with a couch against the wall to the left, two chairs on the opposite wall with a table between them, a chair against the wall on the right as you entered, and a double door in the wall to the right leading out onto a patio. An oval table sat in the middle of it all with a couple large candles already lit for lighting in the room. There was also a lit candle on the table between the two chairs. A bookshelf was in the far corner completely full of books. His uncle loved to read. On the wall above the two chairs was a painting of his aunt and uncle in their younger years. Two battle axes facing each other hung on the wall above the couch and a coat rack stood next to the end of the couch. A door that led into the bedchamber was in the corner between the couch and one of the chairs. It wasn't a big place but now that his uncle was by himself it was perfect.

"Have a seat boy and let's get requainted. Ye want a draft?"

Ogiloth sat on the couch. "Yes."

Durog wandered back into the kitchen and after a lot of noise came back with two drafts. He handed one to his nephew and moved to sit in one of the chairs against the far wall next to the book shelf. Ogiloth remembered that those two chairs were where his aunt and uncle always sat and he knew never to sit in either one. He learned that at an early age.

"What brings ye to Bruston?"

"I'm on a quest."

"And what might that quest be?"

"I'm looking for a man."

Durog started laughing so hard Ogiloth thought he would spill his drink. He remembered that Durog had a very dry sense of humor and knew he'd been misunderstood. After his uncle calmed down he continued.

"Let me restate myself, I'm 'hunting' for a man."

"Oh. And who might this man be?"

"He's the son of the man I work for."

"Yer not still in cahoots with that K'orik fella are ye?"

"Yes I am, and yes he still pays better than mining does. Plus, next to him, I command all his forces. Something my father would have never let me do."

"Command all his forces do ye. I 'spose he's got forces worth reckoning."

"Uncle, you can't imagine."

"So ye came to me fer help then, not just ta visit," he said flatly.

"Yes and no. It's been a while since I visited last and since I was in Bruston I thought 'I should visit my favorite uncle'. I also thought that you were my best chance of getting any help here."

"Well I appreciate that ye came by boy. So what is it ye need me ta do?"

"Chances are that the man I'm looking for came here to report to the sheriff what happened to his village. I was hoping that you could check that out for me."

"And what might he be reportin' happened to his village?"

"It was attacked, burned to the ground, and all the villagers were killed."

"Ye don't say," he paused before continuing. "And did ye have anythin' ta do with this attack?"

"Yes uncle, I was the one that led the attack."

"And why did ye hafta go and burn it down and kill all them folks? They never done nothin' ta ye did they?"

"No, they never did anything to me. The forces I lead are a strange lot and sometimes they can get a little rambunctious." He lied a little, placing the blame on his forces rather than admitting he had ordered it done.

"Ya know, I've hear'd stories lately 'bout this sorta thing happenin' in other places. That be you too?"

"Yes uncle. K'orik wants to find his son, it seems very important to him, and he's charged me with the task."

"And he's told ye to go 'round burnin' their villages and killin'm?" he asked in a gruff tone. "Ya know, this sorta thing doesn't help with relations between yer race and them humans."

"The humans have never really 'liked' our race anyway," he snapped back in disgust. "And as far as the burning and killing, that's something my forces need to sate their appetites."

"What kinda forces ye be leadin' anyway? They be ogres?"

"No. K'orik has a sorcerer friend that's created another race entirely and they're not exactly the prettiest things but they're strong and obedient."

"Another race ye say. So that's why these reports say it's 'monsters' doin' all this damage. Where's yer forces now, boy? They be here in town?"

"No. They're camped along the lake a couple of miles out of town."

"It sounds like a good thing ye didn't bring'm inta town, coulda been trouble. How large be this force ye brought?"

"I started out with ten but one was killed a couple days back. I believe that the man who escaped our last village attack was the one that killed him."

"And ye believe this 'man' is the one yer lookin' for and he's come to Bruston?"

"Yes."

"How sure can ye be he came here?"

"Because this is where I tracked him to. Someone will be travelling with him also."

"Okay boy, I'll do what ye ask of me. Could take more than a day though, I gotta be careful how I go about this. You all right with that?"

"Yes, thank you."

"In the meantime I think it be best that ye stay here while I'm out askin' 'bout yer 'man'. I don't get many visitors but if someone does come a knockin' at the door ye just ignore it."

Ogiloth nodded his assent.

"Now, it's gettin' late and I'm gettin' tired. I'm gettin' old too and I need my beauty sleep." He chuckled at that. "If I'm ta be doin' whatcha want I need ta get ta bed now. Ye can sleep on the couch there." He rose from his chair and took the two empty mugs into the kitchen. Ogiloth had already stretched out on the couch when he came back through the living area.

"Good night uncle and thank you again for your help," he looked at his uncle with a smile.

"Good night boy," he smiled back. "It's good ta see ya again." He blew out the candles and disappeared into his room.

Ogiloth lay there for a while thinking about everything he'd done lately. His uncle was right about one thing, all those people in all those villages didn't deserve to die. They'd never done anything to him or K'orik. They just happened to be in K'orik's way of finding his son and he just happened to be the one leading the way. Sometimes he wondered why he continued but then realized it was because of the way he was raised and the environment he was raised in. Thinking these thoughts, he closed his eyes and fell asleep.

# CHAPTER 10

THEY TALKED CASUALLY as Clare led them down the sidewalk. Actually, Clare did most of the talking. She chattered about her children, her husband, and the work she did at the sheriff's office. As they passed by a dress shop she saw how Lianna eyed the dresses displayed in the window.

"You know what Lianna?" She smiled broadly as Lianna looked at her. "I have a dress at home that I think you would look fabulous in. We're about the same size and I think it would fit you perfect. I'll run home and get it and bring it to you after you've had a chance to clean up at the inn."

Lianna looked down at her own dress and saw that it was pretty tattered and worn from everything she'd been through. She knew Clare was just trying to be nice and she could use a change of clothes. "That would be very nice of you Clare. Somehow I'll find a way to repay you for all your kindness."

"Oh, there's no need for that. After all you've been through it's the least I can do."

They continued talking and walking and it wasn't long before they reached the inn. The sign hanging over the front door had a picture of a red and a blue dragon intertwined in battle. It read 'Dragons' Inn'. J'orik and Lianna looked at each other and wondered if this was some sort of coincidence. They didn't say anything about it as Clare ushered them through the door. Walking into the entry area they stopped suddenly and took in a deep breathe of surprise.

Clare noticed their reaction and asked with some concern, "Is something wrong?"

"No," they both responded slowly.

Looking around they couldn't help but notice how similar this inn looked to the Dragons' Lair in Washoe, almost identical, except for the man behind the counter. He wasn't as rotund as Casper and didn't wear any spectacles but his clothes were the same. Clare led them to the counter and introduced them to the man.

"This is Jake, one of my very good friends. Jake, this is J'orik and Lianna."

"Hello folks, welcome to the Dragons' Inn," he said with a big grin on his face.

Clare proceeded to give Jake a brief explanation of what brought them to Bruston and what they had recently gone through. She told him she had promised them he could put them up in a room for the night. She also explained that they had no way to pay for the room but she thought he would find some way for them to make up for it.

"I think arrangements can be made," he told her. "I have some empty rooms anyway and I don't see that they'll be taken tonight." He turned around and got a key for one of the rooms. "Once you've settled into the room the bath is at the end of the hall." He handed the key to J'orik. "It's room 7. Just down the hall to your right after you get to the top of the stairs. After you're all cleaned up come on back down and

I'll get you set up for a nice hot home-cooked meal. My wife is 'the best' cook in town."

J'orik took the key and they both thanked him. They were still in awe at how similar the two inns were. The walls were painted the same color with paintings of landscapes hanging on them. The chandelier hanging from the ceiling was identical. The counter appeared to be made from the same type of wood and stone. And the mirror behind the counter was the same. The only noticeable difference was the dragon images.

As they were heading up the stairs Clare hollered up to Lianna, "I'll go get that dress I told you about and bring it right back." Then she added, "I think I'll bring one of my husband's shirts for you J'orik."

They both thanked her and disappeared at the top of the stairs.

Jake turned to Clare with a confused look and said, "There's something familiar about that woman."

"You know, I had the same feeling when she was in the sheriff's office waiting for him."

"There's something familiar about that man she's with too. I can't put my finger on it right now but maybe Joice will have some insight after she meets them."

"Well, I better get going so I can get those changes of clothes back for them. I'll see you in a little bit Jake." She turned and waved to him as she headed out the door.

"See you in a while." He waved back.

Jake stood there for a short time with that same confused look on his face trying to figure out what it was that was so familiar about Lianna and J'orik, before going into the kitchen to let his wife know they had two more guests that would be needing a meal.

Clare returned a little while later and Jake told her, as she headed up the stairs, he thought they were done bathing. She walked down the hall to room 7 and knocked on the door.

"It's just Clare. I have the clothes I promised for you."

Lianna opened the door. "Come in Clare."

She stepped into the room and handed the dress to Lianna and the shirt to J'orik. They both thanked her again for her kindness.

Lianna held up the dress to look at it. "It's beautiful Clare. I've never worn anything like it in my life." She looked down at the tattered and worn dress she'd been wearing for the last week. "This is the type of dress I'm used to."

Clare turned to J'orik and asked him, "Do you think the shirt will fit you?"

He held it up to himself. "It'll do just fine Clare. Thank you and tell your husband thanks for me."

"Well, I've got to get back home before the kids drive my husband insane. I'll see you tomorrow." She waved and left the room.

"What a nice woman," Lianna told J'orik as she began slipping out of her tattered dress to change.

He quickly turned his back to her, embarrassment flushing his face. She just smiled at him behind his back as she slipped on the dress Clare had brought. He was changing his shirt at the same time.

"Okay, you can turn around now, I'm done."

When he turned and saw her standing there with her arms slightly raised from her sides he smiled and his face flushed again.

"How does it look?" She looked at him with a smile and slowly spun around.

"It looks beautiful. You look beautiful."

Her smile got even broader. "Why thank you J'orik. My hair is a mess though." She looked over at the vanity in the corner of the room and noticed a brush. She went and sat down at the vanity, took the brush, and began brushing through her hair. It had been over a week since she'd had a chance to do this and her hair was full of knots and rats. She had her back to J'orik but she could see his reflection in the mirror. He sat on the bed watching her the whole time. When she was done she stood up and turned.

"Does it look better now? My hair, I mean?"

"Yes."

"It feels better too. Are you hungry?"

"Yes. I'm starving."

"Well, let's go eat then. I wouldn't want you to die from starvation."

He quickly got to the door and opened it for her. They left the room, walked down the hallway, down the stairs to the entry area, and stopped at the counter to see Jake.

"My, but don't you look pretty," Jake said glancing at Lianna with a smile.

"Thank you Jake." She smiled back.

"I told my wife Joice that you two would be down for dinner. If you go right through the entryway there," he pointed, "and have yourselves a seat at one of the tables, she'll be right out to take your orders."

They did as he suggested and walked into the dining room. Again they were taken aback by the similarities to the Dragons' Lair in Washoe. There were a few other patrons seated at tables, and at the bar, eating their meals. They both took a sniff and were overwhelmed by the wonderful aromas emanating from the kitchen. They wandered over to a table against the wall next to a window that overlooked the street and sat down. They were both looking out the window at all the activity still going on even though night had fallen when a woman walked up to their table and introduced herself.

"Good evening folks. My name is Joice. Have you had a chance to look at the menu and decide what you want?"

J'orik looked up at her with a smile. "No. We've just been sitting here taking in the sights outside."

"You just take your time then, there's no hurry. In the meantime can I get you something to drink?"

"Coffee please," he answered. Lianna indicated the same for herself.

"Okay then, I'll be right back with two cups of hot steaming coffee."

She turned and they watched her go behind the bar and pour two cups of coffee. She returned to their table, set the cups down, and told them again to take their time deciding on their meal.

They sipped the coffee and then picked up the menus.

"J'orik," Lianna whispered across the table, "I don't know how to read."

"That's okay. Just tell me what you want and I'll see if I can find a meal on the menu that's got everything you want."

She told him and he found a meal that fit what she wanted. He also found what he was looking for. They closed the menus and set them back on the table and continued watching the activity outside while sipping their coffees. Joice came back shortly afterwards.

"I see you've decided on a meal."

"Yes," J'orik replied. He told her what they wanted and she left to go start preparing their meals.

They had light conversation while sipping their coffees and watching the streets. Some of the people left while others came in. It wasn't crowded so the noise level wasn't disturbing their conversation. They commented to each other on how similar the two inns were and wondered if there was some relation between the owners or if it was purely coincidence.

"Uncle Casper or Aunt Karin never mentioned having any family in Bruston. But I don't remember Bruston ever being mentioned in our talks except as another town."

"I just get this strange feeling that I should know these people. I got the same feeling with your aunt and uncle when we were at the Dragons' Lair."

"I've only been to Bruston a few times and I don't remember coming to this place or meeting these people."

"Why did you come to Bruston?"

"For my weapons and trade."

"But didn't Falder make your weapons?"

"No. I got all my weapons here. Falder was a good blacksmith but even he told me he couldn't make the type of weapons I have. He said he didn't have the right type of metals for what I was requesting. The crossbow I had made by an expert craftsman that specialized in the making of crossbows."

Joice returned carrying their platters of food and set them on the table. "Can I get you some more coffee?"

"Yes please," Lianna responded. J'orik nodded in agreement.

Lianna looked at J'orik with a wry smile. "I knew that's what you were going to order. You're a through and through meat and potatoes man."

He had ordered a whole rabbit, a large helping of mashed potatoes smothered in gravy, and a couple of dinner rolls. She had quail, diced red potatoes, and sautéed vegetables. They ate their meals without talking. He finished his before she was even halfway through hers. He sat back when he was done and tried to belch as quietly as possible. She just giggled at him and continued eating.

"That hit the spot," he said with a sigh of satisfaction.

"You said you were starving," she reminded him.

When she finally put her utensils down she still hadn't eaten all her meal. She glanced up at J'orik and he was staring gluttonously at what remained on her platter.

"Would you like the rest?"

She already knew the answer so she handed him her platter without waiting for a response and watched him finish it off. She knew what was to come next and just giggled again when he let out with another belch. At least now he was trying to be quieter about it and draw less attention from the other patrons.

Joice returned to take their empty platters. Noticing that both platters were now on J'orik's side she looked at Lianna and commented with a chuckle, "He sure can eat can't he? More coffee?"

"Yes please," they answered in unison.

J'orik then added, "Joice, that meal was absolutely delicious. There's only one other person I know that compares to you when it comes to cooking and that's my Aunt Karin."

"Really. Does she cook for a living or just the family?"

"Both actually. She and my uncle run an inn in Washoe very similar to this one."

"Karin you said her name was?"

"Yes ma'am."

"Is her husband's name Casper and is the name of the inn the Dragons' Lair?"

"Yes. Why, do you know them?" he asked with a startled look. Lianna also looked startled.

"Yes I know them. Karin is my sister."

Both J'orik and Lianna's jaws dropped open.

"Jake!" she hollered. "Jake! Get over here!" She set the platters down on the table next to them, pulled up a chair and sat down. "Jake!" she yelled louder looking towards the entry area.

Jake came running into the dining room with a panicked look on his face. "What is it Joice?"

She pointed at J'orik. "This is Casper and Karin's nephew that they've told us about."

Jake's jaw dropped open in astonishment. He couldn't even respond he was so surprised.

"Close your mouth Jake," she told him. "I told you there was something familiar about him."

Joice knew that all eyes in the dining room were on them. She turned around and told them all to go back to their meals, everything was all right. When she turned back around Jake had been able to compose himself.

He looked down at Joice. "We can't talk about this out here."

"You're right," she told him. She looked at J'orik and Lianna. "I'm going to clean up here. I want you two to follow Jake into his office. We need to talk." Then she turned to Jake and told him, "Have Gerard watch the front counter and take these two into your office and wait for me. I'll tell Kayla she needs to take over in here and then I'll be right there." She got up, grabbed the platters, and disappeared into the kitchen.

"Well, come on," Jake told them. "You heard the woman. Follow me."

He turned to leave and glanced back to make sure they were following him. They were slow getting out of their seats because they were still confused about what had just happened.

"Come on," Jake said again, waving his arm for them to follow.

They finally finished standing and started following Jake out of the dining room. At the front counter he lifted a portion of it at the end against the wall, let them through, set the counter back in place, opened the door to his office, and ushered them in.

"Take a seat. I need to find Gerard and tell him to watch the front counter for me. I'll be right back." Then he shut the door leaving them in his office alone.

"What just happened?" Lianna asked J'orik.

"I don't know."

"If Joice is Karin's sister and Karin is your aunt, wouldn't that make Joice your aunt too?"

"That makes sense. It would also make sense then that Casper and Jake are my uncles, by marriage."

"Is this true?"

"Again, I don't know." He was confused. "I think we need to wait and ask Jake and Joice when they get here." He looked around the office they were in and commented to her, "This office looks almost identical to the office uncle Casper has at the Dragons' Lair."

She looked around and agreed with his assessment.

About then Jake and Joice both walked into the office. Jake took a seat behind the desk and Joice pulled a seat over next to the desk and sat down. They both sat there holding hands, not saying a word, looking at J'orik and Lianna. J'orik and Lianna sat there quietly, waiting for them to start the conversation.

Joice finally broke the silence. "When was the last time you saw your parents Lianna?"

"At my wedding to Falder."

"And how long ago was that?"

"Fourteen years."

"How old was Falder when you two were married?"

"35."

Joice turned to Jake. "He was at prime age." Jake nodded in agreement. Lianna looked at her confused.

"Did you have any children with Falder?" Joice went on.

"Yes, three."

"Did Falder or your parents ever talk to you about what you are?"

"What do you mean 'what I am'?"

Joice turned to Jake. "Apparently none of them ever told her." Jake just shrugged his shoulders.

Lianna leaned forward in her seat and stuttered, "What do you mean 'what I am'? Answer me!" She sounded panicked now.

"Calm down dear. It's nothing to get upset about. You're a dragon," Joice said matter of fact.

J'orik's jaw dropped open. Lianna was stunned.

"Close your mouth J'orik, you look silly. Lianna, dear, you're a dragon. You need to know and understand this so that you can understand some of the things that you might have been wondering about yourself." Joice continued the questioning. "How old are you now?"

"32."

"Ah. You've probably been experiencing some unusual changes going on in your body." Joice glanced over at Jake and he nodded in agreement. She looked back at Lianna. "Have you had any unusual emotions or dreams?"

"Now that you ask, I did sense that something wasn't right on the day our village was attacked and a couple weeks before that I had a most terrible nightmare."

"And in this 'nightmare' did you see the village being attacked?"

"I couldn't really tell if it was our village or just some village somewhere. It was almost as if I was seeing it from above."

"And have you had other 'nightmares' or dreams where you were 'seeing things from above'?"

"Yes."

"How long have you been having these dreams?"

"All my life actually, but they've been occurring more often the last few of years."

Joice looked over at Jake again. "Her body is trying to make the change. She needs someone to guide her." Jake just smiled and nodded in agreement.

"What do you mean 'the change'? And what does this have to do with me being 'a dragon'? And what do you mean 'I need someone to guide me'? Guide me where?" Lianna shot the questions out one right after the other. She was becoming more anxious now.

Jake and J'orik sat in their chairs listening to the whole interrogation. Neither one attempted to interrupt. Jake sat with a very calm expression while J'orik had a dumbfounded look on his face.

"I need you to listen to what I have to say without interruption. This includes you as well J'orik. What I'm going to tell you affects both of you. I'm not going to go into a lot of detail because it's getting late and I need to tell J'orik a few things, but we can certainly talk at length tomorrow when we have more time. Agreed?" She gave them both a stern look.

They both nodded agreement and sat back in their chairs.

"We belong to a race of people known as 'shapeshifters'." She indicated the four of them. "Our normal state is in human form but we have the ability to change our physical shape into something else. A long time ago we could change into anything we desired but that started to cause problems and began to divide our people. The leading council at the time decided it would be wiser and less problematic if the shapeshifting was confined to one secondary form. The human form would always be the normal state but everyone would only be allowed one additional form. That additional form would be a matter of choice. Once that choice was made it would be final and irreversible. Everyone was given one year to decide what their secondary form would be. For the most part it became a family decision. Oh, there were a few who didn't go along with their family's choice but most did. This is the way it's been since that time." She paused momentarily before turning to J'orik and saying, "Now as to you J'orik. There are some things you need to know."

"But what about 'the change' and me needing guidance?" Lianna jumped in quickly.

"Those are things we can talk about tomorrow, there's no hurry. J'orik has been sitting quietly listening to everything and probably wondering how he fits into all of this. I need to abate his curiosity."

Lianna sat back with a huff, like a small child being put off.

Joice turned her attention to J'orik. "Do you know who your father is?"

"No. My mother told me he was dead."

"He's not dead. He's quite alive and kicking. Is your mother still alive or was she killed in the attack on your village?"

"She died when I was 12."

Joice turned to Jake with a stunned look and Jake looked back at her in confusion.

"How did she die?" she asked turning back to J'orik.

"I was told she drowned in the lake."

"I remember that," Lianna said. "That happened the year before Falder and I got married. That was your mother," she looked at J'orik.

"Yes."

"I'm sorry."

Joice continued, "Was her body ever recovered?"

"No. They said they never found her."

Joice smiled. "I'll tell you this much, and you need to understand this as well Lianna, shapeshifters don't 'die', ever. We can be killed but we never just die. Even then we're hard to kill. What happened to you after that? Who raised you?"

"A couple in the village my mother was close friends with."

"How old are you?"

"27."

"Did you ever feel different than those around you?"

"I was always faster and stronger than my friends, even the boys that were bigger than me."

"How did you come to know Casper and Karin as your uncle and aunt?"

"The man and woman that raised me would go to Washoe to trade and I always went with them. They told me that my mother had told them they were my aunt and uncle."

"And did Casper or Karin ever tell you different?"

"No."

"I didn't think so. From the conversations I've had with Karin they loved you like their own son. They knew your mother and knew what she was. Now the next thing I'm about to tell you will come as quite a shock." She paused for a moment to allow J'orik to take everything in. "Your mother is still alive."

J'orik fell back in his chair stunned. He couldn't believe what he was hearing. First, his father is still alive, and now, his mother is still alive. He wasn't quite sure what to think of all this. He glanced at Lianna and then turned back to Joice and just stared blankly at her. "How do you know this?"

"Karin told me. Your mother knew that your father would eventually come looking for you and she didn't want him to ever be able to find you. She faked the drowning, which would have been easy, and disappeared out of your life leaving you in the care of her friends. I don't think you realize how difficult that was for her. She knew she would not be able to protect you from your father, he's much stronger than her and she knew it. The next best thing, in her mind, was to just disappear. Casper and Karin tried to talk her out of it but she didn't feel there was any other way."

"Do you know where she is?"

"No. Neither do Casper or Karin. She thought it was better that way."

Tears began to well up in his eyes. He still couldn't believe what he was hearing. "You said my father is still alive. Where is he?"

"Your father lives in the Castaic Mountains far north of here."

"Can you tell me anything about him?"

"His name is K'orik. He lives in a castle in the mountains. He's not a very nice man. And that's the short version."

"What do you mean 'he's not a very nice man'?"

"Have you heard the stories about other villages besides yours that were burned down and all the people killed that lived in them?"

J'orik nodded his head affirmatively.

"He's the one responsible for all of that."

"What do you mean?"

"He's looking for you, J'orik. He wants to find you, his son. He knows you're coming of age and he wants to be the one who guides you through the 'changing'. He'll do anything and everything in his power to accomplish that. I know you and Lianna probably have more questions about all of this but it's getting late. Jake and I need to get back to business. You and Lianna should go to your room and take some time to think about everything I've said here tonight. Sleep on it, if you can. We'll talk more tomorrow when you've had a good night's rest." She stood up and Jake stood up with her. They waited for him and Lianna to do the same.

They looked back at Jake and Joice as they were going up the stairs and they just smiled back at them.

After she heard the door shut to J'orik and Lianna's room, Joice turned to Jake and said, with a sad look on her face, "Poor kids, they had no idea."

# CHAPTER 11

OGILOTH WOKE THE next morning to the clatter of pans from the kitchen and the smell of bacon. His uncle was already up and had started breakfast. He was hungry enough to eat a whole pig by himself and the smell of bacon just made him all the hungrier. As he rose from the couch he noticed it was raining. It wasn't a hard rain but it was enough to make being in it miserable. The cloud cover kept the sunlight from shining through so it was grey and gloomy outside. Every once in a while he heard the low rumble of thunder. His uncle was making an unbelievable amount of racket. One thing he did know about dwarves was that they made a lot of noise, even when they were trying to be quiet. The noise and the smell of bacon were too much for him to handle so he made his way towards the kitchen. His stomach growled loudly, sounding like a bear, as he stepped into the kitchen entry and his uncle quickly turned with a frying pan in his hand cocked and ready to throw.

"Oh, it be you Ogiloth. I didn't think ye was ever goin' to wake up. Ye was snorin' like a bear, like the noise yer stomach just made. Ye must be hungry. Smelled the bacon did ye?" he ended with a smile.

"Starving," he said, rubbing his stomach. "I can't remember the last time I had bacon. All I've eaten lately is trail food."

"Well, I got biscuits in the oven and sausage gravy cookin' ta top'm. Have a seat boy, it be just 'bout ready." Durog went back to cooking.

He squeezed between his uncle and the counter behind him and sat down at the dining table. This was the problem with being as big as he was, everything was always too small or too tight. He always had to duck going through doors and watch out for things hanging from ceilings, except in K'orik's castle.

Durog opened the oven door and saw that the biscuits were ready. He pulled them out and set them on the table. Ogiloth reached out to take one and got smacked on the back of his hand with the spatula his uncle was holding.

"Boy, ye got ta wait for the rest of the food, and me. Ye just sit there and smell the food and let yer hunger grow."

Ogiloth licked the back of his hand like a wounded animal. The spatula had hot bacon grease on it and that hurt more than being hit by it, but the bacon grease tasted good. He heard the cracking of eggs and the sizzling as they were dumped onto the frying pan. He started slowly reaching for a biscuit again, thinking his uncle was distracted with the eggs.

"Don't even think about it boy. Wud I just say?"

He drew his hand back and grumbled. He didn't have to wait long though. Durog came to the table with two platters mounded with scrambled eggs and half a dozen large strips of thick bacon. He set one down in front of Ogiloth and another across the table for himself. He turned around and grabbed the pot of gravy and set it on the table next to the biscuits and sat down.

He looked at his nephew with a sly grin and said, "Okay boy, ye can dig in now."

Without another word Ogiloth grabbed a couple biscuits, spooned some gravy on them, and started eating like there was no tomorrow.

"So tha plan taday is for me ta go inta town and see what I can find out 'bout yer man?"

Ogiloth just nodded his head yes while shoveling food in his mouth.

"What be his name? I don't remember ye mentionin' it last night."

"J'orik," he said in between bites.

"Do ya know what he looks like?"

"K'orik says he looks just like him."

"Well, I never seen this K'orik fella so that ain't gonna help. Ya gotta give me somethin' more ta work with boy."

"He's twenty seven years old, tall and muscular, and has a birthmark on the back of his head shaped like a phoenix. K'orik's hair is white but I think that's from age. J'orik's hair is probably black or a dark brown and likely long."

"Now that be better. Prob'ly won't be able ta see the birthmark though if he got long hair."

Ogiloth finished what he had on his platter and grabbed a couple more biscuits and spooned some gravy on them. "Is there more bacon?" He looked over at the stove.

"There be a few more slices in the pan. Go ahead, help yerself. So ye think tha first place I should stop is the sheriff's office?"

Ogiloth just shook his head yes.

"Ya know it's rainin' out?"

He stopped chewing and gave his uncle a blank stare. "And?"

"I be gettin' old and this kinda weather makes me bones ache."

"So your saying you want to wait until this blows over?"

"Least 'til the rain stops. I stepped out after I got up an' it looked like it just might clear up by midday."

"That'll be all right. I just don't want to wait too long. I don't want to lose him."

They both finished the food on their platters about the same time. Durog stood, took both platters, and set them in the sink. Grabbed what was left of the pot of gravy and set it on the stove. As he was reaching to pick up the tray of biscuits Ogiloth grabbed two more before he took it away.

"Uncle, that was delicious! Thank you."

"Least ye got some manners. Yer welcome boy. I thought while we was waitin' for the rain ta let up we could play a couple games o' chess. What do ya say ta that?"

"Depends on whether you can handle losing or not," he chuckled.

"Bah! Ye were never that good at the game. What makes ye think I would lose?"

"I've been practicing. K'orik loves to play."

"Okay. So it sounds like we got a challenge."

Ogiloth rose from the table and both of them walked into the living area. Durog pulled his chair closer to the table and sat down. He reached under the table and pulled the game board out with the pieces. Ogiloth dropped onto the couch and they began setting up the pieces for their first game.

By the end of the first game Ogiloth noticed the rain had stopped but it was still grey and gloomy. His uncle had fought the game the whole way through and he could see that he was just a little frustrated with himself. Ogiloth had won, but it was a close game.

"Bah! Ye have been practicin'. Thought I had ye a couple times there but somehow ye managed ta get out o' the pickle I had ye in."

"Are you sure you had me in a pickle?" He just smiled big and chuckled at his uncle.

"Bah!" was the only response Ogiloth got. "Set'm up again, boy. I'll get ye this time."

"The rain's stopped and I haven't heard any thunder for a while."

"Tha only thunder yer gonna hear, boy, is when I stomp me feet after beatin' ya."

"I think the only reason you'll be stomping your feet is because your mad you lost again."

"Bah!" Durog began laughing. Ogiloth joined in the laughter.

"Another game," Durog challenged. "An' if I win, we play again. If ye win, I'll get ta work for ya. Fair enough?"

"Fair enough, uncle."

They set the pieces up and started playing. The advantage went back and forth like the first game. They played for over an hour and in that same time the clouds began breaking up.

S. P. Foster

Sunlight was starting to shine and Ogiloth could see patches of blue sky in the distance as he peered through the double doors leading out onto the patio. He eventually won the game and all his uncle could say was, "Bah!" over and over as he stomped his feet on the floor like thunder. Ogiloth didn't even chuckle this time because he didn't want to make his uncle any madder than he already was at himself.

"Okay boy, ye won fair and square two games in a row. I'll do as ye asked and see what I can find out for ye. But when I get back and tell ye what I found out, we play again." He looked his nephew straight in the eyes, "Okay?"

"Okay, uncle." And then they laughed together.

Durog left his house waving to his nephew as he shut the door. Walking towards the street he looked up into the sky to check the weather again. He'd been right. The clouds were breaking up and the skies would be clear by midday. He closed his eyes and took a big sniff of the air. The rain always left the air clean and this time of year there were an abundance of flowers in bloom making the air smell even sweeter. He loved living in Bruston. He'd lived in Bruston most of his life. It was days like this that he would remember when his wife was still alive. He did miss her, especially her smile and her laugh. He smiled at the memory, took another long sniff of the air, and started down the street towards the humans' side of town.

The weather never slowed the activity in Bruston. Durog's home wasn't that far from the first stop he was going to make. He passed by warehouses and fisheries and was assaulted with a cacophony of aromas. The smell that he first experienced stepping out his front door was gone and buried

137

by those he was passing by now. *Humans and their fishing*, he thought. He was more accustomed to the smell of rock and dirt. He wound his way through the streets until he reached the part that was mostly mercantile. He took a right and headed down the main street through town. It was lined with shops, restaurants, and inns. The sheriff's office was also on this street. Nobody paid too much attention to him because they all knew who he was. After all, he'd lived in Bruston longer than most of these humans had been alive. He didn't have to walk too far before he reached the sheriff's office.

He stopped in front of the door and stood there for a few moments thinking about what he was going to say without sounding too inquisitive. He knew the sheriff and his deputies would probably be out and about in town at this time of day keeping an eye on things. He liked the clerk well enough and he thought she reciprocated the feelings. Clare was her name. He was startled when the door opened. Jack, one of the deputies stepped out.

"Hello, Durog. How're you doing this fine day?"

"I be doin' fine, Jack. An' yerself?" He tried to sound genuinely interested.

"Out for a walk, eh? It's a beautiful day for one," he said as he shut the door.

"Yeah, thought I'd come inta town an' do a little bitta shoppin'. Maybe stop in ta tha Boars' Den fer a pint."

"Well, you have a nice day. Gotta get goin'. Got work to attend to. See ya later." He smiled and waved as he headed off down the sidewalk.

Durog let him get far enough down the sidewalk so he wouldn't hear him open the door. He stepped into the office and shut the door gently behind himself.

Clare was sitting at her desk. "Good morning Durog," she greeted him with a smile. "Or I guess it would be 'good afternoon' now." She giggled. "What can I do for you today?"

"Me nephew's in town and he be lookin' fer an old friend of his use ta be a deputy in one o' the towns on tha far side o' the Great Plains. Got a letter from him sayin' he'd be here 'bout now an' figgered he'd be stoppin' in here ta say hi ta the locals." He lied, not knowing how else to find out.

"What be his name?" she tried to imitate Durog's speech.

"Nephew said it was somethin' like 'Jerik' or 'Jarik'."

"J'orik."

"Yeah, that be it. He been in here?"

"Yes, there was a man that stopped in here with that name but he never mentioned being a deputy from the far side of the Great Plains."

"Maybe he be a diff'rent fella than me nephew's lookin' fer. Happen ta know where he went, just in case?"

"He was looking for a place to stay so I told him about a couple of inns here in town."

Durog didn't think it was wise to pursue the issue any further afraid it might raise some suspicion. "Okay then. Thanks fer the information Clare. I'll let me nephew know what ye tell'd me." He smiled at her, turned and headed back out of the office. "Be talkin' ta ye Clare."

"Bye Durog, have a nice day."

After the door shut Clare walked over to the window and watched as he headed south on the sidewalk towards the end of town where most of the inns were located.

As he walked down the sidewalk he thought to himself how well it had gone. Ogiloth had been right about one thing, this J'orik fellow had stopped in at the sheriff's office, unless there was more than one J'orik wandering about in Bruston. Clare didn't seem to act suspicious about his line of questioning, if she was she didn't show it. He figured he'd just wander towards the inns and see if he spotted a man resembling the description Ogiloth had given him.

After he reached the last inn on the side of the street he was walking without seeing anyone he thought fit the description, he crossed the street and began walking back the other direction. He hadn't walked too far before he noticed one of his favorite places, the Boars' Den, a local drinking hole frequented by dwarves. An old business acquaintance of his from when he worked in the mines had opened the place with the intention of catering specifically to dwarves. He thought he'd stop in and have a pint before returning home, maybe visit with a friend or two. Entering the place he was greeted heartily by just such a friend, another dwarf he'd known for a very long time, Owen. Owen was nearly as old as him. They had mined together in the Castaic Mountains west of town when they were both younger lads.

"Durog," he shouted out with a huge grin on his face. "Haven't seen ye fer a long spell. Sit an' have a pint with an old friend," as he raised his mug and slammed it back down on the table.

Owen was sitting at a table next to a window that looked out onto the street. Durog thought that would be the best spot to sit so he sat down situating himself to see out the window. Before he sat down he hollered over the noise at the waitress bringing drinks to the tables to bring him a pint.

He sat down smacking his old friend on the back, "Owen, old friend, how ye been?"

"Been well old friend. What brings ye ta town?"

He didn't want to give the true reason. "Thought I'd take a little walk an' see if there be any changes in town. Maybe stop in here ta have a pint or two."

"There be no changes I know of an' I'd know. I sit here all tha time watchin' what goes on an' I ain't seen nothin'."

The waitress showed up with his pint and set it on the table. He paid her and she smiled at him and walked away.

He raised the mug to his lips and took a big swig keeping his eyes on the street. "How be yer boys, they still workin' the mines?"

"Yeah. They be gone most o' the time an' me wife and daughter keep up 'round the house. That be why I spend a lot o' me time here, stayin' away from the women. If'n I was ta stay home they'd be wantin' me ta help'm an' I ain't wantin' ta do that." He took a swig of his pint. "How you be, livin' alone like ye do?"

"It be all right. Do a lot o' readin'. Me nephew's in town right now. Played a couple o' games o' chess this mornin' an' he beat me. Boy's been practicin'." He took another swig and as he set the mug down he noticed Clare walking down the sidewalk on the other side of the street. He was curious where she might be going so he got up to leave.

"Where ye goin' so fast? Ye haven't finished yer drink yet." Owen looked at him with a scowl.

"Gotta go, been nice talkin' with ya," he said hurriedly. He took one last swig, set the mug down, and headed out the door.

Before stepping out on the sidewalk he glanced out to make sure Clare was far enough along that she wouldn't see him. There was enough activity on both sidewalks and in the street that he felt comfortable she wouldn't notice him following her from across the street. He hadn't followed her too long before he saw her go into the Dragons' Inn. *That must be the inn J'orik is at*, he thought to himself. *Dern it. She musta been suspicious or she wuda told me which inn he was at.* With that in mind he decided it was time to go home and tell Ogiloth all he had found out.

# CHAPTER 12

SLEEP WAS RESTLESS for both J'orik and Lianna. Neither one got a good night's rest, tossing and turning all night long thinking about what Joice had told them. What she had told them sounded unbelievable. Sometime during the night it started raining, which didn't help. It wasn't a heavy rain but it was enough to interfere with their sleeping. There was one loud rumble of thunder early in the morning that caused them both to decide it wasn't worth trying to sleep any more. It was still dim because of the cloud cover but light enough they figured it was morning. They both just sat on the edge of the bed thinking.

Lianna turned to J'orik and asked, "Do you believe what Joice told us last night?"

He sat there with his back still to her and answered, "I don't know if I believe what she said, but it does help explain some things about myself that make it hard not to believe her."

"She said I'm a dragon and that your parents are both still alive. I wonder if my parents are still alive. If they are why haven't they tried to contact me?"

"If you're a dragon then what am I? Am I a dragon too, or am I something else? She said your body is trying to make this change. Is my body trying to make the same change?" He turned to her with an even more confused look on his face, "Falder never said anything to you about this?"

"No," she said flatly.

"I wonder why he didn't." He paused for a moment then continued. "If he was a dragon and you're a dragon, then that would make your children dragons as well, right?"

"That makes sense."

"Since we didn't find them dead at the village then we could assume they were taken by those that attacked us, right?"

"I guess."

"And if what Joice said about my father being responsible for what happened, we can also assume that your children, and all the children from the other villages, were taken by my father to his castle. What would he want with the children?" He turned away from her and brought his fists down on his knees in frustration.

"Calm down J'orik. Joice said we would talk some more about it this morning. Maybe we should go down stairs and see if she's ready to tell us more."

"Yes, yes, let's do that." He rose from the bed and put on his boots and looked at her with a determined expression, "She needs to tell us more."

She stood up, straightened the wrinkles out of her dress, and put on her shoes. They had both lain down on top of the bed covers without undressing, only removing their shoes. They smiled at each other and then proceeded down stairs to confront Joice with more questions.

It was mid-morning and Joice was already busy preparing meals for the early risers that came in for breakfast, as well as a few patrons that had already wandered down from their rooms. She couldn't help but wonder why J'orik and Lianna hadn't made their way down yet. Maybe with the storm coming in and the clouds keeping the sunlight out, they hadn't woke up yet. She thought to herself that she would have had a million and one questions on her mind and probably wouldn't have slept much at all, anxious to get them answered. Heading back towards the kitchen she stopped momentarily at the bar counter and looked through the opening leading to the front counter. Jake wasn't anywhere to be seen. She figured he was probably in his office so she wandered over and opened the door.

"Jake, are you in here?"

"Yes dear, I'm over here."

She stepped into the office and saw him looking through some books on the shelf in the corner next to his desk. "What are you looking for? Did you know there's no one at the front counter?"

"Yes, I know dear. I was only going to step away for a moment. I didn't think it would matter too much if someone came in and had to wait for a second or two."

"What are you looking for?"

"The sheriff came in earlier and was asking me if I had any record of a certain gentleman that might have stayed here three months back. I told him I would have to look in my guest register from that time. I was busy with something else at the moment so he said he would come back later. I asked him if it was important and that I would take a look when I was done. He said it wasn't and then left."

"You know, those kids haven't come down this morning yet."

"I know. I've been watching for them. Ah, here it is."

"Sounds like you found what you were looking for. I'm heading back to the kitchen. Give me a holler when those kids finally come down."

"Okay dear." Smiling, he walked towards her with the guest register he'd been looking for.

They both exited the office, she going back to the kitchen and he staying at the front counter. Jake set the guest register on the counter and began looking through it for the name the sheriff had left with him.

As J'orik and Lianna came down the stairs they could see Jake at the counter busily looking through a book and humming to himself. He looked up and smiled at them.

"Joice and I were just talking about you wondering when you would be coming down. How did you sleep?"

"Not too good," J'orik grumbled.

"I would imagine not," Jake maintained his smile. "Joice kind of left you hanging last night. If it was me, I probably wouldn't have gotten any sleep."

"We both tried," Lianna smiled back, "but there were just too many questions I had on my mind that I needed answered."

"Well, child, those questions will all be answered today I hope. But first, I think you need to have a bite to eat. Go on into the dining room and have a seat, I'll let Joice know you've come down."

They both walked into the dining room and sat at the same table they'd sat at the day before. Jake stepped into the kitchen to tell Joice they'd come down and were sitting at a table waiting for breakfast. He went back to the front counter and continued looking through the old guest register. Joice came walking out of the kitchen and walked over to the table J'orik and Lianna were sitting at. She had a couple cups of coffee and a big smile for them.

"How are you two this morning?" she asked as she set the cups of coffee down. "Did you sleep well?"

J'orik just grumbled and then Lianna spoke up. "Off and on all night and, when the rain and thunder started, it was almost impossible. He kept twisting and turning," she grimaced at J'orik, "which made it even more difficult."

"You were pretty restless yourself," J'orik interjected, grimacing back at her.

"Okay you two. I know just the thing to help. Eat."

"I am hungry." J'orik relaxed a little and put a smile on his face. The mention of food did seem to make him feel better, even if it was still raining out.

"Just tell me what you want." She looked down at Lianna first.

"I would like some fruit with a nice, warm sweet roll."

"That's not even enough to feed a bird. Are you sure that's all you want?"

She just nodded her head affirmatively.

"Okay then," looking over at J'orik, "I know you'll want more than that. What can I get for you?"

"Scrambled eggs mixed with some vegetables, a couple slabs of grilled ham, and biscuits smothered in gravy."

"My, we are hungry aren't we?"

"Yes, ma'am," he responded with a huge smile. "Oh, and one of those warm sweet rolls sounds good too."

"All right, I'll be right back." She walked away leaving them to gaze out the window.

They sat and watched the people go by, surprised at the activity that still went on even when it was raining. It wasn't a heavy rain but it still made the street muddy. The horses' hooves and wagon wheels splashed the mud about and people would dodge it if it came too close to them. They could see them stamping the mud off their shoes before entering any of the establishments. The waitress came by and refilled their coffee.

"Hi, I'm Kristen. How are you folks this morning?"

"Good morning Kristen. I'm Lianna and this is J'orik," she pointed at him with a smile. "It's nice to meet you. We're still trying to wake up."

"Good morning," J'orik said, with a half-smile on his face. "Thanks for the coffee."

"You're welcome. I'm supposed to do this." Then she quickly added, "Oh, don't get me wrong, I love working here. I get to meet so many different people. And one day I'll probably take over for my mother in the kitchen. Jake and Joice are such nice people."

"Miss, could I have some more coffee too?" came a call from another customer.

"Well, it's nice to meet you." She turned and headed over to the other customer.

As Kristen was walking away Joice came to their table with their breakfast. "I see you met Kristen. Nice girl. Her mother is also a great cook, like me," she said with humility. "Now, when you're done with breakfast we can go into the office and pick up our conversation where we left off last night. I know you both probably have some questions and

I will gladly answer them all. First, you need to eat though. Enjoy your breakfast and we'll talk in a little bit."

Before she could even turn around to leave J'orik practically dove into his food. Lianna just watched with a smile on her face. She knew what he would do after he finished. He did it after every meal they'd eaten together. She giggled to herself and began eating her food. About halfway through breakfast she noticed that it had stopped raining. It was still gloomy looking because the clouds hadn't begun breaking up yet but she noticed there were little bits of sunlight appearing and then disappearing. She figured it would probably clear up and be nice this afternoon. Maybe she and J'orik could take a walk and she could get acquainted with Bruston. She glanced over at him and saw that he was done eating. He picked up his cup and took a drink. She just waited for it. He set the cup down and sat back in his chair to relax. He was quick enough to get his hand up to his mouth before it happened. She heard it coming from deep down and just looked at him and giggled. He belched. Somehow he was able to keep the noise under control this time and it wasn't nearly as loud as it was at dinner last night.

"Excuse me, but her food is so good."

"You know, that wouldn't happen if you didn't eat so fast."

Both of them laughed then. He looked out the window and noticed the clouds were starting to break up and more sunlight was showing through.

"Looks like it just might be a nice afternoon," he commented.

"I thought we could take a walk later and you could show me around town."

"I've only been here a few times and each time the town seems to change. I'm probably not your best choice for a guide."

"Maybe not, but you're my best choice for walking around in strange places." She gave him a smirk. "Besides, I like your company. I've become," she paused for a moment, "'accustomed' to you being around."

"I'll take that as a compliment. You about ready?"

"One more bite and then I think I'll be done."

He sat there and waited for her to finish while he gazed out the window. She finished quick enough. They stood up just as Kristen came walking by.

"All done folks?"

They both nodded yes and J'orik added, "If your mother was the one that fixed breakfast, tell her it was wonderful."

"I'll do that," she confirmed as they walked away.

As they were heading towards the front counter Joice came out of the kitchen with a couple platters of food. She quickly delivered them and then told Kristen that she and Jake would be in his office for a while talking with J'orik and Lianna. She should go tell her mother and then take over handling all the customers. If she needed anything, and her mother couldn't help, she would have to get Gerard to help her, he would be at the front counter.

Joice wiped her hands on her apron and removed it, leaving it behind the bar on her way to the office. She got there shortly after J'orik and Lianna. Jake wasn't there.

"Where's Jake?" she asked them.

"He went to get Gerard to watch the front while we have our talk," Lianna responded. "He said that if you got here before he got back to go ahead and start without him. He would be right back."

Joice lifted the counter gate to let them through and all three went into the office. By the time they'd gotten comfortable in their chairs Jake entered the office. He crossed the floor and sat in the chair behind the desk.

Joice began. "If either one of you have any questions about what I said last night, which I know you do, those questions might be answered by what I'm about to tell you. So, if you can, wait until I'm finished. If you have any questions after that I'll gladly answer them. Okay?"

They reluctantly nodded agreement.

"I'll tell you everything about our people that I know. Like I said last night we belong to a race of people known as 'shapeshifters'. How long we've been in existence, I don't think even the oldest of our race knows. And, like I said, shapeshifters don't die, ever. We can live for eternity if we're not killed. Now, mind you, we can be killed but we never just die. Even then we're hard to kill. We were around before normal humans and all the other races came into existence. There are some of us who believe that normal humans came from a group of our race that decided they no longer wanted to live for eternity. For whatever reason, they felt that living for eternity and being able to change form or shape was wrong. Our normal physical state is human form but we had the ability to change our physical shape into anything we desired. A long time ago changing shape was done for play or sport, but as other, more intelligent races and species began to develop, changing shape became a convenience so that we could more easily interact with them. After a time, though, that started to cause problems and began to divide our people. There were those that started to abuse the ability and began taking advantage of the other races.

"Because of the abuse that was going on the leading council at the time decided it would be wiser and less problematic if the shapeshifting was confined to one secondary form. The council felt that this decision would help alleviate some of the abuse. The human form would always be our normal state but everyone would be allowed only one additional form. That additional form would be a matter of choice. Once that choice was made it would be final and irreversible. Everyone was given one year to decide what their secondary form would be and then they would have to undergo the procedure that had been developed to prevent multiple forms. For the most part it became a family decision. Oh, there were a few who didn't go along with their family's choice but most did. Most of those that didn't go along with the family choice were generally the ones that were the biggest abusers. There were some battles fought and many of our people were killed but eventually the council's decision won out and the single 'changing' was implemented. I'm sure, and there are those that believe like me, that there were a few who escaped the procedure and are still out there with the ability to change into anything.

"What I've told you is just a brief background, but this is the way it's been since that time. Now, I'm sure you're more interested in your own personal abilities and the form that you're able to change into. I need to cover a little background on that too before I can answer more personal questions. What I'm about to tell you is the way it's always been, even before the single changing procedure was implemented.

"When one of our race is born they don't immediately have the necessary qualities to change form. This ability is something that develops over a period of time. It takes the first twenty-five years to develop the 'physical' abilities, skills, and strengths needed to make the change. Then it takes up to an additional five years of practice, usually under the guidance of an elder or someone already familiar with the process, to hone those qualities to make the change instantly with very little effort. The 'physical' development happens without effort, those abilities, skills, and strengths develop naturally. It's the ability to change form that takes some work. This is why it's important to have or find a guide or tutor to help. Someone that's gone through it and understands what it takes. There are additional qualities gained from the other form, depending on what that form is. Also, after fifty years of life, the aging process stops. There is one exception to my last statement. If, at any time, one stops changing for a period of ten years, the aging process begins again and a 'normal' human existence begins. After that there is no turning back and you become human until the day you die.

"As for you Lianna, why Falder decided not to guide you, he must have had his reasons and I would only be guessing at those reasons. He was certainly capable of helping you through that period or your parents would have never left you in his care. Here again, I would only be guessing at the reasons your parents left and never made contact afterwards. I'm sure they had their reasons too. But, if you wish, I have someone in mind that would be happy to help you.

"As for you J'orik, it's understandable why you never received guidance. Your mother went away and left you with normal humans and your father was never in the picture. I'm aware of your particular situation and can understand why your mother went away. She became friends with my sister and her husband and had intended for them to guide you through the changing process. Karin told me the reason they hadn't started yet was that they were unsure how to proceed without your father possibly finding out."

She looked over at Jake. "I think I've covered the basics." He nodded in agreement. She turned back to J'orik and Lianna. "Now I'm ready to answer any questions you have." Before either one could start she immediately added, "Ladies first," and she turned her attention to Lianna.

"I don't understand why Falder wouldn't have helped me. I know you said you would only be guessing but why do you think he wouldn't have helped?"

"Well, it could be a couple of reasons. Maybe he was one of those that decided he no longer wanted to live for eternity and wanted to settle down, have a family, and live a 'normal' human life. It could be, since J'orik and his mother lived in the same village, that he was aware of J'orik's situation and didn't want to draw attention to the village. We do have the ability to sense another of our race but we have to be in close proximity. Falder probably sensed that J'orik and his mother were one of us. He probably confronted her and she explained her situation. It's even possible that he helped her leave. He could have taken you away from the village to help you through the changing which leads me to believe he had probably decided to live a 'normal' human existence. Based on your age, if you don't start the changing within the next three years, your aging will never stop."

"Do you know where my parents are?"

"No. Chances are, though, they live somewhere in the Arrget or Dorguri Mountains. As dragons, when we decide not to interact with those not of our race, we'll find a location that's hard to reach. We love the mountainous areas."

"You said you have someone in mind that will guide me. Who?"

"Clare has offered her services. She took to you almost immediately."

"Is she a dragon also?"

"No, dear, she's a fairy."

"So it doesn't matter who guides us, as long as they're a shapeshifter also?"

"Yes. One that has completed the changing process themselves."

"My children are also dragons?"

"Yes. Here is another issue about our race that you need to understand as well. After the single changing procedure was implemented there was another condition that was enforced. Only like forms could produce children. I've noticed that you and J'orik have taken to each other." She smiled as they blushed with embarrassment. "This is fine. You can marry or just stay friends but, in either case, you will never be able to have children. J'orik is not a dragon."

"What is he?"

"He's a phoenix." Then she added, with a giggle, "And this is why he has such a ravenous appetite."

Lianna sat there for a moment considering everything Joice had said.

"Well, dear, if you don't have any more questions, I can start answering some of J'orik's questions." She glanced at J'orik with a smile. "I can see he's anxious to get started."

She turned back to Lianna. "Why don't you relax and try to absorb everything we've talked about. Maybe some of the questions J'orik has will help answer some of the questions you haven't asked yet. Okay?"

"Okay." She looked over at J'orik and she could see that Joice was right, he did look anxious.

"All right, J'orik," Joice turned her attention to him, "let's get started with you. What's your first question?"

"You've already answered the first question I had. I'm a phoenix. You've already told me where my father is. Where do you think my mother went?"

"Most phoenixes, when they want to get away, will go into the desert or find some other very hot place, like a volcano for example."

"Do you have someone in mind that will guide me through the changing?"

"That all depends on whether or not you plan on staying here in Bruston."

"If I were to stay here, who would you have in mind?"

"Jake said he would be willing to take on that task."

J'orik looked at Jake and he just smiled back at him.

"Son, I would be happy to help."

"When could we get started?"

Jake turned and looked out the window behind him. Turning back he said, "It looks like it's clearing up outside. For you, daytime is the best time. Since we aren't too far from the desert, that would be the best location. We want to be sure that we're far enough away we can't be seen. But, to answer your question, anytime is fine with me."

"What about me?" Lianna jumped in. "When do you think Clare would be able to start guiding me?"

"That will depend on her," Joice responded. "She does have duties at the sheriff's office during the day. As a dragon, though, anytime is okay, day or night. A phoenix, however, generates a lot of light because of the flaming. That's why it's best to practice during the daytime." Joice turned to J'orik. "Do you have any more questions?"

"Most of the questions I had have been answered. There's only one last thing I want to know. Tell me what you know about my father."

"Jake knows more about him than I do. I would only be repeating what he's told me so I'll let him tell you."

Everyone turned their attention to Jake.

"Joice has already told you his name is K'orik and that he lives in the Castaic Mountains. I think I'll begin with your grandfather though. Your grandfather's name is L'orik and he's nearly twice my age. The last I knew he lived in the Arrget Mountains. L'orik was, and as far as I know still is, a good person. K'orik is not his only child. L'orik has had more than one wife in his life and Katreen, his third wife, was K'orik's mother, your grandmother. When I say 'was' his mother I mean she is no longer alive. Something went wrong and she died giving birth to him. In other words, K'orik killed his mother. Remember what Joice said earlier, we don't just die. L'orik knew from that moment on there was something different about K'orik. L'orik's other children, K'orik's half-siblings, never really liked him. He was a mean child and would always fight with them. As hard as he tried, L'orik could never tame him. K'orik just kept getting meaner as he grew. He eventually met a man named J'eren. K'orik was only fifteen at the time and when J'eren offered him an escape from his father and his family he took it. J'eren was very much the same as K'orik and saw something in him that no one else did. He knew that one day K'orik would be a very powerful person and he wanted to capitalize on that before K'orik got older. J'eren was actually a family member of L'orik's second wife. He never approved of her marriage to L'orik and he became a bitter enemy of L'orik's because of that. He felt that by taking K'orik under his wing, so to speak, it was just one more way he could get back at L'orik. Remember, I said L'orik was a good person. He was angry that this happened but felt that by K'orik leaving it was the best thing for the rest of his family. So, L'orik let him go without a fight. J'eren, for all intents and purposes, became K'orik's 'father' from that point on.

"As K'orik got older he became stronger and stronger. J'eren guided him through the changing and taught him how to use his abilities to become even more powerful. The one thing J'eren didn't count on, though, was K'orik turning on him. The day finally came when K'orik felt he could overpower J'eren and a battle ensued between them late one night. The battle was so intense that the sky lit up like the worst lightning storm. It could be seen for miles around. They fought for hours and K'orik finally prevailed. Or so he thought. J'eren just seemed to evaporate into nothingness and K'orik thought he had totally destroyed him. What K'orik didn't realize, though, and probably still doesn't, was that J'eren is an ancient and was one of those that escaped the single change procedure. What J'eren did was become something so minute that he was able to escape detection and that's how he escaped being killed by K'orik.

"Now, you might wonder how I know all of this. I'm old enough that I was around when the battle took place. As far as the knowledge about J'eren, my great-great-grandfather was a member of the council that implemented the procedure. A list was compiled with the names of all those that escaped the procedure and J'eren's name was on that list. Where J'eren is now one can only guess, but I'm guessing he's biding his time until he can come back and combat K'orik. You see, when J'eren 'disappeared', K'orik inherited all of his assets. J'eren is not the type of person that can just let that go."

There was a knock at the office door. Jake stopped his oration and said, "Come in."

Gerard entered. "Clare is here, Mr. Freeman, and she said she needs to talk to you. She said it's important."

"Well, show her in."

Gerard turned to go get Clare but she was already there and stepped by him into the office. He shut the door as he went back to the front counter.

"Yes, Clare, what's so important that it can't wait?" Jake asked.

"It's about J'orik and I thought you should know as soon as possible."

"Go on."

"You remember Durog?"

"Yes."

"He came into the sheriff's office asking about J'orik, if he had come to town and where he was staying. He said his nephew knew him and was in town to meet him. He said J'orik had sent his nephew a letter saying he would be here in town and was wondering if they could get together. Also said he knew J'orik as a deputy from the far side of the Great Plains. None of it sounded right so I thought you should know."

"He didn't happen to mention the name of which nephew he was talking about, did he?"

"No."

"Okay, Clare. Thank you for the information. I know you're probably busy so you should get back to the office."

"One more thing, I think Durog saw me come into the inn. I tried to be discreet but I saw him across the street just as I was shutting the front door behind me."

"That's all right. We can handle it from here. Thank you again. And please keep us informed of anything else you hear or see regarding this matter."

Clare left. Jake was shaking his head back and forth as everyone turned their attention back to him. "This is not good Joice. I think I know which nephew he was referring to, his sister's son Ogiloth. He's the commander of K'orik's army. As far as I know all of his other nephews work in the mines." He turned to J'orik. "He knows where you are now. It won't be long before they come looking for you. I doubt Ogiloth will attempt anything here at the inn or in town, but you just never know." He turned to Joice then. "We need to make preparations and get these kids to a more secure location. You should get word to Casper and Karin."

"It doesn't look like we'll be going for that walk today," Lianna told J'orik.

# CHAPTER 13

AS SOON AS Clare entered the inn and shut the door Durog started making his way back home. He couldn't be sure but he thought she might have spotted him. It didn't matter now. He needed to get back and make his report to his nephew.

He went back the same way he had come to town, passing by the same warehouses and fisheries. The street wasn't as bad now. It hadn't been a heavy rain and the sun had been out long enough that the streets had already begun to dry. He didn't mind slogging through what little mud there was. It kind of reminded him of being in the mines. Memories of his youth passed through his mind. As he passed out of the industrial area and into the dwarf section of town he was, once again, assaulted by the aroma of all the flowers in blossom. His mind began to wander again back to his wife. He was so lost in those memories that he nearly passed by his house. *I must be gettin' old*, he thought to himself.

Ogiloth was sitting at the couch reading one of his uncle's books when he heard stomping at the front door.

He set the book on the table and stood up as his uncle came through the door.

Durog spotted the book on the table. "Whatcha doin' there boy, gettin' some learnin'?"

"Just thought I'd pass the time away and catch up on my reading skills. I haven't read anything written in dwarvish for some time now and I thought I'd refresh my memory on the language. What did you find out?"

Durog finished cleaning the remainder of the mud off his boots and then made his way into the living room. "Sit yerself down, boy," he told his nephew as he stepped around the table and sat down in his chair. "I got some good ta say and I got some bad ta say. That fella, J'orik yer lookin' fer, did stop inta tha sheriff's office just like ye said he would. I think Clare, tha clerk that works there, knew I was a makin' up a story 'bout you knowin' 'im, but she went along with it anyways." Then more to himself than to Ogiloth, "I think there be more ta that Clare than 'pears ta be." Then he continued with his report. "Asked her if she knew where he might be stayin' an' she said she didn't know. I think she lied back at me. After I left tha sheriff's office I took me a stroll down the walk, kinda window shoppin' ya know, seein' if I might spot this J'orik fella. Walked all tha way down ta tha south end o' town, past all tha inns on that side o' the street, an' didn't see anyone lookin' like'm. So I crossed tha street an' started me way back up th'other side, lookin'. Got as far as a place called tha Boars' Den, one o' me favorite places, a place where other dwarves tend ta be. Figgerd I'd have me a pint ta drink an' sit by tha window an' watch. An old friend o' mine was there, so I sat an' talked with him fer a while, still keepin' an eye out. Wasn't long 'fore I seen Clare strollin' down the walk on th'other side. After she got far 'nough by I stepped out so's I could see her better. Whole time tryin' ta make sure she didn't see me. She got to a place called tha Dragons' Inn an' went in there. I think she mighta spotted me watchin' 'er though. My guess is, that J'orik fella be stayin' at tha Dragons' Inn."

"You did good uncle," Ogiloth praised him. "Now, what's the bad news?"

"Well, I kinda worked it all tagether but, an' this be the worst part, it be the Dragons' Inn. I been in tha place ta eat an' that Joice, tha lady what runs tha place an' cooks, she puts out a fine platter o' food. Some o' tha tastiest I ever had. What I be gettin' at though is she an' her husband, Jake, they be some odd folk. They be nice an' all but they be odd."

"What do you mean by odd?"

"Can't rightly put me finger on it, ya know. It just be a feelin' I got when I was 'round'm. Ye know how us dwarves can sense 'magic' an' all? Well that be tha feelin' I got."

"So, is there more or is that all of it?"

Durog sat and thought for a moment. "No, I think that be tha gist of it."

"Again, uncle, you did good."

"Good. I was a hopin' I got enough fer ya ta work with. Now I be gettin' hungry, haven't ate since breakfast. Ye hungry boy?"

"Yes, uncle, I be hungry." He tried to emulate his uncle's speech.

"Whatcha be hungry for? I got rabbit out back in tha hutch. That sound good? Maybe with some more o' me biscuits an' gravy?"

"Yes," he responded with a big grin.

Durog went out back and Ogiloth could hear him trying to catch one of the rabbits. Then he heard a brief squeal. He reached for the book he'd been reading and started in on it again. A short while later Durog reentered the house with the rabbit in hand and headed for the kitchen. He was humming as he walked by.

He tried to read but he couldn't stop thinking about everything his uncle had told him. He set the book back down and began formulating his next plan of action. J'orik was here in Bruston, that was known. According to his uncle he was likely staying at the Dragons' Inn. His uncle hadn't said if he found out whether J'orik was traveling alone or not, he would have to ask him that. And this feeling his uncle had about the people that ran the inn he would need to question him further on that also. He knew of an inn in Washoe called the Dragons' Lair. He wondered if maybe the two places were connected. He also wondered if maybe that was thinking too much and stretching things a little bit. He thought about his team and hoped that Olog would be able to keep them under control. It had only been one day but these creatures that K'orik had for his army needed a very strong hand to keep them from getting out of hand and he didn't know if one of their own would be able to handle it. It was getting too late in the day to really do much more than think about what he was going to do.

Suddenly he was hit with the smell of rabbit coming down the hallway from the kitchen. His stomach grumbled. He stood up and headed towards the kitchen. As he entered he saw his uncle stirring the gravy. He was still humming to himself. He finished stirring and opened the oven door, saw that the biscuits were ready and pulled them out. He set them on the table and as he turned back to close the oven door he spotted Ogiloth standing in the kitchen entryway.

"Couldn't keep away from tha smell, huh?" He smiled big at his nephew. "Tha rabbit'll be done in a couple o' minutes. Grab yerself a seat." Ogiloth squeezed by again. "But remember, don't start without me."

He eyed the biscuits as he sat down, but the last thing he wanted was for his uncle to smack his hand again. Instead, to take his mind away from the biscuits, he decided to question his uncle further.

"Did you find out if J'orik was travelling alone?"

Durog turned the stove off and stirred the gravy one more time before putting it on the table. "No. I didn't want ta ask too many questions. Didn't want ta sound suspicious. Clare didn't say nothin' 'bout' 'im bein' with someone else neither." He went back and opened the oven door and pulled the rabbit out. "Ye goin' ta set some plates an' utensils fer us ta eat on or we just goin' ta eat off tha table?" he asked as he set the rabbit down on the table.

Ogiloth quickly got up and did as asked while Durog began slicing the rabbit.

Looking up at his uncle he probed, "Tell me more about the feelings you have about the people that run the Dragons' Inn."

Durog set some slices of rabbit on both their plates and sat down. They both began to eat. "I'm not sure, boy. Ye know us dwarves have a sense fer magic, but this ain't magic, it be somethin' diff'rent, somethin' more than magic."

"What do you mean 'more than magic'?"

"It be hard to explain. Yer half dwarf, ye should have some sense fer magic. Take this K'orik fella fer example. Is he some sorta warlock or sorcerer?"

"I don't think so."

"Do ye feel he be diff'rent than other humans ye met?"

"Yes."

"Y'ever seen him use magic?"

"I've seen him touch people and things and burn them. I've seen flames come from him and shoot out of his hands. Sometimes, when he gets angry, it gets really hot around him."

"Y'ever seen him do anythin' else?"

"Like what?"

"Like make the ground shake, make things disappear or appear or change inta somethin' else? Does he use a staff or wand ta make things happen?"

"No."

"This feelin' ya have that he be diff'rent, does it feel close up or kinda far off?"

"Kind of far off I guess."

"That be what I'm talkin' 'bout. The feelin' I get 'bout these folk at tha Dragons' Inn be far off. Magic feels like it be right there. I get tha same feelin' 'bout Clare too. Now that I think 'bout it, I've had this feelin' 'bout other folk I pass by in town too. Never really thought much 'bout it 'afore."

There were no more biscuits and gravy left and the rabbit was almost a skeleton. Between the two of them they had eaten all the food while talking and hadn't even noticed. Durog got up from the table and started cleaning up. Ogiloth just sat there and thought about their conversation.

"So, what be yer next move?"

"I need to find out for sure if J'orik is staying at the inn or not before I do anything else."

"Yer not plannin' on goin' inta town, are ye?"

"How else am I going to find out, unless you do it for me?"

"Well, I don't think it be a good idea if ye go inta town. Dwarves be okay, tha humans have accepted us bein' 'round. They be aware that ogres exist but they won't tolerate'm bein' in town. And you, boy, are one big ogre. They wouldn't see ye any other way."

"Then what am I supposed to do?"

"I got some friends, human friends, that might be willin' ta help. Their goin' ta wanta be paid though."

"I brought some gold along with me just in case there was a need for it. Will that work?"

"Yes. These friends will take gold fer payment."

"Then it's settled. Set up a meeting for me with these friends of yours and I'll tell them what I need them to do."

"It's not that simple. These friends will be wantin' ta take their direction from me. They think ogres be stupid an' won't even give ye a chance ta start. Besides, I know how ta handle'm. Ye just tell me what ye want'm ta do an' then I'll take it from there."

The fact that humans thought ogres were stupid just infuriated him. He almost told his uncle it wasn't worth it to him but realized his uncle was probably right. He thought about what he should do immediately while helping his uncle finish cleaning up. They went into the living room and sat down to relax.

"How 'bout a game o' chess, boy?"

"Not right now, uncle. If J'orik is at the inn I need to place a watch on it. I don't want him to get away. It's not too late yet. Can you gather at least three of your friends to help with that?"

"I can do that. How do ye want ta set them up?"

"One should be inside, one to watch the front, and one to watch the back. I'm assuming the inn has a back entrance?"

"Yeah, most places do. There be alleys."

"If he's there and decides to run it's more likely he'll go out the back, especially if he thinks he's being watched. If what you say is true and this Clare saw you watching her then he won't leave by the front."

"If they spot'm leavin' you want'm to follow'm?"

"Only if they can do it without being spotted themselves, and only far enough to let me know which direction he goes. Are these friends trustworthy enough to follow my instructions?"

"As long as they be paid they'll do whatever ye ask'm ta do. Anythin' else?"

"I want them to keep watch all night if necessary. If they see anything I want them to report it immediately."

"Okay, I'll set it up but when I get back my pay will be at least one game o' chess."

"All right, uncle, I promise."

Durog got up and left to make the arrangements discussed.

# CHAPTER 14

$A$ S THEY WALKED out of the office Joice told J'orik and Lianna, "You kids go to your room and pack your things. I'm going to discuss with Jake what we need to do. When you're done come on back down to the office. By then we should have some sort of plan. Okay?"

They both nodded yes and started up the stairs for their room. Once in their room they began packing their things like Joice had told them to.

"What do you think about all this?" Lianna asked.

"About what? The fact that we're both 'shapeshifters' or that my father has someone looking for me?"

"That your father has sent someone to find you."

"I'm not sure what to think. I'm told that my father isn't a good person and the people telling me this seem to want to keep me from him. From what they've told me I probably should stay away from him, but he's my father. I've always believed my father was dead. My mother, who I find out now is probably still alive, must have had her reasons for telling me my father was dead, probably the same reasons Jake and Joice have. After what happened to our village I tend to believe what I've been told. So, what do I think? I don't know. I'm a little confused."

"Well I think they're right."

"How do you feel about your parents now? Knowing that they as much as abandoned you."

"I'm sad. I can't understand why they would do that."

"Are you going to try to find them?"

"One day I will but for now I'm going to learn how to be who I really am and I think you should do the same."

"Yes, you're probably right. Let's just finish packing and go find out what they've decided to do."

They both got quiet again and finished packing. As they were coming down the stairs they saw the sheriff at the front counter talking with Jake.

He turned to them asking, "So how'd you two like your first night in Bruston?" Then he noticed they had their things with them. "Are you planning to leave already?"

They stopped and glanced at Jake. He was nodding his head back and forth with a stern look on his face. The sheriff was looking at them so he didn't notice Jake's action.

Unsure what to say, J'orik lied. "No. Lianna and I are planning on taking a walk and doing some shopping. I wanted to have my pack with me so I could replace the things I've used out of it and carry anything she might decide to get."

"Good. I wouldn't want to think you were already done with our wonderful little town here. One day doesn't give you time enough to see everything it has to offer." Then he turned back to Jake. "Right, Jake?"

"Right, sheriff." Then he added, "I'm sorry I couldn't help you with that person you were asking about. Have you asked the other innkeepers?"

"Yes, Jake, I've asked them all and no one has any record or recollection of him staying at their inn. I guess it's just going to be one of those mysteries that never gets solved. If you do happen to recall anything later just let me know." He turned to go. "Hope to see you two around. Enjoy your stay." And he was out the door.

"Okay you two, Joice is in the office waiting."

They followed him into the office and took their seats again. J'orik set his pack down beside the chair. He and Lianna sat quietly waiting for the plan to be laid out.

"Jake and I have talked about a couple different things we can do but I think the one we finally decided on is the best. We considered taking you to Washoe but that would take you too far away to accomplish some of the things we've already discussed, the most important one being providing some guidance for both of you for making the change which, in both your cases, should start soon. The other reason would be we think you would like living here, but that's just selfish on our part.

"What we finally decided was that we would take you up into the Castaic Mountains. Jake and I have a place we go when we want to get away ourselves and it would serve to provide a place for you to learn. It also provides to appease our selfishness to keep you here. I know you've only been here one day but Jake and I have come to like you both very much and want to see you grow in your new-found life. We want to be part of that process.

"The final decision, however, is up to you. If you have an alternative plan that you'd rather follow then we'll help as much as we can to make that happen. Regardless of what is decided action needs to be taken now before Ogiloth acts and things get out of hand." She looked directly at J'orik and said, "We're hoping that he doesn't decide to just barge in and try to take you by force. Things would get ugly then. We have no idea how large a force he brought with him and a battle in town would not go over too well with the townspeople." She sat back in her chair with a gentle smile on her face and looked at both of them. "So, what shall it be?"

Without hesitation Lianna spoke up. "I like it here. I like Clare too and would be grateful to have her as a teacher. I'm in agreement with your plan."

Then all eyes fell on J'orik. Lianna had more of a pleading look.

"Well, nothing like a little pressure." He glanced at each one of them.

"I assure you J'orik, there's no pressure from Joice or me on this matter," Jake assured him. "All we want to do is help you and Lianna and avoid any direct conflict here in town."

J'orik sat back in his chair and thought for a moment. Everyone stayed quiet waiting for him to come to a decision.

He looked at Lianna. "It's easy for you. You don't have someone chasing you. This Ogiloth person isn't concerned about you, all he wants is me." Then he looked down at the floor. "You're all probably better off if I was just to go as far away as possible."

"You're being childish," Lianna snapped. "You remind me of my children when they don't get what they want. You know you'd be better off staying here. Besides, where would you go? Who would you have teach you what you need to learn?"

"I could go to Washoe and have Casper or Karin be my teacher."

"I don't think that would work out J'orik," Jake interrupted.

"And why not? You said we could be taught by anyone else."

"Yes, I did. But your particular form is a little more difficult to work with. Remember, you're a phoenix. Do you know what a phoenix is?"

"Isn't it like a fire bird?"

"Yes. A phoenix emanates a tremendous amount of heat and flames and most other forms aren't able to withstand that much heat or that amount of flames."

"Then what makes you a good choice for a teacher? You're a dragon aren't you?"

"Yes, but not all dragons are the same. I happen to be a red dragon. I'm a fire creature myself and the heat and flames don't bother me."

"What kind of dragons are Casper and Karin?"

"Both of them are blue dragons. And if you're thinking about their son Jarrell, he's not of age yet, he's younger than you and his type hasn't been determined yet."

J'orik sat back in his chair with a sigh of defeat.

Lianna looked over at him. "Besides, I don't want you to go away." She had tears in her eyes. "I want you to stay here with me."

He just looked at her. His eyes began to well up with tears also. With all they'd been through together recently he'd come to care for this woman very much. He wanted to stay with her too. "It's decided then. We go to the Castaic Mountains."

Lianna smiled huge. She wiped the tears from her face, leaned over, and gave him a big hug. He hugged her back.

Jake and Joice looked at each other with smiles. Joice had tears rolling down her face as well.

"Who will be taking us?" asked J'orik.

"I will," Joice replied. "Jake needs to stay here to keep up appearances. Nobody will notice me being gone for a day. I spend most of my time in the kitchen anyway. Kayla cooks as good as I do so no one will notice a difference. I haven't seen my sister for some time now and someone needs to let them know what's going on. So, it's me you get to have a ride with."

"What do mean 'ride with'? Are we taking horses?" Lianna asked excitedly.

"No, we're not taking horses. Actually you'll be riding on me."

"What do you mean by that?" J'orik showed a little concern.

"It'll be more fun to show you than tell you. You'll like it, just wait and see. Are we ready?"

"Yes," they both answered together.

"We're going to walk out of town for a ways until we reach the foothills. There, we'll be out of sight and then I can show you what I mean. The sun's starting to go down so we need to get going." Joice leaned over and kissed Jake on the cheek. "Take care. I'll be back early tomorrow morning after I've dropped these two off and gone to talk with Karin."

"Okay, dear. Be careful and say hello to Casper and Karin for me."

Joice stood and indicated for J'orik and Lianna to do the same. They followed her out of the office and into the kitchen. She had J'orik put some food in his pack then she led them to the back door of the inn. She checked the alleyway before leading them out. From there she led them south out of town then turned west towards the foothills. They walked for a little over an hour until they couldn't see Bruston when they looked back. The sun was beginning its descent below the tops of the mountains when she stopped in a small valley surrounded by rolling hills. The only way someone could see them now is if they stood on top of any one of the small mounds around them.

"This is the place," she seemed to say to herself. "I need you two to stay right here for a moment."

"Where are you going?" J'orik wanted to know.

"It's all right. You'll be able to see me the whole time," she assured him. "Don't let what you're about to see scare you. It's something you'll eventually get accustomed to. I'm going to change into my dragon form, which is much larger than my human form. That's why I'm going to move away from you a little bit. Once I've changed you'll climb onto my back and I'll fly you the rest of the way."

"Fly?" J'orik asked with concern as his eyes opened wide. Lianna had the same reaction.

"Yes, fly. It's something you'll both need to become comfortable with because you're both flying creatures in your second forms. My body is covered with feathers so hang onto those while you're on my back." Then she stressed, "Don't let go."

"How far will we be flying?" he wanted to know.

Joice pointed to the west. "See that mountain peak right there?" They both nodded yes. "There's a cave about half way up the slope. That's where I'll be taking you. The flight only lasts about a quarter hour but since it's your first time it may seem longer. Like I just said, don't let go."

She walked about twenty yards away, turned and smiled at them, and suddenly she was a dragon. J'orik and Lianna stepped back stunned. Neither one had ever seen anything like it before and were completely surprised at how quick it happened. Joice's body was as large as a small cottage and covered in a brilliant array of red, yellow, orange, and green feathers. There was a light breeze and her feathers fluttered as it swept across her body. Her feathers sparkled as they caught the sunlight that remained. What startled them the most, though, was when she spoke. Her voice seemed to soothe their nerves. It sounded so calm and serene. Then she moved towards them, dipping a wing down for them to climb on.

"Okay, kids, it's time to fly. Climb on."

Hesitantly, they both stepped onto her wing. It surprised them both how strong it was. They quickly made it to her back and sat down, J'orik in front.

She turned her head and looked back at them. "Remember, hold tight. I won't be talking much during the flight because the wind is kind of loud and it isn't the easiest thing to do turning my neck in flight. I'll try to keep as level as I can so you don't feel like you're going to fall off. Hold on tight," she said one more time. "Ready?"

They both nodded that they were. She turned her head forward, spread her wings, and lifted off the ground. They had a sudden feeling of dizziness as the ground disappeared under her body. They found themselves gripping her feathers like vises. As she gained altitude she began to level out and the mountaintops came back into view. They felt the wind hard in their faces as it whipped through their hair. As they settled in to the ride they started looking about. To the north they saw Lake Wishik with the Castaic Mountains stretching along the western bank and Murwood Forest along the eastern bank. Behind them, to the east, they could see the Great Plains over the tree tops of Murwood Forest. To the south they saw the Great Desert stretching for as far as the eye could see and further. As they turned back to look ahead, the mountain peak Joice had pointed out earlier seemed to suddenly be right there. They could feel Joice slowing and beginning to descend. The mountainside seemed to come straight at them. Her head suddenly rose, she flapped her wings hard a few times, and then they were on the ground. She dropped her body, low to the ground, stretched her wing out, and they climbed down.

"Now step away towards the cave opening."

They stepped away a couple paces and turned towards her and by that time she'd changed back into her human form.

"Follow me kids," as she walked towards the cave opening in the side of the mountain.

They followed her in. She would have never fit through the opening in her dragon form. By now it was dark outside and even darker inside the tunnel they were in. Joice lit the torch that was set in the wall of the opening, took it in her hand, and continued further in. They followed. The tunnel curved slightly to the left and then to the right. About fifty yards in it opened into a large cave. Joice stopped just as it opened up and lit torches on either side of the tunnel opening. She walked around the cave and lit three more torches. As their eyes adjusted to the torchlight they saw that the cave was large enough to hold the whole of the Dragons' Inn. In the center there was a pit for a fire, which Joice also lit. There was a pile of wood already stacked about five yards from the pit. Two large tree trunks about man–height had been split in half and were surrounding the fire pit to sit on.

"There's enough firewood to last several nights. When you get ready to bed down you should go around and extinguish the torches. You can leave the fire burning all night if you want. The tunnel leading in is designed so that no light can be seen from outside. There's bedding in that large chest over there." She pointed it out. "It's difficult to get here without flying so you should be safe. Don't try to leave. You have enough food to last until I come back tomorrow evening. Any questions?"

"You're leaving?" J'orik asked.

"Yes. I need to go see Casper and Karin and let them know what's going on. You'll be fine. Just relax and enjoy each other's company. By the way, how'd you like the ride?"

"It was exhilarating," Lianna said with a big smile.

"To say the least," J'orik remarked.

"I'm glad you liked it. You need to get used to the feeling of flying. I've got to go now so take care and I'll see you tomorrow."

"Good night," Lianna said.

Joice disappeared down the tunnel and the torch light disappeared with her.

They spent the next couple of hours sitting around the fire pit talking more about everything Jake and Joice had told them and their recent experience flying atop a dragon's back. Eventually they got tired and retrieved some bedding out of the chest Joice had pointed out and laid it out next to the fire pit. They lay there in thought as the fire burned low and they finally fell asleep.

# CHAPTER 15

WHEN DUROG RETURNED home there were still a couple hours of sunlight remaining. Ogiloth was reclined on the couch reading again.

As he shut the door he informed his nephew that it was all set up. "Got one inside an' th'other two outside, front and back. Promised'm a pound o' gold to split between'm so's ta be sure they stay all night if necessary. That be okay with you?"

"Yes."

"Now set up that chess game boy an' prepare ta be beaten."

"Thanks for your help, uncle, and it's you that needs to prepare to be beaten," he chuckled.

He set the book down and pulled out the chess game as his uncle came in and sat in his chair. Durog had a grim look on his face as the game began. He was determined to beat his nephew this time. He had to win at least one game. Like most dwarves, he couldn't stand to lose.

They had been playing for some time and Durog seemed to have the advantage when a sharp rap came at the door.

"Who be there?" Durog hollered.

"Jenner," came the reply. "He's on the move Durog."

"Just a minute!" Durog hollered. He looked at Ogiloth and whispered to him, "You should prob'ly go in me room and wait there while I talk with Jenner. Leave tha door open a crack so's ye can hear all he says."

Ogiloth did as his uncle said.

Durog went to the door and opened it. All three men were standing outside.

"Only one o' ye be comin' in," he said in a stern voice. "Which one o' ye has tha tale ta tell?"

"Me." Jenner raised his hand.

Durog stepped aside and let him in. He looked at the other two. "You two wait right there while Jenner tells me his tale. When he comes back out ye'll get yer pay." He shut the door.

He led Jenner into the living room and indicated he sit on the couch. Durog sat in his chair directly across from him.

"Now tell me whatcha got boy," he said gruffly.

Jenner noticed the chess game set up and saw that the pieces had been moved like a game was in progress. "Were you playing a game with someone? Is there someone else here?" he asked concerned, looking around the room.

"No. I just like ta play meself once in a while ta keep me skills honed. Now tell me whatcha got, I said."

"Okay. I was watching out back of the place and he came out that way, just like you said he would. Only he wasn't alone. There were two women with him. I think one of them was the lady that runs the inn. Anyway, they headed south down the alley. I waited until they were far enough ahead before I started following them. They went all the way out of town and then turned west towards the mountains. I stopped following them then because there wasn't anything to hide behind. I just watched them go until they were out of sight then I went and got Cory and Lance and headed over here to your place."

"Ye sure they din't spot ye?"

"Positive. They never even looked back."

"Okay. Now 'fore I pay ye I want ye ta promise, an' make sure th'other two understand, not a word 'bout this to no one." Durog looked him square in the eyes and waited for a response.

"Not a word."

Durog reached into his shirt pocket and pulled out a bag with the pound of gold he'd promised to pay. As he handed it to Jenner he said one more time, "Not a word, boy, or none o' ye will see tha light o' day ever again."

"Not a word." He took the bag and peered inside to see that it was really gold. A smile crossed his face.

Durog escorted him to the door and let him out. He walked out with a smile still on his face. The other two started smiling too. He raised the bag up for the others to see as they all started walking away.

"Make sure ye let'm know what I said Jenner. Not a word." Then he shut the door.

Ogiloth came out of the bedroom and walked into the kitchen. He looked out the window and watched them walking away while Durog watched them through the small opening in the door.

"Did ye hear all that nephew?"

"Yes. I got it all. I hope they take what you said seriously about not telling anyone."

"If I hear they been flappin' their gums 'bout where they got that gold an' what they done ta get it I'll help ye make sure they never see tha light o' day ever again."

"Well, it's getting dark and it's too late now to do anything more. How about we finish that game of chess you were playing with yourself?"

They both laughed heartily and returned to the game.

Ogiloth woke to the crashing and clattering of pots and pans again. He wondered if his uncle ever slept. He hefted himself off the couch and down the hallway. Peering into the kitchen he saw that his uncle hadn't even started cooking yet, he seemed to be just banging his pots and pans just to be banging them.

"What're you doing uncle?" he asked, rubbing the sleep out of his eyes.

"I be lookin' fer me muffin pan. I was goin' ta bake ye some muffins ta take on tha road."

"What makes you think I was going on the road again?"

"Well, this J'orik character's on tha run again an' I just figgered ye'd be off after'm again. So, I thought I'd be nice an' have some muffins ready fer ye ta take along. There it be."

"I'll stick around long enough for the muffins to be ready. I need to wake up anyway."

"Hard night?"

"Long night. We played three games last night."

"An' I won two," he said proudly with a smile.

"Yes, you won two, but I put up a good fight."

"Ye did. Now sit down an' let me get these muffins started."

Ogiloth squeezed by his uncle again while he was making up the batter. He yawned while sitting down. Durog finished mixing and started pouring the batter into the muffin pan.

"Cinnamon muffins topped with yer aunt's special sweet sauce glaze. Perfect ta start a road trip."

"Sounds good to me. I remember those from when I was little."

"Boy, I don't think ye was ever 'little'." They both laughed at that.

He slid the pan in the oven, closed the oven door, and then sat down at the table.

"So fill me in on yer plan fer taday."

"I'll be heading west along the lake shore until I find my team. They should be about a couple miles out of town. Head south from there, along the foothills, until I pick up J'orik's trail and follow it until I find him."

"Ye make it sound easy. Ye a tracker now too?"

"No, but I have two of the best trackers I've ever known."

"Think they'll be able ta pick up tha right tracks?"

"Yes. They know what their looking for. They followed them before."

"Yeah, but now there be three tracks not just two."

"Which should make it even easier. I doubt too many people wander out of town and up into the foothills anyway. So, I'm thinking it won't be too difficult to find them. I could probably find them myself."

"Then whatcha need yer team fer?"

"It's been two days now, uncle, and they're probably getting antsy. Besides, it's not that I need them, I don't want them to be wandering into town."

"I see whatcha mean." He stood up and went to pull the muffins out of the oven.

The smell of cinnamon wafted towards him as his uncle set the pan down on the counter and he took a big sniff. He watched as his uncle spread the sweet sauce glaze over the tops of them.

Returning to the table Durog said, "Gotta let'm cool now, should only take a few minutes. Think ye'll be stoppin' back by 'fore headin' north again?"

"I don't know. I'd like to, I really enjoyed my stay, but I have no idea what's ahead."

"Well, yer welcome here anytime, boy, I enjoyed yer comp'ny too."

"There is one more thing I have to ask of you."

"Anythin', boy, ye just name it."

"Keep your eyes and ears open for anything, and I mean anything that you see or hear regarding this matter. If you feel it's important enough that I should know, find a way to get it to me."

"Done."

"Thanks again for all your help." He glanced over at the muffins. "Are the muffins ready yet?"

Durog got up and touched the top of one of the muffins. "They be ready." He put six of them in a bag for Ogiloth and kept six for himself. He handed the bag to his nephew. "Now ye best be on yer way 'fore the day's gone."

He rose from the table, reached out and shook his uncle's hand, and headed for the door. Durog followed behind him.

Ogiloth looked out the kitchen window as he passed by it checking for anyone that might be outside. He didn't see anyone nearby so he continued out the door. They waved farewell to each other as Ogiloth turned towards the lake. Durog smiled and went back in his home shutting the door. Neither one saw him but Jenner was watching. When Ogiloth was far enough away Jenner set in to following him.

He walked for about a mile out of town then stopped and sat down on a rock near the water's edge. He opened the bag of muffins and began eating. There was a slight breeze coming down the shore from the northwest and he could hear the leaves rustling in the trees behind him. The waves lapped against the shoreline and helped soothe his nerves. He continued eating the muffins wanting to finish them all before he arrived at his team's camp. The last thing he wanted was for them to think he had eaten better than them, even though they probably realized he had. Finishing the last muffin he stood and walked to the water's edge to get a drink, that's when he heard the snap of a branch. Whoever was following him wasn't very good at it. He ignored it and continued his walk like he hadn't heard anything.

It didn't take him long to reach the camp even though the shore was somewhat rocky. His team had made camp a little more than three miles from town. It was the first place they came to that had a beach area large enough to accommodate the boat and a campsite. The Castaic Mountains lined this side of Lake Wishik. Looking further north along the shore he could see that they came all the way down to the edge of the lake. He was hailed by Lorith, one of the trackers, who happened to be on watch at the time. It was good to know that Olog knew how to do his job thoroughly. He explained quietly to Lorith that he had been followed and should stay on watch. Also that he didn't want his stalker to be killed, if caught, he wanted him brought in alive. He walked into camp and was greeted by all with a loud "Huh! Huh! Huh!"

He found Olog and explained to him that he had been followed. He wanted his stalker captured, not killed. They were all to act like they weren't aware of an outsider being close by. Two warriors were to be sent out to circle around behind him. Olog said that wouldn't be necessary and pointed behind Ogiloth back down the shore. He turned and saw that his stalker had already been captured. He looked back at Olog with a huge grin.

"I'm impressed Olog."

"Thank you, sir. Besides the guards I stationed along the shore on either side of camp I also placed a secondary set of guards up in the trees."

That's when Ogiloth looked around camp and realized that there were only five warriors in camp. "Again, I'm very impressed Olog. It appears that from this point on all I need to do is tell you what I need done and you'll take it from there." Then he gave Olog a very stern look. "But remember, never countermand one of my orders. Don't let my praise go to your head and wipe that grin off your face."

"Yes, sir."

The captured human was brought to Ogiloth and forced to his knees. He was shaking with fear and looking all about. He saw that there were more of these creatures and figured his life would come to an end soon. The large one standing in front of him, the one he had followed from town, frightened him the most though, he was huge compared to the others.

He knew he was big but he hadn't gotten close enough to really see how big. He looked up into Ogiloth's eyes.

"Please don't kill me," he pleaded.

"Get on your feet!" Ogiloth roared.

The man winced and tried to stand up but fell back to his knees. The warrior behind him grabbed his arms and lifted him to his feet.

"Why did you follow me?" he asked in his normal tone.

"I was curious."

"Curious? About what?"

"You."

"Enough small talk, explain yourself or I'll let my men have you to play with before they kill you."

All the warriors chuckled at that and the man started shaking even more.

"I saw you come out of Durog's house . . ."

"Why were you watching Durog's house?" he interrupted the man. "Who are you?"

"Jenner. My name is Jenner."

"You're one of the men Durog hired to do some surveillance for him. I thought you looked familiar. What made you decide to follow me though?"

"When I was in Durog's house telling him what I had seen I had a feeling we weren't alone, that someone else was in the house too." He looked around again at the creatures that surrounded him. He was still shaking with fear.

"Stop looking around and look at me," Ogiloth commanded. The man did. "Now finish your story."

"After we split up the gold and Cory and Lance went home I decided to go back and watch Durog's house. I wanted to see if what I felt was true. I stayed there all night watching and waiting and you finally came out this morning. Like I said, I was curious and decided to follow you to see where you would go."

"And that's all, nothing more?"

"Yes."

"Did you think you might be able to rob me at some point, maybe as I slept at night?"

"No, no, no, nothing like that."

"You were the one that saw those three people leave town and walk up into the mountains, right?"

Jenner stopped shaking and looked up at Ogiloth stunned. "Yes."

"Would you remember where it was you last saw them before you went running to Durog's house?"

"Yes"

"Would you be willing to help me, especially if it meant saving your own life?"

"Yes," he responded with more conviction.

"All right then, you work for me now." He looked at the warrior standing behind the man, "Cut him loose."

Jenner stood there with his arms hanging at his sides unsure what to do next. He looked at all those around him and then back at Ogiloth. "What do I do now?"

"Make yourself comfortable but stay close by and do as you're told." Then to his team he spoke loudly. "If any of you see this miserable creature trying to escape, KILL HIM." Then he turned back to Jenner and looked down on him with an evil grin. "Understood?" He didn't even wait for a response, he just turned his back on the man and walked away with Olog.

Jenner just stood there shaking his head up and down for a moment until he was able to calm down enough to walk over and sit on a rock by the edge of the lake.

# CHAPTER 16

JOICE FLEW THROUGH the night high in the sky heading towards Washoe to see her sister. She loved being in her dragon form and flying, it always gave her a sense of freedom and serenity, the wind in her face and flowing across her body. She was alone way up here and everything looked so small way down there. Usually Jake was with her but sometimes it was nice to get away and be alone. It seemed like she could see forever and beyond. She saw the lights of Bruston as she passed over and the darkness of Murwood Forest approaching. Off in the distance she could just make out the lights of Washoe. It never took long to get somewhere when flying. She didn't mind travelling on land but this, this was definitely the way to travel.

It took about an hour to fly from the mountain cave to Washoe but it only seemed like minutes to her. Before she knew it, it was time to make her descent. She needed to be on the ground at least a mile out of town so no one would see her in her dragon form. The walk was short enough and it helped her relax after the flight.

She landed with a big whoosh of air as her wings came down to stop her descent. Instantly she shifted back into her human form. She and Jake had found a good place south of town to land when they flew here at night to visit with Casper and Karin. They rarely flew during the day because they were more likely to be seen. Shapeshifters had decided long ago that it would be best not to change shape in the presence of non-shapeshifters unless it was a matter of life and death. For the most part this policy had been upheld.

She walked into town unnoticed and headed for the Dragons' Lair. She hadn't seen her sister for some time now and was very excited about it. She opened the front door and stepped into the entry way. Casper was behind the counter and smiled broad when he looked up and saw her. He rushed around the end of the counter almost forgetting to lift the gate and ran to give her a big hug.

"Joice, it's so good to see you again. Karin will be so surprised. What brings you to Washoe?"

"Something that would be best talked about in private."

"Okay." He got a serious look on his face. "I'll go tell Karin you're here."

She stopped him as he turned to go. "No. I want to surprise her myself if that's all right."

"By all means. You haven't seen each other for a while she'll probably scream when you walk in. Where's Jake?"

"He didn't come with me this time. I'll explain later."

Joice prepared herself and walked into the dining area. She didn't see Karin anywhere so she headed towards the kitchen. Just like Joice, Karin spent a lot of time in the kitchen. She made it as far as the bar and Karin walked through the kitchen door carrying a platter of food. Karin stopped suddenly, shocked, when she saw her sister. She screamed, like Casper said she would, and nearly dropped the platter of food. She quickly set it down on the bar and gave her sister a big hug.

"Joice, it's so good to see you again." She turned to Casper, "Would you be a dear and take this platter to the customer sitting over there." She pointed.

"My pleasure dear." He picked up the platter and delivered it.

"How long has it been Joice?"

"Too long, little sister. We should try to see each other more often."

"So, what brings you to Washoe, business or pleasure or both?"

"Business, but it's definitely a pleasure seeing you again."

"If its business I imagine it's something best talked about in private."

"That's what I was just telling Casper."

"That was the last platter of food for the night so I'm free to talk now. Just give me a minute to find Jarrell to have him watch the dining room and clean up after the last customer leaves."

"No hurry but I do need to get back to Bruston before the sun comes up."

"Jake, where's Jarrell?"

"I believe he's out back. He took the trash out. He should be back any moment now."

Right then Jarrell came walking out of the kitchen and saw Joice. He smiled. "Aunt Joice, it's good to see you." He gave her a big hug.

"How've you been, Jarrell?"

"Mother and father keep me busy. I keep telling them they need to hire someone to help out," he looked at his mother with a sly grin. "Father seems to agree but I don't think mother is listening to us."

"We've been very busy around here," she conceded to Joice. "Jarrell's right, we do need to hire someone. More and more people keep moving here and the business that comes through town is increasing, which brings a lot of people that just pass through needing not only accommodations but are looking for a place to eat. Casper keeps saying the same thing so I may have to just give in and hire someone to help."

Casper and Jarrell both just stood there listening with an 'I told you so' look.

Karin glanced at them and gave in. "Okay, okay, enough. Tomorrow we can start interviewing for more help. Right now you need you to watch the place and clean up after the last customer leaves," she told Jarrell. "Joice has come here to talk business with your father and me."

Jarrell's shoulders slumped and he looked at his aunt. "See, Aunt Joice, it never ends."

"We'll be in the office if something comes up you can't handle and you need us."

They all three headed towards the office leaving Jarrell to tend the inn.

Once in the office and they were all comfortable Karin asked her sister, "So. What's this business that brings you here? I hope there's nothing wrong."

"It's not really 'business', it's more of a family matter." Casper and Karin got a concerned look on their faces and Joice continued. "J'orik has been to the inn with his friend Lianna." She paused and waited for their reaction.

"J'orik and Lianna?" Karin sounded worried. "They were here a while back and stayed the night. They told us what happened in their village. They left the next morning to go back and see if there was anything they could salvage. Are they in some sort of trouble?"

"Let's just say they've been through a lot since they left here and arrived in Bruston." Then she informed them of everything she knew that had happened since the time they left Washoe and came to Bruston.

They listened intently and asked questions once in a while to clarify points they were confused about. When Joice was done relaying everything up until she left them at the cave in the mountains she could see that Casper and Karin were both concerned and wanted to help in any way they could.

"It sounds like this Ogiloth character won't give up until he's captured J'orik and taken him back to his father," Casper remarked. "I knew K'orik was a bad egg, but to destroy all those villages and kill all those people," he shuddered, "that's just plain disturbing. So, what do you propose we do next?"

Joice shrugged her shoulders. "That's why I came here. I thought that if we all put our heads together we could come up with a plan of action to protect J'orik and Lianna from not only Ogiloth, but from K'orik as well."

"K'orik is not likely to just give up," Casper said bluntly. "From what little I know about him he's probably told this Ogiloth not to come back empty-handed, which is why he seems to be so relentless in his search. I don't think Lianna has anything to worry about other than being with J'orik if Ogiloth ever does find him. I think what you've done by moving them out of town and into the mountains should slow Ogiloth's search a little. Right now I can't think of a better plan." He looked at Karin for input. "Do you have anything in mind?"

"No. I think what Jake and Joice have done is the best plan of action for now. We'll just have to wait and see what happens next."

"Okay then." Joice stood up and Casper and Karin followed. "It's time I start back. I'll keep you informed of what's going on, when I can." She started for the door. "It was nice seeing both of you again. I would love to stay longer and visit but I'll do that when this is over and Jake can come with me."

They all headed out into the entry area. There were no more customers in the dining room and Jarrell had finished cleaning up. He was standing behind the front counter when they came out.

"You have to leave, Aunt Joice?"

"Yes, Jarrell, I have things I need to do and they can't wait. Besides, I need to get back to Bruston before daylight. It was good to see you though." She smiled at him and then gave him a big hug. She hugged Casper and Karin and waved at them all as she headed out the front door. "Good-bye everyone."

They all waved back and said good-bye.

Joice walked back to the same place she'd landed, changed form, and began the flight home. Again, she felt the freedom and serenity that flying gave her. The flight was uneventful and she landed in a spot about a mile out of Bruston where the Murwood Forest started to thin as it bordered the Great Desert. When she got back to the inn, Jake was still up waiting for her. He reported that nothing had happened while she was gone and asked about Karin and her family as they headed to bed.

"The visit was much too short, though. I told them we would come and visit after all of this was over."

"That sounds like a great idea."

"Jarrell is growing up so fast. He reminds me a lot of Jerome." She got a distant look in her eyes. "You know Jake, we need to take some time and visit our own children. I miss the grandkids too."

"I do too, dear," he smiled.

# CHAPTER 17

OGILOTH TOOK OLOG aside to explain what they were going to do next. Now that Jenner was there he had revised his plan a little. It wouldn't be as difficult to find J'orik's trail, as long as Jenner was capable of pointing it out.

"J'orik has headed into the mountains. It won't be necessary to take him in the town now. With the human, Jenner, and his knowledge of where they're headed, it shouldn't be difficult to find J'orik's trail and track him down. I don't want an incident like we had with Gorog so two warriors are to stay behind with the boat and maintain camp. We'll be travelling by land now so we only need enough supplies to last a few days. We'll skirt along the edge of the mountains west of town, but we'll avoid town. Once we're beyond the south end of town, Jenner will be brought forward to indicate where he last saw J'orik and the general direction he was heading. Jenner said he was travelling with two women now. I suspect that one of them is the travelling companion he's had all along. I'm not sure what part the other one plays other than she appears to be aiding him. After Herg and Lorith confirm we're following the right tracks I want Jenner disposed of. When I say 'disposed of' I mean I don't want any evidence left that he even existed." He paused and looked Olog square in the eyes trying to determine if he understood everything he'd said. "Understood?"

Olog shook his head up and down.

"You have no questions?"

Olog shook his head side to side.

"Okay, I'm leaving it up to you to carry out these orders. We leave as soon as you have the team organized. Be quick about it though, I don't want to waste any time."

"Yes, sir." Olog went off to initiate Ogiloth's orders.

Jenner was calming down now and most of his fear was beginning to subside. He heard a lot of activity occurring behind him but he forced himself to keep looking out over the lake, he didn't want to see what was going on. The fear, however, suddenly returned when he heard a sharp, gravelly voice close behind him.

"Human. It's time to move. Get up and fall in," Olog barked at him.

He didn't hesitate. He jumped to his feet and joined the others. He tried to get past the fear of being surrounded by these monstrous looking creatures and think. He needed to figure out a way to escape but now was neither the place nor the time. He would follow along and look for the right moment, hoping it would come soon. He knew that it was likely they would kill him once he'd done what they wanted. He noticed that two of them stayed behind, that left only the big one and seven others. He knew his chances were slim but if the right moment came along he was going to take it. He couldn't understand why they didn't bind him or at least harness him to one of them. Maybe they thought the fear he'd exhibited for them was enough to keep him from considering escape.

All the next day J'orik and Lianna just enjoyed each other's company and the fabulous view they had from this high up. They spent most of their time at the cave opening. It was too stuffy inside.

Joice was right. Access to the cave was very difficult. The cave opening was on the face of a steep, rocky slope. The ledge in front of it was large enough to accommodate Joice's dragon form with some space to maneuver. She and Jake probably took turns landing and taking off. They wouldn't have been able to both fit on the ledge at the same time. Murwood Forest could be seen in the distance and the Great Desert stretched out forever to the southeast. Bruston couldn't be seen from here nor could Lake Wishik.

The day seemed to pass slowly as they waited for Joice, or Jake, to return.

Jake and Joice spent the next day as usual. They'd discussed what they would do after retiring to bed the night before. Jake would be the one to visit J'orik and Lianna regularly each night until they could resolve the problem of Ogiloth. This way he could start the process of guiding them through the changing. Clare could go along when she was able. Joice would speak with her about that. All of them would need to be discreet since this type of activity would not be perceived as normal by those that knew them or anyone that might be watching them. They were more concerned with someone watching them. After what Clare had told them they would have to assume they were being watched.

After Ogiloth left, Durog went back inside, grabbed the tray of muffins, and made himself comfortable in his chair. He sat there eating the muffins thinking about the last couple days. He'd really enjoyed his nephew's visit, especially playing chess. He thought about how sedentary his life had become since his wife was gone and he no longer worked in the mines. He spent most of his time at home either reading or working in his garden. He had few friends and didn't see them very often. He thought about the short visit he had with Owen at the Boars' Den when he was looking for this J'orik fellow and regretted having been so short with him. He decided to make a point of making it up to him. He liked the intrigue that Ogiloth had brought into his life. His nephew had asked him to keep his eyes and ears open for any activity regarding J'orik so he decided he would make daily trips into town and watch for anything unusual. He would especially keep an eye on what Clare did and any goings on at the Dragons' Inn. It would also give him a chance to visit with his old friend Owen and not have to drink alone.

He finished the muffins, brushed the crumbs out of his beard, and set the tray on the kitchen counter as he headed out the door. Today would be a different day.

Once they got under way and were walking back towards Bruston, Olog checked to make sure that Jenner was in the middle of the pack so that he would always have eyes on him. He made his way up next to Ogiloth at the front of the line. They were far enough ahead that he felt it was safe to talk without being heard by Jenner.

"Sir, I do have a question."

Ogiloth looked down at Olog with a scowl. "I didn't think you had any questions. What's bothering you now?"

He hesitated slightly before continuing. "I was just wondering why we don't bind or harness the human so he has no way to escape."

Ogiloth sighed, but he knew Olog had a legitimate concern. "Since you're doing so well as a leader and you don't understand the reasoning I will help you. If we were to bind him then he would know we were treating him as a prisoner and he would be less cooperative. By letting him walk freely he will believe he is part of the group and be more likely to cooperate."

"But why do we need him at all? Herg and Lorith will be able to find the trail we're looking for."

"You're right, but this human knows exactly where the trail is. Time is important and Herg and Lorith would need time to find the trail. Understand?"

Olog's eyes widened in realization, "Yes, I understand now."

"You need to learn to use all the resources at hand as wisely as possible to attain your end goal. Once he has shown us where the trail is and Herg and Lorith have confirmed it then his presence will no longer be necessary. Any more questions?"

"One. What if he tries to escape before he shows us where the trail is?" Olog could see that Ogiloth was becoming irritated but he needed to know.

"Do not kill him. If he is able to escape," he looked at Olog with fire in his eyes, "then I will know I chose the wrong warriors, and lieutenant, to aid me with my search."

Ogiloth looked away from Olog dismissing any further questions or concerns he might have.

Olog stopped and let the group walk by. He eyed Jenner hard as he walked by attempting to convey that he was keeping his eyes on him, and he was. He wasn't sure what Ogiloth meant by his last remark but he didn't want to find out. He meant to make sure that Jenner did not escape. He decided he would take up walking behind him so that he could keep watch over him.

When Jenner passed by Olog he knew something was up by the way Olog looked at him. He was sure the two of them had been talking about him. He glanced back and saw that Olog was watching him. He knew escape would not be easy if it was even possible.

Ogiloth stopped the group short of a wide trail ahead. Upon closer investigation it was wider than a normal foot trail and had a double set of grooves in. He remembered the mining operation that went on up in the mountains and realized that this must be the access road to and from Bruston. There wasn't any traffic currently on it so they continued their journey south.

He had them stop when he felt he was at a point due west of the south end of Bruston. They were in some low rolling hills with the mountains behind them and the forest was beginning to thin. He knew that any further south the land would start to level out and eventually turn into desert. He had Olog bring Jenner forward.

"I'm glad you did not try to escape Jenner." He grinned at him.

Jenner tried to act fearless. "I would have but I couldn't with him watching me." He jerked his thumb at Olog.

"Ahh, Jenner, you disappoint me. Have we treated you badly?" He spoke with some sarcasm in his voice and continued without letting him answer. "All I want you to do is show me where those three people you were watching went after they left Bruston and then I'll let you go." He looked at him with a wry grin. "Unless you decide you want to stay with us." Then he laughed out loud and the others laughed with him.

Jenner looked around and chuckled sarcastically trying to comfort his own fear. He looked up at Ogiloth with a blank face. "I just might do that."

Ogiloth stopped laughing abruptly and growled, "ENOUGH!" Everyone stopped laughing. "You will show me where this trail is and then your fate will be decided."

Jenner thought he'd push his luck as far as he could. "And if I don't?"

Ogiloth had fire in his eyes now. "I crush you right here with my bare hands." He raised his hands up and with an evil grin he brought them together slowly like he was already crushing him. Jenner's fear returned.

"How much further?" Ogiloth growled.

Jenner pointed and said, "About another half mile."

"Herg, Lorith, you two will lead with Jenner here until we find the trail."

They rushed to the front and started off with Jenner between them. They looked at him with smiles and chuckled.

Jenner had been right. It was only about a half mile before they came across some tracks. They were out in flatland now covered mostly by low lying brush and dried grass. The soil was a mixture of dirt and sand being this close to the desert. The sun had already started its descent to the mountaintops and a warm breeze was blowing from the southwest. When they stopped, Ogiloth came to the front.

"Are these the tracks?"

"I'm pretty sure they are," Jenner replied.

Ogiloth looked at Herg and Lorith. "There are three sets of prints," Herg told him. "We'll have to take a closer look to confirm them."

Ogiloth nodded his head and the two of them went about their business. Within minutes they returned and informed Ogiloth that two sets were similar to the ones they had seen going out into the plains earlier. They were certain that these were the tracks they were looking for. They were heading in a westerly direction leading back into the mountains. Ogiloth told them to lead on.

They reached the foothills after walking for about a half hour and continued up into the hills. About a half hour later Herg and Lorith both stopped. They had come down into a small valley and discovered something unusual. The tracks ended and they'd found prints from a large, four-toed creature. The ground had been stirred up as if by some huge gust of wind. They told Ogiloth they had never seen anything like it.

"The tracks just stop?" he asked Herg.

"Yes, sir, they end right here." He pointed, moving his hand in a circular motion. "There are no other tracks beyond this area."

"What do you make of the large prints?"

"We're not sure, sir, neither one of us has ever seen anything like them. Whatever it is it must be huge and it only walks on two legs."

Ogiloth turned to the group behind him. "We make camp. Find a place in the trees over the hills there to the north," he pointed, "where we can't be seen from here." Everyone began moving in that direcron. "Olog, I want three guards posted, one on the ridge between camp and here, one on the ridge along the eastern entrance to this valley, and one on the ridge along the western side." He pointed to all three locations.

"Okay, you heard, follow me." Olog took command leaving Ogiloth to consider what they would do next.

No one had been paying any attention to Jenner and when Ogiloth turned to question him he saw him running back the way they had come.

"Herg, Lorith," he yelled. "Our prisoner is escaping, after him."

They both turned and saw Jenner heading up the hillside. Both carried crossbows and immediately brought them to bear. Both fired and immediately started after Jenner. He was hit in the leg by one and went down. Before he could get back up and start running again Herg and Lorith were on him. They each grabbed an arm and roughly lifted him to his feet. They practically dragged him back and threw him down in front of Ogiloth.

"Did you really think you could escape?" He didn't give him time to answer. "Well, I guess you decided your own fate." He looked at Herg and Lorith. "Finish him and dispose of the body." Then he walked away to join the rest of his team.

Ogiloth had his suspicions of what this large creature might be that his trackers had found prints of. He knew what

K'orik was. He'd seen him change into his phoenix form many times over the years of service he'd put in. He'd even questioned K'orik about it and K'orik had explained some of the history of his kind. This was part of the reason he was being so cautious hunting for J'orik. He knew J'orik was like his father and was afraid he would have trouble capturing him. He also knew that the prints Herg had described were not those that would be left behind by a creature like K'orik, or J'orik. There was another large creature involved in the game now. Based on the descriptions K'orik had given him of some of the various forms his kind could change into he suspected this one was a dragon. The four toes, the ground appearing like a large gust of wind had disturbed it, and the fact that the only tracks left at the location were those of the four-toed creature. This creature could fly or there would have been more tracks found further beyond. He decided he was going to have to be even more cautious. He wasn't sure if he should say anything to his team fearing that they would abandon him so he decided to keep that information to himself. When the time came they would find out anyway and he hoped they wouldn't just run.

The sun was beginning to set behind the mountaintops when one of the guards came rushing into camp.

"There's a human headed this way," he told Ogiloth. "I could just make him out with what light there is and he's still some distance away."

Ogiloth figured he had about a half hour. "Go back and return to camp when he reaches the foot of the hills." Then he turned to Olog. "Have the campfire put out and the other guards brought in. I don't want any noise. If this human comes into the valley he can't know we're here. Make it clear that there is to be no noise. Other than myself everyone is to stay in camp." Then he turned and made his way to the ridge overlooking the valley to wait. He stood next to a large tree to block his presence from view.

He saw the guard from the south return to camp and within a few minutes he saw the human come over the hills to the east. The sun had already gone down behind the mountains. He watched him walk down into the valley near the spot they had found the large prints. He noticed him looking around almost as if he suspected he was being watched. As Ogiloth watched, the man changed into a dragon and flew away to the west. The change did not surprise him. He'd seen K'orik do it and had become accustomed to it. This dragon, however, was nearly four times the size of K'orik's form and from what little light remained he appeared red in color. He knew the color of the dragon was important. K'orik had explained to him that it determined the type of dragon. Red meant fire. This dragon's breath was fire. He also knew that dragons were very difficult to kill. Their scales were like a thick coat of armor and protected them from all the known weapons. He watched until the dragon was far enough out and then he emerged from the trees to watch where he might be headed. It was dark now and all he could make out was a shadow in the sky, but he saw that he was headed generally due west from the valley he was in. He watched until he completely lost sight of the shadow.

Returning to camp he found everyone waiting anxiously to find out what he'd seen. By the looks on their faces he could tell they were wondering why he hadn't returned with the human. Wondering why he had wanted them all to stay back. What it was he didn't want them to see. After all, it was only one human and there were eight of them. He knew they'd heard the dragon take off. When he spread his wings and lifted off the ground the sound was like the distant *thump*, *thump* of a drum beat. He wasn't sure how he was going to explain it.

Olog was the first to raise the question. "What was that noise? It sounded like a drum beat."

Ogiloth decided it would probably be best just to come right out and tell them. "It was a dragon."

He could see by the looks of confusion on their faces that they weren't sure what to make of what he had just said. Olog was the only one that didn't seem confused.

"Is that what we're hunting, a dragon?" Olog asked.

"No," Ogiloth answered flatly. "What we're hunting is much smaller but still just as dangerous."

The others stayed quiet and figured it would be best to let Olog speak for them.

"What are we hunting for?"

"Nothing different than what we've been hunting for all along, K'orik's son."

"But nothing was ever said about dragons. Is K'orik's son a dragon?"

"No. But it seems that he may have made friends with one." He thought, at this point, that he might be able to get away without telling them everything by circumventing the truth and redirecting their curiosity. He also hoped that none of them knew what he knew about K'orik. "Have any of you ever seen a dragon?"

They shook their heads no, all except Olog. "I've never seen one but I've been told about them."

"And what have you been told?"

"That they're big, dangerous, and I should stay away from them."

"What would you do if you were to meet one?"

"Run as fast as I could." The others shook their heads in agreement.

"So, what I'm hearing now is that you're all planning to run and hide. Is that right?"

They all looked at each other still confused, except for Olog. "Not me, sir. If you're willing to go up against a dragon then I'm with you."

"That's what I like to hear," he said with a grin. "The sign of a *real* warrior." Then he asked the rest with sarcasm in his voice, "Do you all feel the same or are you going to run and hide like little children? I thought I chose *warriors* to follow me."

He could see that the confusion had compounded but he thought as long as he had one with him the rest would follow. He could tell now that all the praise he had rained on Olog was beginning to pay off.

Then Olog turned to them and surprised him even more. "Ogiloth is right, if you're not a *real* warrior then leave now. I only want someone with me that I can trust to have my back. If you can't do that then I don't want you here. If Ogiloth isn't afraid to face a dragon then I'm not afraid either." Then he looked at Ogiloth with a smile and drew his shoulders back, puffing out his chest. Little did he know, Ogiloth was petrified, but he was a leader and leaders don't show fear or they lose control.

Ogiloth followed up with, "You heard him. Now's the time to decide, you're either in or out. You're either a warrior or not. If you're out then I want you gone—NOW." He waited for a few moments. No one moved to leave. "Good. You'll need a good night's rest. Tomorrow we head west into the mountains. I'll stand first watch. Whoever's standing watch when that dragon comes back, if he comes back, I want you to come and get me immediately." He turned and walked away from camp.

# CHAPTER 18

J AKE LEFT TOWN while he still had a little over an hour's worth of daylight left. He headed west for the small valley he and Joice used to change into their dragon forms before flying up to their mountain cave. About a half hour out of town he noticed a lot of foot prints on the path they normally took. He started examining them and found that they came from the north, intersected their path, and then followed it west. He had a strong suspicion that this was no coincidence. This had to be Ogiloth and he appeared to be travelling with a large group. Someone must have been watching them and seen Joice leave town with J'orik and Lianna yesterday. He would have to stay alert and be ready if he was attacked. He was just glad that Joice wasn't the one returning to check on the kids.

Paying more attention to his surroundings he happened to notice smoke curling up out of the trees to the north of the small valley he was headed for. As he got closer he saw that the smoke had stopped. Whoever it was must have spotted him coming and put their fire out. He had to assume it would be Ogiloth and his group. From the amount of tracks it couldn't be more than a dozen of them. He would be ready if they moved on him otherwise he would play it off as if he didn't know they were there. He would still have to change form to complete his journey but that wouldn't be a hindrance. If anything, he figured it would act in his favor.

He came up over the ridge and headed down into the valley. The sun had gone down behind the mountains and it was dark now He hadn't seen anyone. He could smell the residue left from the fire and he saw a thin cloud of smoke off in the trees to the north over that ridge. That's where they must be and he was sure he was being watched. He could almost feel the eyes on him. He took one last look around and then changed. Pumping his wings he took off.

As he gained altitude he looked back and spotted the thin cloud of smoke he'd seen while on the ground. He saw several bodies clustered around the center of the smoke cloud and one that had come out of the trees on the ridge. He knew he'd been watched and was still being watched. They wanted to see where he went but he knew they wouldn't be able to see where he ended his flight because it was night now and he would be too far away. He decided to just enjoy the flight and the peace he felt.

It didn't take long to get to the cave, which disappointed him a little. He really wanted to fly a little longer and even considered it. He doubted the kids would mind but then he remembered that they'd pretty much been trapped there all day. Without the ability to fly, access to and from the cave was near impossible. He and Joice had chosen it for that reason.

As he neared the ledge outside he noticed the kids were outside on it. He made one pass to let them know he was coming in and they should get back off the ledge to allow him room to land. He was larger than Joice and needed the whole ledge to make a landing. When he came back around he saw that they'd cleared the ledge and he made his landing. Once settled he changed back into human form. J'orik and Lianna both came walking over to greet him. Lianna ran more than walked and almost knocked him down as she wrapped her arms around him and gave him a big hug. J'orik greeted him with a strong handshake. He was really beginning to like these two kids and he felt they liked him too.

J'orik had a torch in his hand and Jake said they needed to get inside with it before anyone saw it. Even from a distance and this high up, a light could be seen. They all walked into the cave. There was a fire going in the fire pit and they all sat down around it.

"So tell me how your first day was trapped in this cave."

Lianna didn't hesitate. "At first it was wonderful, almost peaceful. We sat out on the ledge and wondered at the view from up here. We talked and enjoyed each other's company. But as the day passed it started to get a little boring. Like you said, we were trapped. I'll be glad when I can fly then I can come and go as I please."

"Well, that's something you're going to have to learn, you can't just come and go as you please, not during the day anyway. At night it's another story, you don't have to be as concerned about being seen. How about you J'orik?"

"I feel the same way Lianna does. I enjoyed the time up here but I'll be glad when I can fly too."

"Don't worry, all in good time. Now, I take it from your responses that Joice didn't show you the back door."

"The back door," they said in unison, looking at each other and then back at Jake.

"Yes, behind the chest that holds all the bedding is an opening that leads to another larger cavern further in the mountain. From there, are several tunnels that eventually lead to the outside. Some just open out to a sheer cliff face similar to this one, only without the ledge, and others lead to safer exits."

"No, she neglected to mention that," J'orik told him.

"I think she was just so excited she was going to see her sister that it just slipped her mind. It's probably a good thing though. It would be better, and safer, after someone has shown you around and you become more familiar with everything so you don't get lost. If you would like, that can be what we do today. The other choice was to begin guiding you through the change. Which would you prefer?"

"First, will we be staying here for a while?" J'orik asked.

"Yes. I think it's the best option right now. It's safe and secure."

"Then I'm up for some exploring first."

Jake looked at Lianna for her opinion. She nodded her agreement with J'orik.

"Then that's what we'll do. Before we get started, though, there's something I need to let you know. On my way here I spotted a group that was watching that small valley Joice took you to before bringing you here. I believe it's Ogiloth and his group." They looked at each other with concern as Jake continued. "They saw me change and the direction I flew but it was dark and they couldn't have seen where I flew to. I don't think they knew I was aware of them. You don't have anything to worry about. If they do try to follow it'll take days for them to reach the foot of this mountain. Even then they would have to scale the rocky cliff leading up to the ledge outside. You'd see them coming. Having said that, in the next day or two, start keeping your eyes open for any movement nearby. The most likely sign will be smoke curling up out of the trees from their campfire."

"What if they find one of the other entrances you just mentioned?" J'orik asked, concerned.

"Even if they do it's a maze of tunnels. They could spend weeks wandering around before they found the cavern this tunnel drops into." He pointed at the chest against the wall. "And if they did find it, they would still have to figure out which tunnel to take from there to find this cave. I don't think you need to be concerned with them coming through the back door." They both relaxed with the thought and Jake continued. "Now getting back to the back door tunnel, I just said it 'drops' into the other cavern. The opening at the other end is high up on the wall of the cavern. You either have to be able to fly or you need a rope to climb." He looked at J'orik. "I noticed that you carry a length of rope in your pack."

"Yes, I do."

"You're going to need that and a torch. Today I'm only going to take you as far as the other cavern and let you do a little exploring there. Afterwards, we'll start your tutoring. Sound good?"

They both smiled and nodded in agreement. While Jake went to move the chest, J'orik got the rope out of his pack and Lianna got a torch. The opening behind the chest was not much smaller than the chest but still large enough they could walk through it. Jake took the torch from Lianna and led the way followed by Lianna then J'orik. The tunnel wound around but slowly sloped down. There were no other tunnels leading off of it. After walking for almost a half hour Jake finally stopped. They could feel a slight breeze coming up the tunnel shortly before they got to the end and it started to widen.

"Here we are." Jake said as he placed the torch in a notch on the wall of the tunnel.

The opening was much larger than the one at the other end in the cave. All three of them could stand side by side as they looked out into the cavern. There was a ledge that jutted out slightly from the cavern wall. They were about a hundred feet above the floor. Looking up, the ceiling disappeared in the darkness. The cavern was more than large, J'orik and Lianna thought, it was enormous. They could hear the echo of running water that sounded like a small river.

"Is there a river in here?" Lianna asked curiously.

"Yes. There are several springs that bubble up on the floor and then flow out an opening on the other side of the cavern. The river eventually leads to the west side of the mountain and opens out on the side as a waterfall that drops about eight hundred feet. I would suggest avoiding getting caught in the river or using it as an exit until you can fly. How long is your rope, J'orik?"

"I carry a hundred foot length."

"Good, that should be long enough to reach the floor." He set the torch in the side of the tunnel. "You can secure it to the torch, it'll hold. I'll go down first and then you can climb down the rope. I need you to stand back a little while I take off."

J'orik and Lianna stood next to the torch and they watched Jake. He started a ways back up the tunnel and took a running leap off the ledge. Lianna sucked in her breathe as she watched. Just before Jake began to drop down from his leap he changed into a dragon and pumped his wings hard. He dropped to the floor slowly and changed back after landing.

"Okay, you can climb down now," he hollered up at them. "Make sure you extinguish the torch first."

J'orik went first just to make sure the torch would hold. Lianna followed after he hollered up that he was on the floor. Jake had already lit another torch that was kept hidden nearby. Jake led them over to the edge of the underground lake. They passed by several stalagmites varying in size on their way. The lake was very large. Standing on the floor, the echo from the river was even louder.

"You can walk around on either side of the lake but once you reach the far side," he pointed, "there is no easy way to cross without getting in the river and swimming. I would not suggest doing that unless you have no other choice. The current is very strong and likely to pull you out of the cavern before you could reach the opposite side. There are several openings for tunnels leading out on either side as well. Joice and I have explored them all and followed them to their ends. I'm sure the two of you will do the same the more time you spend here." His voiced echoed through the cavern as he spoke. "Right now, though, I'm going to show you one that leads out to a safe exit on the west side of the mountain we're in." He started off around the left side of the lake.

The tunnel Jake was leading them to was almost all the way around to where the river exited the cavern. Being that close, he decided he would also show them the river. He continued past the tunnel about twenty yards and stopped at the edge of the river.

"The tunnel I'm going to show you is back a little but I thought I'd show you the river."

At the bank of the river he held the torch up as high as he could so they could see more. The bank on the other side of the river was right at the edge of the torchlight and was about twenty yards away. The river was flowing fairly fast through the opening where it exited the cavern. He was right when he said there was no easy way across. They turned around and went back to the tunnel.

"Before we go in I need to tell you that it's a long walk to the outside. If we go all the way we won't be back here until early morning and we won't have enough time to start with the tutoring. Are you okay with that?"

They both nodded their assent.

"There are other tunnels that branch off this one so it's important that you pay attention to the route we take."

"Are there some kind of markings that'll help?" J'orik asked.

"Sort of," he responded, "but the more you walk it the more familiar you'll become with it. Like I said earlier, you should have me or Joice with you until you do become more familiar."

As they walked Jake talked about how he and Joice had discovered their cave and explored the multitude of tunnels that branched off the larger cavern. At the same time he would point out ways to identify the tunnel branches so they could keep on the main one they were travelling. He briefly explained where a few of the other tunnels led. He told them it took many years of exploring, and sometimes getting twisted around, before they finally had it all mapped out in their heads. It seemed like they'd been walking all night before they reached the end and were standing outside but Jake told them they'd only been walking for about two hours. He extinguished the torch and set it in a notch in the tunnel wall. They let their eyes adjust to the natural lighting provided by the stars in the night sky before walking about.

Lianna heard rushing water in the distance to the north of the tunnel and asked Jake, "I hear rushing water. Is that the river coming out of the mountain?"

"Yes, it is. It's about three hundred yards away. It comes out of the mountain and falls into a large pool then continues down through the trees."

"Is this where we'll come to learn how to change?" J'orik asked.

"Eventually, after you learn to control it better. I thought we would start in the large cavern where we have a lot of room and you can't be seen. Initially we'll be practicing at night because that'll be the only time I can get away from the inn."

"Will Clare be teaching me or will you?"

"Unless Clare comes along then I will and I can teach both of you at the same time. Okay, kids, we need to start heading back. I need to make sure that I get back to town before sunrise. I can't be seen in my dragon form flying about in the daylight." He relit the torch and waited for them to fall in behind him.

They both stood there staring at him with stunned looks on their faces.

"Is something wrong?" he asked.

They just stood there for a moment. J'orik finally spoke. "How did you just light that torch?"

"Oh, that," he chuckled. "I'm a creature of fire. I have the natural ability to generate a flame at will much like you, J'orik, once you learn."

"But how can you do that without changing form?" he asked.

"Ahh, now that I think about it, that's one thing Joice didn't mention. The abilities you have can be used in either form, except, of course, the ability to fly. For that you need to make a complete transformation. We, however," he indicated J'orik and himself, "since we're creatures of fire, we can generate heat and fire. It comes in handy sometimes, like now. I guess you can consider this part of your learning process."

"What about me?" Lianna asked.

"Well, dear, until we determine what *type* of dragon you are, I can't answer that. Any more questions?" he waited for a moment. When neither one responded he turned towards the tunnel. "Okay, let's get going then."

He pointed out the tunnel markers again on the way back. The echo of the underground river could be heard as they neared the cavern. They came out into the cavern and walked around the lake back to where the rope was hanging. Jake told them both to climb back up and pull the rope up behind them.

J'orik looked at Jake. "Why don't you just climb back up the rope with us?"

"Because I'm going to let you see how tricky it is to make it onto the ledge from flying."

"I was wondering about that. The ledge is nowhere large enough to hold your dragon form."

"Watch and learn. The only thing I need you to do is make sure you're inside the tunnel."

After they climbed back up the rope and pull it in they stepped inside the tunnel, relit the torch, and told Jake they were clear. He suddenly appeared outside the opening flapping his wings and hovering about twenty yards away and higher than the ledge. He made one last downward motion with his wings, dipped his body forward, and appeared like he was going to swoop straight into the tunnel. Just before it looked like he was going to smash into the cavern wall he changed into human form, kicked his legs forward, and landed on his feet.

"That was impressive," J'orik commented.

"It's only impressive to someone that's never seen it done. Eventually both of you will learn to do it and it will seem less impressive."

They walked back to the cave they were staying in, through the tunnel, and out onto the ledge. Jake said his good-byes, told them he'd be back tomorrow night, changed into his dragon form, and flew away. From the height they were at the distant horizon was starting to glow with the rising sun. They both yawned and went back into the cave. They had had a long day and they were both tired. They fell fast asleep as soon as they lay down.

Jake thought it would be best if he didn't land where he usually did. He knew that he would be watched for and didn't want to take any chances with a confrontation. He flew a little further north looking for a clearing that was close to the mining road. He would walk back into town that way. He had a higher chance of being seen coming back into town but that was better than the alternative.

# CHAPTER 19

OGILOTH WAS AWAKENED by the last guard on watch at sunrise. "No sign of a dragon, sir."

"Have you got the others up yet?"

"No need, sir, they were up when I came into camp."

"Good. I'll be out in a moment."

The warrior left him and rejoined the others. When Ogiloth came out of his tent two of them immediately rushed over to break it down. *Olog must be on top of things*, he thought. *That's good.* Olog seemed to be a natural leader, which is what he wanted, but it was something he would have to keep in check. If things went well he would definitely consider promoting him.

*No sign of the dragon*, he thought to himself. *If he did return during the night he must have chosen a different place to land. He must have known we were here and watching. We'll have to be more careful next time.*

Olog walked over to him. "We're all packed and ready to go, sir."

"Good, let's get moving."

They all walked down into the small valley. Ogiloth took the lead and started heading west. He wasn't quite sure where he was going. He chose the mountain peak the dragon appeared to be heading towards when he saw him last night. By the looks of it, foregoing any major obstacles, he figured it would take about two hard days of walking to get there. In the meantime, if Olog asked, he would tell him that dragons usually chose the tallest mountains because it was harder to reach them. The mountainside would be rocky and steep and their cave would be high up and difficult to get to. Once they got closer these would be the things they would look for.

K'orik got up that morning in a wicked mood. It had been a week since Ogiloth had left and he hadn't heard anything from him. He thought that after this much time he would have sent word of his progress. He was becoming concerned. He'd told Ogiloth not to come back empty-handed and he'd been rather harsh about it.

His son was twenty-seven now and if he had anyone tutoring him he would be fairly strong by now. Strong enough that Ogiloth wouldn't be able to capture him easily, even with ten warriors to help him.

He wondered if J'orik's mother was the one tutoring him. K'orik remembered how much Jalana hated him and wanted to get away. When she finally escaped, left him, the boy was only five months old. He didn't care that she left but when he found out she'd taken his son with her, he was furious. He nearly burned everything in his room before he got himself under control. That was twenty-seven years ago and he still remembered it like it happened yesterday.

He needed to find out what was going on. He couldn't stand not knowing.

*Maybe Sarguroth can help*, he thought to himself. *He's a sorcerer. He was able to create these damnable creatures that make up my army. He should be able to see what's going on with them somehow. I should pay him a visit anyway and see what he's up to.*

He summoned one of his servants and told him to have his carriage readied. He would be leaving within the hour. Sarguroth's tower was half a day's ride from his castle and it was already mid-morning. Chances were he would have to stay the night there. Sarguroth loved to hear his own voice and K'orik knew he would waste more time talking about nothing of interest than doing what he wanted him to do.

He continued wondering about Ogiloth and the quest he'd sent him on while he changed into his travelling clothes. He liked wearing elaborate clothes that helped to give the appearance of power. Calf-length suede trousers made from the finest hides held at the waist with a black leather belt. The buckle, of course, was of polished gold and silver with an image of a phoenix on it. Knee high boots made from fox furs. A long-sleeved white shirt under a red velvet vest with gold buttons that also had an image of a phoenix on them, all covered by a full-length, bear-hide coat trimmed with fox fur. The hide was stamped with images of phoenixes. He didn't wear a hat because he felt that his snow-white hair spoke for itself. He also carried a hardened steel short sword plated in silver clasped to his belt, the handle, of course, had the image of a phoenix on it as well.

About the time he finished dressing himself the servant returned informing him that his carriage was ready. He made his way down to the courtyard and climbed into the carriage. The carriage was built with ash wood, painted red, and framed in hardened steel. The framing was plated with gold and emblazoned with phoenixes. The undercarriage was designed to give the rider the smoothest ride possible. The interior was red velvet and the bench seats stuffed with eider down to make the ride even smoother. It was pulled by two of the sturdiest and largest draft horses available. The driver was human of course, K'orik would not have one of those creatures that Sarguroth created driving him about.

The driver turned and asked K'orik, "Where are we off to today, sir?"

"Take me to Sarguroth's tower," he snapped.

"Yes, sir."

The driver whipped the horses into action and the carriage started off.

Sarguroth's tower was north of K'orik's castle high in the Castaic Mountains near a large lake named after the mountains, Castaic Lake. It was nowhere near the size of Lake Wishik but still considered large. Sarguroth liked the location because during the winter months it would snow and he enjoyed the snow. K'orik, on the other hand, despised the snow. He didn't like cold weather. Fortunately for him he would be visiting during the summer months when it was the warmest.

When Jake returned that morning Joice could see that he was concerned about something. "Are the kids okay? Did something happen?" She had a worried look on her face.

"The kids are fine, dear," he told her. "What concerns me more, though, is this Ogiloth."

"Did you run into him?"

"Sort of, I think. I didn't see him but I knew I was being watched when I changed form, I could feel the presence of others. He wasn't alone either. There must be almost a dozen of them. I could smell the fire they tried to put out and there was a thin cloud of smoke in the trees. They must have seen me coming and were trying to hide their presence. After I took flight I looked back and I could see several forms on the ground. The sun had already gone behind the mountains so I don't think it's likely they were able to see where I went, but they could have seen the general direction I was going if they were watching, which I'm sure they were."

"So, where did you land when you came back?"

"I found a clearing near the mining road and came in that way."

"What do you think we should do?"

"For the next couple of days I don't think we need to worry about it. It'll take them that long to even reach the foot of the mountain our cave is in, assuming that's what they do. I think he had someone watching the inn and you and the kids were seen leaving town heading into the mountains." He paused for a moment, thinking. Then continued, "I think for right now, I'll continue making visits with the kids and begin their training. I'll keep a watch on Ogiloth's progress on my way there and back."

"And if he gets too close to the kids?"

"I'll confront him and his group."

"As a dragon of course."

"Yes, as a dragon. If he was watching, he saw me change and saw what I changed into."

"When the time comes, will you want me to go with you?"

"No. I can handle them alone. There's no need for you to show yourself unnecessarily."

"It sounds like you've thought this through already so I'll let you do what you think needs to be done. Just keep me up on what's happening." Then she got a different kind of worried look. "You look tired, dear. Maybe you should get some rest so you'll be fresh when you visit the kids tonight."

"You're right. I think I'll get a few hours of sleep. I'll grab a bite to eat first, I'm hungry. If I'm not awake by mid-afternoon come and rouse me. Okay?"

"Okay, dear, you have a good rest."

J'orik and Lianna slept until midday. Their tour of the mountain underground had taken all their energy out of them, especially since they'd been up all day. They decided that if this was going to be their routine for a while they would try to get as much sleep as possible during the daytime. If Jake was going to be coming here every night to tutor them they would need as much energy as possible. They figured that after they got up in the afternoon they could do some exploring in the larger cavern, no tunnels yet, and be back to meet Jake in the evening. They thought they should be back early enough so they could keep an eye out for this Ogiloth and his group.

They had a bite to eat and then made their way down to the larger cavern to do some exploring.

# CHAPTER 20

SARGUROTH SAW K'ORIK'S wagon coming from a distance and when he arrived at the base of his tower he had him met by his servants. His servants were human, of course. He was a human himself and did not feel comfortable using the creatures he had created for K'orik as servants. He stayed in the top of his tower and waited for K'orik to be shown up. He wasn't sure why he had come to visit him, he thought it might be to create some more of those damnable creatures he so loved. He knew K'orik was in the process of building an army but he didn't know for what. He would have to figure out some way to get that information out of him without asking him outright. He didn't want to sound nosy.

Sarguroth was a sorcerer of the highest caliber and he had many people in places of power that desired his assistance in one form or another. His services did not come cheap and he generally didn't ask questions not relevant to the task he was asked to perform.

He'd seen how K'orik was attired and decided that he would put on something a little more appropriate than the heavy leather robe he was wearing. He always wore this robe when he was working. It helped protect him from any inadvertent splashes from the chemicals he used or the fires that would flame up. He was currently working on creating a love potion for one of the minor land lords that lived near the ocean to the west. This lord was not one of the best looking men and he'd decided to marry one of the most beautiful women in a rival family. He was tired of the fighting and figured if he could marry her that the fighting would stop.

He stripped the leather robe off and donned his best white velvet robe. It was trimmed in white rabbit fur and decorated with silver stars that sparkled in the sunlight streaming through the windows. He placed a silver medallion, of a star inside a circle, around his neck. He never wore a hat. He was proud of his long, snow-white hair that hung to his waist. His eyes were an hypnotic sky blue with thick, snow-white brows over them. His nose was of moderate size, sharp but not pointed, and they were flanked by high cheek bones. He had full lips the color of pink roses and other than his eyebrows he had no facial hair. Regardless of what clothes he wore he always wore calf-high, thick leather boots. Each boot had a knife sheathed in them. He was much older than he looked. Early in his career he had developed a potion that prolonged life. Actually, what it did was slow the aging process. He was, after all, human and humans have finite lives. He wanted to live longer than that.

He made sure the door to his laboratory was closed. There was no need for K'orik to know about that. His laboratory was actually above the room he would be meeting K'orik in. The meeting room was not overly elaborate. Bookcases lined a quarter of the room and were filled with books he'd collected over the years. An arched opening, strung with beads and leading to his bedchamber, was between two of the bookcases on the northeast side of the room. A large oaken desk and chair set against the wall underneath a window that looked southeast. To the left of the desk was a case filled with wine bottles and to the right was a cabinet that contained a variety of goblets. A couch set against the wall opposite the desk with small end tables that had a variety of knick knacks on them. There were two windows above the couch that looked out over Castaic Lake. A rectangular oak table, the length of the couch, set in front of the couch and had a large silver bowl in the middle that was filled daily with fresh fruit. Today it contained red apples, nectarines, and green grapes. There were large candles on either side of it. Two chairs set at either end of the table. There were no rugs on the floor, it was bare stone. In the middle of the room was a brazier attached to the floor covered by a sheet of leather that hung to the floor. The door to his laboratory was actually one of the book cases. He opened the windows and, with a wave of his hands, he cleared the room of any lingering odors from his laboratory. He lit a stick of incense, waved it around the room, and set it atop his desk to finish burning. The scent was of roses, one of his favorites. The room was kept clean, like all the rooms in his tower. He was a very fastidious man and he loathed dust, it interfered with his work. He looked around the room to make sure everything was in its place. He was standing in the middle of the room next to the brazier and ready to meet with K'orik.

A knock came at the door and Sarguroth spoke loudly, "Enter."

The door opened and the servant that had brought K'orik up ushered him into the room.

"That'll be all," he said to the servant and waved him away.

The servant bowed and left the room, closing the door and leaving the two of them alone.

"Would you care for some fruit," he indicated the bowl on the table, "or a goblet of wine?" he indicated the case of wine bottles. "Or do you want to just get right down to business?"

K'orik headed for one of the chairs and sat down. "A goblet of wine will do to start."

"Red, white, or somewhere between?"

"Red, of course."

"Of course," he said with a smile. As he prepared the goblets of wine he asked, "So, what brings you here today, K'orik?"

"I need some information and I believe that you can obtain it for me."

Sarguroth walked across the room and handed K'orik his goblet of wine, then sat down in the other chair. "What is this information you need that only I can obtain?"

"I need to know where Ogiloth is."

"Ahh, Ogiloth. He's the commander of your army, isn't he?"

"Yes. I've sent him on a mission and I haven't heard from him since. He's been gone a week now and I'm getting concerned that something may have happened."

"And what makes you think I have the ability to find him?"

"You're a sorcerer, damn it." K'orik was beginning to get irritated. "You must have some way of doing that."

Sarguroth could see that he had pushed K'orik to the edge with his idle chit chat and decided to back off before things got out of hand. K'orik was quick to anger and, from past experience he didn't want to push him over the edge. He'd been around when K'orik and J'eren had battled it out. He witnessed the light show they'd put on. He was friends with J'eren before K'orik came into the picture. J'eren had helped him build his tower. He knew what J'eren was and he knew what K'orik was. He also knew how K'orik could be, especially when he didn't get his way.

He took a drink of his wine and set the goblet on the table. "Straight to business then."

He stood up and walked over to the brazier. He removed the sheet of leather and hung it on the back of the chair at the desk. The kettle setting on the brazier was already filled with water. He always kept it filled because he used it often to keep an eye on things. He lit the coals in the brazier.

"It'll take a few minutes for the water to heat so why don't we relax and enjoy our wine while we wait." Sarguroth returned to his chair. He picked up a bunch of grapes and started popping them in his mouth. "So, what is this mission you sent Ogiloth on?" he asked in between grapes.

"I don't think that's any of your concern."

"Fair enough," he conceded. "How's the weather been at your place?" He tried to be civil but he could see that it wasn't going to be easy. "I thought that last big storm that came through was going to drop some snow here."

"You know I don't care much for cold weather, Sarguroth. That storm was miserable."

Sarguroth heard the water beginning to bubble. He was relieved. He popped the last grape into his mouth, took a drink of wine, stood up, and walked over to the brazier. K'orik got up and followed him. With a wave of his hands the coals went out. He slid a lid over them closing them off. With another wave of his hands the little bit of smoke there was dissipated. The water was really starting to bubble now. He walked over to his desk and picked up a bag. Inside the bag was the special dust he sprinkled in the water which allowed him to use the water as a looking glass of sorts. He walked back to the bubbling water, took a pinch of the dust, and sprinkled it over the middle of the kettle of bubbling water. The dust instantly started spreading out in a perfect circle. As the dust circle spread, the water stopped bubbling and developed a glass-like smoothness. With an image of Ogiloth in his mind he waved his hands over the kettle of water. As they watched an image of mountains began to appear on the surface of the water. At first it was from high above as if they were flying and looking down on it. Near the edges they could see what looked like a body of water, a forest, and a desert. They decided those must be Lake Wishik, Murwood Forest, and the Great Desert. They had to be looking at the southern end of the Castaic Mountains. Then the image began to swoop down getting closer to the mountains and trees started appearing. As it got closer they could make out bodies moving through the trees. They could tell they were moving west. Then the image began to circle around as it got even closer. Ogiloth could be made out now. He was leading the group. The image circled all the way around and centered Ogiloth's face in the kettle. Then it zoomed in on his face and the image dissolved leaving nothing but K'orik and Sarguroth looking at their reflections.

"How old is this image?" K'orik asked.

"The image is of Ogiloth right now."

"He must have lost three of his warriors. I only counted seven besides Ogiloth. Something has happened. And why would he be in the mountains at the southern end of the Castaics? Something is wrong."

"I'm afraid I can't help you with any of that."

"Can you do this again with someone else?" K'orik asked hopefully.

"Only if I've seen the person with my own eyes. Who is it?"

"You haven't ever seen this person." He turned away from the brazier disappointedly. "I have to go now," he said abruptly.

"What about payment for my services?"

"What is it you want?"

"Who is it you're looking for?"

K'orik jerked his head around and looked at Sarguroth with a glare. "Why do you want to know?"

Sarguroth stepped back a little. "No particular reason. Curiosity I guess."

K'orik looked hard at him and decided it would be of no consequence if he knew who he was looking for. "My son," he said slowly.

Sarguroth stepped back a little more with a stunned look. "You have a son?"

"Yes, I have a son. Is that so hard to believe?"

"No," he half stuttered. "I just never knew. How old is he?"

"Now you're asking too many questions," he snapped. "I gave you your payment. Now I must go." He headed towards the door to leave.

"It's been nice visiting with you K'orik. Come back again soon."

K'orik just grumbled and waved a hand at him as he shut the door behind him. Sarguroth rushed to the top of his tower, which was just above his laboratory, to watch as K'orik rode away. "I don't like that man at all," he mumbled to himself.

# CHAPTER 21

J OICE ROUSED JAKE from sleep about mid-afternoon and he spent the rest of the day doing business for the inn. She prepared him a full course meal for dinner so he could energize himself for the evening. While he was eating she sat and talked with him about his plans.

"I'm assuming that you're going to use the clearing you found near the mining road for a while instead of our usual location."

"For now I think that would be the wise choice. I know there's more of a chance that Durog, or whoever he has watching us, will see me but that's the chance I'll have to take. I'll be careful."

"I've prepared a meal for the kids to take with you. They should be close to running out of food, especially with the appetite J'orik has." They both chuckled at that.

"It's a little bit more of a walk the way I have to go now so I should be getting ready to leave. I don't want to be in the air until it's dark. I don't want to take the chance that Ogiloth will see me. I'll be looking for him so that I can watch his progress though."

"Do you think there's a possibility he'll find where the kids are?"

"Eventually he's going to find them but it won't be because he saw me. I think from now on I'll fly around to the west side of the mountain and walk up through the tunnel."

"Won't that take you even longer?"

"What choice do I have? I can't lead him to them." He sounded frustrated. "I need to get going, dear."

"You know, there's always the option of taking them far away. Maybe Jerome or Janice will take them in."

"I can't burden our kids with this. Besides, neither one can tutor J'orik. We can discuss this more tomorrow. I have to go now."

They both stood up and gave each other a kiss. She handed him the bag with the kids' meal in it. He left through the back door again, being careful that he didn't see anyone. He headed south down the alley and skirted the south side of town until he got past the dwarves' section and then headed northwest across the foothills towards the mining road. After reaching the road he headed up into the mountains to the clearing he'd found. The sun had gone down behind the mountaintops and it was dark by the time he got there. Most of the traffic on the mining road was during the day so that wasn't a concern for him. He checked to make sure he was alone and then changed into a dragon. He took off and didn't see anyone as he gained altitude. He flew due west and about half way to the cave he noticed smoke curling up out of the trees. *That has to be Ogiloth and his group*, he thought to himself. He flew over the top of the mountains, swung south, and dropped down when he spotted the waterfall coming out of the mountainside. He spotted a clearing about fifty yards from the tunnel entrance he was looking for and landed. He walked to the entrance, lit a torch, and began the trek into the mountain. Since he was alone he moved much faster and was able to cut the time into half of what it took when he was with J'orik and Lianna. Once inside the cavern he crossed it to the tunnel leading to the cave. He extinguished the torch, changed form, flew up to the next tunnel opening, and made that tricky landing on the ledge he'd shown the kids the night before. He lit the torch there and walked the short distance up that tunnel to their cave. When he stepped out into the cave the kids weren't there. He figured they were out on the ledge waiting for him. They were probably wondering where he was. He was later getting there than last night. He set the bag containing the meal Joice had prepared on the floor next to the fire pit and headed out the tunnel. He extinguished the torch before he got to the ledge. As he walked out onto the ledge he didn't see either one of the kids.

"It's just Jake," J'orik sounded relieved.

Jake jumped a little as he turned and saw them against the wall. They both giggled.

"Did we startle you?" Lianna asked him, still giggling.

"Yes, you did. I didn't see you anywhere in the cave so I expected to find you out here waiting for me."

"We were out here waiting for you," she told him, "but we both heard you coming up the tunnel. Since we weren't expecting you from that direction we weren't sure who it was so we got up against the wall."

"Why didn't you come in the front here?" J'orik asked.

"With Ogiloth and his group coming this way I didn't want them to see me so I flew around the other side of the mountain and came in the back way. Sorry I'm late."

"It's all right, Jake," Lianna said. "We did notice some smoke curling up out of the trees off in the distance. Other than that we were just out here enjoying the night sky together. It's beautiful, don't you agree?"

"Yes, it is." He looked up and sighed. "Joice sent me with a fresh meal for you. I left it back in the cave next to the fire pit. Let's go in and talk while you eat."

J'orik didn't hesitate. He started into the tunnel ahead of both of them. About ten yards in Jake relit the torch he was carrying so they could see the rest of their way in. Once in the cave he lit the fire pit, extinguished the torch, and sat down to watch them eat. J'orik reminded him of himself with that ravenous appetite. He couldn't wait to see him eat once they started the tutoring. He would probably need twice the amount of food.

"So, did you have another relaxing day?"

J'orik just shook his head up and down while devouring his food.

Lianna was a little more bird-like with her eating habits and responded, "We went back down to the other cavern and did some exploring there."

"You didn't attempt to explore any of the tunnels did you?"

"No, we were good kids. We remembered what you said and just hung out in the cavern. The water in the lake is ice cold."

"Yes. It comes straight out of the core of the mountain. Did you see where it bubbles up?"

"We saw a couple spots where it looked like it was bubbling."

J'orik belched loud, which was a sign that he was done eating. Jake seemed to expect it but Lianna was still appalled.

He looked over at J'orik. "Sounds like we're ready to start some tutoring?"

Lianna giggled. "I'm ready too."

All three stood up and made their way over to the tunnel leading down to the larger cavern. Jake lit the torch and they made their way down. J'orik and Lianna were no longer surprised by the way Jake lit the torches. Lianna, however, was still awed by the way he would leap off the ledge and instantly change his form. She couldn't wait until she was able to do the same.

After J'orik and Lianna climbed down to the floor of the cavern Jake asked, "Who's going to start first?"

J'orik, being the gentleman that he always was to Lianna, indicated that she should start.

"Okay then," Jake began, "the first thing you need to do is provide yourself with enough room as if you were actually going to change form."

Lianna moved away from Jake and J'orik.

"Good," he continued. "Now you need to work on learning how to shut out the sounds and images around you. See an image in your mind of the form you will be changing into and focus on that image. You've seen what Joice and I look like so just imagine you're one of us. You need to focus. At first it helps to close your eyes. You should also try to control your breathing. Close your mouth and take slow, even breathes through your nose."

She did as he said. She closed her eyes and got an image of Joice in her mind. She closed her mouth and concentrated on her breathing.

Jake continued speaking only with a calm, easy, and even tone. "Focus. Breathe slow and even. See the image."

He kept repeating this mantra over and over. Her breathing became more even and her body visibly seemed to relax. She appeared almost serene and at peace. Jake kept repeating the mantra.

She fell deeper and deeper within herself. The only sound she heard was Jake's voice and that seemed to be getting further and further away. She could see herself as a dragon, flying through the air, the wind in her face, her wings pumping up and down. She felt free.

Jake stopped speaking and he and J'orik watched as she smiled and her arms began to move up and down slowly. She was leaning forward slightly and her hair and dress were fluttering as if in a wind. Jake was surprised at how quickly she was able to fall into this trance-like state. He could tell she thought she was flying. He let her continue like this for a while before attempting to bring her back down.

"Lianna?" he spoke loud but gentle. "Lianna?" He had to say her name several more times before he saw that she responded. "It's time to come back now." She got a look of disappointment on her face but he continued anyway. "Come back," he began repeating over and over.

Her hair and dress slowly stopped fluttering and her arms came back down to her side as she stood straight. The look of peace slowly faded from her face and she opened her eyes. She looked around at Jake and J'orik.

"That was wonderful," she said with a deep breath and a smile on her face. "I want to do that again."

"You will," Jake told her. "This is just the first step, 'imagining' what you will become. The more you practice this, the sooner physical changes will start happening. It's okay to practice this without a tutor but remember, if anything other than what you were feeling in your mind begins to happen, you need to stop and wait for more tutoring. When that happens you'll be ready to move on to the second step." Then he turned to J'orik. "It's your turn now. Are you ready?"

"As ready as I'll ever be," he replied.

"Okay. All the same things I told Lianna apply to you also. The only part that might be a little more difficult is that you've never seen a phoenix. Am I right?"

"Yes."

"You already know what it's like to fly, just like Lianna knew. You've been on Joice's back when she was a dragon and flew you up here. The hard part will be imagining you're a phoenix, having never seen one. What I'm going to do is help you develop that image by using things you're already familiar with. First things first though." Then he turned his attention to Lianna. "Working with J'orik is a little different than with you. You won't be able to stand idly by and watch. J'orik, being a creature of fire, might possibly emanate some heat and that heat might be more than your human form can withstand. I don't want you to get hurt. You'll need to be far enough behind me so that I can change and create a barrier between you and J'orik if necessary. This will be the case, *at all times*, whenever J'orik is practicing. And, if I'm not here, it would be best if you got no closer than the ledge up there."

He pointed to the ledge for the opening leading back to their cave. Then he stressed, "This is important, all right?"

She nodded her assent and did as he said.

He turned his attention back to J'orik, who had moved to where Lianna had been standing when she was being tutored. "Okay, J'orik, are you ready?" J'orik indicated he was. "You know what a hawk looks like?" He nodded he did. "You also know what a fire looks like, right?" Again he nodded he did. "Do you think you can imagine a hawk *emanating* fire from its body? Not being *on* fire but *emanating* flames from its body?"

"I can give it my best shot," he replied.

"Just like I did with Lianna you need to work on learning how to shut out the sounds and images around you. See an image in your mind of the form you will be changing into and focus on that image, in this case the hawk emanating flames from its body. You need to focus. Again, it helps to close your eyes. Try to control your breathing. Close your mouth and take slow, even breathes through your nose."

He did as Jake said. He closed her eyes and imagined a hawk emanating flames. He closed his mouth and concentrated on his breathing.

Jake continued speaking only with a calm, easy, and even tone. "Focus. Breathe slow and even. See the image." He kept repeating this mantra over and over like he did with Lianna.

His breathing became more even and his body visibly seemed to relax. Jake kept repeating the mantra.

J'orik fell deeper and deeper within himself. The only sound he heard was Jake's voice which seemed to be getting further and further away. He could see himself as the hawk, flying through the air, the wind in his face, his wings pumping up and down. He felt, heat. His eyes snapped open and he saw Jake in front of him, only he was in dragon form. He felt hot and his body was drenched in sweat. "What happened?" he asked with a concerned look.

Jake changed back to human form. "That was incredible," he said wide-eyed. "I've never seen that happen before."

Again J'orik asked, "What happened?"

"You changed form, J'orik."

"What do you mean 'I changed form'? You said it would take time for that to happen."

"No. I said it would take time for it to happen instantly, with little thought. I never expected you to change form on your first attempt."

"You were beautiful, J'orik," Lianna said as she stepped out from behind Jake.

"Yes," Jake said. "It was an awesome sight to behold."

"What did I look like?"

"I only caught a glimpse of you before you disappeared behind Jake, but you were almost as big as Joice's dragon form," Lianna began describing. "Mostly red but there were hints of orange, yellow, white and even blue. The only thing I've ever seen close to it is when we saw Joice for the first time. The whole cavern seemed to light up too."

"What does this mean, Jake?" J'orik looked at him imploringly.

"On the surface it means you're past the first step and ready to move on to the second step in the process. But as for the underlying meaning, I can only guess."

"Well, guess," J'orik urged.

"I would say that your father, or anyone else for that matter, should be careful and never make you angry," he laughed. "I would even venture to say that you'll become one of the strongest and most powerful phoenixes in existence. And as for you, young lady," he looked at Lianna, "you shouldn't be around when he's practicing, at least until we find out if you're the type of dragon that can withstand the heat, even then, not until you can observe while in your changed form."

"So, what's the next step?" he asked Jake.

"Learning to not fear the change, holding the form, and making the change faster. It was apparent something frightened you. What was it?"

"I thought I was on fire."

"You were. That's why you need to learn not to fear it." Then he looked at both of them. "I think that's enough for tonight. I need to start heading home. Going the back way takes a little longer and I need to make sure I'm not seen. I don't want you to practice, J'orik, unless I'm here. I don't think it's a good idea right now. Lianna, you can practice all you want, just remember what I said. I'm going to leave from here, so I'll see you kids tomorrow night." He shook J'orik's hand and kissed Lianna on the forehead. Then he headed towards the other side of the cavern. They both watched him go until the torchlight disappeared in the tunnel. They climbed back up the rope and made their way back to the cave.

Jake quickly made his way through the tunnel and out the back side of the mountain. He walked down to the clearing he had found, changed into dragon form, and took off. The whole time he thought about the tutoring session. He was amazed at how quickly both of them picked up on the process, especially J'orik. He certainly didn't expect either one of them to make the change on the first attempt. He considered the possibilities and the implications of J'orik's ability to make the change so soon. He'd never heard of anyone in the history of their kind doing what J'orik did. He would have to discuss this with Joice and get her opinion.

He cleared the top of the mountain and continued gaining altitude as he headed east towards town. From this height he could see the glow on the horizon as the sun was beginning to rise behind the Dorguri Mountains. Glancing down, he saw smoke curling up out of the trees in the same place it was on his way in. *At least they don't travel during the night*, he thought to himself.

He landed in the clearing near the mining road, changed into human form, and walked back to town. He didn't notice them, but Cory and Lance both saw him coming back into town.

# CHAPTER 22

J ACK ERENSON OWNED and operated the largest warehouse used for storing the ores mined in the Castaic Mountains by the dwarves. He owned an assay house, a tailor shop, and a restaurant, all of them preceded by his last name. He also owned the Boars' Den, a local pub frequented by dwarves, and the Tigress Inn, which also had a restaurant. He was considered to be one of the wealthiest men in Bruston. Everyone knew him and everyone liked him. To see him walking down the sidewalk, though, you wouldn't be able to tell he had such wealth, he didn't dress the part. He dressed more like a warehouseman, which is where he spent most of his time. He wore a blue long-sleeved, button-up cotton shirt, usually keeping the sleeves rolled up to his elbows, and a dark brown leather vest. His pants were heavy cotton and full-length held up by a black leather belt. The belt buckle was made from silver and embossed with the image of a unicorn. His last name was engraved across the top of it. He wore soft-soled, brown leather boots stamped with the same unicorn image that was on his belt buckle. Each boot had a hardened steel knife sheathed in the side. The handle of each knife was plated with gold and silver and the image of a unicorn was emblazoned on each blade. On his head he wore a black suede wide-brimmed hat with a brown leather band around it stamped with the same unicorn image. Since he was primarily in the ore business he wore three rings on each hand made from gold and silver and encrusted with diamonds, rubies, and emeralds. The rings were the only things he wore that indicated he might have some wealth. He was well-built and strong from hard work in the warehouse. He wasn't afraid to get down on the floor with the men that worked for him. His hair was coal black and neatly trimmed. He had sharp facial features but no facial hair. His eyes were an hypnotic pale green and captured the attention of anyone that looked at him.

He had lived in Bruston for so long that no one knew where he came from. He was a single man and had no family in town. He spent most of his time in his warehouse, which was located on the east side of town just as the road from Washoe entered. It set between the road and the lake. Once a week he would leave the warehouse to check on his other businesses. They were all on the east side of the main road and he would stop at each one on his way through town spending time talking with the managers and employees and finally ending up at the Tigress Inn. His inn was directly across the street from the Dragons' Inn. He would have an early lunch at the inn's restaurant while having casual conversation with some of the patrons. Afterwards he would cross the street, stop in to say good afternoon to the owners of the Dragons' Inn, and then start back up the street towards the north end of town.

He would stop at the Sweet Shoppe and buy three large lollipops which he gave to Clare at the sheriff's office when he stopped in there. The lollipops were for Clare's three children and he stopped to talk with the sheriff if he was in. He had an ulterior motive for keeping in touch with the sheriff. Owning several businesses in town he wanted to be on the sheriff's best side hoping that it would encourage him to keep a closer eye on his businesses.

After leaving the sheriff's office he would walk over into the dwarves' section of town and visit his old friend Durog. Jack had a long history with him. Durog was the chief of mining operations for the dwarves in the Castaic Mountains when Jack first started his warehouse business in Bruston. He had helped Jack build his business by directing most, if not all, of the ore shipments through his warehouse. Even after Durog retired, most of the shipments still came through his warehouse. By then, though, he had already started the other businesses in town, including the Boars' Den, which he started specifically to service the dwarves. He considered it a gesture of friendship for all the business they had directed his way.

This particular day, though, he heard several interesting pieces of information that not only grabbed his attention but brought back a flood of old memories. His visit with Durog at the end of the day just seemed to tie all of it together.

The first thing he heard was when he visited the Boars' Den. After spending time with the manager and employees he saw Owen, a good friend of Durog's, as he was making his way out. He decided to sit and have a pint with the old codger.

"Owen. Mind if I have a seat?" He sat down without waiting for an answer.

Owen looked up at him. "Jack, how ya be? Sure, have a seat, and a pint."

Before Jack even had a chance to wave the waitress over, she showed up with a pint and set it down in front of him.

"Now that be what I call service," Owen said, eyeing the waitress. "But I guess when ye own tha place that be what happens."

"How ya been old man?"

"I been well. An' yerself?"

"Things have been very good for me. Your friends in the mountains keep bringing me business. Have you seen your old friend Durog lately?"

"Funny ye should mention'm. He was in here jes' th'other day."

"Really, did you two have a good talk?"

"Din't really talk much. He seemed a bit preoccupied ta me. Din't even finish his pint. He got up, said his goodbye, an' walked outta tha place in a hurry-like."

"Really?"

"Yeah. I watched'm fer a while. He walked down a ways, seemed ta be lookin' fer somethin'. Musta seen what he was a lookin' fer cuz he came walkin' back by an' I watched'm head back up tha street. Musta been headin' home I guess."

"That's interesting. Well, I'm out on my weekly visit with my businesses and I have one more to go." He downed the rest of the pint. "You take care." He smiled and patted Owen on the shoulder as he stood up. "I'll see you next week when I come through and we'll sit and have two pints, I'm buying."

Owen smiled at that. "Sounds good ta me." He raised the pint he had and drank down the last of it. He turned and waved the mug in the air for the waitress to see, indicating he needed another one.

Jack left the Boars' Den and continued his walk down to the Tigress Inn for his early lunch. He stepped through the inn's front door and into the entry area. Harold Jane, the innkeeper, was behind the front counter and greeted him with a big smile.

"Good to see you Jack. You must be making your weekly visit into town."

"Yes I am, Harry. It's good to see you too. How's business doing?"

"It's doing very good. The rooms are staying full and people are coming in to eat."

"That's what I like to hear. What's the special on the lunch menu today?"

"Katy has a couple things she's put together. Go on in and have a seat, I'll let her know you're here."

"Thanks Harry."

Harry went back into the kitchen to tell Katy that he was there and taking a seat in the dining room. He made his way in and found a table next to the window so he could look out onto the street. He liked watching the people and all the activity that went on in town. He was gazing out the window when Katy walked up to the table.

"Jack. How nice to see you again. Harry tells me you were asking about today's lunch specials."

"Yes. He said you had a couple things prepared. Which one would you suggest? Oh, and it's good to see you again too Katy." He smiled up at her.

"My choice would be the fruit and spinach salad."

"Mmm. Tell me more."

"It's a bed of spinach leaves topped with blueberries, strawberries, caramelized pecans, and sliced grilled chicken breast. Then we drizzle a strawberry, balsamic vinaigrette over it and serve it with a cinnamon-carrot muffin."

"Sounds deliciously wonderful. You have me convinced."

"What would you like to drink with that?"

"I'll just have a strong cup of coffee please."

"Okay. I'll get your coffee right now and then get that salad made."

She came right back with the coffee then turned around and went back into the kitchen. Jack took a sip of the coffee and continued gazing out the window. He kept wondering what Durog had been up to the other day. He would have to make a point of asking him about it when he got to his place for his weekly visit. He was lost in thought when Katy returned with his salad.

"Here you go Jack. And the muffin is hot out of the oven."

"Looks fabulous Katy," he complimented her. Taking a big sniff he said, "Smells wonderful too."

She smiled and then walked away.

He ate slowly as he watched outside. The salad was delicious and he ate every last bit of it, as well as the muffin. After what Owen had told him about Durog he didn't feel much like mingling with the patrons like he usually did. As he was finishing the last of the muffin Katy came to his table.

"What did you think?"

"I thought it was delicious. You need to keep this on the menu."

"I'll do that. Was there anything else?"

"No. I think I'm done," he told her as he took the last drink of his coffee.

She picked up his empty platter and coffee cup. "It was good seeing you again Jack." She walked away.

He stood up wiping his mouth with his napkin and proceeded out of the dining room. He stopped at the front counter to speak with Harry before he left.

"Harry. You haven't heard of anything unusual going on in town, have you?"

"Nope. Why do you ask?"

"No reason in particular. You know me. I spend all my time in the warehouse. I don't get out much except when I make my weekly trips into town."

"It's business as usual around here, Jack."

"Okay. Well I'll see you next week then." He smiled and waved at Harry as he went out the door.

He stepped up to the rail in front of the inn and stood there for a while watching the townspeople go about their business. Delivery wagons were rolling up and down the street bringing goods from the warehouses to the local businesses. The sky was a bright blue with a few wispy clouds. The sun hadn't quite reached midday yet but it was starting to warm up. He decided it was time to roll up his shirt sleeves. There was a slight breeze blowing from the south, not enough to blow the dust around, but enough to make the day comfortable. He looked over at the Dragons' Inn, his next stop for the day, and crossed the street. Jake and Joice were a nice couple. He enjoyed stopping by their inn and chatting about the inn business. Mostly it was to check on the competition. The other inns in town seemed to do all right but his and theirs always attracted more business, probably because theirs were the only inns with restaurants attached. He walked through the front door expecting to be greeted by Jake, but he saw that Gerard was behind the counter today. Gerard was a nice fellow, he was also very handy. Jack would sometimes hire him to do repairs around his inn when things needed repairing. It worked out good for Harry too because he was always right across the street. Gerard glanced up and saw Jack walking through the door.

"Good morning, Mr. Erenson. I see you're on your weekly rounds. How are you today?"

"I'm doing well, Gerard, thanks for asking. Where's Jake today?"

"Oh, he's still asleep. He's been out late the last couple of nights."

"Really, what's the old man been up to?"

Gerard didn't get a chance to answer. Joice stepped out from the dining room. "Good morning, Jack."

Jack turned to greet Joice with a smile. "Good morning to you Joice. You look ravishing today, as always."

Even though she was standing there wiping her hands on her apron, which had a few food stains on it, he always thought she had a glow about her, and to him she did, he could actually see it. They knew about each other, of course, which was another reason he would stop in and visit with them. He liked the company of his own kind more.

"Would you care to sit and chat over a cup of coffee? I have a few minutes to spare."

"Actually, I was hoping to talk with Jake about a business matter we discussed a few weeks back," he lied, "but I see that he's 'indisposed' at the moment."

"Yes, he's been staying up late the last few nights going over the books," she lied. "He does this every year and it usually takes him about a week to finish. Are you sure you don't want to have a cup of coffee? I'll be getting him up soon."

"No, that's all right. What I need to talk with him about isn't that important. It can wait until I come in next week. I need to get going anyway, finish up business in town before I head back to the warehouse."

"Okay. I'll let him know you were here. Have a nice day." She smiled and headed back into the kitchen.

"Well, Gerard, you have a nice day and maybe I'll see you next week."

"You have a nice day too Mr. Erenson."

They waved good–bye to each other as Jack headed back out onto the sidewalk.

*Something's going on here*, he was thinking to himself as he walked up the sidewalk. *She lied to me, I could feel it. But then I lied to her too. I wonder what Jake is up to. And Durog, Owen said he was acting peculiar, preoccupied he said. Well, that's something I can discuss with him when I get to his place.* He was in front of the Sweet Shoppe now and he stepped in to get the lollipops for Clare's children. Leaving the Sweet Shoppe, he continued his walk. He got to the sheriff's office and walked in with a big smile already on his face.

He held up the lollipops and greeted Clare. "Good morning Clare."

Clare looked up and saw Jack standing there with the lollipops. "Good morning Mr. Erenson," she smiled back. "Out on your weekly rounds I see."

"Am I that predictable?" he chuckled. "I don't see the sheriff, or his deputies. They must be out and about keeping the peace in town." He handed her the lollipops. "As always, I brought some treats for your children. Another predictable thing I do, I suppose."

"Yes, it is. But the kids so look forward to getting their weekly treat from Mr. Erenson. How's your morning been?"

"It's a beautiful day, perfect day for a walk. Oh, if you get a chance, you need to stop in at the Tigress. Katy has put together the most wonderful salad. It's heaven on a platter."

"Really?" her eyebrows lifted. "I'll have to take the family in there and try it out."

"So, besides Katy's new salad, is there anything else new happening in town?" he asked casually.

"Let's see," she thought for a moment. "Other than a couple new arrivals in town, no."

"New arrivals in town? Business? Pleasure? Did you send them to the Tigress?"

"Actually, their story is quite sad. Have you heard about all the villages that have been attacked lately?"

"You know, I've heard bits and pieces."

"Well, theirs was attacked about a week ago and they were the only ones to survive. A man and a woman named J'orik and Lianna, real nice couple. I sent them down the street and I believe they ended up at the Dragons' Inn."

"That is sad. No one should have to go through something like that. You should have sent them to the Tigress, I'm sure Harry and Katy would have set them up, especially if they knew what happened." Then, without giving Clare a chance to interject, "Well, gotta go. Give your kids my best and I'll see you next week." He turned and headed for the door.

"Thanks again for the lollipops," she was able to say before he shut the door.

He started walking towards Durog's house and thinking about all he had heard today. *Why did Joice and Clare lie to me? They must know I knew they were lying. And Durog, why would he be acting so peculiar? Something's going on here they don't want to tell me about. And this name J'orik, it sounds so familiar.* He had reached the north end of town where all the warehouses were and turned to leave the main street and head into the dwarves section of town. *That's it, K'orik, I haven't thought about him for years. I wonder if this J'orik fellow is related to him somehow and what would it have to do with all these villages being attacked? Maybe when I get to Durog's and talk with him, he might be able to help.* He was so deep in thought that he almost passed Durog's house.

He stood at the end of the walk for a moment breathing in the aroma of all the flowers that were blossoming in Durog's yard. He remembered Durog's wife and how she'd kept flowers and saw that Durog was keeping them up. He figured that he was doing it in remembrance and maybe just so that he could feel close to her. He came out of his reverie, walked up to the door, and knocked.

"Who be there?" Jack heard Durog's voice through the kitchen window.

He stepped back and looked through the window and saw Durog heading towards the door. "It be yer good friend Jack." He liked trying to emulate Durog's speech. He thought it helped keep them closer.

The door swung open and Durog stood there with a huge smile. "Me good friend Jack, come in." he stepped aside and let him enter. "How ye be taday me friend?"

"I be well. And how might ye be taday Durog, me friend?"

"I be well too," he answered. "Have a seat on tha couch there an' I be right with ya." Durog went back into the kitchen while Jack took a seat on the couch. "I be bakin' some o' me wife's special berry muffins. Want one?" he hollered from the kitchen.

"Yeah, 'course I be wantin' one." Jack hollered back. "Care fer a game o' chess ole man?"

"Course, I thought that be why ye was here."

"Ya know that not be tha only reason I come ta visit ya. Don't care what others say, I like yer comp'ny."

Durog was coming down the hallway with a platter full of steaming muffins. "Whadaya mean 'what others say'? They be sayin' things 'bout me?" he chuckled as he set the platter of muffins on the table.

Jack just chuckled back as he reached under the table and pulled the chess game out.

Durog slid his chair over in front of the table. "Wanna cup o' me mud?"

"Sure, it probly go good with tha muffins."

Jack began setting up the pieces as Durog went to get coffee for the two of them.

"Had a talk with our good friend Owen at tha Boars' Den when I stopped in there earlier taday."

Durog set the cups of coffee down and sat in his chair. "Yeah, wud he hafta say?"

"Not much, jes that ye was actin' mighty peculiar th'other day when ye was in there."

"Me thinks Owen drinks a bit too much. Me thinks Owen *lives* at tha Boars' Den." He and Jack both laughed hard at that.

Jack had the chess pieces all set up and took the first move. The ritual was that whoever set up the pieces got the first move.

"Okay, I be givin' ya a heads up here. Me nephew was here th'other day an' spent a couple days. He plays a mean game an' he showed me a thing or two. So I'm a warnin' ya, watch yer moves."

"Which nephew this be?"

"Ogiloth. He be me favorite nephew."

"Ogiloth." Jack was thoughtful for a moment. "He be the one that be half an' half?"

"That be him, big boy but nice as cud be. Tha only thing I don't like 'bout'm be his work."

"Why, what's he do?"

"He works fer that no-good K'orik fella up north."

Jack tried not to show his emotions when Durog mentioned K'orik's name. Everything he'd heard today seemed to be coming together and he didn't like the sound of any of it. He needed to be careful how he proceeded with the conversation. He didn't want Durog to think he was being too nosy about his business, but he needed to find out more.

"Who be this K'orik fella? Sounds like ye don't like'm."

Jack wasn't sure what it was, the way he asked the question, how Durog felt about his nephew working for K'orik, the smell of his wife's special berry muffins, their relationship, or maybe he just needed to tell someone about it. Whatever it was, Durog opened up and told him everything that had happened. Durog was so distracted by telling his story that by the time he was done Jack looked up at him and said, "Checkmate."

"Dern ye," Durog grumbled. "Ye took advantage o' me."

Jack started laughing to help break the tension and Durog joined in. They set up the pieces for another game. They played four games that afternoon while talking about everything except the story Durog had conveyed. They each won two games making them even for the day. There was nothing but crumbs left on the platter when Jack said he needed to get going. He thanked Durog for the games and the muffins and said he would see him again the next week.

The sun was getting low in the sky when Jack walked away from Durog's house. He enjoyed spending time with his old friend and looked forward to seeing him again the following week. Walking down the street towards his warehouse he kept thinking about the story Durog had told him. He was wondering if maybe it was time for him to start interfering with K'orik's life. Now that he knew J'orik was K'orik's son and that K'orik was looking for him, if he played his cards right he might be able to turn this to his advantage. The key seemed to be Jake and Joice. Somehow they were helping J'orik. He decided he needed to keep an eye on them, so instead of going back to his warehouse he turned down the alley that led to the backside of the Dragons' Inn, made sure no one was watching, and changed into a cat. He headed towards the Dragons' Inn planning on sneaking in to watch Jake and Joice.

As he neared the inn he saw a couple other cats rummaging through the trash. It was starting to get dim in the alley with night coming on. The back door of the inn opened. He quickly started poking around in the nearest trash container so he would look more like a normal cat. Jake poked his head out and looked up and down the alley. Seeing only the cats, he stepped out and started walking south down the alley. He was obviously acting like he didn't want to be seen. Jack waited until Jake had turned out of the alley. He looked around, again to be sure no one was watching, and he turned into a blue jay. He quickly took flight to avoid the cats, which had suddenly turned their attention on him, the bird. He flew to the west because that was the way Jake had turned when he exited the alley. As he gained altitude he noticed two men running along the rooftops. It appeared as if their course would intersect with Jake's. He flew a little higher and was able to spot Jake walking west along the southern edge of town. He watched as the two men climbed down off the rooftop near the south end of an alley just before the dwarves' section of town and fall in behind Jake. They followed him until he left out of the dwarves' section and headed across the foothills in a northwest direction. Jake's course looked like it was going to intersect with the mining road. Jack continued flying around watching both Jake and the two men. It was starting to get too dark for him to be flying around as a blue jay so he decided he would fly into the trees and turn into something with a little bit better night vision. Once on the ground he changed into a wolf. By then Jake had already started walking up the mining road and the two men had started heading for the road to catch up. He figured being a wolf would serve two purposes. He had better night vision and the two men would probably be frightened by him.

He walked through the trees stalking the two men on a parallel course. He wondered how long they would walk in the dark before turning back for town. He thought he would prompt them and at the same time have a little fun.

He growled loud enough that they could hear him. They stopped suddenly, looked at each other, and cocked their heads to listen. He growled again. They looked at each other with frightened looks, turned, and started running back towards town. Jack ran out into the road and started chasing them, growling. He didn't want to bark fearing that Jake would hear him. He chased them all the way back until the tree line stopped and then he stopped. He watched as they ran the rest of the way into town and then he turned back into his human form and started laughing. *That was fun*, he thought to himself as he continued laughing.

He'd gotten so involved in chasing the two men that he'd almost forgotten about Jake. He quickly turned into a hawk and took flight. He knew Jake was going somewhere to change form and he didn't want to miss it when he took off. He knew Jake and Joice were both dragons. He gained altitude as quick as possible while at the same time flying back the direction he'd come. He followed the mining road and it wasn't long before he saw a huge creature lifting up out of the trees. It was too dark to tell for sure but he knew it was no bird, not that size. It had to be Jake. He followed as best he could but he couldn't keep up and he didn't want to change into a dragon himself, afraid he would catch Jake's attention. He watched as Jake flew over the mountaintops and disappeared in the distance. He was about to turn back when he also noticed a bright, fiery light appear from the north and land atop one of the highest peaks. He decided to land on top of the tallest tree and watch for a while to see what would happen next, if anything. Moments later he saw the same bright, fiery light reappear atop the mountain peak. As he watched, it descended into the trees and then it went out. *That must be K'orik,* he thought. *He must have decided to come help Ogiloth with his search. If he was watching he had to have seen Jake.*

He started thinking about what his next move would be as he turned and flew back to his warehouse. Landing on the roof and confirming that he wasn't being watched, he changed back into his human form and climbed down the side of the building. He walked around to the front of the warehouse and entered through the entry door and made his way to his room. He lived in the warehouse. There was a living area and a bedchamber built for him in the upper corner of the building for this purpose. He didn't see any sense in having a home built if he was going to live alone. He spent most of his time at the warehouse anyway.

Walking by his office he thought maybe he should write an anonymous note letting Jake know he was watched by those two men. Sitting at his desk he penned a short note to that affect and decided he would deliver it early in the morning before the sun came up and the town woke up. He folded the note and wrote Jake's name on the outside.

Tomorrow night he would make sure to follow Jake all the way to wherever he went while at the same time keeping an eye out for K'orik. If he spotted those two men again he would make sure to scare them off sooner. Maybe he would change into a bear tomorrow. He laughed to himself as he crawled into bed.

That night he dreamt about K'orik. It was a restless sleep, so restless that he finally decided to just get up. Looking out his window he saw that it was still dark. *Good,* he thought, *maybe now would be a good time to deliver that note. I can't sleep anyway.* He picked up the note off his desk on the way out.

Making his way to the Dragons' Inn would not be easy, it was necessary to cross the open street at least twice and walk up the sidewalk. Then a thought occurred to him. *Why not change into a hawk and carry the note there? I'll be able to see if anyone is about that way and avoid them. Once I'm at the inn I can quickly change into human form, sneak in and leave the note, sneak back out, and fly away as a hawk. Brilliant.* He did exactly that and completed the task without any problems. It made it even easier that no one was at the front counter of the inn when he snuck inside.

Flying above town on his way back to the warehouse he decided to just circle about for a while. He so loved flying. There was such a feeling of serenity and peace about flying. Then he caught a glimpse of a dark, shadowy shape to the south of town flying low and towards Murwood Forest. The sun still hadn't come up yet but there was a glow on the eastern horizon precluding the sun's rise. He watched as the dark shape disappeared into the forest. A few moments later a man appeared out of the forest walking towards town. *That's got to be Jake*, he said to himself. *I'll just watch for a while to be sure.* He continued to circle above town watching the lone figure. The man walked into town and up the alley leading to the Dragons' Inn. Jack didn't see any figures on the rooftops this time. He continued watching and the man did go into the inn. The man had glanced up in his direction a few times so he knew he'd been seen, as a hawk, so he wasn't overly concerned. He knew Jake would get his note soon so he flew back to his warehouse.

# CHAPTER 23

K'ORIK HAD PLENTY of time to think about what he had seen in Sarguroth's brazier as he rode back to his castle. Night had already fallen by the time he got back. There was nothing more he could do right now. He would have to wait until morning. At least he didn't have to stay the night at Sarguroth's. He couldn't take another moment in that man's presence. He would have left anyway, regardless of the time.

He made his way back to his room and changed into his lounging robe. His robe felt less constraining than the clothes he wore when he went out to meet people or show himself in public. His servants had a meal waiting for him in his room when he got there so he sat down to eat after changing. He went to bed early that night and had a restless sleep.

He dreamt about the night he had *taken* Jalana, J'orik's mother. She was not a willing lover but she gave in to him anyway. She knew it was useless to fight with him. He wanted to have a child, a male child, and he would have made as many attempts as necessary to that end. When she finally became pregnant he was anxious to find out if it would be a male child or not. The waiting was interminable. To help take his mind off the wait he had a nursery built in a corner of the castle. He would spend hours helping with the design and layout. Then came the day the child was born. There was nothing that would have kept him from being present at the birth. He needed to see the child born. All his anxiety dissipated when a male child was produced. And then came the day he found out Jalana had run away and taken J'orik with her. He was furious and had destroyed everything in her room. Then came the searching, he had searched relentlessly for a decade before he finally gave up and decided to wait until some piece of evidence came to his attention. It wouldn't be for another decade before he discovered she had been hiding away in some small village in or around Murwood Forest. That's when the destruction of villages began. He didn't care how many villages and people were destroyed and killed. All he wanted was to find his son. He hadn't been with another woman since Jalana and J'orik was his only child. He wanted, needed, to find him.

He woke in a cold sweat. Sunlight was streaming through the windows. He crawled out of bed and walked over to the window. Looking out the window he saw the sun was already halfway across the sky. Angry with himself for oversleeping he turned and practically screamed for a servant. The door immediately opened and one stepped in.

"Bring me some coffee!" he yelled, "the whole pot!"

The servant bowed while backing out and shut the door. Moments later he returned with a pot of coffee and a mug. He came in and set it on the table. "Will that be all, sir?" he asked meekly.

K'orik was sprawled on his couch. He glared at the servant. "Yes. Now leave me." He waved him away.

Just as the servant was closing the door K'orik had a second thought. "Wait." He paused as the servant stopped in mid-stride and spun around. "Have Derek come to my room." Then he waved him away again.

Derek Menderhoff was one of the few humans living in his castle that wasn't considered a servant. He was slight of stature with plain facial features. His hair was a dark brown that hung down below his shoulders. Other than the small moustache he wore, he had no other facial hair. He wore rounded spectacles set in thin wire silver frames. His robe was black velvet trimmed with a multi-colored, hand-width ribbon. His sandals were leather, open-toed, and laced to his knees. On his left hand he wore one gold and silver ring embossed with a phoenix that indicated his status in the castle and was used to stamp approval for all services issued from his office. He had been brought there as an accountant to replace the last man that K'orik had doing the job. The last man had been caught by K'orik embezzling. So that others could see they wouldn't be able to go against K'orik, he was hanged in the courtyard and left hanging for a week. Less than half an hour later Derek was knocking at the door.

"Enter," K'orik yelled.

Derek came in closing the door behind him. He walked over to stand near the table in front of K'orik. "What is it I can do for you, sire?"

"Ogiloth has five lieutenants to help him with the army, one of which he took with him. I'm sure he took the best of the five. Of the four remaining, did Ogiloth indicate which would be best to leave in command during his absence?"

"He did not inform me, sire. It might be better to ask them."

"I need your opinion then, Derek. Which one *appears* to have taken command? I'll never get a straight answer from them. They'll bicker back and forth with each other and I'll never know which one to choose."

"In my opinion, sire, Draiger would be the choice. From what I've observed he seems to be the one that takes control in most instances."

"Thank you. Go find Draiger and the two of you return to my quarters." He waved Derek away.

"As you wish, sire."

Somehow he couldn't help but talk civil with Derek. He had come to trust and like Derek and often used him for advice in matters involving castle operations.

It was almost another half hour before Draiger and Derek returned. Derek knocked at K'orik's door.

"Come in," K'orik yelled.

The two of them entered closing the door behind them. Draiger was larger than most of the other creatures in K'orik's army but not near as imposing as Ogiloth. Standing next to Derek, though, he was an imposing figure.

"I'm leaving today and I'm not sure how long I'll be away. I need someone I can count on to keep control of the daily operations of the castle. This task I'll be leaving to you Derek. Now, Ogiloth obviously trusts you," he turned his attention to Draiger, "otherwise he would not have given you the position you hold. I'm going to trust that he made the right choice and leave you in command of my army during my absence. Is this something you feel you can take on?"

Draiger stood erect with his arms at his sides and a slight grin, "Yes, sir," he snapped with some pride in his voice.

K'orik then looked him straight in the eyes. "Remember, failure in this task is not acceptable."

"I will not fail," he replied with sureness.

"The two of you shall work together to assure that my wishes are upheld. To make things easier for you, gather my army in the courtyard and I will make it clear to them that you have been left in command of them. I will be leaving soon so be quick." He waved Draiger in dismissal. "Now go."

"Yes, sir," he snapped. He left K'orik's room with more pride in his stride than when he entered.

Derek started to turn to leave behind Draiger but K'orik called him back. "Derek, stay a moment." K'orik waited for Draiger to leave the room and close the door before continuing. "You appear to have gained the trust of the castle staff and they seem to come to you for advice on most matters. I don't believe it will be necessary to do with you what I'll be doing for Draiger. He and his kind are more difficult to control and they need someone telling them exactly the way things are to be. You, on the other hand, don't seem to need that help. I can trust that you'll be able to manage things in my absence, correct?"

"I don't think it will be a problem, sire."

"Good. I also want you to keep an eye on Draiger, and his activities, and report on them when I return. I don't plan on being gone more than two or three days so it shouldn't be too much of a problem. Do you have any questions?"

"Shall I have your carriage readied, sire?"

"No, I won't need my carriage on this trip."

"Good enough sire. Is there anything more?"

"No, Derek, you may go."

"Thank you, sire, and have a good journey." Derek turned and left K'orik to himself.

By now it was nearly mid-afternoon. K'orik knew he would need a meal before he left so he summoned the servant back in and told him to have a meal brought to him. It should consist of a whole roasted rabbit, a large serving of mashed potatoes, and three large biscuits smothered in sausage gravy. After ordering his meal he changed out of his robe into his travel clothes. Just as he finished changing there was a knock at his door.

"Enter." The servant with his meal came in. "Leave it on the table."

The servant set the tray on the table and left the room. K'orik made himself comfortable on his couch and ate. After he was finished he rose and made his way to the courtyard. Walking through the main hall he could hear the rabble outside. As he came out the doors and walked out onto the landing of the stairs that led down to the courtyard, Draiger and Derek were both standing there waiting for him. The other three lieutenants were standing at the bottom of the stairs with his army spread out behind them in rank and file awaiting his arrival. As soon as he came out Draiger signaled for the two warriors on either side of the landing to sound their horns. It immediately became quiet. K'orik looked out on his army with a slight smile. Sarguroth had created over five hundred warriors for him. It had cost him much in gold but he felt it was worth every ounce. He stood there silently, looking at them for a few moments before beginning.

He spoke loudly. "I will be leaving for a few days and in my and Ogiloth's absence Draiger," he pointed at him, "will be in command." He glanced down at the other three lieutenants and saw the angry looks on their faces. "I expect there to be no problems and if there are," he paused for a moment, "I will deal with them personally when I return." Then he turned and walked back into the main hall. He indicated for Derek to follow him as Draiger dispersed the army to go back about their usual activities.

Once inside K'orik stopped and turned to Derek. "I need you to have a horse prepared for my departure and brought to the south side of the castle outside the wall, I'll be waiting there. Make sure it's one that knows its way back. Be quick, I want to be gone within half an hour's time."

"As you wish, sire."

Derek left to do as told and K'orik made his way to the south side of the castle.

The sun had already begun its descent behind the mountains when Derek arrived at the south side of the castle. The horse was being led by one of the horsemen. K'orik mounted the horse and made ready to leave.

"Good journey, sire." Derek yelled, waving his hand as K'orik road away. He didn't even look back or respond to the farewell.

K'orik rode for over two hours before he decided he was far enough from the castle to change form and finish the journey by air. He dismounted the horse, turned it around, and slapped it on the rump to send it home. The horse ran off towards the castle.

He knew Ogiloth was somewhere in the southern part of the mountains but he didn't know exactly where. He did know, however, that his trail was pretty much due west of the town of Bruston. He figured that if he flew to the top of one of the mountains in the general area he would be able to spot their location after they stopped to camp and built a fire. He figured that if he flew in with the sun relatively behind him he was likely not to be noticed. He picked one of the higher peaks to land on and wait. He landed as the sun was making its descent below the mountaintops. As the mountains started to overshadow the land east of them he spotted a thin curl of smoke coming up out of the trees. *That has to be them*, he thought to himself. *There can't be others out in the mountains or I would see other signs of smoke*. Feeling confident that this had to be Ogiloth he decided he would change form and fly as close to the treetops as possible, getting close enough to the location he'd spotted before changing back to human form and hiking the rest of the way. He would need to find a large open area to land so as not to ignite any of the trees. Just as he was about to change form, he noticed a large dark form in the sky coming from the east. As he watched it he could tell it was no ordinary bird, it was much larger than that. He continued watching it as it flew over the top of a mountain to the south. The sun hadn't gone down completely on the west side of the mountains yet and as it got to the sun side of the mountain, just before it dropped back down, he got a glimpse of what it was. He was surprised by what he did see. It was a very large red dragon. Then it dropped out of sight. *Ogiloth must have found out that J'orik is somewhere in these mountains, that's why he's out here. That red dragon must be involved somehow*. He was thinking about what he had just seen and was trying to pinpoint the particular mountain the red dragon had dropped down behind. From his vantage point it appeared to be one of the taller peaks and its slopes were more rocky and sheer on the east side, but it was getting dark and he couldn't be sure. He thought it was about time for him to fly down and find Ogiloth and his group. He changed form and began his descent off the mountain peak he was on towards the spiral of smoke he'd spotted coming up out of the trees. Within a few minutes he could make out the light of the fire. He spotted a large enough clearing nearby and landed.

They'd been walking through the mountains for two days now and hadn't seen any sign of the dragon or J'orik. Ogiloth wasn't sure if they were even headed towards the right mountain but, without any other options, he would continue in the direction they were heading. He had an idea of what to be looking for so he was going to stay with that until something better came along.

It had gotten dark and he already had two guards on duty just outside the camp. The rest of them were sitting around the campfire talking casually. Ogiloth was in his tent wrestling with himself about what he should do next when he heard a commotion outside. He opened the flap of his tent just as Olog came running up.

"Sir, there's been a bright, fiery light spotted in the north coming our way." He had a look of concern. "Both guards reported seeing it descend over the mountaintop and dropped down into the trees not two hundred yards from here."

Ogiloth had an idea what, or who, it was. Besides the possibility of it being J'orik, there was only one other person he knew of that would have that appearance. He came out of his tent and walked over near the campfire. Other than Olog and himself the others seemed to be shaking in their boots with fear. With everything that had been happening lately he wasn't surprised. First a dragon and now this bright fiery light, they were rather stupid creatures. Without him and Olog there to hold them together they probably would have already scattered into the trees.

"All right, hold your positions," he commanded in a gruff tone. "Keep your weapons ready but don't attack."

They were all facing north, the direction the light had been seen coming from. He stepped out three paces in front of them placing himself between them and whatever might come through the trees. He figured if he was in front of them they would be less likely to attack without him making the first move.

They stood there quietly for a few minutes before Ogiloth heard a branch snap. He looked in the direction of the sound and saw a shadow moving in the trees.

"Halt," he yelled out. "Who goes there?"

"Ogiloth, is that you?" K'orik spoke out.

Ogiloth recognized the voice as K'orik's. He turned to his warriors. "Stand down. Put your weapons away."

"Yes, have them put their weapons away," K'orik said as he appeared out of the trees. "We wouldn't want anyone hurt now would we?" He had a sarcastic tone in his voice.

"K'orik, what are you doing out here?"

"I might ask you the same question. In fact, I will. What *are* you doing out here?" A wry grin appeared on his face as he waited for an answer.

Ogiloth turned to see what the others were doing. They were all standing there watching him and K'orik and listening to their conversation.

Ogiloth glared at them. "Guards, back on duty," he snapped. "The rest of you, back to whatever it was you were doing."

The guards took off to where they were stationed earlier and the rest did as told.

He started walking back to his tent. "Can we talk about this with a little more privacy?"

"Of course." K'orik followed him into his tent.

His tent had few things in it. His pack in one corner, a bedroll along one wall, and his weapons stood in another corner when he wasn't wearing them. He sat down on his bedroll and offered K'orik a seat at the other end.

"I apologize for the lack of accommodations but when you're hiking out in the woods it's wise not to carry too much weight."

K'orik sat down. "I understand. Now, back to my question, what *are* you doing out here?"

"I'm doing what you asked, looking for J'orik."

"And you think he's out here in the mountains?"

"I know he is. I followed him from his village, to Washoe, to Bruston, and then out here."

"What makes you so sure he's still out here?"

"He's being aided by a dragon and that dragon has made several trips out here. I'm just not sure which mountain it is he's been going to. Whichever one it is, though, is the one where I'll find J'orik."

"A dragon you say?" He asked with a wide smile. "What if I were to tell you I saw a dragon also and that I know which mountain he's going to?"

"I would say, tell me and I'll go get J'orik for you."

"You think it'll be that easy with a dragon around?"

"The dragon isn't always around. He's only around at night."

"Are you sure of this?"

"With the information I've gathered and the dragon's activity I've seen, yes. Plus, why else would he return to the mountain every evening after the sun goes down? Where is he before that?" He paused for a moment and looked K'orik in the eyes. "He's in Bruston," answering his own question.

"What would he be doing in Bruston? There are no dragons in Bruston."

"But there are." Ogiloth stated emphatically. "He's like you. He can change his form. In Bruston he runs an inn." Then he chuckled to himself. "And the inn is called the Dragons' Inn."

"And you know all this for fact?"

"No, I have not seen this with my own eyes but with all I have heard and seen, how could it not be?"

"You've always been a smart one Ogiloth. This is why I chose you. I believe what you're saying to be true. Tomorrow I'll show you which mountain. Chances are, though, since J'orik is being aided by a dragon that he's *inside* the mountain, not on it. We'll need to discover where the entrance is. Now, do you have an extra bedroll?"

He let K'orik have his tent for the night. He used the tent of one of the guards on duty and told him to share with the others.

# CHAPTER 24

J AKE LEFT OUT the back door of the inn again. He didn't pay any attention to the cats rummaging in the trash, they were always there. He was unaware that one of the cats was watching him and that he was also being watched by Cory and Lance. He hadn't seen them hiding on the rooftops. He walked out of town the way he had come in the morning before, planning on going to the clearing he'd found off the mining road. Cory and Lance ran along the rooftops until they came to a spot they could climb down to the ground and continue following Jake. They were unaware they were also being watched by someone that was not only watching them, but someone that had planned on following Jake also. They watched as Jake left town walking across the foothills heading for the mining road. As soon as he disappeared up the road they took off running across the foothills to catch up, they didn't want to lose him.

It was getting dark when they heard the growl just inside the trees off the road. They looked at each other, shrugged their shoulders, and decided it wasn't anything to be concerned about. They continued trying to catch up with Jake and then the growl came again. This time, though, the growl persisted and they could hear branches snapping. Something was running their direction and it sounded big. They didn't wait to see what it was. They didn't want to see what it was. They just turned and started running back towards town. They didn't even look back.

Jake was unaware of all this activity, he just continued up the road until he reached the clearing. He glanced around, didn't see or hear anything, and changed form. He took off and started heading towards the mountain with the cave in it not noticing the hawk that appeared behind him.

Nearing the mountain he was flying for he noticed a bright, fiery light come from the north and land atop the highest peak around. *That must be K'orik come to help Ogiloth*, he thought, *I need to make sure he doesn't see where I land*. He quickly swooped over the mountaintop and down into the trees towards the clearing he'd picked out on the west side of the mountain. On his way down he looked back and saw that the mountains were such that the peak he'd spotted K'orik on could not be seen from his position. He breathed a sigh of relief. He landed, changed into his human form, and started the trek into the mountain.

When he arrived in the larger cavern, J'orik and Lianna were already there waiting for him. He could see that both of them were excited for more tutoring. After the pleasantries he sat them down and told them he had some *not so good* news.

"Your father has come and he is outside the mountain," he informed J'orik. "He's probably looking for Ogiloth to help him with the search. How he knew where to even find Ogiloth is a mystery which concerns me almost as much as his presence. If he can find Ogiloth this easily then it's likely he'll be able to locate you."

"Do you think he saw you?" J'orik asked with as much concern.

"The sun had gone down and it was fairly dark but it's possible he may have seen me before I flew behind the mountain. Phoenixes have very good vision and there was nothing I could do by the time I noticed him."

"How did you notice him?"

"He was still in his phoenix form and I saw him land atop the highest peak around this area. I'm sure he chose that spot for a reason and it probably paid off."

"What will we do if he finds us?" Lianna interjected.

"Most likely there will be a confrontation. He's here for one thing and one thing only, J'orik, his son. Nothing else matters to him. We'll just be in his way of getting what he wants and he'll destroy us if he has to. Remember the story we told you about him and J'eren? J'eren should have been able to destroy him but he didn't, or couldn't. Instead, K'orik destroyed him and took everything he had."

J'orik looked at Lianna and then back to Jake. "I don't want anything to happen to you or Lianna. What if I were to just go with him?"

"That's an option only you can make a decision on. It would certainly prevent a straight on confrontation and anyone getting hurt."

Lianna looked at J'orik with sad eyes. "If you go with him I may never see you again."

"Think of this though. If I go with him willingly then no one gets hurt. Also, if he does have your children I might be able to find them and save them from harm." Her eyes lit up at that. He continued. "And, if what Jake says about me is true, there may come a time when I'll be able to defeat him."

"But he's your father," she said emphatically. "Could you really do that?"

"I never knew him as my father. I always believed my father was dead. K'orik is just another man to me and if he's as bad as I've been led to believe then yes, I could do that."

There was a silent pause as they all seemed to be absorbing everything that had been said.

Jake was the first to speak again. "Well, like I said J'orik, that's a decision only you can make. But, to defeat K'orik, you'll have to practice and if you go with him then he will most likely become your tutor. Do you think you'll be able to resist the temptations he'll surely place in front of you?"

"I can't say, Jake. But I can say," he looked deep into Lianna's eyes, "that I have something that'll help me fight those temptations." Then he smiled gently at her. She smiled back knowingly.

It was obvious to Jake that they'd developed a very close bond with each other since their journey began together. They'd been through some harrowing experiences and come out stronger for them. Maybe the bond they had would be enough for J'orik to resist any temptations his father had.

Jake broke the silence again. "In the meantime, I don't think there is any immediate threat. We should continue with your tutoring."

They both looked at him and agreed.

"Did you practice any while I was gone?"

"No," Lianna nodded. "After what happened last night I convinced J'orik we should wait until you were here. Instead, I talked him into some exploring."

Jake smiled, remembering when he and Joice had explored the tunnels. "Since you're both here, I see that you were careful. Okay, let's start with you again, Lianna."

The experience for Lianna was pretty much the same as it was the night before. Jake did notice, however, that her body took on a more ethereal appearance which was more normal for someone just learning. She was proud of herself. And, like the night before, she expressed how wonderful and serene the experience was.

When it was time for J'orik, Jake told her he would feel better if she wasn't so close by. He suggested she climb back up into the tunnel leading to the cave. Once she was safe he changed into his dragon form for his own protection before J'orik began. The experience for J'orik, this time, was a little different. He was expecting what happened. He was even able to hold the change longer before it became too much for him. After he was done, Lianna climbed back down to join them.

"You kids are doing wonderful," Jake spoke with some pride. "I think I'm going to leave a little earlier than last night. I want to build a camouflage for the entrance of the tunnel on the west side of the mountain. Since K'orik saw me fly to that side it's likely he'll lead Ogiloth and his group over there to start their search for an entrance. I'm sure that if he saw me, in my dragon form, he'll think the most likely place to hide you will be inside the mountain. I think as long as you kids don't expose yourselves by going outside, the chances of him not finding you will be better or at least take him longer."

"I don't think that'll be a problem," Lianna told him. "We like to explore anyway."

"Good. You kids be safe and I'll see you tomorrow night."

They both waved as he headed out across the cavern to leave.

When Jake made it to the western tunnel entrance he put together the camouflage he'd talked about. Once it was in place and he was satisfied, he walked down to the clearing. He thought about how he was going to go home and decided he should fly south, out over the desert, and land somewhere near Murwood Forest. He knew K'orik would be watching for him so he decided he would also be flying low, trying to stay below the treetops as much as possible.

After landing in Murwood Forest and making the walk back to Bruston he noticed a lone hawk circling above town. Arriving back at the inn he was greeted by Joice. She had already been up preparing for the day and waiting for his return.

"How did it go last night, dear?"

"Both of them are coming along quite well," responding with a smile and a morning kiss. "J'orik is doing exceptionally well. He's already able to change form, and last night he was able to hold it for longer than the first time. Lianna is beginning the change but I think it'll take a while longer before she can make a complete change."

"Are you hungry?" she asked, as she began to prepare him breakfast.

"Ravished." He paused, thinking.

Looking concerned, Joice asked, "Did something happen?"

"I think K'orik has come to help Ogiloth search for J'orik. I believe I spotted him last night as I was flying over the mountain."

"Well, if it is him, that's just one of the problems that's come up." Jake looked at her questioningly as she continued. "When I got up this morning and came down stairs I found a note on the front counter. It was folded, and on the outside it had your name written on it." She took the note out of an inside pocket in her apron and handed it to him. "I already read it but, here, you can read it for yourself." Then she went back to preparing his breakfast.

He took the letter and unfolded it. On the inside it said:

Jake,

Just wanted to let you know, there were two men watching you when you left the inn last night. They followed you as far as the mining road. I was able to scare them off.

A friend

"Gerard wasn't at the counter this morning when I found the note," Joice told him. "I was going to ask him about it later. Maybe he saw who brought it in."

"Another strange thing happened. As I was walking back to town I noticed a lone hawk flying above town. If I read this note correctly it appears these two men aren't the only ones watching me. And then there's Durog, we know he's involved because of his nephew. Maybe these two men were hired by Durog to keep an eye on me."

"Whatever's going on, we're going to have to be more careful now. We have too many eyes on us."

She finished making his breakfast and put the food on a platter for him. He followed her into the dining room with the note still in his hand and sat at the bar. She set the platter in front of him and he started eating.

# CHAPTER 25

K'ORIK WAS UP at first light the next morning. Coming out of the tent he found that all the others were up as well. They were sitting around the campfire having their morning meal which consisted of dried vegetables boiled in a broth to make a soup and dried biscuits. It wasn't the most appetizing meal but, when you're out in the wilderness and weight is an issue, you put up with what you can carry. Someone must have thought to bring along a spice or two because the soup smelled pretty good.

He wandered over to the campfire and was greeted heartily by them all. He was offered a tin of the soup and a biscuit, which he took and began eating. He did like he saw the others doing and dipped the biscuit in the soup broth to soften it. All in all it wasn't as bad as he thought it would be.

Ogiloth finished his and the others quickly finished theirs. "Okay, boys, let's pack up and get ready to move out."

They all started breaking camp while Ogiloth put the campfire out.

K'orik finished his meal and looked over at Ogiloth. "So, what was your plan of action today?"

"That was something I thought we could discuss this morning. You said you knew which mountain it was, so I thought I'd let you lead us to it. From there we could begin searching for an entrance into the mountain, unless, of course, you have another suggestion."

"Do you even know what to begin looking for?"

"I have a fair idea. After all, I spent my youth working with my uncle in the mines above Bruston before I came to work for you. I'm familiar with tunnels and caves and how to move about in them. The biggest problem I have is determining which mountain to even start with. This is where you come in."

"And if I hadn't come, what would you have done?"

"Continue moving forward and keeping an eye out for that dragon."

"So you're saying you would have wandered the mountains until you just happened upon what you were looking for?" he asked incredulously.

"No." Ogiloth was beginning to get angry with K'orik's line of questioning but he held that anger in and attempted to qualify his search methods. "I know a little about dragons from the stories my uncle used to tell me. They like caverns hidden inside the mountains. The mountain they choose will generally be one with little growth on it *and* one of the taller peaks. The cavern will be large and most likely have a source of water in it, such as a lake or spring. There's a high chance that a waterfall will be coming out the side of the mountain with no apparent source. The source of that water will be inside the mountain and the opening for it will be a likely place to start if another one is not found. Short of spotting the dragon and seeing where it enters the mountain, this is how I would go about searching." He paused and looked K'orik in the eyes. "Is there anything you have to add?" he asked, trying not to sound smug.

K'orik looked straight back into his eyes. "No. Your methodology is sound Ogiloth. Short of being led by your hand you have a sound plan of action. The next thing I have to ask is, are your warriors willing to follow you? Do they know what they're up against?"

"Yes," he responded with confidence. "They will follow me. They know what we're up against. This has already been discussed. I gave them the chance to run and they didn't take it."

"So they are aware of the dragon?" He raised his eyebrows.

"Yes."

K'orik moved in closer to Ogiloth before continuing the next line of questions and lowered his voice. He didn't want the others to hear. "Do they know what else they might be up against?" he asked with some skepticism.

"What do you mean by that?" He had a questioning look on his face.

"My son, of course. Do they know what he is?"

"No. I have not informed them of that. One unusual creature is enough. Another one and they would flee for their lives."

"Don't you think that that's what will happen when they're confronted by both?"

"By then it will be too late and they'll have no other choice but to fight."

"Well, just so that you're aware, my son may not be a problem. He may not have developed the ability to change yet. This is the reason I am so anxious to find him, and soon, so that I can be the one that helps him develop that ability. Do understand now the reason for my aggressiveness?"

"Yes."

"This is also why I decided I would come and join you on the search." He stepped back and spoke normally again. "Now that we've had our discussion it's time to get moving, don't you think?"

"Yes."

K'orik moved to a spot where he was able to see the mountain they would be heading for, the one he thought he saw the dragon heading for. He pointed to it and called Ogiloth's attention to it. "That's the mountain we're headed for. I believe it meets a couple of the conditions you mentioned."

Ogiloth moved so he could see where he was pointing and looked.

"Only we'll be going to the other side," he told Ogiloth. "That's the side I saw the dragon go to. Our quickest and easiest route will be around the south side. The mountains get lower that way and we should be able to find a pass between them which will shorten the journey some. It'll take another couple of days to get to the other side but I don't see a better choice."

Ogiloth saw that his warriors had finished breaking camp and were ready to go. "Okay, fall in behind me. Move out." He took the lead with K'orik.

They spent the day hiking across the mountains and through the trees. Just as K'orik had said, the mountains were lower to the south and they did find a pass. By the time they crested the pass, though, night was already coming on. The daylight lasted a little longer than it had when they were on the east side of the mountain and in its shadow. They stopped to make camp and prepare for the night watch. This was the third day since he'd left two of his warriors behind to watch over the boat. He was beginning to wonder if they would still be there or if they had decided to return to the castle. At this point it didn't really matter. He had other, more pressing issues to deal with. He would deal with them later when the time came. After camp was set up and the evening meal prepared K'orik came over next to him.

"I was just thinking. Didn't you leave the castle with ten warriors? I only count seven in the group. What happened to the other three?"

"Funny you should mention that. I was just thinking about it. Can you read minds too?" He tried to be smug but all it did was draw an angry glare from K'orik.

"Answer my questions," K'orik said brusquely.

"Yes, I did leave with ten. One was killed at the landing near the village shortly after arriving. I had left him behind to guard the boat and our things. I have a suspicion it was J'orik that killed him. The other two I left behind to guard the boat that's shored about three miles west of Bruston."

"The boat was that important that you left two behind to guard it?" he asked derisively.

Ogiloth gave him a sideways glance before answering. "Yes. The boat will cut days off the journey when we return with your son."

"You could have hidden the boat and then you would have two additional warriors to assist you when we confront the dragon." K'orik sounded even more condescending.

He felt like an idiot. K'orik was right so he admitted as much. "Hiding the boat would have been a better choice."

Then he tried to reason his way out. "But it would have taken more time to find a place to properly hide it. Besides, given the coming confrontation, I don't think two more will make that much difference."

K'orik conceded Ogiloth's point. "You're probably right about that, two more of *them* probably won't make any difference." He chuckled and Ogiloth joined him.

The sun had completely set and the only light was being provided by the campfire. Before they both retired to their tents Ogiloth told Olog to make sure the guards kept their eyes to the sky and wake him and K'orik immediately if they saw anything.

# CHAPTER 26

HEEDING THE NOTE that had been left for him, Jake decided to go to the roof of the inn and take a look around before leaving that evening. He didn't see anyone on the rooftops nor did he see the hawk he'd seen earlier. He went back down to say good-bye to Joice before he left. She'd prepared another food package for him to take to the kids. He'd done some thinking about which way he would go to the mountain tonight and had decided to use the original route. It wasn't likely that K'orik would try to enter from the east side since he'd seen him fly over the mountain to the west side. He would probably lead Ogiloth and his group around the mountain and look for an entrance on that side. Going around the south side of the mountain made the most sense. The mountains were less treacherous that way. As far as taking the mining road, Jake decided against that because if the two men were watching out for him they could do that from the ground and from the edge of town. They might even be in the trees near the road waiting for him to pass by. The only real unknown was the anonymous note he'd gotten. Questions were going through his mind.

*Was that person also watching his movements? Who was it and why were they watching? Were they really a friend? Did the hawk have anything to do with it or was it just a hawk?* He didn't have an answer for any of those questions. He still needed to make the visit with the kids, deliver food to them, and tutor them. They needed to be assured that everything was still okay.

He kissed Joice before heading out the back door. She wished him good luck. Checking the alley all he saw were the alley cats rummaging through the trash. He walked south down the alley, around the south end of town, and west towards the small valley he and Joice always used. On his way there he didn't see anything unusual. The sun had already dropped below the mountaintops by the time he got to the small valley. He changed into his dragon form and lifted off. He decided he would fly north first and circle west, coming south along the mountains hoping this would prevent him from being spotted by Ogiloth's group. He didn't see any spots of light on the ground from campfires. That was a good sign. He flew below the mountaintops and as close to the mountainside as possible to provide less of a profile to be seen. After landing on the ledge he changed back to his human form and made his way into the cave. J'orik and Lianna weren't there, but he didn't expect them to be. They would be expecting him to come in through the western entrance and meet them in the larger cavern as he had the last two nights. When he showed up in the opening to the passage leading down from the smaller cave they were completely surprised.

He stepped out onto the ledge in the larger cavern and yelled down at them. "Hello down there." He saw them both jump with surprise and look up at him. "Didn't mean to startle you," he chuckled. "Give me a moment and I'll be right down. Clear some room for me."

They moved back against the wall and he leapt off the ledge and changed into a dragon. Dropping down, he landed and changed back into a human. He walked over to them and handed the bag with the meals in it to J'orik.

"Joice has prepared another meal for you. Why don't you have a seat, eat, and we can talk before we get started."

While they were eating Jake told them everything that had happened since the last time he was there. The note he'd received from *a friend* saying that he was being watched, apparently by more than one pair of eyes. K'orik, Ogiloth, and his group must be coming around from the south to look for an entrance on the west side of the mountain. The hawk that seemed to just show up suddenly from nowhere. The general overall feelings he'd been having.

"But why did you come in from the front again?" Lianna asked curiously.

"It seemed to be the wisest choice with K'orik going around the south side of the mountain."

"What about the hawk you mentioned? Do you think it has any significance?"

"The hawk and the note are the two things that concern me the most. The hawk may not even have any significance. I just might be a little edgy and anything out of the ordinary raises a red flag. The note, however, is significant. It appeared on the front counter of the inn some time during the night. It's signed from *a friend* and provides a warning. The warning I believe is two-fold. First, the explicit statement that I'm being watched by two men, and second, the implication that I'm being watched by the friend. My question would be, why doesn't this friend make themselves known? Are they afraid? I'm not sure what to think."

Lianna noticed that J'orik had finished eating. She put her hand up towards Jake indicating for him to wait. A few moments past and then J'orik did the expected, he belched. It echoed off the walls in the cavern like thunder in a storm. Lianna and Jake both started laughing heartily.

J'orik looked at them dumbfounded and said, "What, it was good." Then he joined in their laughter.

"Did you do some more tunnel exploring in my absence?"

"Yes," Lianna answered excitedly. "What we've done is chosen one tunnel to explore to its end."

"Which one?"

She pointed to the opposite side of the cavern from the tunnel they use to exit on the west side of the mountain. "It's on that side of the cavern, way in the back."

"Is it the furthest one back?"

"Yes. Why? Is it not a good one?"

"Oh, it's the best one."

"Where does it lead?"

"If you're able to stay on the main path it will eventually lead out to a ledge on the north side of the waterfall." Jake's eyes suddenly went wide.

Lianna looked at him concerned. "What's wrong?"

"That'll probably be the one they use to get inside. They'll come around to the west side and find the waterfall, you can't miss it. It's obvious that it flows from inside the mountain because it exits out the side of the mountain with no apparent source. They'll climb up to investigate and find where the tunnel you just mentioned opens. If you know the route and are walking normally, it takes about a half hour to make the walk. Exploring would take longer because of the other tunnels that lead off of it, but no more than a few days. Less time if you're familiar with tunneling and Ogiloth will be with them."

"What about Ogiloth?" J'orik interjected.

"Before Ogiloth went to work for K'orik he worked in the mines. Plus he's half dwarf. Dwarves naturally have a strong sense in the underground and with the tunneling experience he has I doubt it would take him more than half a day to find his way in here."

"How long do you think that gives us before they're here?" J'orik queried.

"Given the last place I saw them and the route I believe they're taking," he paused to think, "I'd say two to three days at the most."

"Why don't we just leave here and go somewhere else?" Lianna asked suggestively.

"We could do that but do you really want to just keep running? Now that K'orik has found J'orik's trail he's not going to give up. He'll keep coming until he catches him."

"He's right, Lianna," J'orik conceded, looking her in the eyes. "I don't want to spend the rest of my life running and hiding. Besides, this is probably the best place to face him." Then he turned to Jake. "Don't you think so?"

"It's a confined space." He looked around the cavern. "And if he decides to change form it would make it difficult for Ogiloth and his group to assist him. They wouldn't be able to withstand the amount of heat he would generate and if J'orik were to respond by changing form also it would be impossible for anyone but the two of them to be in here."

"Like I said," J'orik sighed, looking at Lianna, "I don't want anyone, especially you and Jake, to get hurt."

Jake had a slight look of defeat and decided it was time to help Lianna realize she needed to let go. "If K'orik was able to defeat an ancient like J'eren, the chances of me and J'orik together defeating him are slim, especially in a confined space like this. I wouldn't be able to do it alone and J'orik hasn't developed enough to hold his phoenix form as long as would be necessary. I think J'orik's idea is the best one."

"But I don't want him to go," she pleaded and started crying. She looked up into J'orik's eyes. "Do you have to?"

His eyes began to tear also. "I don't want to go either but I don't think there's any other option at this point. Jake is right, he won't give up."

Jake's eyes were starting to tear as well. He could tell this was tearing them apart inside.

Lianna lunged at J'orik and wrapped her arms around him. "Will I ever see you again?" She was sobbing now.

"Yes. I would never just go away. I will find a way to see you again. Eventually I'll become strong enough that even K'orik won't be able to stop me," he said with confidence. "And if he has your children, I'll find them and bring them to you."

She leaned her head back and looked into his eyes. "I hope you're right." Then she buried her face in his chest again and continued crying. He just held her tight.

They all sat there for a time until Lianna's sobbing subsided. Once she calmed down enough, Jake suggested they start with their tutoring. To give Lianna a little more time he said he would start with J'orik. The tutoring went as before, only J'orik was able to hold the change longer and

Lianna's body took on a more ethereal appearance. Jake told them they were progressing along more each time he was with them. They both smiled at his praise but the smiles were more distant because of what they had decided would happen when K'orik arrived. They followed Jake out to the ledge on the east side of the mountain and said their good-byes. He told them to enjoy the little time they had left together and that he would see them when he returned the following night. They should also discuss how J'orik was going to be able to recognize Lianna's children. They stood back as Jake changed form and lifted off to fly back home. After he was gone they stayed on the ledge for a while holding each other quietly and looking into the sky.

Back in the cave she provided him with her children's names and a brief description of what each of them looked like.

"Neeco, my son, is the oldest. He's twelve now with dark brown hair that hangs to his shoulders. He looks a lot like Falder only he's thin. His eyes look a lot like yours, a dark green. Leira, my oldest daughter, looks like me when I was a little girl. Her hair is coal black and shoulder length. Her eyes are pale blue like the sky. She's ten and thin like her brother. She's very outgoing and can talk your ears off. She's a regular chatterbox. Helena, the youngest, is six. Her hair is the same color as her brother's and hangs down to her waist. Her eyes are a darker blue than Leira's. She still carries around a little of her baby fat. She's shyer than her sister and brother and tends to hang on Neeco. I'm afraid for them J'orik. Neeco's strong willed like his father was and he'll probably do everything he can to protect his sisters but, I don't know how he'll handle being in such a different environment. All the children from the village will be there but I don't know if they'll be together. I hope K'orik treats them well." She paused in thought for a moment then continued. "I wonder what he wants with all the children."

"I'm not sure what use he would have for the children but at least he kept them alive. Like Joice said, shapeshifters can sense other shapeshifters. Even though they're young I should still be able to sense them if I'm near them, especially if they're all together."

"I still don't like the idea of you going away." She looked longingly into his eyes.

"I know. I'm not too happy about it either but I still think it's the best option. I'll do my best to keep in touch and let you know what's happening with me and your children." He tried to reassure her.

She started to cry again and put her arms around him. "I miss my children," he heard her whisper into his chest.

They held each other until they fell asleep.

After leaving J'orik and Lianna, Jake decided to confirm that K'orik and the others were going around the south side of the mountain. He flew north first and then up over the top of the mountains to the west side before heading south. If he was spotted he wanted them to see him coming from that side. Knowing that they knew he existed and was out there and would be watching for him, he wasn't concerned if they saw him. Coming around the south side of the mountain he spotted the light of their campfire. It had to be theirs. It was unlikely that anyone else would be out here but he wanted to make absolutely sure. He swooped down low enough that he could make out several tents near the campfire. He heard some voices yelling and saw two figures outside the camp running in. *Those must be the guards on duty,* he thought. *Good, they spotted me. Now they can run and tell K'orik.* He flew over the camp just above the tree tops and then began gaining altitude again.

He flew back to the small valley in the foothills, changed back into human form, and walked back to town. At this point in the game he was no longer concerned who saw him. This would all be over soon and he could get back to his normal routine and it wouldn't matter anymore. He was sad for J'orik and Lianna and he would miss all the excitement they had brought to him but he would be glad to return to normalcy. He and Joice had made a life for themselves in Bruston, a good life, and he was happy and content with it.

He would hand over the tutoring of Lianna to Joice and Clare now. He was sure that Lianna would stay with them after J'orik left with his father. It would be easier for him to reach her with information of what was happening with him and her children if he knew where she was. He would go back to running the Dragons' Inn and life would be as it was before.

Joice met him in the kitchen when he got back to the inn and fed him breakfast. He told her about everything he and the kids had discussed and the decision J'orik had made. He could see she was as sad as he was about it but realized it was probably all for the best. He finished eating, gave her a kiss, and went off to bed.

# CHAPTER 27

JACK HAD WATCHED Jake's activities long enough that he knew he left late in the evening and returned early in the morning, all after the sun set and before it rose again. Jake was being careful not to be seen outside his normal routine except, of course, by those that were watching him.

Jack went about his normal routine that day in his warehouse anxious for the day to end. He was excited about the upcoming evening. Tonight, he planned on following Jake all the way to where he went at night. He wasn't concerned about the two men he'd chased off on the mining road figuring they would think twice before following Jake that way again. The only thing he wasn't sure of was the route Jake would be taking. Jake seemed to change it for some reason and he would need to be nearby when Jake left the inn tonight. The only thing that was consistent was that Jake came and went through the back entrance of the inn.

A large shipment from the mines came in late that day and he knew it would take longer than he was willing to take to check it in. It would be almost dark before it would be done so he informed George, the head warehouseman, he would have to finish the job without him. There was something more important he had to attend to in town. George told him it wouldn't be a problem and Jack trusted that he would get the job done. The man had been working for him for quite a few years and knew what he was doing. He'd proven himself many times over the years.

He excused himself and left the warehouse. The sun was just starting to make its descent behind the mountains. He walked around to the side of the warehouse, confirmed that no one was watching, and climbed to the top of the building. Once on top he changed into a blue jay again. Blue jays were common in Bruston so he felt he would draw less attention that way. He flew across town and perched on a weather vane atop one of the buildings at the south end of the alley that Jake would be coming down. He set there and waited and watched.

As the sun disappeared below the mountaintops he saw Jake come out the back door of the inn. He watched as he walked down the alley. Jack didn't see the other two men anywhere. Jake exited the alley, skirted the south side of town, and headed due west out of town instead of towards the mining road. *A change of route*, Jack thought. *Let's see where you go tonight*. As soon as Jake was a good distance out Jack took flight and flew parallel to Jake's path, to the north of him. He flew past him and landed in the top of a tree about a half mile ahead of him where he could still see him. He knew his note had been received because Jake would look around once in a while checking for anyone following him. He walked across the low rolling foothills and continued west. He was out in the open now but would glance back periodically to check for followers. After Jake was out of sight

Jack took flight again. He spotted him walking over the rise of a hill that led down into a small valley. Jack flew past there and continued flying west. Once he was out of sight again he quickly changed into a swift, one of the fastest birds he knew of. He needed to be fast to get ahead of Jake. He sped west towards the taller mountains, staying low to the treetops, glancing back and up frequently to see where Jake was. He saw him high above and gaining on him. Jake was a little north of him so he adjusted his route and angled his flight in that direction. Jake passed above him and was now in front of him. He flew as fast as he could to keep up, watching Jake the whole time. As he watched, Jake neared the side of one of the mountains and looked like he was going to crash into it, but then he swung his legs out in front and pumped his wings as he landed on a ledge halfway up the rocky side of the mountain. Jack gained altitude quickly and was able to see Jake change back into his human form and enter an opening in the side of the mountain at the back of the ledge. He swooped down, landed on the ledge, and changed into human form.

Silently he walked over to the opening and stood there for a moment listening. He could hear Jake in the distance down the tunnel. Entering the tunnel, his eyes adjusted to the lack of light. Even in human form Jack's night vision was excellent. Walking as quietly as possible he began making his way down the tunnel, listening as he walked. He heard the echo of footsteps and figured that Jake was no longer in the tunnel and walking through a cave. It only lasted for a short period and then he didn't hear anymore sound. He stopped, unsure as to why there was no more sound. After a few moments of hearing nothing more he continued through the tunnel. A short distance from where he'd stopped he saw that the tunnel ended and opened into a cave, the one he must have heard Jake in. Staying against the wall of the tunnel he made his way slowly to the cave entrance and stopped. He peeked in and didn't see Jake or anyone else. There was a fire pit in the middle of the cavern surrounded by log benches. Some bedding lay next to the fire pit. Against the wall to his right was a large standing chest that had been pulled away from the wall. Behind it he noticed a dark hole, another opening. He walked across the cavern and listened at the opening. This tunnel appeared to have a downward slope and he heard faint footsteps in the distance. He stepped into the tunnel and quietly started making his way down. About ten yards into the tunnel he heard a voice call out 'clear some room for me' followed by a loud, thunderous whoosh and the thumping of what sounded like large wings flapping. He stopped in his tracks. *Did Jake just change into a dragon?* He wondered to himself. *If he did, then he must be in a very large cavern.* He continued walking down the tunnel until he saw light up ahead and decided it was time to change into something smaller and less conspicuous. He could hear voices in the cavern ahead echoing off the walls. Changing into a black cat, he crept the rest of the way down the tunnel until it ended, opening into a *very* large cavern. He made himself comfortable close enough to the edge of the ledge so that he could see Jake and the other two people with him and hear what they were saying.

He learned that the other two people were J'orik and Lianna. From the conversation it became apparent to him that Lianna and J'orik were more than just friends, they had become quite close. J'orik had decided to leave with his father, K'orik, to prevent harm from coming to Lianna and Jake, or anyone else. He was also doing this to save Lianna's children from K'orik. After some crying and hugging Jake suggested they get to their tutoring, which Jack knew all about. Lianna got up and walked towards the wall directly under the ledge he was on. He hadn't really paid too much attention but there was a rope running over the ledge and it started to shake. A sudden thought occurred to him. *She must be climbing up the rope. I've got to get out of here.* He scooted backwards a little, stood up, and started running back up the tunnel. He didn't even stop to look behind him, he just kept running. Up the tunnel, across the cave, through the first tunnel he'd come in, across the ledge, and a leap into the air changing into a hawk. He figured he'd seen and heard enough for the night and it was time to leave anyway.

As he was flying away he remembered hearing Jake say that K'orik and his group were going around the south side of the mountain. *Maybe I'll fly over that way and see if I can spot them*, thinking to himself. So he swung south and headed in that direction. As he came around the south side of the mountain he spotted a campfire in the trees. Getting closer, he noticed several tents. He considered changing into a red dragon like Jake and giving them a real scare, but then he thought better of it and didn't. The last thing he wanted to do was interfere with the plan he'd overheard. Up to now he was just an innocuous figure in the scheme of things and he didn't want to jeopardize that position, yet. He turned around and headed home, back to his warehouse. It was a fruitful evening, he'd learned a lot.

# CHAPTER 28

THE TWO GUARDS came running into camp yelling, "The dragon, the dragon!" They were pointing east.

Everyone woke up to their yelling and rushed out of their tents looking skyward. K'orik and Ogiloth were already awake in their tents and had heard him fly over. They could tell he had come in as low as possible. When they came out of their tents they saw the guards pointing east and looked in that direction. They could see the large shadow of the dragon flying away.

K'orik cursed under his breathe, "Damn him, he knows where we are." He looked over at Ogiloth. "Calm them down," he commanded. "He was just trying to put a scare in them and it seems to have worked."

Ogiloth smiled and walked over to his warriors. "All right everyone, calm down," he commanded in a harsh tone. "He's gone now."

They all settled down except the two guards who were still out of breath from the close encounter. Ogiloth could not believe how excitable these creatures he called warriors could get. K'orik was beginning to wonder if his purchase had been worth what it cost him. He'd watched them in action and, under normal circumstances, they were superb, but when it came to something like this they became like children. He was going to have to talk with Sarguroth about making some adjustments either in price or in the mental capacity of his creations.

Eventually they all calmed down to normal. Olog was the only one of the bunch that didn't seem to be affected by what happened. He reacted similar to K'orik and Ogiloth who both noticed it. Ogiloth was really beginning to grow attached to him. He was strong not only in body but in mind as well. Something he would be able to take advantage of later on. K'orik saw how he looked at Olog compared to the others and realized why he had chosen him to be one of his lieutenants but also why he chose him to be with him on this journey.

"All right," Ogiloth commanded, "quick bite to eat, break camp, and then move out."

They all moved to his direction and in less than half an hour they were moving through the mountains again with K'orik and Ogiloth in the lead.

As they came around to the west side of the mountain they were under its shadow. It was still early and the sun had only begun to rise in the east. It wouldn't be until late afternoon before they would see it again. Unfortunately the brush on this side was a little thicker which slowed them down some. Olog had two of the warriors go up front and start hacking through some of the thicker parts that couldn't just be pushed aside. Shortly after the sun made its appearance over the mountaintop the brush started to thin some and they were able to walk a little faster and easier. They stopped one time to eat and take a short rest.

By the time the sun had gotten low enough in the sky to cast shadows taller than their height the sound of rushing water was heard in the distance. Ogiloth glanced at K'orik with a knowing look. He had a suspicion that what they heard was a waterfall. K'orik just sneered back at him. Regardless, it was water up ahead.

They reached the river first as the sky was beginning to dim. The pounding of water falling could be heard further upstream. Ogiloth decided they would set up camp near the river while he and K'orik walked upstream to look for the waterfall. It didn't sound like it was that far away and they had been walking along the foot of the mountain.

It was only about a half a mile upstream and they came out of the trees and saw the waterfall. It was set in an indentation in the mountain and spilled out the side of it about eight hundred feet up. The mountainside continued above it so it was obvious the waterfall originated from inside the mountain. There was a large pool at the bottom of it where the river started. Ogiloth had a smile on his face when K'orik turned and looked at him. K'orik just smiled back. They found what they had come looking for but it was too dark now to see much more so they headed back to camp. They got back just as the sun set.

Camp was set up, a campfire had been started, and the evening meal was ready to serve. Another good thing about Olog, he was efficient.

K'orik pulled Ogiloth aside after they had eaten. "The sun won't be on this side of the mountain tomorrow until the afternoon," stating the obvious. "There won't be enough light to see anything from the bottom of the waterfall so I want you to keep everyone here in camp while I go alone to look for a way in."

"You're going to change into your firebird and fly up around the waterfall, aren't you?" sounding somewhat dejected.

"Yes. And it's called a phoenix," he corrected him angrily. "I never want to hear you say 'firebird' again." He glared at Ogiloth. He calmed down a little and continued. "I have two advantages. One, I have light. Two, I can deal with heights without assistance. Once I've located a way in I'll come back and get the rest of you. Agreed?"

"Agreed," Ogiloth conceded. Of course he knew he didn't have a choice in the matter.


Cory and Lance decided it was time to pay a visit with Durog. They hadn't seen or heard from Jenner for several days now and they were getting concerned. Maybe Durog had him doing something alone, without them, and they wanted to be part of it. After all, the pay was good and the work wasn't that hard. A little more gold in their pockets couldn't hurt and they had been keeping an eye on the owner of the Dragons' Inn. Even though they'd been doing this on their own initiative, they felt something was due them.

They made their way over into the dwarves section of town that afternoon after spending the morning in the Winged Horse, one of the local pubs in town. They found Durog's house and stood out front at the end of the walk discussing how they were going to approach him. They were barely able to stand straight and looked like they would fall over any second.

"Ya know he should give us somethin' for what we done," Lance stated matter-of-fact, looking at his friend with bloodshot eyes. "After all, we been keepin' an eye on that feller what owns tha inn." His speech was somewhat slurred.

"Yeah, yer right," Cory responded with a slur in his speech as well. His eyes were just as bloodshot.

"He might know where Jenner is too."

"Yeah, he dis'peared tha nex' day an' we haven't seen'm since. Ya 'spose he's been workin' for'm all this time?"

"Don' know, but I 'tend ta find out, cuz if he has we should get a piece a tha action."

"Yeah," Cory replied, reaching over and grabbing Lance's shoulder to steady himself.

"Okay. How we gonna do this?"

"Jus' walk up an' tell'm we should be paid for watchin'. He did say ta keep an eye open." He looked at Lance with one bloodshot eye open and the other one closed and giggled. "An' that's what we been doin'."

Lance looked back and giggled. "Thas right. Let's go."

Durog had been watching them through his kitchen window and could see that they'd been drinking. When they turned to come up the walk he went and opened the door. Standing there looking at the two of them with disgust he hollered at them in a gruff voice. "What ye boys doin'?"

"We come ta get paid," Lance hollered back.

"Yeah," Cory hollered in agreement. "An' where's Jenner?" he added.

Durog didn't want the whole neighborhood to hear their conversation. "Get yer drunkin' hides up here," he grumbled at them. He stepped back and opened the door all the way.

Holding each other up, they stumbled up the walk and into the house. Durog shut the door behind them. "Ye boys jes' stop right there, now." He had a mean tone in his voice. "Tell me what ye want."

They both stopped in the hallway and turned to look at him. "We come ta get paid," Lance repeated. "Jus' like I said."

"Yeah, an' ta find out where Jenner is." Cory added.

"Get paid fer what?" He was getting angry now.

"Watchin' that feller what owns tha Dragons' Inn, like ya ast us to," Lance replied.

"Yeah, like ya ast us to," Cory added, giggling. "An' where's Jenner?" he repeated again.

Durog was getting more irritated by the second. He decided it was time to end this. "Okay, I'll pay ye boys but ye got ta give me some information. What do ye have ta say?" He looked at Cory. "An' no repeatin' what th'other one says," he added with a glare.

"Can we sit down?" they asked in unison. Then they looked at each other and started to laugh.

Durog could see it wasn't going to go any further until they were sitting down. "Sure. Have a seat on tha couch 'fore ye fall down."

He followed them into the living room and watched them practically fall into the couch. He took a seat in his chair and looked at them with a huge sigh.

"Okay, tell me what ye know, an' only one of ye talk."

They looked at each other with a smile and Cory sat back in the couch. Lance stayed sitting up and began telling him what they'd seen.

"That feller what owns tha Dragons' Inn, he been makin' reg'lar trips inta the mountains. We been followin'm as far as we can but he always dis'pears an' gets away from us. He leaves at sunset an' comes back early in tha mornin' ev'ry day. He never goes an' comes tha same way either. Sometimes he goes out south a town an' sometimes he uses tha minin' road. Sometimes he comes back on tha minin' road an' sometimes he comes back from tha forest. But he always goes an' comes through tha back door of tha inn and tha alley. Thas jus' 'bout all." He turned and looked at Cory. "Right?"

Cory looked like he was almost ready to pass out but he opened his bloodshot eyes and said, "Right. 'Cept where's Jenner?"

Lance turned back to Durog. "Yeah, right, we haven't seen Jenner since tha first day ya had us doin' this. Where izzee?"

Cory leaned forward and they both sat there with a dumbfounded look waiting for Durog to respond.

He sat in thought for a moment before he replied. "I don't know where Jenner is boys, sorry, but I will pay ya fer tha watchin' ye done." He dug in his pocket, took out some silver coins, and set three on the table in front of each of them.

They looked down at the three coins and then back up at Durog. He added one more coin each and they smiled.

"Now, ye boys be done workin' fer me. I don't need yer services no more. Okay?" He looked at them hard.

They took the coins, put them in their own pockets, and responded in unison, "Okay."

"Now git yer hides outta me home an' I don't wanna see ye agin'." He stood up and waved his arm towards the door.

They stumbled up out of the couch and headed towards the door stumbling down the hallway. Durog followed them and watched as they stumbled down the walk and out into the street heading for town. *They're prob'ly headin' back ta tha pub*, he thought to himself as he shut the door.

There was a loud banging on his door and Jack snapped awake. He'd had a very eventful night and hadn't gotten back until early in the morning. He swung his legs over the edge of the bed and sat up rubbing the sleep out of his eyes. The loud banging on his door came again.

"Come in," he yelled.

The door opened and George, the head warehouseman, entered his room. George was a large man standing nearly six and half feet tall and broad at the shoulders. He had graying hair with a trim beard and mustache. His clothes were similar to what Jack had on. A white long-sleeved cotton shirt with the sleeves rolled to the elbow, heavy cotton pants held up with suspenders, and hard-soled leather boots. All covered with a heavy leather apron that was knee length. His gloves were off and stuffed in one of the pockets in his apron.

"Boss, there's a ruckus downstairs in the main office. One of the dwarves is arguing about a load of empty crates he's hauling back up into the mines."

"All right, I'll be right down, just give me a few moments. Try to calm him down until I get there."

George left and Jack heard him stomping down the stairs. He stood up off the bed and realized he still had his clothes on. He hadn't even taken his boots off. His hat wasn't on his head, though, and looking around he found it on the floor at the head of his bed. He picked it up, smoothed his hair back, and placed it on his head. He was ready for the day but he still felt tired.

Heading down the stairs he could hear some yelling. Apparently George wasn't able to calm this dwarf down. It must be awful important. Of course, dwarves were hard to calm down once they got steamed about something. He entered the main office and saw George making his best attempt to calm the dwarf but failing miserably. George was a big man and he towered over the dwarf standing in front of him. They both had a piece of paper in their hands and the dwarf was shaking his as much as his beard was shaking with every word he spoke. Bryce, the clerk behind the counter, just sat there watching the whole affair.

Jack stepped closer to the two arguing. "Hey," he said. No response from the dwarf, but George looked at him with a helpless shrug of his shoulders. "Hey," he yelled straight at the dwarf. The dwarf went quiet. "What seems to be the problem here?"

The dwarf turned his way. "There's to be one more crate than this big oaf say there be."

Jack looked at George and he showed him the invoice. Then he asked for the invoice from the dwarf. Looking at the two invoices he found them to be identical.

"Did you load the number of crates indicated on the invoice?" he asked George.

Before George could respond the dwarf yelled, "No he did not." Then he gave George an angry look.

Jack knew that sometimes dwarves had a hard time counting, especially when the count went higher than ten. The invoice he was looking at indicated there should be twenty-three crates.

Jack looked down at the dwarf. "Let's just see about this. Where's your wagon?"

The dwarf turned and headed out to the front of the warehouse. Jack and George followed him. When they got to the wagon Jack did a quick count, which wasn't hard. He counted three rows, four long, two high, with only two crates instead of three on the top in the back.

Jack looked at the dwarf again. "The invoice says twenty-three crates, right?"

The dwarf nodded agreement.

"That's how many I count. What's the problem?"

"Ya see how them crates be stacked in tha back there?" He pointed to the two on top in the back.

Jack nodded indicating he did.

"Should be three 'cross, not two. Ain't right."

"If we were to do that you would have twenty-four crates, not twenty-three."

"Ain't right. There be room fer one more."

"But that's not what the invoice calls for."

The dwarf huffed and looked Jack in the eyes. "Well, there be room fer one more. But ye always been good to us an' ne'er cheated us so I'm a goin' ta trust ye on this Jack."

"Good, because I would never cheat you, never have and never will," he said with a smile.

Jack handed the invoice back to the dwarf. He walked to the front of the wagon, got up on the bench with his partner, and grabbed the reins. Slapping the horses on their backs and the wagon slowly pulled away.

George gave Jack a resigned look. "Sometimes those dwarves are hard to deal with."

"Sometimes they are George but they're our bread and butter. I started the business with them and I won't ever jeopardize that relationship."

"Now that that's over I can get back to work." He sounded relieved as he turned to head back into the warehouse, but he stopped and turned back when Jack called his name.

"George. I need to leave again later this afternoon and I won't be back until tomorrow morning. Are you okay with handling the warehouse while I'm gone?"

"Sure, that's not a problem. Is there something wrong?"

"No, just some personal business I need to take care of."

"Well, you take as much time as you need, boss, I can handle things just fine. Besides, the place pretty much runs itself. Everyone knows what they're supposed to do and they do it."

"Good. I'm glad to hear that. Thanks George."

"Sure thing," he smiled at Jack and headed back into the warehouse.

Jack walked back up to his office and sat at his desk thinking for a time. There were windows on the two walls that faced out into the warehouse so he could watch the activity that was going on. He just sat there with a blank look staring out the windows thinking. He was remembering more than thinking, remembering back to a different time in his life. He must have sat there for a couple hours before he woke from his reverie. He got up and walked to the window that faced outside and saw that the day was getting late. The sun was halfway down the sky heading towards the mountaintops. He thought he should get a bite to eat before he started the evening fun he had planned. Katy's salad came to mind and he decided he would walk to the Tigress.

He left the warehouse and strolled down the sidewalk watching the townspeople go about their business. There were a few wagons that rolled up and down the street as he made his way to the inn. As he passed by the Boars' Den he saw Owen sitting at the table nearest the window and he waved at him with a smile. Owen smiled and waved back. As he neared the Tigress he glanced over at the Dragons' Inn across the street. *I wonder if Jake has figured out who gave him that note yet*, he wondered. Then the thought of Katy's salad came back and he went into the Tigress.

Harry greeted him with a smile as he entered. "I didn't figure on seeing you for a few more days Jack, something wrong?"

"No, everything's fine. I just got hungry and I couldn't get Katy's salad out of my mind."

"You know, she did add it to the menu as a regular offering after what you said. There were plenty other people that said the same thing as you."

A young couple came in and walked up to the front counter and Harry turned his attention to them.

Jack continued in to the dining room and took a seat at his regular table. Katy spotted him, came over with a mug of hot coffee, and set it on the table.

"Well, good evening Jack," she said with a smile. "What brings you in today?"

He looked up at her and smiled back. "That wonderful salad of yours."

"Well, I'll go get one made up for you. That was what you wanted, right?" He nodded and she hurried off to the kitchen.

He took a sip of the coffee and stared out the window next to the table. *First George, then Harry, and now Katy. Has my life become that routine and predictable?* He wondered. As he watched the passersby he found himself staring across the street at the Dragons' Inn. *Since J'orik came to town he seems to have broken the routine of everyone he's come in contact with, direct or indirect, including mine. Not that I mind, the change has actually been quite refreshing.*

He jerked in his chair slightly when Katy returned with his salad. "I'm sorry, did I startle you?" as she set the platter on the table.

"A little, I was just deep in thought."

"Is everything all right?" she asked, concerned.

"Yes, everything's fine, thank you."

"Good. Now, you enjoy your salad." She turned and went back about her daily routine.

He ate the salad and drank his coffee as he watched the sun slowly sink behind the mountaintops. When he was finished he got up and made his way back out to the sidewalk, thanking Katy for the salad and saying good night to Harry. He walked down the sidewalk towards the south end of town. Then he headed west, out of town and up into the foothills. About a mile out of town he saw a large shadow rise up out of the hills and fly off towards the higher mountains. *There goes Jake, off to see J'orik and Lianna*, he thought. *This'll probably be the last night he does this and then he'll go back to his regular routine.* He continued walking until he was out of view of town. Then he changed into a hawk and flew towards the mountain where J'orik and Lianna were. He had planned on looking in on K'orik and his group to see where they were.

Flying around the south side of the mountain he didn't see any campfire light so he continued around to the west side. He spotted their campfire next to a river and, as he got closer, he heard the sound of a waterfall. Flying a little closer to the waterfall he noticed that it came straight out the side of the mountain. *That must be where the river from the underground lake comes out*, he was thinking. *K'orik must be planning on finding an entrance into the mountain that way.* He flew back out to where he'd spotted them and perched high on a treetop so he could watch. They all seemed to be gathered around the campfire having their evening meal. He counted nine figures. There were no guards out yet. He dropped to the ground about two hundred yards north of them and changed into a wolf. *This could be fun*, he thought as he began to howl. Then he ran off to the west a ways, stopped, and howled again. Changing back into a hawk he flew to the south of them about two hundred yards and landed on the ground. He changed into a wolf again and began to howl. Then he ran off to the west a ways, stopped, and howled again. He changed back into a hawk again, flew back to the tree he'd perched on earlier, and watched what his activity had initiated. He only saw seven figures at the campfire now. K'orik must have had two guards posted. Good, it had worked.

He remained perched in the tree until he saw the ones in camp retire to their tents for the night. This left the two guards out alone. He knew they would be staying alert after the howling they'd heard so he would have to be silent sneaking up on them. The sound from the waterfall and the rushing river would help to cover any noise he would make. The guards had been posted on the west side of the camp, one near the river, the other south. They were about thirty yards outside the camp. He would take the one near the river first. He flew down from the tree, landed between the guard and the camp, and waited quietly for a moment. He saw that the guard had heard what little noise he'd made so he stopped in his tracks. When the guard figured that it was probably just some small night creature he went back to his duty. Jack changed into his human form and snuck up behind the guard, reached around to cover his mouth, and slit his throat to prevent him from yelling out. *One down, one to go*, he smiled. The other guard was about fifty yards away. He would have to move slow and careful making sure not to step on any branches or twigs. He knew that the guards worked in two-hour segments, so he would have to move as quickly as possible. He was only a couple yards away when he stepped on a twig and it snapped. The guard turned and Jack leapt towards him thrusting his knife to the hilt in his throat. The guard was only able to groan as he fell to the ground. Jack quickly grabbed him and helped him fall. *Good, both guards out leaving K'orik with only six. It feels good to be doing something non-routine and unpredictable. It should be interesting to see the reaction of the others when they find these guards in the morning.* He was pleased with himself. He wiped the blade off on the guards clothing, re-sheathed it, changed into a hawk, and flew back to his perch in the tree above their camp to wait until morning.

The morning came quick enough. He was awakened by a thumping sound and a huge gust of wind. Then there was a loud roar. When he opened his eyes it was still dark and the tree was still swaying from the gust of wind that had passed by. He wasn't surprised by what he saw. Jake had flown close overhead and was heading south on his way home. He watched as he began to gain altitude and noticed a figure riding on his back. *J'orik's alone now inside the mountain. Jake's taking Lianna back to town with him*, he was thinking as he looked down on the camp below. *Now for today's fun and games, but I should find a better hiding place before they find those dead guards.* He flew off towards the waterfall and found a ledge to perch on and wait. As he set there waiting he heard a second roar, only this time it sounded more like an animal. *That must be Ogiloth*, he thought. *They must have found the dead guards.*

The ledge he was on was about three hundred feet above the pool and about fifty feet away from the waterfall itself. He had a good clear view of the whole side of the mountain.

# CHAPTER 29

J AKE GOT UP later in the afternoon than he had the last several days. When he came down to the dining room he noticed it was already starting to get dark outside. Joice spotted him and had Kayla start preparing his meal. In the meantime, she prepared a meal for him to take to J'orik and Lianna. He popped his head into the kitchen and Joice told him to have a seat, she'd be right out with his evening meal. While he ate, they talked casually about how business had been going. She mentioned that Clare had come in asking about Lianna, wondering if she would be helping her with tutoring. The sheriff had stopped in asking about J'orik and Lianna, wanting to know if everything was all right with them. Gerard seemed to like working the front desk as much as he had been recently. She was missing his company.

"It'll all be over in a few days, dear," he reassured her. "J'orik will be going away with his father and Lianna will be returning here."

"I'm sad that J'orik will be leaving. I won't even get a chance to say good–bye. When do you think all this will happen?"

"Lianna will most likely be returning with me in the morning."

"That soon?"

"Yes. I don't think she should be there when K'orik and his group arrive. Chances are, they'll be there late tomorrow afternoon and I think it best if J'orik is there alone to meet them."

"How are the kids taking all this, especially Lianna?"

"I think Lianna's taking it the hardest. J'orik doesn't seem too happy about it either but he knows it's probably for the best. He has a point though. He doesn't want anyone to get hurt."

"And the tutoring, how's that going?"

"J'orik is doing superb. If he keeps practicing he should be able to change instantly within a year. Lianna is moving along too. She hasn't been able to change form yet, but her body is etherealizing. She still has to concentrate on it though. Still no indication of the type of dragon she'll be."

"Well, I'm looking forward to seeing her again. Give J'orik my best when you see him. It's getting late and you should be on your way."

He glanced out the window and saw that she was right. He finished his meal and Joice picked up the platter as she stood. He followed her into the kitchen and she handed him the meal she'd made for J'orik and Lianna. They kissed and he slipped out the back door, checking the alley first as usual. He walked south down the alley keeping his eyes and ears open for anything unusual.

The anonymous note that had been left on the front counter and the appearance of the lone hawk around the same time still bothered him. *Those two things have to be connected in some way*, he thought. *They can't be just merely coincidence. And coming at this time, whoever it is must have some vested interest in the outcome. I wonder what that interest could be. Is it J'orik, Lianna, or both, or something else not related to either one? The note was signed* a friend. *What could that mean? Is it someone I know?*

He walked west out of town thinking about all the questions he had on his mind. By the time he reached the small valley in the foothills it was completely dark out. He changed into his dragon form and headed towards the mountain cave. J'orik and Lianna were out on the ledge when he arrived. He presented them with the meal Joice had prepared and they walked back into the cave. J'orik had already built a small fire in the pit. They all sat and Jake watched as the two of them ate. Nothing was said while they ate. Jake suspected that Lianna knew it would be her last meal with J'orik for a while and just wanted to enjoy watching him eat and waiting for his usual belch. J'orik put the last bite of food in his mouth and sat up as it went down his throat. Lianna sat up waiting. Jake watched them and waited too.

J'orik looked at both of them. "What?" he said with a knowing smile. Then he closed his mouth and put his fist to it. There was a low rumble from deep in his stomach and then his cheeks puffed out.

"You ruined it," Lianna moaned.

"Ruined what?" He just smiled.

Before she could say another word he let go with a second belch and it echoed off the walls. All three of them started laughing heartily.

"There. Are you happy?" He smiled even bigger at her.

"Yes. I'm going to miss that," she said with sadness.

Jake hadn't said a word the whole time knowing this would be their last evening and meal together.

"Are we ready for some tutoring now?" he asked, placing his hands on his knees and making ready to stand.

They both looked at him smiling and nodded their heads yes.

So they all stood up and made their way down to the larger cavern. Lianna stopped at the ledge and told Jake she would climb down after he finished with J'orik. He acknowledged her request, turned, leapt off the ledge changing into his dragon form, and settling on the cavern floor. He didn't bother changing back to his human form since J'orik would be going first. J'orik climbed down behind him and prepared.

"Now, I want you to hold the change as long as possible this time," he told J'orik.

J'orik nodded. "I'll do my best."

"And if you can, try to lift yourself off the floor." He turned and yelled up at Lianna. "If he starts to rise, you should back up the tunnel some. Okay?"

"Okay," she yelled back down at him.

Jake turned his attention back to J'orik. J'orik closed his eyes and began concentrating. He quickly changed into a phoenix, bright flaming colors emitting from his body.

Jake let him stay in that state for a few moments and then he encouraged him to lift off the floor. "Raise your wings and pump them," he spoke loud but calm.

His wings started to open and spread. They spread all the way open and he pumped them once. The flames died down and he changed back into his human form.

"That was a good start," Jake told him.

"I want to try it again," he told Jake excitedly. "I think I can do this."

"Okay, give it a try."

J'orik closed his eyes tightly and concentrated. He changed form, his wings came open, and he pumped them. He lifted off the floor as he continued pumping his wings. It lasted a few moments and then he dropped back to the floor and changed back to human form.

"That was very good," Jake said encouragingly. "You're moving along splendidly."

"I was flying wasn't I?" he asked excitedly.

"Yes you were. Did you want to try again?"

"Yes!"

J'orik was so excited that before Jake could say another word he had changed form and started pumping his wings.

Jake quickly spoke up. "Not too high. Try to hover. Remember, you're inside a cavern, not outside."

J'orik did as Jake said. He hovered about twenty feet off the cavern floor for a longer time than the first and then he floated back down maintaining his phoenix form. Folding his wings back in, he changed back to human form.

"That was nearly flawless, J'orik"

"It felt fantastic."

"Now, don't do it again. I'm going to change into my human form."

"Okay."

Jake changed and walked over to J'orik, who had a huge smile on his face. Lianna could see that they were done so she climbed down from the ledge and ran over to J'orik. She went to fling her arms around him but Jake quickly grabbed her and held her back.

"Why'd you do that?" she asked him, somewhat hurt.

"He's still warm and I didn't want you to get hurt. He needs to cool down before you can touch him."

J'orik still had a smile on his face as he moved to sit down. He was also breathing heavily.

"You still have a lot of practicing to do, but you're doing very well. I've never seen anyone move along as quickly as you have."

J'orik started gaining control of his breathing and calmed down. The smile, however, never left his face.

Jake turned to Lianna. "Are you ready?"

"Yes," she replied with as much excitement as J'orik had shown.

Moving out away from them to give herself room, she closed her eyes and began concentrating. Her body slowly became translucent. Her clothing and hair were blowing back as if she was in a wind. She spread her arms out and seemed to lift off the floor slightly. A smile appeared on her face and she looked serene, peaceful. Suddenly she began sparkling. Small, multicolored flashes of light appeared inside her body. Then she dropped to the floor on her knees and became solid-looking again. Jake went to her side.

"What happened?" she asked, confused. "It felt different this time." She stood up.

"It was, dear. Your body wants to make the change now."

"I want to try again."

Jake nodded and backed away. She tried two more times with the same result. Jake could see the frustration in her face and suggested that it was time to stop.

"We should probably be on our way. The sun will be rising soon and we need to be back to town before then." Then he looked at Lianna, regretting the next thing he would have to say. "You do realize that you're leaving with me, right?"

"No. Not yet," she pleaded. Tears began welling in her eyes.

"K'orik will be here soon, tomorrow most likely, and we agreed that J'orik would have to be here alone when he arrived."

She started crying. "But I'm not ready to leave him yet," she pleaded some more.

J'orik stood and reached out with his hand to cup her chin. He lifted her head and looked deep in her eyes. He knew he had to be strong for her to do this. "I'm not ready to leave you yet either Lianna, but Jake is right and you know it. We've discussed this and this is the way it has to be. I don't like it any more than you do." He stepped close and wrapped his arms around her. She hugged him back, tightly.

"I'll leave you two alone for a moment, but only a moment. We need to be on our way." He turned and walked away. Instead of changing form he climbed up the rope and ran up to the cave. He gathered J'orik's things together, organized them in his pack, and ran back down to the ledge.

They held their embrace until J'orik backed away. She tried to hold him tight, not wanting to let go, but he gently pushed her back. She reached up, grabbed hold of his head, and pulled him down to give him a kiss. After the kiss she ran to the rope crying and climbed up to the ledge. She looked back at him one more time and disappeared up the tunnel.

Jake called down to him as he was pulling up the rope. "I have your pack with all your things in it. I'm going to lower it down and then drop the rope. Joice sends her love. Take care of yourself J'orik. I hope to see you soon." He had tears in his eyes now as he let go of the rope.

"Thanks for all you've done Jake. Tell Joice the same. Take care of Lianna for me and I will see you all again, soon."

Jake waved and then turned to head back up the tunnel.

J'orik was alone now waiting for what would happen next.


Jake walked out onto the ledge outside the mountain ahead of Lianna and changed into his dragon form. He'd brought a length of rope along for her to wrap around his neck to give her something to hold onto. He told her where to place it and that she needed to cinch it as tight as possible. His body wasn't like Joice's. He didn't have feathers to hold onto. His body was made up of smooth scales. After she had the rope in place he opened a wing for her to climb up on his back. Once she confirmed she was in place and ready to go he leapt off the ledge and took flight. He had explained that he was going to fly to the other side of the mountain to see exactly where K'orik and his group were.

Lianna reveled in the flight. She loved the wind in her face and the fact that you could see forever. She looked forward to the time when she would be flying herself.

Coming over the top of the mountain Jake began the descent on the other side. He thought he knew about where they would be by now. He flew close to the treetops once he reached the foot of the mountain and spotted their campfire next to the river. Flying right over the top of the campsite he let out a roar of defiance and then started gaining altitude. *That should wake them up*, he thought. Lianna smiled at his bravado and held on tight as he started upwards.

They flew around the south side of the mountain and headed back to the small valley in the foothills. Jake landed, let Lianna climb off his back, and then changed back into human form. They began the walk back to town.

"You know that Joice will be happy to see you again." He tried to take her mind off J'orik.

"I suppose Clare will be glad too. It seems like we've been gone for a long time but it hasn't even been a week yet." They walked in silence for a moment and then she looked wonderingly at Jake. "What do you think will happen when J'orik finally meets his father?"

"I don't know, dear."

"Have you ever met his father?"

"No."

They spent the rest of the walk without speaking. By the time they reached town the sun was just starting to peek over the tops of the trees in Murwood Forest. They walked up the alley and entered the kitchen. Joice was there waiting with open arms and a smile. Lianna ran and threw her arms around her weeping.

"I know child, it's hard to leave someone you love." She had tears in her eyes now as she hugged back.

"I do love him Joice, I do."

"You two have been through a lot together and it was bound to happen."

Even Kayla had tears in her eyes and had to stop working. She didn't understand what was going on but watching Joice and Lianna she couldn't help herself. Jake's eyes were tearing as well.

"You'll be fine child. You'll see him again soon enough." She tried consoling her as best as she could.

They stood there for a while longer holding each other until Lianna finally calmed down. Jake and Kayla both wiped the tears from their eyes and Kayla went back to work.

Joice walked Lianna up to the room she had held for her knowing she would be coming back and sat down on the bed with her.

"Now, you take your time and relax before coming back downstairs. You should take a long hot bath, it'll help. Clare brought by another one of her dresses she thought you would like. It's hanging in the closet. I'm going to leave now but you come back down when you're ready. I'll fix you something to eat when you do."

Joice stood up and looked down at Lianna. She just sat there looking down at her hands cupped between her legs and sagging shoulders.

Joice reached down and put her hand on Lianna's shoulder. "There are people here that care for you very much, Lianna." Then she left the room.

Coming back into the dining room she went and sat with Jake. Kayla had prepared his breakfast for him.

"So, how did things go?"

"She was pretty much the same there as she was here. She's very emotional. He took it pretty well given the circumstances. I could tell neither one of them liked what was happening but they both knew it had to happen."

"When do you think K'orik will find him?"

"Today. Probably late this afternoon. He's at the base of the waterfall. I'm sure they'll find the tunnel quick enough and, with Ogiloth, it won't take much longer before they find the cavern." He finished eating. "Joice, we've done what we can. He's made up his mind to go with his father. He plans to rescue Lianna's children and thinks this is the best way to accomplish that. I agree with his decision."

"You're probably right. He needs to stop running at some point and face his father. K'orik will never stop until that time comes. What I can't figure out is why he's so adamant about finding his son. He was never in his life. But, then again, he was never allowed in his life either."

"Who knows, Joice? Maybe he feels he owes something to J'orik for never being there. Maybe his life feels empty and he thinks J'orik will fill that void. Who knows? Maybe he's decided he wants to change his ways. All we can do is hope for the best and wait to see what happens. In the meantime, Lianna's here and we can do something with that."

She looked at him and could tell he needed some rest. "And how do you feel?"

"I'm tired," he sighed. "I'll probably sleep all day." Then he looked her in the eyes, "But don't let me. It's going to take me a few days to get back to normal and sleeping all day won't help. Make sure I'm up shortly after midday."

"Okay, dear." She smiled.

He stood up and went off to his room. She picked up his empty platter and went back into the kitchen.

# CHAPTER 30

THERE WAS A thumping sound and a whoosh of air followed by a loud roar. The leaves in the trees rattled like chimes. Everyone woke up startled by the sounds and rushed out to see what it was. The campfire appeared to have been blown out but there were no sparks anywhere. K'orik and Ogiloth already knew what it was and looked at each other knowingly as they came out of their tents. All eyes went to the sky but it was still dark and the trees were too thick to see what it was. The tree branches were still swaying and continued for several moments afterwards.

Olog looked over at Ogiloth. "It's the dragon again, isn't it?"

He just nodded yes.

K'orik had a scowl on his face. "That damn thing. Why does he do that?"

"Because he knows it irritates you," Ogiloth replied. Then he realized there were no sparks from the fire. He quickly counted the warriors and only came up with five. "Where are the guards?" he roared.

Olog quickly dispatched two of the warriors to go get them. They were only gone a few moments and came running back wide-eyed. Both reported the guard they had gone for was dead.

"What do you mean 'dead'?" Ogiloth roared with anger. "That could not have killed them. Bring them to me!" he ordered.

Olog sent the four remaining warriors in twos to collect the bodies. When they were brought back and examined Olog found that their throats had been slit open. He also realized they were the first ones put on guard duty which explained why the fire was out. He went and reported his findings to Ogiloth.

He roared with anger again. "Who could have done this?"

K'orik walked over next to him and looked down at the bodies. "Apparently there's someone following us that we're completely unaware of. Someone that's sneaky and quiet." Then he looked at the rest of the group. "Did anyone hear the guards yell out during the night or hear any strange noises?"

They all shook their heads no.

"Whoever or whatever it is, they're very good at what they do," he continued. "Looks like guard duty may be useless." Then he glanced at Ogiloth. "Or maybe it's the guards that are useless," he smirked.

Ogiloth growled at his remark.

"Well, now that I'm up, I'll be on my way to examine the waterfall," he said to no one in particular. Then to Ogiloth, "Have this mess cleaned up and be ready to move out when

I come back." Then he walked off into the trees towards the waterfall.

"Have those two buried quickly," Ogiloth ordered, "and then break camp. Time to eat only if you're ready to move out before K'orik returns and I don't expect him to take long." Then in a more angry tone and manner, "Move!" clenching his fists and gritting his teeth. "Now!"

While the others were doing as ordered, he prepared four torches for their walk inside the mountain.

K'orik walked to the edge of the pool and looked up the waterfall. He examined it from the ground first looking for anything out of the ordinary along either side of it. Since it was still dim out he was unable to see much of anything. As he had thought, he was going to have to examine it close up. The first thing he did was look for a way to get around the pool to the base of the waterfall. The sides of the mountain came down almost vertical all the way to the edge of the pool. After a closer examination it became apparent that the only way was to swim, and he wasn't going to do that. He was going to have to change into his phoenix form. He did notice, though, that on the north side of the pool near the base of the waterfall was a relatively flat area of rocks large enough to accommodate him as a phoenix, so he changed form, flew over to that spot, landed, and changed back to human form. The pounding of the water was incredibly loud. It was all he could hear.

He flattened his back against the rock face and carefully stepped behind the falling water. He felt along the rock face ahead of him with his left hand and eventually felt the rock bending away from the falling water. As he moved further in he found he was walking on sand instead of rock. He was able to make out what appeared to be a large opening with a sandy beach area behind the base of the waterfall. Feeling confident there was enough room he changed into his phoenix form and the cavern lit up. Fortunately it was large enough to accommodate him. He examined the whole interior and found that that's all it was, a large indentation with a sandy beach behind the base of the waterfall. No openings in any of the walls. He was a little disappointed. Changing back into his human form, he made his way back out,

Once outside, he leapt off the rocks and changed into a phoenix and began examining the face of the mountain adjacent to either side of the waterfall. It wasn't long before he spotted an opening along the north side of the waterfall about three hundred feet up with a ledge not quite large enough to accommodate him. He continued looking for other openings but found none. Returning to the one he had found, he noticed a narrow path along the face of the mountainside leading away from the ledge. He followed it as it led down towards the trees. Once he saw that it was less than a hundred feet above the river, he landed and changed back into his human form. Then he walked back to the camp.

He found Ogiloth and the others waiting for him, ready to go as he had directed them to be.

"I've found a way in but it won't be easy getting to it. The first thing we need to do is get to the other side of the river. We should be able to do that right here," he pointed at the river. "The water isn't moving too fast and it doesn't appear to be more than waist deep. Are we ready to go?"

They all stood and in unison they grunted, "Huh! Huh! Huh!"

K'orik gave a wry smile at Ogiloth and asked with some sarcasm, "I guess that means they're ready?" Then he walked to the river's edge and began crossing. They all followed behind him.

They crossed the river without incident. K'orik led them back to the path they would take to reach the opening he'd found. To reach the path it would be necessary for them to scale the slope up to it. Olog volunteered to climb first and then he would drop a rope for the others to use. Everyone watched as he climbed. Again, Olog impressed Ogiloth with his skills. He made it without any difficulty. He secured the rope to his waist and threw the other end down. The four warriors went first, one at a time, followed by Ogiloth, and then K'orik. The path was narrow, about two to three feet wide, so as each one came up they fell into line in the order they would be walking, K'orik, of course, in the lead, followed by Ogiloth, Olog, and then the others. Once they were all up on the path K'orik led them to the opening. There were a couple of narrower spots and one of the warriors almost fell but they all made it to the ledge next to the waterfall.

Ogiloth lit two of the torches and had one handed back to the warrior in the back of the line. He would carry one since he would be leading them. The sun hadn't appeared over the mountaintop yet as they entered the tunnel.

About fifty yards in the tunnel began to slope steeply upwards and turn at the same time. They hadn't passed any side tunnels yet. The noise from the waterfall had died away behind them and the only thing they could hear were their footsteps. The tunnel leveled out and split into three. Ogiloth stopped.

"Which way now?" K'orik asked with a smirk.

"Give me a moment." Then to the rest of the group, "Keep quiet." He handed the torch to K'orik. "Hold this at the opening of the tunnel that I'm in."

K'orik did as told and Ogiloth walked up each tunnel as far as the torchlight allowed. When he came back from the last tunnel he took the torch from K'orik and headed up the one on the left.

"Are you sure?" K'orik seemed doubtful about Ogiloth's choice.

"Yes," he answered with confidence.

The tunnel began to slope steeply upwards again. Ogiloth had to do this three more times. As they neared the large cavern J'orik was waiting in, they could hear the roar of a river. Stepping out into the cavern, Ogiloth turned and looked at K'orik with a smile.

K'orik just looked back with a glare. "The question now is will you remember the way back?"

Ogiloth just chuckled.

Jack watched below as K'orik flew over to the bottom of the waterfall, landed on the rocky area next to it, changed back into his human form, and slipped behind the rushing water. Moments later he came back out and Jack could see he had a look of disappointment. Then K'orik changed back into his phoenix form and began flying up the waterfall, searching. Jack was undecided what he would do so he just continued watching.

He saw that K'orik finally found a way in and watched him go back to get the rest of his group. They came back and climbed up to a narrow rocky path leading to the tunnel opening K'orik had found. Jack just continued watching from the perch he'd found on the opposite side of the pool. He thought about making their passage difficult but decided not to. He didn't want to expose himself to K'orik unnecessarily. One of them slipped and almost fell. He just laughed to himself.

They finally made it to the tunnel opening and he watched them disappear inside one by one. Eventually they would find their way in to the cavern and find J'orik there waiting for them. He figured he'd just wait for them to come back out so he made himself comfortable for the wait.

J'orik decided to take a short rest while he waited for K'orik to arrive. Jake had told him they probably wouldn't be there until late afternoon anyway. Not having the sun to judge time by, he had no idea when that would be.

While he slept he dreamed about the attack on the village. How he first met Lianna in Murwood Forest and their journey together over the last couple of weeks. The experiences they'd both had, people they'd met, and things they'd learned. He was going to miss her presence in his life.

His eyes snapped open. There was noise coming from the far end of the cavern. Listening carefully, he was able to discern voices. K'orik must be here and he wasn't being very quiet about it. Mentally, he prepared himself for the meeting. He didn't have a torch lit so he was sitting in the dark and was able to see the light from the torches K'orik's group was carrying. They stopped as they entered the cavern and he could hear them talking. He wasn't able to make out what they were saying but thought they were probably trying to figure out their next move. Then the talking stopped and the lights began moving his direction. He sat there and waited, in the dark, silent.

Eventually he was able to make out figures as they got closer. The one leading was huge, that must be Ogiloth. Behind him he saw a man with snow white hair. That must be K'orik. The others behind looked just like the monsters that had attacked his village. Suddenly he had an overwhelming feeling of rage but kept it under control. He knew that if he let the rage take over he would probably change form and attempt to slaughter them. K'orik would be the only one able to fight back and he knew it, but that's not the way he wanted to handle the situation. He had decided to go willingly without a fight.

They finally got close enough and spotted him sitting there, alone in the dark. Ogiloth halted, startled, and the rest of them stopped behind him. K'orik looked at him and stepped forward.

"Are you J'orik?"

He just nodded his head yes and K'orik stepped closer looking about the cavern.

"Are you alone in here?"

Again he nodded his head yes. This time, however, he stood up. The first thing he noticed was that he was nearly a head taller than K'orik, which surprised him. He had imagined him being similar in size and stature.

"I've decided to stop running," and very hesitantly he added, "father."

K'orik smiled and stepped closer with his arms open but J'orik stepped back.

"Yes," K'orik dropped his arms to his sides, "I guess we're not quite ready for that yet," sounding disappointed. "I suppose it'll take some time for us to get to know one another first. I'm just glad to finally meet you."

"I'm ready to go back with you."

"Good, good. It's almost a six-day journey back to the castle and we'll have some time to talk on the way. We should get started though. I'd like to be back outside the mountain before dark." He smiled up at J'orik again. Then he turned to Ogiloth and the others and waved his arm. "Okay, let's start back," he ordered.

Ogiloth went to take the lead and K'orik indicated for J'orik to walk in front of him behind Ogiloth. They crossed the cavern and entered the tunnel. They were back outside in little more than an hour. K'orik was impressed with Ogiloth.

They walked the narrow rocky path back to where they'd climbed up, without incident. Then they climbed down, hiked back to where they'd crossed the river, crossed, and stopped where they'd made camp earlier. There were still a couple hours of sunlight left but K'orik decided they would make camp anyway. While the others set up camp he took J'orik aside and found a quiet place where they could talk.

"I'm glad we finally have a chance to meet. I've thought about you often over the years wondering what you would be like, who you had become." K'orik was being as genuine as he possibly could. "Did you ever wonder about me?"

"Mother told me you were dead," he said in a flat tone.

K'orik looked down so the anger he had could not be seen. Recovering his composure he looked back in J'orik's eyes with a smile. "Well, I'm here now and I'm not dead," he said as gently as he could. "Where is your mother now?"

Even though J'orik knew the truth now, he lied. "She drowned when I was twelve."

K'orik knew that this was likely not true but he went along with it anyway. "I'm sorry to hear that. Who raised you after her death?"

"There was a couple in the village mother was close with that took me in." Anger rose inside him thinking about how that couple had been slaughtered with the others in the village when it was attacked and before he could stop himself he blurted out, "Why did you destroy my village and have all those people killed?" He looked at K'orik with tears in his eyes. "There was no reason for that. Those people did nothing to you." His anger was growing.

K'orik could see the anger in him and realized he needed to do or say something to calm him down. He could also feel more heat radiating from J'orik's body. He knew he would have to be careful what he said next, so he lied. "I was not there and had no control over what happened. I was disobeyed."

"You mean to tell me that you did not order the destruction and the killing?"

"That is correct. I only sent them to look for you."

"Then why send such a large force?"

"I didn't know what they would be going up against and wanted to assure they would have no problems."

J'orik looked away. "I don't believe you."

K'orik sighed and reached out to touch J'orik's shoulder. "You can believe what you want but that's the truth."

J'orik jerked away from his touch. "I still don't believe you." He turned on K'orik with anger. "The people in my village were peaceful people. They did not deserve what happened to them."

"I agree. But, what is done is done. There's nothing I can do about it now." K'orik was beginning to get frustrated and wanted to end this before it got out of control. "It's getting late now and we should have a bite to eat." He tried to interject a little humor. "I don't know about you but I'm famished." He stood up to go back to camp and waited for J'orik to stand. He stayed seated. "Okay, you sit here for a while and come into camp when you're ready."

J'orik didn't see the sad smile K'orik gave him before he turned and walked away. He sat there alone for the longest time listening to the crackle of the fire and the others' talking. He didn't go back into camp. Instead he lay down on the ground where he was and fell asleep. Again, he dreamt of the attack on the village. He never knew that K'orik came back and stood over him for a time before retiring to his tent for the night.

Neither one of them realized there was another pair of ears listening to their whole conversation.

Jack waited for several hours before he saw them come back out. J'orik was with them. He watched as they made their way back to the same spot they'd camped the night before. As camp was being set up, K'orik and his son walked away from the activity and sat down to talk. He found himself a place to perch close enough to hear their conversation. He listened to K'orik lie to his son. They talked for about a half hour before K'orik stood and tried to get his son to go back to camp to eat. J'orik refused and stayed where he was.

Eventually J'orik laid down and fell asleep. He watched K'orik return and stand over him for a while before going to his tent. He decided he would just watch them over the next few days as they made their way back to K'orik's castle. Quietly he took off and flew back to his warehouse in Bruston.

# CHAPTER 31

S HORTLY AFTER MIDDAY Joice decided it was time for Jake to get up. On her way to wake him she stopped in at Lianna's room to check on her. She hadn't come downstairs to eat and Joice was a little concerned. Opening the door quietly she peeked in. She was asleep. Joice could tell she hadn't moved from the bed since she left her. She still had the same clothes on that she'd come back in. Deciding to let her continue sleeping, she quietly shut the door and went to get Jake.

Jake was sitting up on the edge of the bed yawning and stretching his arms when she entered the room.

"I see you're awake already. Are you ready for some lunch?"

"Yes. For some reason I'm starving." He stood up, shook himself, and started dressing. "Did Lianna ever go downstairs and eat?"

"No. She's still asleep. I just checked on her. I think she passed out right after I left her this morning."

"Poor girl, this last day has been pretty rough for her." He finished dressing and they headed down the hall.

"She'll come out of it, Jake. There are people here that'll help take her mind off her troubles. Clare has already stopped in to see her."

Gerard was behind the front counter when they came down the stairs.

"Good afternoon, Mr. Freeman. Did you have a good rest?"

"Yes, Gerard. Thanks for asking and thanks for watching the front counter these last few days."

"Not a problem, Mr. Freeman, I rather enjoyed it," he smiled.

They continued into the dining room. There weren't too many people since it was between lunch and dinner time. Jake sat down at a table near a window. Joice brought him a mug of hot coffee then went off to the kitchen to get him something to eat. He sipped on his coffee and stared out the window. *Things are going back to normal now*, he thought.

He was still staring out the window lost in his thoughts when Joice returned with a platter of food for him. She set it on the table with a cup of orange juice.

He looked down at the food and then up at her. "What do we have here, dear? It looks really good."

"I thought a large turkey sandwich, a green salad, and a hot bowl of turkey soup would do you good. I also made a cup of fresh squeezed orange juice. And for dessert, I thought you'd like a couple of cinnamon rolls. How's that sound?"

He smiled. "Perfect."

"I'm going to let you eat in peace today. Besides, I have to start prepping for the evening dinner crowd. But, before I do that, I think I'll go make sure Lianna's up. She shouldn't sleep all day."

He smiled at her as she walked away. *I don't know what I'd do without that woman.* She turned and smiled back at him like she knew what he was thinking.

Joice decided to knock this time. There was no response so she slowly opened the door and peered in. Lianna was nowhere to be seen. *I wonder if she's gone to take a bath.* She walked down the hallway to the communal bathrooms. Only one appeared to be in use. She knocked on the door.

"Who is it?" Lianna asked.

She recognized Lianna's voice. "It's me, Joice. I was just checking on you. I thought if you were up you could tell me what you'd like to eat and I could get it fixed for you."

"I've only been in here a few moments. You were right, it feels wonderful."

"Well, I'll leave you alone then. You can decide later when you come downstairs what you want to eat."

"Okay, thank you."

She left and on her way back downstairs she heard a commotion going on outside. Gerard wasn't at the front counter. When she walked into the dining room she saw all the customers gathered at the windows staring out at something in wonder. She went to the window at Jake's table and looked out. There, in the street just outside the inn, were four camels, each bearing a rider dressed in puffy white pants and shirt. Around their waists they wore a wide black belt with a large curved sword attached, unsheathed. The silver blade glinted in the sunlight and the handles were ornately decorated in gold and silver relief of a phoenix. Their hats looked like upside down red buckets banded in gold lace. They weren't wearing shoes. The camels' reins and mounts were just as ornately decorated in red and gold with images of phoenixes. Behind the camels was a red carriage similarly decorated and drawn by four huge white horses with long, dark brown, braided manes. The windows of the carriage had the curtains drawn closed. There were two coachmen sitting on the bench of the carriage dressed the same as the camel riders only without the swords and wearing red vests. Behind them, on top of the carriage, was a large chest similarly decorated. The carriage was parked right outside the front door to the inn. All activity outside had stopped as the townspeople watched and waited for the occupants of the carriage to step out. The camel riders got down and walked over to stand near the carriage door, two on either side. The one nearest the handle reached up and opened the door. A woman dressed in more colorful clothing stepped out of the carriage. Her clothes were sheerer and appeared to be layered. Her hat was smaller and fit closer to her head. It was encrusted with jewels. She had a veil across her face but it did not cover her long, thick black hair. As she walked towards the front door of the inn one of the camel riders rushed to open the door for her. The two coachmen hefted the large chest from the roof of the carriage down to two of the camel riders. Gerard, Jake, and Joice all rushed to the entry area arriving just as she came through the door. The customers all ran and crowded around the entry to the dining room. The two camel riders carrying the chest came in with the woman and shut the door. They set the chest down and stood in front of the door as if to prevent it from being opened again. The woman walked over and stood in front of Gerard, Jake, and Joice.

"I wish to speak with Jake and Joice Freeman," she said in a soft, heavily accented voice.

Jake stepped forward. "I'm Jake Freeman. What can I do for you?"

She looked over at Joice. "And you would be Joice Freeman, sister of Karin Drake?"

Joice nodded. "Yes. What can we do for you?"

"My name is Jalana Khameer. I need to speak with you about my son, J'orik."

Jake and Joice's mouths dropped open. They could not believe what they just heard. They closed their mouths and composed themselves.

"Let's get some privacy," Joice said. "Follow me."

She lifted her arm towards the office and started walking. Jake stepped aside and let her pass then followed behind her. Everyone in the inn just watched as she walked by and disappeared into Jake's office. After the door was shut they all went back to their seats and started talking about the new arrival. Some of them went to the windows and looked outside at the unusual animals. No one in Bruston had ever seen a camel. Horses they had seen but nothing like the horses that had just come into town. They were almost as unusual as the camels. Everyone was wondering where they came from. The townspeople outside were reacting in a similar way.

Joice ushered Jalana to a chair and then sat down herself. Jake shut the office door and made his way around to his chair behind the desk and sat.

"Now that we have some privacy," Joice began, "what is it you need to speak with us about?"

Jalana removed her veil to speak. "I was led to believe that J'orik was here. Is that true?"

"Well, he 'was' here. Who told you this?" she asked curiously.

"Your sister, she came to visit me and told me that J'orik was in trouble. She said he was staying here with you and Jake. Where is he now? It is important that I find him."

"He's with K'orik by now," Jake responded.

A look of fear and sadness came across Jalana's face. "I was afraid of that. Karin told me he was looking for J'orik and that J'orik had come here. How is it he came to be with K'orik?"

"I didn't think Karin knew where you were," Joice stated with confusion.

"Karin has always known where I was and I asked her to keep it secret. I told her so that she could contact me if the need arose. Now, how is it he came to be with K'orik?"

"When he came here, he was running from some dangerous creatures that K'orik had sent after him." Joice told her. "We didn't know who he was at first. Clare, the woman that works at the sheriff's office, brought him here to stay. That was the first place he stopped when he came to town, the sheriff's office. He went there to report what had happened at his village and then Clare brought him here. Did Karin explain what happened at the village?"

"Yes, and that is why I came here as quickly as possible. She also said he was travelling with a woman, Lianna. She also survived."

"Yes, Clare brought them both here. Like I said, we didn't know who he was at first. We took them in, gave them a room, and fed them. We could sense they were both of our race. I was talking with them while they were eating in the dining room and that's when it came out who he was.

I decided Jake and I should have a longer and more private conversation with them. We explained what we knew about him, how we knew him, and that we would do everything we could to help him. We thought it best if he left town. There's a place in the mountains that Jake and I go so we took him and Lianna there thinking it would be a safer place for him to stay. As you probably know, K'orik is relentless. Somehow he was able to track J'orik here and we knew it was only a matter of time before he would track him to our place in the mountains. It was J'orik's decision to go with K'orik. He didn't want to spend the rest of his life running so he decided to face him and, like Jake just said, he's with K'orik now."

"Are they still in the mountains or has he returned to his castle?"

"They're still in the mountains but are on their way back to K'orik's castle," Jake replied.

"Do you know where in the mountains they are?"

"I have a pretty good idea."

"Can you lead me to them?"

"I could," he replied, "but I don't know if that would be such a good idea."

"Are you refusing to help me?"

"I didn't say that. I just said . . ."

"I know what you just said," interrupting him, "and I am telling you that K'orik cannot have my son. I will not allow it," she said angrily. Then in a calmer tone, "Will you help me?"

Jake and Joice looked at each other and then sighed in resignation. Before either one could respond, though, there was a knock at the door. Joice got up to see who it was. When she opened the door Lianna was standing outside.

"Come in, dear, there's someone here I think you should meet." She stood aside allowing Lianna to enter.

She came into the office and stopped just inside the door when she saw Jalana. Joice shut the door and gently pushed her towards the empty chair next to Jalana. Hesitantly she sat down. Joice introduced them after she was in the chair.

"Jalana, this is Lianna. Lianna, this is Jalana, J'orik's mother."

They stared at each other for a moment then at the same time they said, "Hello," and smiled.

Jalana looked at Jake and Joice. "Now, I need to know, will you help me?"

"Yes," Joice answered, "but we need to have a little more information."

"What is it you need to know?"

"First of all, why is it so important? After all, you haven't been in J'orik's life for quite some time now," she said bluntly.

Lianna looked confused but continued sitting quietly.

Jalana looked at her and then back at Jake and Joice. "How much do you know about J'orik's past?"

"Just what little my sister has told us. K'orik kidnapped you and forced himself on you. You bore him a son and shortly after his birth you ran away with him to the village he grew up in. When he was twelve, you faked your own drowning and left him to be raised by a couple in the village. During your time in the village, you made many visits to Washoe and became close friends with my sister. She and Casper treated him like family and he grew up knowing them as his aunt and uncle. Until recently he didn't know otherwise. Is there more you have to add to that?"

"Yes." She paused in thought before continuing. "My father is the ruler of the land I come from. My family has ruled there for as long as there is memory. I am a princess in my land and J'orik would be a prince. When K'orik kidnapped me, my father sent search parties looking for me. He told me that he looked for ten years before he resigned himself to the fact that I was probably dead or lost to him forever. There was never a ransom request for my return. He said he never really gave up though, thinking that one day his lost daughter would return home.

"K'orik kept me locked away deep inside his castle. He treated me well because I would be the mother of his child. He swore he would let me free after the child was born. On the day of J'orik's birth there was a great celebration in his castle. He was especially happy that the child was a boy. He wanted a son so badly. He kept his promise and let me free to move about the castle, even telling me that I was free to leave if I wanted. But, I could not take J'orik with me. I swore to myself that I would never leave until I could take him with me. I planned and planned our escape for months. Finally a chance came. K'orik left to make a visit with Sarguroth," she said his name with distaste, "and with the help of one of the nursemaids we snuck out of the castle with J'orik that night and ran. She led me to the village where J'orik grew up. She eventually married a man in the village and when I left, she and her husband were the ones I left him with. They, along with a man named Falder, helped me fake my drowning so that no one would think I just abandoned my son.

"I left the village and went to Washoe to visit your sister. I explained everything to her then I started my journey back to my home in the Great Desert. Because of the way my father is, I knew he would not be receptive to me returning with a child from the man that kidnapped me. That is why I left J'orik behind. When I arrived home my father was so happy to see me. There was a celebration and then I settled back into the life that I had been taken from. It took me many years before I was able to confess to my father everything that had happened. And, as I had known, he was not happy that I had had a child out of wedlock. It took my several more years to convince him to allow me to bring J'orik home. Shortly after that is when your sister came to me and told me what happened. I knew I needed to act quickly before I lost J'orik to his father.

"Now do you understand why it is important for me to find J'orik?"

"Yes," Joice said sadly. Jake nodded in agreement.

Then Lianna looked at Jake and Joice. "What about my children?" she asked with an angry tone. Turning to Jalana she said, "J'orik decided to go with K'orik not only to prevent any further harm to anyone but also to rescue my children. K'orik took all the children from my village and probably all the children from the other villages he destroyed in his search for J'orik. What about them?" She was leaning forward in her chair, near rage, when she ended.

Jake quickly interceded. "Lianna calm down now. We understand why J'orik made the choice he did. This is why we haven't promised anything to Jalana."

"But you said you would help her," she reacted with frustration.

"Yes we did," he conceded, "but Jalana doesn't know everything that's been going on nor does she understand fully why J'orik made the decision he did."

Lianna fell back in her chair exasperated.

"Perhaps if I understood J'orik's reason for going with his father I would not be so forceful about my needs," Jalana tried to console Lianna. "It sounds as if K'orik has wrought much destruction in his relentless search for J'orik. Perhaps, by working together, we can find a solution for all of our needs." Jalana was sounding more diplomatic now.

"I think you're right, Jalana," Joice volunteered. "I think J'orik can handle himself just fine with his father. The important issue right now is rescuing the children that were taken, all of them. My question, though, is why did K'orik spare the children and take them back to his castle?"

"He raises them to be his servants," Jalana responded. "K'orik has always been a kidnapper and he enjoys having servants around. All the children, whether born to his existing servants or children he has taken, are put in a nursery and raised to serve him. He is a very arrogant man."

Jake and Joice looked at each other and chuckled. "Don't we all know that," Jake jokingly opined.

It was starting to get dim in the room and Jake stood to light a lamp. "It's getting late and the sun will be down soon. Do we have any rooms available?" he asked Joice.

"I'll have to check with Gerard, but I believe there's one room left." She got up and went out to the front desk. A moment later she returned. "There's one room left. We would love to have you stay the night Jalana."

"What about my men outside? There are six of them."

"I can check the other inns, starting with the Tigress across the street," Jake offered. "Jack has more rooms than we do. I'm sure he has a couple open. The stables are just down the way. I can show your men the way."

"Thank you Jake, that's very kind of you. Only one of them speaks your language though. His name is Sayid."

He nodded his head and smiled, then left to do as he said.

"Lianna, it has been a pleasure to meet you. I apologize for my selfishness and hope that you will forgive me. I would enjoy your company for an evening meal before we all retire. What do you say?"

"I would like that."

Joice smiled, glad that they were able to get past their personal needs and work towards a common goal. "Why don't you two go have a seat in the dining room and figure out what you want to eat, I'll be out to check on you in a moment."

Jake showed Jalana's men to the stables and was able to secure rooms for them at the Tigress Inn. One of the men, however, decided to stay with the camels at the stables. The stable hand had no experience with camels and indicated it would be better if someone stayed with them that did. It was dark by the time Jake returned. He let Jalana know what had been set up. She thanked him and continued enjoying her meal and conversation with Lianna. He walked back to the kitchen where Joice was.

"Well, that was strange," he told her. "I'm just glad it all worked out."

"It's not over yet, dear. We haven't really discussed what our next move will be. I think Jalana was just being very diplomatic since it was her against us. Tomorrow when we sit down to talk will be when we find out how cooperative everyone will be with each other." Joice looked at him sidelong and then went back to cooking.

He headed back out to the front counter with Gerard. He glanced over at Jalana and Lianna as he passed through the dining room. It looked like they were getting along fine.

# CHAPTER 32

AFTER A FULL night's rest Jack got up for a normal day at the warehouse. He walked downstairs and found George.

"Everything go all right yesterday while I was gone?"

"Yeah, we didn't have any more problems after those dwarves left. There was some excitement late yesterday before we closed up shop though."

"Really, what happened?" His eyebrows went up with curiosity.

"I didn't see it myself but one of the delivery drivers came in all excited. Said a rich looking carriage being pulled by two huge horses stopped at the Dragons' Inn. There were four other strange looking creatures, each with a rider all decked out in white wearing funny looking hats and long curved swords. He thought he heard someone say they were camels or something like that. Some lady all dressed in frilly clothes, wearing a veil over her face, got out of the carriage and went inside the inn. He watched for a little while longer and then figured he should get back here before we closed up."

"I might have to go down there and see what's going on." Then he changed to business. "What do we have going on here for today?"

George took out his daily log and started reading. Jack stopped him when he got to the delivery to Washoe.

"Good. I was hoping we had something going to Washoe today. I have a letter I need delivered. When Sammy or Tommy get here, make sure they understand I want them to hand deliver it to the person whose name is on the envelope. I've also written the place it needs to be delivered to on the envelope. I'll go get it and leave it with Bryce and tell him the same thing. I want you to make sure that whichever one it is, they understand it's to be hand delivered and given only to the person named on the envelope."

"Sure thing, boss."

"Okay, what's left?"

George finished reading his log. When he was done, Jack left to go get the letter he needed delivered. After he dropped it off with Bryce and explained to him what he'd told George, he decided to walk down the street and see what all the excitement was from yesterday. He figured he'd stop at the Tigress first for something to eat before walking across the street to the Dragons' Inn. On his way, he saw Owen already at the Boars' Den starting the day with a pint. He waved at him and smiled. Owen smiled and waved back. *I wonder if he even goes home at night or if they just let him sit at that table all night and sleep.*

He glanced over at the Dragons' Inn before going inside the Tigress and didn't see anything unusual. *Jake must have taken the wagon and those other animals George was talking about down to the stables for the night. Was it camels he called them? If they were truly camels, then there's only one place they could have come from. Some place in the Great Desert.* It had been years since Jack had seen camels. The last place he expected to see them was here in Bruston.

He entered the Tigress and greeted Harry on his way into the dining room. Harry stopped him before he went in.

"Jack. We had some unusual guests stay last night. They're in eating right now."

"Yeah, I heard there was some excitement yesterday. George told me about it."

"Just thought I'd tell you so you wouldn't look surprised when you walked in and saw them."

"Thanks Harry."

He walked into the dining room and spotted the new guests without any problem. They were dressed just like George had described. He continued over to his usual table by the window and sat down. Katy came over with a hot mug of coffee for him.

"Did Harry tell you about them?" she spoke softly and nodded her head towards them without looking.

"Yeah, he said they were in here. I don't see the woman with them."

"She stayed across the street. Have you ever seen the likes of them before?"

He didn't let on that he had. He just smiled up at her. "Any specials for breakfast?"

"No. Just the usual stuff."

"How about some scrambled eggs, half a dozen slices of bacon, and biscuits smothered in your special gravy?"

"I can do that. Be right back."

He glanced over at the new guests for a moment and then stared out the window while sipping his coffee. *So the woman stayed at Jake's inn. I wonder what this is all about. I wonder if it has something to do with J'orik or Lianna.* He was still staring out the window deep in thought when Katy came back with his breakfast. She set the platter of food down and refilled his coffee.

"I added a cinnamon carrot muffin on the side."

"Thanks Katy. You sure know how to win a man over." He smiled at her as she turned to go.

He tried to focus on the conversation the new guests were having. It was in a different language but he recognized it. He hadn't heard it for a long time so it took him a few moments to remember. They were having a casual conversation, nothing specific. It centered mostly on the weather and how much cooler it was here than in the desert. They made comments about how differently the people looked and dressed. The other guests and patrons in the room ignored them, simply because they couldn't understand what they were saying. He ate slowly so that he could see what they would do when they were finished. Looking closely at their attire he noticed that their swords, belts, and hats were ornately decorated with the image of a phoenix. *This has to have something to do with J'orik, or maybe even K'orik.*

Eventually they finished with their meals and got up to leave. He watched two of them cross the street and go inside the Dragons' Inn. The other four headed down the street. *They're probably headed for the stables to check on the camels*, he thought. He finished his breakfast, drank down the last of his coffee, and proceeded to make his way outside.

He stood on the sidewalk just outside the Tigress for a while watching the activity going on before he crossed the street to the Dragons' Inn. He was greeted by Gerard as he came in.

"Good morning Mr. Erenson. How're you today?"

"I'm doing great Gerard. Is Jake in?"

"He is, but he's in his office with Joice and our newest guest."

"I heard about that. They came into town with, camels, was it?"

"That's what I was told they were. Strange looking creatures if I ever saw one," he half chuckled. "Have you ever seen one?"

"Yes, a long time ago."

"Do you know where they come from?"

"I saw them when I was in the desert."

"In the desert?" his eyebrows went up.

"There's something I need to discuss with Jake. Would you let him know I was in and that I'll be over at the Boars' Den for a while?"

"Certainly will Mr. Erenson."

"Thanks, Gerard," and he stepped back outside.

He stood on the sidewalk outside the inn for a while thinking about what he would talk to Jake about before heading over to the Boars' Den. While at the pub he figured he'd just sit and talk with Owen to pass the time. When he got there, Durog happened to be sitting with Owen. *Good*, he thought, *two good friends to pass the time with*. He walked in and they both hollered at him to sit down with them.

"Jack, how ye be me friend?" Durog growled.

"I be fine me friend," he responded in their slang.

"Have a seat an' join us."

He pulled a chair over and sat down across the table from them positioning himself so that he could watch the Dragons' Inn. The waitress immediately showed up with a pint for him."

Durog looked over at Owen and winked. "Tha advantages of ownin' tha place, eh? Served quick an' coin free." He and Owen let out with a loud round of laughter, smacked their mugs together, and took a long swig ending with an 'Ah'.

"Whatcha be up to taday me friend, out fer a stroll?"

"I heared 'bout all tha excitement yesterday an' thought I'd come in ta see what it be all about." He took a long swig of his ale. He looked at Owen. "Do ya know anythin' 'bout it Owen, me friend?"

"I was a sittin' right 'ere when they rolled in." He took a swig. "Mighty funny lookin' creatures they be ridin' too. An' them riders, they be dressed funnier than I ever seen afore too. Wearin' buckets upside down on their heads." He started laughing and Durog joined him. They both took swigs. "Poofy pants an' a long curved sword. Never seen nothin' like'm afore."

"What about ye, Durog? Ever seen anythin' like'm yerself?" Jack asked and then took another swig. As he was bringing the mug back down he saw the two coachmen come walking back out of the Dragons' Inn with Gerard in the lead. *He must be taking them down to the stables*, he thought.

"Wasn't 'ere meself. But from what Owen 'ere says sounds like they come from tha desert." He took another swig. "I heared tell they got some mighty odd creatures livin' out there in tha desert." He went to take another swig but found his mug was empty. He turned and hollered, "Waitress, filler up would ye."

"Me too," Owen spoke up. "What 'bout ye Jack, ready fer some more?"

Jack tipped his mug to take a swig, finished it off, and replied, "Me too. An' this round be on me," he added, putting a smile on his friends faces.

The three of them drank and talked for over an hour before Jack decided it was time for him to leave. The last thing he wanted was to be drunk when he talked with Jake. Unlike his friends, he couldn't hold his liquor like a dwarf. Dwarves could drink all night long without sleeping and go right back to mining again. He knew. He'd watched them do it. They were a stout race, just like the ale they drank.

Before he left he told Durog, "If'n ya see Jake come in, tell'm I be at me warehouse, would ye."

"Sure will." He and Owen lifted their mugs together and then downed what was in them. "Dern humans can't take their liquor." Then he and Owen laughed out loud again.

Jack left the Boars' Den and headed back to his warehouse thinking about what he might talk to Jake about. He hadn't decided yet and the drinking didn't help.

# CHAPTER 33

JAKE WAS ALREADY at the front counter when Jalana and Lianna came downstairs the next morning.

"Good morning ladies, how're we doing today? Did you sleep well?"

"I'm feeling a lot better," Lianna responded with a smile. "That's the first full night's rest I've had in a while and it felt wonderful, especially sleeping on a real bed."

"You have a very nice inn, Jake," Jalana replied. "I had a restful sleep as well. Thank you for asking." Her smile wasn't near as broad as Lianna's.

"Joice is already in the kitchen prepping for breakfast. Why don't you ladies head on into the dining room and decide what you'd like to eat. I'll let her know you're up."

He followed them into the dining room. They went and sat at the same table they'd used the night before. He continued on into the kitchen.

"The girls are up, dear."

"Okay, thanks. I'll get to them in a moment." She and Kayla were still busy prepping. "If Kristen hasn't already, would you take them some coffee?"

On his way back out he noticed that Kristen had already taken them some coffee and was standing at their table talking with them, so he went back out to the front counter.

Kristen set the coffee down and handed each of them a menu. "Good morning," she smiled and looked out the window. "It looks like it's going to be another beautiful day."

"Yes it does, Kristen," Lianna agreed. "I don't believe you've met Jalana yet. I didn't see you in here last night when we had dinner."

"I was here during all the excitement of her arrival but I left shortly afterwards. I usually only help get things set up for the dinner crowd then I go home," she explained. "Hello Jalana, I'm Kristen," she offered her hand with a broad smile on her face and Jalana reached up and shook it.

"You remember J'orik, right?" Lianna asked. Kristen nodded yes. "This is his mother."

"It's very nice to meet you."

"It is very nice to meet you also, Kristen."

"Is this your first time in Bruston?"

"Yes."

"I love your outfit, it's very colorful. You can't find anything like it here in Bruston."

"Thank you."

"Well, I should leave you ladies to decide what you want for breakfast. If you need anything more just give me a holler. Again, it was nice meeting you Jalana." Then she walked away to check on the other patrons that had already come down for breakfast.

Jalana and Lianna talked casually while reviewing the menu and sipping their coffee. Soon enough Joice came out of the kitchen and wandered over to their table.

"Good morning ladies. Have we decided what we're having for breakfast yet?"

"I think I'll go with the bowl of fruit, a cinnamon carrot muffin, and a glass of fresh squeezed orange juice," Lianna replied.

"I will have the same," Jalana told her.

"You girls are too easy," she chuckled. "All right, a bowl of fruit, a cinnamon carrot muffin, and a glass of fresh squeezed orange juice coming right up."

Jalana looked at Lianna with a bigger smile than earlier. "Joice appears to be in a very happy mood today," she observed, watching Joice walk back into the kitchen.

"Yes, she does," she agreed with a chuckle. "Almost bouncy."

"Is she always like this?"

"I haven't been around her long enough to see if that's the way she always is, but I imagine having to serve people all the time you need to be in a positive mood."

"I imagine you are right," as she looked out the window. "Is there always this much activity in Bruston?"

"Yes. From what I understand a lot of commercial and industrial business flows through here. The dwarves have a mining operation in the mountains west of town and, with the lake, there's a lot of fishing."

"I remember living in the village and the people fishing there also. Where I live in the desert we must import the fish."

Joice returned to their table carrying a platter with their orders. "Here you go ladies," as she set everything down. "I brought along some butter and honey for the muffins just in case. Is there anything else I can get you?" They both nodded no. "Well, if there is, just let me or Kristen know. Enjoy." She smiled and left them to eat.

They continued with more casual conversation while eating and when they finished Joice came back to their table. "How was everything?"

"It was delicious," Jalana responded.

"Good. Now that you've eaten we can continue our discussion from yesterday. I'll clean up here and then meet you and Jake in his office."

They both got up as Joice was clearing the table and headed for the front desk. Jake was behind the counter assisting a couple checking out. He thanked them for staying at the inn and then turned his attention to Jalana and Lianna.

"How was your breakfast?"

"It was very good," Jalana answered.

"Good, I'm glad. Are we ready to sit down and talk now?" They both nodded yes. He ushered them into his office. "You ladies have a seat. I need to go get Gerard to watch the front desk. I'll be right back."

He shut the door and Lianna sat down. Jalana walked over and started inspecting the variety of books Jake had in his collection before taking a seat. They were only in the office for a few moments before Joice arrived. She was no longer wearing her apron. She walked across the room and sat down just as Jake entered. He did the same.

"Okay," he said, "where'd we leave off yesterday?"

"We were discussing what we would do about my son," Jalana replied.

"Yes, yes. Have you had time to think on the matter?"

"I was hoping you would have a solution to the dilemma."

"Joice and I talked about it last night and we did come up with an idea but I thought if you had decided on something we would listen to what you have to offer first."

"I would prefer to hear your idea first," she stated flatly.

"All right, here it is then," he began, with his elbows on the chair arms, his hands clasped together, and a serious look on his face. "We believe J'orik should go with his father at this time. Your son has a very strong will and we don't believe he'll be easily influenced by his father. After spending the last week with him and tutoring him with the changing process I believe he'll eventually be much, much stronger than his father. He has obviously been raised in a positive and good environment and this is reflected in his behavior. He shows a desire to help rather than destroy and because of the decision he made to go with his father, we don't believe he would want us to interfere with that decision. We understand your desire to reunite with your son but, under the circumstances, we don't believe that to be the right choice at this time. We know this will be a hard choice for you but it is the right choice. It was hard for Lianna to let him go too but she did." Jake paused for a moment as Jalana and Lianna looked at each other with half smiles.

"Now, as to the matter of the children," he continued. "There were many villages destroyed by K'orik's forces and all those villages had children that were taken. If there is any hope of recovering those children, J'orik is the best option. This is part of the reason Lianna was able to go along with his decision. Her children were three of those taken. J'orik has said that he'll keep in touch with us and keep us informed on his progress, not only regarding the children but his progress with the changing. Understand, though, that he will now be tutored by his father." There came a knock at the door. "Excuse me for a moment." Jake got up to see who it was.

Gerard was at the door. "Jalana's coachmen are here. What should I do?"

"Just a moment," he turned to Jalana. "Your coachmen are out in the entry area. Would you like to speak with them?"

She got up and walked towards the door. "Yes, let me talk with them for a moment. I will be right back."

Jake stood at the door holding it ajar while Joice and Lianna stayed seated. He could hear them talking but was unable to understand them.

When she came back in the office she asked Jake, "I told them to go to the stables and see about the animals and come back here when they were done. Can your man take them down there?"

"Yes, of course. It'll take a moment or two because I'll have to have Kristen watch the front desk while he's gone." He turned to Joice. "Kayla will be all right watching the dining room by herself, right?"

"Yes. I'll go talk to her."

Jake went to have Gerard escort Jalana's men to the stables then he went to have Kristen watch the front desk until Gerard got back. Joice got up and went to inform Kayla that she would be alone watching the kitchen and the dining room while Kristen was watching the front desk for Gerard.

They both returned and took their seats again.

"Now where was I?" Jake questioned himself. "Oh yes. Joice and I have even considered the possibility that having J'orik around might be a good thing for K'orik. Maybe he feels his life is empty and having J'orik, his son, around will help fill that emptiness. Maybe he's tired of his evil ways and is looking to make a change himself. J'orik could be the catalyst for that. We're trying to keep an open mind about the possibilities and think more optimistically. We were hoping that you could to the same." He stopped and waited for a response, or input, from Jalana. Other than the interruption from her men, she had listened quietly to everything he said.

Several moments passed before she responded. "I see the points you are making, Jake, and I agree with your reasoning. I do have a question for you though. Do you know where J'orik is right now?"

"After today he should be coming around to the east side of the mountains and heading back in this direction."

"Do you know how long it will take them to get back to K'orik's castle?"

"Not exactly, but I'm guessing it could take them up to a week, or more, depending on the route they take."

She sat in thought for a few moments. "For the sake of the children I will agree to your plan. Based on what you have told me I agree that J'orik is their best hope. I will return home and wait for news of his progress. Karin knows where to find me. You can send messages through her. If this issue has not been resolved before a year's time, I will return here and we can discuss what will be done next. Agreed?"

He looked at Joice and Lianna and they indicated agreement. "Agreed," he answered.

"I would like to stay one more night, if that is not a problem, before leaving for home. I have come to enjoy Lianna's company and would like to spend the day with her visiting your town of Bruston."

"That's not a problem. I'll go secure the rooms at the Tigress again for your men." He got up immediately and left.

"Do you mind spending the day with me Lianna?"

"No, not at all, in fact I'm looking forward to it," she smiled.

The two of them got up and looked at Joice. "No, don't you worry about me. You two go enjoy yourselves. Someone has to stick around and watch this place anyway." She got up and followed them out. "I'll have Jake go down to the stables when he gets back and let your men know you'll be staying another night."

Jalana nodded acknowledgement and she and Lianna left the inn to enjoy a day on the town.

Jake returned shortly after they left and Joice sent him down to the stables. About half way there he met Gerard on his way back.

"Is everything all right?" he asked Gerard.

"Yeah, the stable hand was able to understand the one okay enough. They wanted to tend to those camels of theirs and I thought it would be okay if I went back to the inn."

"They'll be spending another night so I'm going to tell them. You go ahead on back to the inn. Joice could probably use your help anyway. I'll be back quick enough."

"Oh, one more thing, Mr. Erenson stopped by and said he wanted to talk with you. Have you seen him yet?"

"No. Did he say it was important?"

"No, just said he wanted to talk with you. He said he was going to be at the Boars' Den for a while, though."

"Okay, thanks Gerard. I'll be back to the inn quick enough. You go on ahead."

Jake continued on to the stables and informed Jalana's men they would be staying at the Tigress Inn again. On his way back he decided he'd take the time and stop by the Boars' Den to talk with Jack. When he walked in Durog hailed him.

"Jake, how ye be me friend?"

"I'm doing good, Durog. Hey, have you seen Jack Erenson?"

"He was in 'ere a while back. We had a few pints an' then he left. Said ta tell ya he'd be at his warehouse if'n we saw ya. Ain't that right, Owen?" Owen just nodded his head in agreement.

"Did he say what it was about?"

"Now why wud he be tellin' us that? That be betwixt tha two o' ya." He and Owen laughed at the use of the word 'betwixt' and took a swig of their ale. "Who be that gal in them perdy clothes stayin' at yer inn?" He looked around and Jake was gone.

He didn't even hear Durog's last question as he walked back out on the busy sidewalk and headed back to his inn. He figured that if it was that important Jack would come back to the inn. He had things to take care of there.

Jalana and Lianna strolled down the sidewalk talking casually and watching the townspeople go about their daily business. Of course, Jalana drew a lot of looks herself. People remembered her arrival the night before and recognized her clothes. She and Lianna just laughed about it. They stopped into one of the dress shops and wandered around inside looking at the dresses, hats, shoes, parasols, and other items in the shop. Jalana drew several compliments about her clothes from the other women shopping there. Their next stop was at the Sweet Shoppe. The aroma is what attracted them. They could smell chocolate, cinnamon, and sugar among other lesser aromas. They spent some time in there as well walking around all the barrels of candies.

Their next stop was at the sheriff's office. Lianna wanted Jalana to meet Clare.

"Good afternoon, Lianna." Clare stood and gave her a big smile. She came around her desk, through the gate, and gave her a big hug. "I'm so glad to see you again. I was wondering when you would get back. Did everything turn out okay?" She kept eyeing Jalana, not sure what to make of her.

"Yes," answering her question. "Clare, I'd like you to meet Jalana. This is J'orik's mother."

"Hello Jalana, it's nice to meet you."

"It is nice to meet you too Clare. Lianna has told me so much about you on our walk."

"Really. I hope it was all good."

"Of course. Lianna thinks highly of you."

Lianna blushed at her remark.

"I love your outfit," Clare commented. "You created quite a stir yesterday when you got here. A couple people stopped in and told me about the unusual animals travelling with you. I had to lock up and go down to see for myself. What kind of animals are they?"

"They are called camels."

"Camels. I've never seen one before. Where do they come from?"

"They live in the desert where my home is."

"You live in the Great Desert? It must be terribly hot out there."

"Yes, it can get very hot sometimes."

"I suppose that's why you wear the clothes you do."

"Yes, they help."

"Well, I'm guessing that Lianna is showing you around town. Have you ever been here before?"

"No, this is my first visit."

"Are you planning on staying long? Oh, forgive me. Working for the sheriff I tend to ask a lot of questions."

"That is all right. I understand," accepting her apology. "No, I will be leaving in the morning tomorrow to return home."

"Well, I won't take up any more of your time then. It was very nice meeting you Jalana." She turned to Lianna. "Come down and see me tomorrow." Then she walked over and opened the door for them. "I hope you enjoy our little town."

They walked out onto the sidewalk, crossed the street, and stepped into the bakery. Again, it was the aromas that attracted them in, the heavy smell of cinnamon and sugar. They scanned the trays of pastries, pies, and cakes commenting how pretty the decorations were. Leaving the bakery, they stopped in at two more dress shops. They attracted hoots and whistles as they passed the Boars' Den. Lianna attributed that to Jalana. They finally reached the Tigress Inn late in the day as the sun was making its descent towards the mountaintops. Crossing the street, they arrived back at the Dragons' Inn.

"Ah, you're back," Jake greeted them. "Did you have a nice walk?"

"Yes," Jalana replied. "Lianna showed me many shops and introduced me to Clare. Were you able to secure rooms across the street for my men?"

"Yes, that wasn't a problem. They ended up with the same rooms they had last night."

"Are they over there now?"

"Yes. They took care of the camels and horses too."

"Good. They understand we will be leaving in the morning?"

"Yes. Sayid said they would get your carriage ready and be here first thing in the morning."

"Thank you Jake."

"My pleasure. Now, if you ladies want to take some time to wash the street dust off I'll let Joice know you're back. She has a special meal planned for you, Jalana, as sort of a 'going away' gift."

They went upstairs, bathed, and changed into clean clothes. They met in the hallway and went back downstairs into the dining room together. There was a round table set in a corner decorated with one of Joice's fancy lace tablecloths and set with her finest dishes and silverware. A large bouquet of freshly picked flowers set in the middle of the table with two large, scented candles on either side of it. Jake and Joice had also changed into more formal attire. All four of them sat down and Kristen began serving them.

She brought out four crystal wine glasses, set them in front of each 'guest', and filled them with some red wine. Kayla came in with a platter holding four dinner salads and served them around the table. As she was walking away Kristen returned with a plate containing freshly baked bread already sliced and a dish containing a cube of honey butter. The four of them talked casually about their day while eating their salads.

After they finished their salads, Kristen cleared the dishes and refilled their wine glasses. She went back in the kitchen and returned with Kayla, each carrying two platters covered with domed lids and set them in front of each 'guest'. Then they removed the dome lids and left to let them eat.

Joice then proceeded to tell them what had been prepared.

"Tonight I thought we could have roast duck, steamed vegetables fresh out of the garden, and chunky mashed potatoes flavored with garlic and thyme topped with brown gravy." She had a big smile on her face. "I hope you all enjoy." And, to get things started, she was the first one to take a bite.

The other three just giggled a little and began to eat their meals also. There wasn't much talking this time. Everyone seemed to be doing what Joice had wanted, enjoying their meal.

After they finished the main course, Kristen and Kayla cleared the dishes and returned with dessert.

"And for dessert, Kayla has prepared a cinnamon bread pudding topped with a warm cherry sauce and whipped cream."

Smiles went around the table as everyone started in on dessert. After everyone was finished, Kristen came and cleared those dishes and returned to refill their wine glasses again.

"That was a most wonderful meal Joice, thank you," Jalana complimented.

"Yes, Joice, that was fantastic," Lianna also complimented. Then she giggled and remarked, "And we all know what would have happened next if J'orik had been here."

They all laughed except Jalana who looked at them curiously. "And what is that?"

Lianna stopped laughing long enough to tell her and Jalana giggled at how her son would have reacted to the meal.

"Hopefully when he meets my father, his grandfather, he will be able to contain himself," she said between giggles.

They talked for a while longer and then Jake and Joice excused themselves, leaving Jalana and Lianna alone at the table. They discussed their day some more before retiring to their rooms for the night.

The next morning they all gathered in the entry area to say their good-byes to Jalana. Two of the camel riders had brought her travelling chest downstairs. She had them open it and she brought out one of her outfits.

Handing it to Lianna she said, "I hope you like the colors. We are about the same size, it should fit you."

"Thank you." She took the outfit and held it up, looking at the array of colors in it. "Thank you very much."

Next she brought out a small jewelry box made of teak and banded in gold. She handed it to Joice. "This is for you Joice, for being such a gracious hostess."

"Thank you Jalana, it's beautiful." She took the box and opened it. Inside was a gold ring with the image of a phoenix on it and encrusted with rubies. "Oh my," she said smiling and looking at the others. "This is gorgeous." She set the box on the front counter, took the ring out, and placed it on her finger. She held her hand out and admired the ring.

Finally she brought out a notebook bound in black leather, trimmed in gold, and embossed with the image of a phoenix. She handed it to Jake. "And this is for you Jake, for helping my son when he was in trouble."

"Thank you Jalana. I was in need of a new journal and this will be perfect."

"Well, I must be on my way now."

"Wait," Joice interrupted. "I have a small gift for you too." She rushed into the kitchen and came back with a small wooden box. She handed it to Jalana. "You seemed to really enjoy the dessert last night so I had Kayla make up a dish for your trip home. The cherry sauce is in there too. Sorry there's no whipped cream. I'm afraid it wouldn't keep."

Jalana smiled and accepted the gift. She handed the box to one of her men and they took it and her travelling chest out to the carriage. She turned back to give them all hugs.

"I have enjoyed my stay here, thank you. Please keep me informed about J'orik. Remember, unless things change I will be back in one year's time." Then she turned to Lianna. "Please come visit me sometime. Joice's sister knows where to find me."

"I will."

Then she turned to leave. Her carriage was waiting outside along with the camels and their riders and many of the townspeople. The coachmen helped her up into the carriage, climbed up on their bench, and the whole entourage began moving out of town. Once they were out of sight, Jake, Joice, and Lianna went back inside the inn.

Jack Erenson had been in the crowd watching as Jalana left and followed them inside.

# CHAPTER 34

J ACK SPENT THE rest of the day considering what he would talk to Jake about. He wasn't sure if he should tell him who he really was or if he should just offer his help as the friend he had become to him. With everything that had been happening lately there were a lot of bad memories coming back. He'd lived a very long life and the one he was living now had been very satisfying. People liked who he was and he'd come to enjoy that feeling. He'd made many friends over the last couple decades living in Bruston and ran a profitable business operation. Things were much different now than long ago.

He remembered when the council had first suggested the single form change option. Their reasoning had been sound but he wasn't too keen on the limitations it created. There were many others that felt the same way. They didn't believe their race should have to change to accommodate the other races that were developing. They argued adamantly against the process, but the council would not listen. In the end, he, and others like him, had to run and hide so they wouldn't be put through the process. Their names had been put on a list and they were hunted as outlaws. The others that had gone through the process perceived those that hadn't as evil. Eventually, enough time passed and the hunters ceased hunting. Many had been captured and forced to undergo the process but Jack was able to escape being found. He'd spent centuries running and now, he was tired of running and hiding. Besides, he felt he could trust Jake. Jake was an infant compared to him and all he knew about what happened back then were simply stories handed down through the millennia. Jake would never truly understand what really happened and why. Jack felt, that given enough time with Jake, he could help him understand.

And now, with K'orik back on the rampage, all those memories came flooding back. He knew, from the relationship he'd developed with him, that K'orik was a wicked and evil soul and would never change. He was afraid he would take his son J'orik and turn him into the same type of person. All Jack wanted to do was prevent that from happening. He needed to convince Jake of that. He needed to make him understand that he was satisfied with the life he'd created for himself in Bruston and that he did not intend to take back what K'orik had taken from him years before.

Jack went to bed that night with all these thoughts and memories running through his head, still undecided what he would tell Jake or even if he would say anything at all.

The next morning Jack woke up refreshed. Somehow he'd gone the whole night without dreaming, or at least remembering dreaming. It was still dim outside as he sat on the side of his bed thinking. He could hear the activity starting in the warehouse below and knew he should at least check in with George before he went to visit Jake.

Making his way downstairs he looked around the warehouse and felt a sense of satisfaction with what he had accomplished over the last couple decades. He'd developed a strong relationship with the dwarves that mined the mountains west of town, attributing that to the relationship he'd developed with Durog. Even after Durog retired they continued most of their shipments through his warehouse. The dwarves were hard to deal with at times but he'd learned how to handle them.

He saw George, with two of his foremen, standing on the platform overlooking the warehouse going over his log book with the daily shipments that would be coming and going for the day. He let him finish before he made his way over to talk with him.

"Good morning George. How're we doing today?"

"Fine, Jack. Did you have a good rest?"

Even with his employees he'd developed that sense of a more personal relationship. They all called him by his first name and not 'Mr. Erenson'.

"Yes, very good rest, thank you. Lots of shipments today?"

"No more than usual. It looks like that same wagon we had trouble with the other day will be in for more empty crates. Hope it isn't the same driver."

"Come on George, it wasn't that bad. You saw how I handled him, right? Just do the same thing I did and everything will go just fine. Always remember to be 'nice' and people will respond to you."

"I don't know Jack. I have to put up with these men here." He waved his arm out into the warehouse. "And they're an ornery lot as it is," he chuckled.

Jack smiled back at him. "You can handle it George, otherwise I wouldn't have chosen you for the job."

"Thanks, Jack." He paused for a moment. "Are you going to be around today?"

"I have something I need to do in town this morning but I'll be here the rest of the day. Why?"

"I just feel better when you're around and those dwarves show up. I don't think they like me too well."

"Have you ever taken time out and mingled with them at the Boars' Den? That might help. They like to drink and if you can handle your liquor with them they'll cuddle up to you like great big teddy bears."

"Yeah, I suppose. But I've listened to you talk with them. You can talk like they do."

"Get a little liquor in you and you'll start talking like them too," he chuckled. "Well, I think I'm going to head on into town. I'll see you later. Oh, did that letter of mine get out okay yesterday?"

"Yes. Sammy was the one that picked it up."

"Good. Okay, I'll see you later then."

"Okay boss." He went back to his log as Jack walked away.

The sun had come up over the treetops in Murwood Forest and was shining brightly when Jack came out the front door. He stood on the landing and watched as the business slowly started in town. One thing he did notice was there were only a few people walking about and the ones he did see seemed to be heading south. A curious look came over his face as he wondered what might be attracting all the attention. Then he realized it had to be the woman that had come into town the other day. He stepped off the landing, walked down the street, came around the corner, and looked down the main street of town. Down at the Dragons' Inn he saw her carriage and the camels she had with her. There was already a crowd of people gathering on both sides of the street to watch. He crossed over to the west side of the main street and started making his way down the sidewalk. He'd planned on visiting with Jake anyway.

He stood in the crowd and watched as the coachmen brought a large chest out and loaded it on the carriage. They were soon followed by the woman, Jake, Joice, and Lianna. He watched as they said their good-byes and she climbed up into the carriage. She waved one more time and the whole entourage started out of town. The others went back inside and the crowd slowly dispersed. When there was room enough he made his way to the front door and stepped into the Dragons' Inn.

Jake, Joice, and Lianna were still standing in the entry area talking. They all looked when he came in and he smiled at them.

"Good morning folks. Pretty exciting morning, huh?"

They all smiled back at him and nodded their heads yes.

"Good morning Jack. I'm sorry I didn't get back to you yesterday. Things have been a little hectic around here. Gerard told me you stopped in and wanted to talk with me. What can I do for you?"

"Actually, I was hoping we could talk privately Jake. But first, who is this lovely young lady?" he asked looking at Lianna.

"Oh, you two haven't met yet. I'm sorry. This is Lianna." Then he turned to Lianna and said, "This is Jack Erenson. He's the only real competition I have in town and a long time friend."

"It's nice to meet you Lianna."

"Nice to meet you too, Mr. Erenson." She smiled and extended her hand in greeting.

"Oh, by all means call me Jack," he said taking her hand and smiling back.

Looking into his eyes Lianna was overwhelmed by the strong presence he exuded.

"I don't mean to be short but I do need to speak with Jake. Again, it's been very nice meeting you and I hope to see you around town." He turned to Jake, "Are you ready?"

"Sure thing Jack, come on into my office." He gestured with his arm for Jack to follow and he headed towards his office.

He followed him in and Jake shut the door behind him. Jack took a seat as Jake made his way around his desk to his chair.

"What can I do for you Jack? Is everything okay?"

"For the most part Jake. I've had something on my mind for a while now and I finally decided it was time you and I had a talk about it."

Jake got a serious look on his face. "I hope it's nothing terrible."

"It isn't anything terrible, but it is a serious matter."

"Okay, I'm listening."

Jack sat for a moment, thinking about how he was going to say it and decided the best way was to just come right out and say it.

"We both know we're shapeshifters but I don't think you know who I really am."

Jake leaned forward in his chair and got an even more serious look on his face. "Who you really are. What do you mean by that?"

"Well," he hesitated, "everyone here knows me as Jack Erenson. That's just the name I've chosen to go by. I feel that you and I have developed a stronger, more trusting relationship, and I think it's time I told you who I really am. Have you ever heard the name J'eren?" He paused, looking straight into Jake's eyes, and waited for a response.

Jake's eyes went wide. "Yes, I know the name. Why do you ask?"

"I am J'eren," he said bluntly.

Jake fell back in his chair for a moment and then leaned forward again. "That can't be. J'eren was killed by K'orik decades ago."

"That's what I wanted everyone to think, Jake. K'orik was much stronger than me when we fought years ago so, rather than fight to the death, I simply disappeared."

"This is amazing." He sat back in his chair again. "I can't believe it."

"Well, you can believe it Jake, it's true."

"Can you prove this?"

"Yes."

And without even hesitating he changed into the hawk Jake had seen flying above town. Then he changed into a monarch and fluttered about the office. Then, landing on the floor near the door, he changed into a wolf and sat on his haunches. Then he changed back into his human form and sat back down in the chair. Jake's eyes grew wide in amazement at each change.

"See, Jake, I can change into anything I desire. Who else do you know can do that?"

"No one," he admitted. "That hasn't been possible for eons now."

"So just imagine how old I really am."

Jake sat there considering what had just happened. "Why tell me now then?"

"Because I believe K'orik is back on the rampage and he wanted to find his son to enlist his help. We can't let that happen. You've been with J'orik long enough now to know he's nothing like his father, correct?"

"Yes."

"We can't allow K'orik to corrupt him. If he does, then the two of them together will be a most formidable force. That can't be allowed to happen. I felt that if I exposed my true self to you I could get your help in preventing that from happening."

"But the stories I've heard about you."

"They're all just stories, Jake," he interjected quickly. "I'm not the person those stories have portrayed me to be. Just think about the relationship we've had the last few decades. That should say something about who I really am," he pleaded.

Jake was flabbergasted by what he'd just heard, and seen. He wasn't sure how to respond. Jack just waited, wondering how he would respond. Moments went by and neither one said anything. Jack could tell Jake was still undecided on how to react. He probably would be too if he'd grown up with the stories about him Jake had grown up with.

Jake finally settled down. "Okay, okay. If what you say is true, what do you propose?"

"I know what J'orik has proposed and I'm willing to let him proceed. All I'm asking of you is to help me intercede if he is unable to follow through. I've watched J'orik make the change and I can feel that he is, and will be, much stronger than his father. If K'orik is able to corrupt him, then all will be lost and I'm afraid what the world will be like if that happens. What I'm proposing is to keep an eye on the situation and intercede if need be."

"How do you propose keeping an eye on things?"

"You've seen what I can do," he smiled. "I can change into anything. I can make periodic checks and keep you informed on what I see and hear. Between the two of us we can decide if it becomes necessary for us to step in. You are a formidable creature yourself, Jake, and the two of us together, fighting for the same cause, would be an even more formidable force. The only other thing I ask of you is that you tell no one about this, not even Joice. Can you do that?"

"Yes. But if it does become necessary for us to step in I will bring her in on it. Agreed?"

"I'm okay with that," he conceded. "With all of us together, K'orik wouldn't stand a chance."

They both stood. Jack put his hand out and Jake extended his. They shook hands in agreement.

"I'm glad we had this talk, Jake. I feel as if a huge weight has been lifted off my shoulders."

"I'm still taken aback by your confession."

"You're all right with it though, aren't you?"

"Yes. I'm fine with it. It's just going to take some time to get used to the idea."

Jack smiled and turned to leave. "Well, I have business to attend to, Jake. Again, I'm glad we had this talk. You have a nice day and I'll keep in touch." He left Jake standing in his office.